HOSACK'S FOLLY

HOSACK'S FOLLY

A Novel of Old New York

Gillen D'Arcy Wood

Other Press • New York

Production Editor: Robert D. Hack
Text Designer: Kaoru Tamura
This book was set in AGaramond by Alpha Graphics of Pittsfield, NH.

10 9 8 7 6 5 4 3 2 1

Library of Congress Cataloging-in-Publication Data

Wood, Gillen D'Arcy.
    Hosack's folly : a novel of old New York / Gillen D'Arcy Wood.
        p. cm.
    ISBN 1-59051-162-X (hardcover : alk. paper)   1. Hosack, David, 1769-1835–Fiction.   2. New York (N.Y.)–History–1775-1865–Fiction. 3. Yellow fever–Fiction.   4. Physicians–Fiction.   I. Title.
    PS3623.O625H675 2005
    813'.6–dc22

                                                                    2004015383

For the three thousand innocent dead

PROLOGUE

Weehawken, July 11, 1804

The only sound was the dipping of the oars. The soft working of the wood against the gunnels, then a soft slap on the invisible water. Regular as a man's heart still beating. The oarsman's face barely registered the strain of the boat's course through the gray mist. That steady gaze said he was a Navy man, who would keep his own counsel. No doubt he was a veteran of dawn encounters. Sailors, after all, were a bloody-minded set of men.

But the young doctor sitting at the stern had taken the ancient oath to heal men, not kill them or see them killed. He was a tall man and felt awkward in the small boat, with his long legs bent upward almost to his chest. His hands were shaking. To steady them, he reached under his seat and felt for his new leather bag. He fingered the cold brass clasp, intending to check its contents for the hundredth time: the cotton swabs and bandages, the iron clamps for extraction, and the steel-toothed saw if a quick amputation were necessary. But, looking over at Hamilton, he stopped just in time and wondered at himself for thinking of such an ill-omened act.

They were now halfway across the river. Hamilton sat bareheaded on the starboard side of their little craft. He was looking down at the water, running his hand in the swell like an idling child waiting for a fish. His steel gray hair was tied back in a club. He wore a blue coat with a thin wool shirt visible beneath the lapels. The doctor regretted the wool shirt and wished he had been more insistent. Wool was a devil of a fabric in a wound.

Hamilton! Was there a man more admired in New York? In America? Washington's thwarted lieutenant, who had become a political meteor in the years after the Revolution, the financial genius of the young Republic. Without him and his banking system to build commercial confidence and trade, the fledgling union would have been stillborn. It was Hamilton who taught those Virginia farmers how to make a nation out of a mere idea.

Was Hamilton crying? Or was it the morning mist rising off the river, clouding his spectacles? Sure enough, he took them off now and wiped them with his sleeve in that studied way of his. His face half-obscured in the mist, head bent in thought, Hamilton reminded the doctor for a moment of his glory days. When he had strode about Wall Street like a God—Prosperity Incarnate. Then the doctor looked more closely and observed the crow's lines about his eyes and the unkempt gray streaks in his hair. The death of his son in a duel some years back had broken him. His enemies had seen it and begun closing in. They made him pettish and resentful, until there was no world for him beyond their intrigues. Though they had not yet destroyed him, they had made him mortal.

Hamilton looked over at him suddenly, and the doctor felt a creeping irrational conviction that he had read his thoughts. He blushed. But Hamilton only smiled.

"Don't worry, David. I'm sure we will both fire in the air, or the seconds will call it off. His man has said as much. Mr. Bayard will speak to him."

Bayard stood forward as a lookout, directing the boat through the folds of mist and the sleeping fishing vessels at anchor. A flat wooden case lay on the seat beside him. He looked back at the mention of his name, then at the doctor, but said nothing.

Weehawken Bluff loomed through the predawn darkness. The sun rising behind them caught only the tops of the trees: little fingers of orange flame shooting up into the gray immensity.

The bow scraping on the sand was a strangely ordinary sound. They might have been a weekend party arriving to picnic on the bluff. But there was no women's laughter to fill the air, no quick, light talk. It was only men in the boat and their deadly, determined silence.

Hamilton was first to step on shore. But he stopped immediately to take off his spectacles once more and wipe his eyes.

"Is the bad light bothering you, Mr. Hamilton?" asked the doctor.

"You can't fight if you can't see," said Bayard, stepping forward.

But Hamilton waved them away. He seemed to have withdrawn into himself. Everything he did from that moment on had an almost mechanical air. First, he removed the blue jacket and gave it to Bayard, who folded it carefully on his arm. Then Bayard handed him the case. Hamilton took it, opened it and removed the pistol. He ran his finger along the barrel and tested the flintlock. Not hurried actions, but strangely perfunctory, without the least show of nerves. It was as if Hamilton were reading from a script he had already composed in his mind.

The doctor thought they had arrived first. But then he saw two figures near the trees on the left, stepping silently out of the gloom.

Bayard sniffed the air and looked over at the men in the trees.

"That's powder, by God—I do believe that devil has been practicing!"

They looked back at Hamilton, who was wiping his eyes again, this time with a kerchief drawn from his pocket.

"For God's sake, Hosack, speak to him. You're the doctor," hissed Bayard. "The man can't see."

But by the time the doctor stepped forward to say something, Hamilton had already climbed over the small crop of rocks to the strip of bare sand under the bluff. In the dim shell of dawn light, the doctor could see the crisscross of footprints leading in opposite directions.

Hamilton gestured to Bayard, who climbed up to him. They conversed in low, inaudible tones and were clearly at odds over some point. After a minute or so, Bayard seemed to concede and he walked over toward the other second, who met him halfway along the strip of sand.

The doctor's heart leapt up. Here was where the deal would be struck! Bayard would offer that Hamilton write a letter of explanation, or apologize on the spot and shake his old comrade's hand. They would all laugh about it over breakfast at the Shakespeare Tavern that very morning.

But Bayard was already turning around! He and the other second had spoken no more than five words together, and now he was walking away! Something was wrong. If only Bayard had looked over to him, given some signal, he surely would have done something. But he only turned away and took up a place on the other side of Hamilton, at a short distance under the arch of the bluff.

The two men stood appallingly close, not twenty feet apart. Bayard began the count. His gruff voice broke the silence like a cannon shot, and a flock of birds mounted wheeling from the trees to the left. They seemed to distract Hamilton. He was squinting into the sky. Two, three numbers in the count passed when the doctor again thought he should say something. His arm tingled. The words formed in his throat. He would have the count restarted. Or postpone the duel until the light was better. At the least, he must swab Hamilton's weeping eyes so he could see properly. But the counts passed, and he did nothing. Now it was too late. With a gust of panic, the doctor saw that Hamilton was *still looking into the sky. Only at the very last moment did he lift his gun, at the very last number of the count.*

Burr fired first. Burr definitely fired first. But Hamilton fired too. Two streaks of orange flame licked across the sand, and twin balls of smoke plumed into the air.

There was a moment's echoing pause while the two men held their places like figures in a tableau. Hamilton was staring straight at Burr, gun still raised. Burr lowered his weapon and staggered forward. Then, with his eyes still on Burr, the doctor heard a sound he never forgot. An inhuman groan. He looked back to see Hamilton lying on his elbow in the sand. Bayard was holding his head.

The doctor leapt up the rocks. He lifted Hamilton's shirt. He was at first unsure of the situation of the bullet, hoping it might have passed clean through. But then he looked at Hamilton's face and his heart sank. His cheeks were a glassy white, and the brilliant blue-green eyes were gone entirely, rolled back in his head.

The doctor picked up the wounded man in his long arms, treading carefully but swiftly down the rocks to the boat. They heard a call and turned to see Burr clambering across the rocks toward them. He called out to them. Bayard shouted something in reply—angry words, so that Burr's man reached out and restrained him, held him there on the rocks. Standing in the shallows of the Hudson River, the doctor laid Hamilton down into the boat as gently as a baby into its cradle. Then he stepped in, still nursing the pale head. In the same instant, the oarsman began his stroke, teeth clenched.

That night, in Bayard's bed at his house in Greenwich Village, Alexander Hamilton still lay in David Hosack's arms. The medical bag sat open on the table, its contents bloodied and useless. The doctor thought more than once of hastening the end, but even now he felt paralyzed by uncertainty and inexperience and he did nothing. Visitors came to the house throughout the day, but Bayard turned them away or kept them in the parlor—for dignity's sake. Only the presumptive widow and her sons stood by, weeping quietly in the monstrous shadows of the candlelight. By midnight, Hamilton was exhausted. Blood bubbled with his every breath and, during the endless dark hours that followed, the doctor had only his strong, young arms to oppose the racking pain, the pointless agony, as the great man slowly dragged himself into death.

Twenty Years Later

CHAPTER ONE

Day after day into the second week of July, the heat beat fiercely down as it had the whole hot wet month of June. Each morning the sun, as if refreshed from its travels through the night, emerged above the horizon like an angry phoenix and set itself ablaze, flooding Manhattan in a blinding glare. To deepen New Yorkers' misery, plagues of airborne insects—flies, mosquitoes, unknown tribes of gnats and mites—had appeared as if from nowhere after the recent rains and swarmed across the island like over an old mutton bone.

On the Brooklyn Ferry, passengers sat slumped on their seats, while children who had sneaked aboard without paying lay in small heaps on the deck. Not a breath refreshed the sails. Not that anyone cared for their destination, only the chance of escape from the stifling haze of the city. But there was no relief even on the water. The exhausted passengers could feel the heat under their feet as the boat bobbed like a cork on the East River, barely able to clear Peck Slip. An endless half-hour passed, and still they wilted mid-river in the windless haze. In their overheated imaginations, the Brooklyn Ferry slowly assumed the character of an infernal transport, ferrying the Damned on a never-ending circuit of the lake of fire.

A young man stood alone at the prow, cursing the captain for the faults of the wind. To his fellow passengers, he presented a certain mystery. On the one hand, his face was pale and his hands unmarked by scars or welts. This was not a laboring man, his complexion colored by years on the open docks or at sea. Nor did he squint and stoop, as did even very young men in the city who spent their days in dim rooms counting stores, drawing up accounts, or making endless copies of all the legal documents of trade and exchange. But his status as a young man of leisure was equally uncertain. He wore a strange battered cap rather than the requisite stovepipe hat, and his morning coat was worn at the elbows and did not fit him. His boots were scuffed beyond even minimal notions of respectability, and the cuffs of his shirt were strangely compounded with dirt, as if he spent his days digging in a ditch or tramping though forests. Gentleman or barroom fancy man? Broadway or the Bowery? Those passengers who considered the question to this extent returned to his face, with its handsome Dutch lines and keen, open expression, and gave the young man the benefit of the doubt.

To distract himself from his impatient fury, Albert Dash turned and looked back toward Manhattan. The brick warehouses along the wharf on South Street were almost invisible behind a forest of masts. Ships crowded and bounced against the slips like a herd at a watering hole. The continuous bustle and shouting from there had faded, the close-up chaos giving way to an impression of mathematical order in the steady accretion of stock on the dockside. Bales of wool and cotton, hogsheads of rum and sugar, barrels of rice, flour, and tobacco, and crates of calico and timber—a small army attended to the piles, their rapid disposal of objects of all sizes giving the New York port an air of remorseless, abstract efficiency.

Further north, shipyards dotted the banks of the East River. Albert counted eleven ships on stocks at Corlear's Hook, overlooked by the plain low-slung facades of the breweries and tanning factories. The tanners' horrible work was hidden from sight, but it could be smelled in the air: the acrid tang of burnt animal hide. Boys fished, undeterred by the filth, from little skiffs in the shallows. Beyond the Hook, in the distance, Grand and Broome Streets appeared like country lanes. From the height of the prow he could make out the purple band of lilacs in the hedgerows linking the scattered Dutch cottages, with their high-pitched roofs shaped like hands in prayer. Further beyond these stretched the green swath of the old Delancey farm until, at some indistinguishable point near the horizon, the Manhattan of agriculture and industry merged into primeval forest, shimmering in the heat under a great blue canopy of summer sky.

Albert had received the urgent message from Dr. Hosack before the sun was up, before even his aunt was up. She had not forgiven his hurried departure, though she had persuaded him to bathe (a pail of brown water, which she deposited over his head in the yard) and to put on a clean shirt. But he had undone these efforts by running all the way from Franklin Street to Peck Slip. Now he was as damp in his clothes as if he'd chosen to swim the East River.

I should have swum, he thought bitterly. *I'd be in Brooklyn by now.*

Dr. Hosack had always impressed upon his students the medical implications of time. "An hour lost, a life lost," he would say. Now that the doctor had chosen *him*, of all his students, to assist him on this day, the importance of a speedy arrival loomed in Albert's mind like a Biblical commandment. "A minute gained, a patient saved."

At last, a luff of wind awakened the sails, and they broke the line of ships on the Brooklyn side. East India merchantmen, brigs from Jamaica, Havana, San Domingo and trim-waisted packets from Liverpool, bunched against the dock.

One ship sat apart. An old West Indian—the gold lettering on her side, *Belladonna*, chipped away, barely legible. She lay downwind at a distance, strangely deserted. On all the other ships, stevedores hauled sacks from the hold and put ropes and swinging nets over the side. But not *Belladonna*. He stared at her for a long minute, as a chill settled over his heart.

The ferry captain gave the call to disembark, but caulking wax from the seams of the deck had melted on Albert's shoes. As he disengaged the sticky mess with the help of his handkerchief, he felt the rage of impatience rise inside him once more. He burst through the crowd on the ramp—turning a deaf ear to the ripple of protest behind him—and set out at a run along the dockside.

All around him the working men of Brooklyn grunted under crates and bullied their horses, while barefoot boys darted up and down like chicks. Hammering sounds ahead of him. Another new warehouse reaching to the sky. The workmen's bare backs glistened in the heat as they set cross beams, lattice-like, across a single open floor for the accommodation of ceiling-high stacks of sugar and cotton bound for Europe and cases of rum for the western frontier.

A stone's throw beyond, through the dust and glare, a boardinghouse with a small porch. Two sharp raps on the door—a child's questioning face—his hat spinning on the kitchen table—and he attacked the stairs three at a time to the upstairs landing.

There, through the crack in a door, Albert saw a man in a bed. Only the patient's pale, drained face was visible above the sheet wrapped tightly around him. He recognized the smell at once. The sweet-sour odor of rotted fruit, even with the windows open.

A stout woman in an apron was seated next to the bed. Across from her, his back turned, sat a broad, bald man. He did not even turn his head, did not look at him. As a young man, Dr. Hosack had been known for his height and stork-like gait. But he had filled out substantially in middle age. His girth, together with his gleaming bald head and short-cropped red beard, put Albert in mind of Henry the Eighth, an impression strengthened by the doctor's air of kingly disdain.

"I've been here all morning. What kept you?"

Albert apologized quickly, though the doctor's sharp tone gladdened him—it was the gratification of the apprentice who realizes he has become indispensable to the master.

"Thank you, Mrs. Little," said Dr. Hosack. "Mr. Dash has arrived at last. You must leave the house now and take the little boy with you. Leave Brooklyn if you can."

Albert took his place in Mrs. Little's chair.

"I have always known the yellow fever to progress by the odd days." Dr. Hosack sat back in his chair, as if talking to himself. "On the first it appears no more than a common debility without apparent special cause. On the third day, a violent fever and an uncommon despondency of spirits—a phenomenon our good nurse, Mrs. Little, observed—are accompanied by a depressed pulse and fearful hallucinations. The eyes also, you will have noticed, protrude unnaturally. It is now the fifth day. The matter will be resolved by tonight. If favorable symptoms develop today, he will recover on Thursday. But if the signs progress to the definitive phase, he will be dead by tomorrow—nothing is more certain."

"What can we do to influence this result?"

"Very little. Nothing."

The patient, a shipwright from Jackson's Yard named Duggan, was weak and delirious. They bled him first. Albert almost wept to see the small pod of blood on the doctor's tray, its crust inflamed. He watched the doctor take a linen rag from his bag and dip an end in the dark serum. He held it to the light, and they saw the white cloth stain bright yellow. They threw buckets of cold water over Duggan as he lay prostrate. Had he been aboard the *Belladonna*? But there wasn't time for such questions, not while the man lay groaning and clutching his belly like he was on fire.

Down in the kitchen, Albert rattled about in the doctor's old leather bag for another of his little tin trays. On the table, he set tiny slices of tamarind, shrunk in the heat, and a small bowl of liquefied rhubarb and rose syrup. It looked like supper for a bird or a hare. He found a bowl of whey among Mrs. Little's stores. He mixed it together and boiled it over a fire. The heat was so bad he felt the pores of his skin open to the size of pennies. He took the mixture to Duggan, but it failed. No emetic Dr. Hosack knew could help him. Duggan grasped at his stomach and moaned piteously.

When night fell, Albert lit two lamps beside the bed to illuminate the patient. The yellow tint began in the eyes, deep in the pupils. The eyes were watery, too, as if he were crying. Albert and the doctor watched as the golden frost spread across the skin of Duggan's face and down along his body. He sweated great streams onto the bedclothes and threw up a grainy fluid as black as cocoa beans. The colors of the fever were yellow and black. Molten gold and coffee.

After sleeping some hours, Duggan woke looking fresher. It was dawn, but Albert and the doctor hadn't slept. Duggan turned his still yellow eyes to the doctor and smiled. The doctor said nothing, had said nothing for hours.

"Thank you," said Duggan. But the Doctor didn't answer, only rubbed his bearded chin and stared straight ahead. Suddenly, miraculously, Duggan got up and walked to the window bracing his arms, a spring in his step.

"I'm hungry," he announced.

Then in one slow instant, the life left him. His body wilted to the floor with a strange grace, right at the doctor's feet.

"Quickly, Albert," cried the doctor, "we must burn this bedding, and wrap and bury him. He will putrefy within an hour."

They had not passed a man-made structure for more than a mile. It had been an anxious ride because Albert's young mare (borrowed from the doctor's private stable on Church Street) felt her required station behind and to the right of the doctor to be an affront to her dignity and strained to be given her head. Meanwhile, old Coriolanus plodded along under the doctor's broad eighteen stone. Once out of the city, their journey had become more peaceful, even scenic. Heading northward on First Avenue, they rode past the lordly stone mansions of New York's trade barons who, having made their fortunes on the docks, had made sure to place a hygienic distance between that neighborhood and their families.

They rode through pools of water left by the overnight rain, and soon both they and their horses were splattered with streaks of mud. Beyond this northern rim of Manhattan, green-grassed meadows stretched to the horizon. But at each twentieth of a mile, surveyor's red flags marked out the city's destined conquest of the island wilderness. Fourteenth Street. Fifteenth Street. The future here was already imagined, the way cleared for the city to spill, like a teeming Babylon, into the birch groves and geese ponds and to pave over the clam-filled streams. Albert had spent much of his boyhood here, hunting and trapping and playing fort with his friends. But he gave no thought to such things now. They were scenes from someone else's childhood.

At Twenty-sixth Street, the grand, double-storied brick facade of Bellevue Hospital stood alone in the open fields, fronted by a sweeping arc of steps in gray Westchester stone. People had called it a white elephant—Hosack's Folly—but its size and location were indispensable to its mission. An epidemic hospital had to be large enough to accommodate a flood of victims and far enough from the city to avoid infection of the healthy. If it stood partly empty much of the time, with only a single ward open for the ordinary traffic of consumption, dysentery and the always sickly children of the poor, then the city should count it a blessing. But for some reason—Dr. Hosack called it the inverse proportion of public newspapers to the sensible workings of citizens' minds—the fact that Bellevue had been so little used had been looked upon as a public waste. The paradoxical effect of Dr. Hosack's tireless efforts to prevent the return of the yellow fever, but to ensure the city's readiness if it did, had been to diminish his stature in the public eye. Where once he was never mentioned in the newspapers but with some mark of veneration, more and more he found himself subject to a skeptical scrutiny, like any common ward politician.

Albert had never been admitted to the doctor's rooms at Bellevue before and he felt the honor so keenly that he had to fight not to appear overwhelmed. The entire office, floor and desk, was strewn with papers and medical curiosities, from skeletal fingers used as paperweights to a mysterious box of powder half-opened on the arm of the doctor's chair. A head portrait of a man (Hippocrates? Alexander Hamilton?) hung on the wall, next to a certificate of honor from the city for his "valiant service" in the yellow fever epidemic of 1814.

The doctor caught him looking at it and seemed embarrassed.

"I did not ask for that, you know. It was no more than cynical flattery on the mayor's part. He thought he could puff me up enough that I would forget to demand he build this hospital for the *next* fever. I know I did not do enough in the '14 epidemic."

Albert looked away, and there was an awkward silence. Finally, the doctor spoke.

"Which brings us to our rather better situation now. Now that we have the hospital, it will be different. If the yellow fever comes to Manhattan this summer—"

"If?"

"I will restrict myself to observable facts for the moment—*If* the yellow fever comes, we have porters and orderlies enough to transport twenty victims an hour from the city to here. We can fit three hundred beds in a squeeze and are far enough north to effectively quarantine the sick from the well. In 1814, the fever raged for seven weeks. Only the October frosts relieved us. With the measures we have taken since then, I believe we can forestall an epidemic altogether. The fever under control in a week, eliminated in two. Deaths in the few dozens, not multiples of hundreds. The city returned to prosperous health in a month, not devastated for years."

Once again, the doctor stopped himself too late and he shot another glance at Albert. But the young man's face was lit with excitement: he looked ready to leap out of his chair and rush to the bedside of fever patients who did not yet even exist.

"So, I have Bellevue now," the doctor repeated. "But I will also have you."

Albert looked up to find the doctor's eyes fixed on him.

"You have become very valuable to me, Albert. And your work today with poor Duggan—it was exemplary. No one knows the botanical compounds as you do, with your deft hand for mixture.

Certainly no one with a stomach for this kind of nursing. I cannot handle a major outbreak on my own. I learned that in '14. You must be my special assistant. Beginning tomorrow, with this outbreak in Brooklyn, I will begin delegating responsibilities to you. I will tell the mayor this very evening that, in the event of yellow fever breaking out here in Manhattan, you will speak for me and represent my authority in the city."

The doctor paused, as if considering one last time whether this commission did not represent some failing on his part, an abdication of the responsibilities he had assumed in New York from a very young age. But he got to his feet at last, a broad smile across his face.

For a moment, Albert thought the grin meant the offer had been a joke and that he was supposed to laugh. But the doctor reached out and offered him his hand. No student Albert knew at Columbia had ever shaken Doctor Hosack's hand. Even the mayor was lucky to get a short nod of the head by way of greeting.

The doctor said, "It will be the last time we shake hands for a while I'm afraid. I do not believe the yellow fever is communicable through the skin, but it is best to take no unnecessary risks when our theory of airborne contamination is still not proven."

Albert nodded and smiled, so stupid with happiness that he forgot to ask whether his new position came with a salary.

"Now, Albert. I will leave you in charge here for the night. I must pay a visit to the mayor. Poor Duggan cannot be our little secret for ever. The yellow fever lurks on our very doorstep."

"What will you tell the mayor?"

"First, to not be a fool, whatever his inmost nature commands him. And second, that he must shut down this port!"

CHAPTER TWO

"I don't think it necessary to quarantine the port for now, for all Doctor Hosack says," said Mayor Van Ness the next morning, leaning back into his chair.

Eamonn Casey looked at him in surprise, but said nothing. He looked out the window of the mayor's office and saw a single closed carriage with fancy brass trim clattering north up Broadway toward City Hall, raising great clouds of dust in its wake. He was hardly in a position to challenge the mayor, after all, not when he had just asked for his endorsement for governor in November.

Mayor Van Ness was a broad-beamed man with a flabby face who looked as if he had at one time been squashed from above by some object of even greater dimensions than himself, and had his stuffing squeezed out in odd places. He joined Casey at the window. "This fever outbreak in Brooklyn has a silver lining for us, you know, Eamonn. It puts sanitation in the city at the front of people's minds. We need fresh water from your aqueduct to drink, yes, but we need it to protect us from the fever, too. Sanitation, Eamonn! Sanitation will be our catch cry!"

Casey nodded serenely. So confident did he feel of winning the election now that the legislature had given all tax-paying men in New York state the vote, that he wondered if he actually needed the mayor's support any longer. The days of Tory gentlemen ruling New York were over. History had placed him in the breach. Looking at the mayor, he felt almost ashamed of his own advantages. Old Van Ness was a man of the past now, though he knew the little Dutchman would fight his obsolescence to the very death. He, by contrast, held an office more powerful than any mayor's. He could stoke outrage in a thousand hearts with a single metaphor, bring riots to the streets by the stroke of his pen. Given these talents, was he not in fact made for governor of this *new* New York?

It was with this happy conviction that he watched the expensive-looking carriage turn the corner by the old Bridewell Jail and draw up in front of the steps of City Hall. A slim man in a dark suit and beaver hat emerged, instantly adding an air of wealth and importance to what was a very meager tableau. A small herd of swine rooted through an upturned barrel of potage on the steps, while a solitary water cart labored south along Broadway on its unhappy trek from the dried-up wells near the old Dutch canal to the homes of the wealthy Westsiders, who preferred a private supply of tea-colored water to the irregular, evil-smelling flow from the street pumps.

Two sets of footsteps in the hall, and the mayor shot Casey a glance, eyebrows raised.

The mayor's secretary appeared at the door, wearing a significant expression.

"Thank you, Mr. Fry."

Though a large man in a stout, overfed way, Mayor Van Ness moved swiftly out from behind his desk, hand extended in greeting, as Mr. John Laidlaw entered the room.

"This is a happy event indeed, sir. We are very grateful you could come. Great things afoot. Great things!" He ushered Casey forward. "You know Mr. Eamonn Casey by reputation, I'm sure."

"Indeed," said Laidlaw, accepting Casey's hand with a grin. "I've often had reason to curse your name, Mr. Casey, at least in your capacity as editor of the *Herald*." Laidlaw was a slender, almost fragile-looking man, so the strength of his grasp surprised Casey. For a brief instant they eyed each other, more like two beasts of the field than successful city gentlemen making their acquaintance in the office of the mayor.

"I don't doubt you have had reason, sir," Casey replied with a careful smile, "as any man might curse me who is blessed with riches like yourself, but thinks little of the working men who labor for them."

"An uncommon alliance this is, to be sure, gentlemen," said Mayor Van Ness with a big laugh and a slap on the shoulder for each of them. "But it is the beauty of our democratic republic, is it not, that two men of differing views can come together for the public good? Please, let us sit down. We will be more comfortable over here."

The mayor led them to a circle of capacious velvet divans by the empty marble fireplace, conspicuously redundant in the heat. Above the mantel hung a lordly portrait of Alexander Hamilton, taken in his days as first treasurer of the Republic. Perhaps it was only Eamonn Casey's anxiety at soliciting a partnership with John Laidlaw, but Hamilton appeared to look down on their clandestine Sabbath meeting with an expression of distrust in his pale eyes.

For a moment, all three men stared at the empty grate, as if not knowing how to embark on the weighty matters that lay before them.

At last, John Laidlaw spoke. "I am surprised we have not met before, Mr. Casey, our daughters being such firm friends at school. Your Virginia gained high marks in her time at Miss Piper's Academy, I hear. I'm afraid my Vera idled her time away there for no gain but in vanity and a few sentimental French sayings."

They all laughed, and the tension eased slightly.

"How *is* Miss Vera?" asked the mayor, who could not prevent his eyebrow raising a half-inch.

"Wonderful as ever," Laidlaw replied, with a complacent smile. He could be relied upon to regard any mention of his daughter as a compliment to himself. The mayor pursued this lucky theme.

"Her debut in *Hamlet* at the Bowery Theater—it is coming together well I trust? She is to play opposite Mr. Digby, I hear. We are all in a fever of anticipation about it, you know." *And thoroughly enjoying the scandal too*, he thought. He blessed himself that he and Mrs. Van Ness did not have Vera Laidlaw for a daughter. Their Margaret was fat and docile and could barely be persuaded to move herself from the couch in this heat, let alone conceive the ridiculous notion of going on the stage.

Some mysterious social mechanism now communicated to the three men that polite chat must give way to matters of business. So it was no surprise when John Laidlaw leaned forward, directed his gaze at Eamonn Casey and said, "The mayor tells me you wish to run for governor, Mr. Casey."

Casey had been well prepared for his meeting with Manhattan's richest man, but he gave a small start nevertheless. The idea of his running for governor was perfectly familiar to his own mind, but he had yet to get used to it as a topic of daily conversation.

"I am exploring the possibility, sir."

"Have you made an announcement?"

"Not yet. But I hope to be in a position to, in a few days' time."

"After today, we hope," said the mayor, with a glint in his eye toward Laidlaw.

Casey noticed Laidlaw's amused look. "I realize that many obstacles stand in the way of a man of my background."

"You are a Papist, yes?"

"By birth, not by practice. It is no secret."

"And you were not born in this country?" Mr. Laidlaw posed these questions in clipped English vowels that suggested he himself was no True American either. But instead of Casey finding solidarity with the man in this, the effect was only to make him feel all the more Irish. Very Irish. Like the Blarney Stone on a divan.

"I came over from Dublin when I was eight, sir, with only a sickly aunt for company and not a penny to my name."

Laidlaw sat back in his chair, pressing the tips of his fingers together. "A sentimental biography, then. You could rely at least on my daughter's vote, were she enfranchised."

The mayor caught Casey's black look. "The immigrant vote should not be scorned, Mr. Laidlaw," he said quickly. "Manhattan is now a city of two hundred thousand souls, twice what it was a decade ago. The Irish make up a fifth of our numbers, and every packet that arrives from Belfast ups their portion. But what is most important is not Mr. Casey's heritage—it is his newspaper. The *Herald* has fifteen thousand readers, sir. Fifteen thousand! The biggest circulation in the city. Most of these are voting men, what's more."

"To buy a man's newspaper is one thing, to vote for him quite another. How can we know Mr. Casey is capable of making one of the other?"

The mayor clearly saw it his duty to argue Casey's case for him. "Mr. Casey may not be well known on the hustings, but he is no political novice either. He has influence on the street, sir. The Bowery in particular. Time and again he has carried the fourth and fifth wards for me. It is not where your banker friends live, to be sure, but with our new Voting Rights Act, one man's vote is as good as another's. Politics has changed here forever, and Mr. Casey is a coming man you would be very wise to back. He already has a band of loyal subordinates in this city who can be relied upon to, shall we say, 'demoralize' the opposition, and are second-to-none for barrels of beer and beef stew on polling day to bring the voters in."

"It will take more than thuggery and Tammany Hall tricks to install Mr. Casey in Albany, with or without your Voting Rights Act," Laidlaw replied. "He must win in the western wards, in Brooklyn, and make a good showing in the upstate farm counties where he is presently unknown."

Casey was impressed. For a Wall Street businessman, Laidlaw appeared to know a great deal about politics. He leaned his large frame across the mayor toward him.

"I would not waste your valuable time on a foolish fancy, Mr. Laidlaw. My newspaper might bring me fifteen thousand votes, but I will need ten times that number to win. I am under no illusions, I think. To succeed, I must have a winning platform—a cause to rally the people to me in great numbers."

Laidlaw scoffed. "It is barely three months until election day. Look around you—the city is booming! New warehouses are built by the day, and the demand for new dwellings is so great that respectable families think nothing of moving into half-built houses and placing their domestic lives on public view as the walls are erected around them. Ships anchor in the harbor because there is no room for them at our crowded slips. Our share of the Atlantic trade is now greater than either Boston or Philadelphia. And the Erie Canal has opened the interior to us, as well as uniting the interests of New York and Albany for generations to come. What cause could you find in this short time to defeat a governor who has presided over all this?"

"Water." Casey allowed a beat of silence to follow his pronouncement of the word. "We cannot sustain this boom without water. Fresh water from upstate rivers brought down to Manhattan. An endless, renewable supply of water."

"I suppose you mean this aqueduct plan of yours," said Laidlaw carelessly.

Casey gave a start of surprise. He turned to the mayor, who looked suddenly uncomfortable. "Ah, yes, Eamonn. I did mean to tell you that I had already dropped hints that way to Mr. Laidlaw. I'm afraid it was necessary to persuade him of your bona fides."

A blush of anger crossed Casey's face but he said nothing, and after a moment he leaned back on the cushions of the divan. This Englishman had played him like a cheap violin so far.

"Please do not be angry with the mayor," said Laidlaw. The amused smile had returned. "I think it is an inspired idea—in principle. I have taken the liberty of consulting with a friend of mine about it. An engineer with experience in the Erie Canal project, and a long-time advocate of an aqueduct for this city."

"Do you mean Sam Geyer?" said the Mayor.

"The very gentleman. Mr. Geyer has explained to me that to build a structure capable of bringing the millions of gallons of water a day this city needs, across dozens of miles of rough terrain, will run costs into the many millions. Then there is compensation for the farmers whose lands the aqueduct will cross. Very handsome compensation, too, or we will have upstate against us and lawsuits out of our ears."

It was Casey's turn to indulge a smile. "I see we have been consulting the same man. I myself have enlisted Mr. Geyer to draw up preliminary plans, and to begin surveying possible routes for the aqueduct. But the material point is, as you suggest, that a work of such magnitude is clearly beyond the reach of private financiers."

"However wealthy and civic-minded," added the mayor, with a nod to Laidlaw.

"That being the case," continued Casey, "I intend to propose a public subscription to raise the necessary funds, to be managed by a consortium of reputable men with accountability to the governor and legislature."

"You mean to raise a tax on the city?" said Laidlaw.

"A public *subscription*," said the mayor.

"A compulsory public subscription?"

"The aqueduct will serve the entire city of Manhattan," said Casey. "It will not be the private holding of the western wards, who at present drink ninety per cent of our potable water from our wells simply because they can afford to. I think I can guarantee that the working men of this city will be prepared to pay their share."

Laidlaw gazed at Casey for a moment, then turned back to the mayor as if he had never spoken. "Mr. Casey means to win an election by proposing a heavy new tax for a project that many will not live to see completed?" He sounded incredulous.

Casey now raised his voice, forcing Laidlaw's attention back to him. "I mean to win by promising a future for the city of Manhattan, a future that cannot be secured without new sources of fresh water! Everyone knows the old Collect Pond is now putrid, and our wells are almost dried up. With the situation as it is, we will face crisis after crisis, each summer worse than the last. Hundreds in this city, perhaps thousands, die every year from diseases related to the poor water supply. In the poor wards, they add brandy to their water just to get it down. I put it to you, Mr. Laidlaw, that this is a disgraceful situation for a city with pretensions to being the Atlantic's most important port! And if some year there is a drought, God forbid, the rich and the poor will suffer alike. We'll be chewing the dry grass together like cattle."

"Eamonn is right," said the mayor. "If a water tax it is, then New Yorkers will welcome it with open arms—if it is put to them in the right way. Lord knows it will be worth any kind of tax to them to drink water that isn't smelling of old boots and don't poison them and their children."

"It is certainly a noble notion, gentlemen," said Laidlaw, holding up his hands against their twin assault. "But as a man of business, I am used only to consulting the raw truth of numbers. If the numbers Mr. Geyer has given me are correct—and I have gone over them carefully myself—then your project will certainly ruin the city you mean to save. And if I can support that conclusion with sums on a page, I'm sure the governor can, and you can be sure he will beat you with them in this election. He will beat you hollow."

Casey looked at the mayor, who gave a small shrug.

Laidlaw now took the advantage. "Your plan of a public company board, funded only by public monies, must be abandoned."

"In favor of what?" said the mayor, leaning forward again. Casey felt a vague unease rising in him, but he hung on Laidlaw's words nevertheless.

"A water company—a company charged with management of public funds, but with the freedom to invest those funds for profit and to accept investment from private individuals in the purchase of shares. Such a company would make a sensation on Wall Street, I am sure of it. And with Mr. Casey in the governor's seat to promote the project everyday to the press and fix all the legal snags, the company's share price—well, I would set no ceiling for it."

The mayor clapped his hands, while Eamonn Casey experienced another strange feeling: that the aqueduct project—his Grand Idea—was being sold back to him, at a loss.

He spoke as coolly as he could. "Mr. Laidlaw, I am a Democrat, a Jackson man. My newspaper represents the common worker. After a lifetime of championing his interests in this city, how can I now encourage him to give up a stiff portion of his wages to the speculative schemes of the monopoly-loving merchants who would no doubt make up your company board, the very kind of men I have educated him to hate and distrust?"

Laidlaw gave a short laugh. "But Mr. Casey, you are too modest! Your skills as a rhetorician are famous. I'm sure you will find some way of explaining to the *Herald*'s readers where their true interests lie, without compromising your principles. I suggest an abundance of water imagery."

"You weren't expecting a walk in the park, were you Eamonn?" cried the mayor, reaching over to slap him on the knee. "If Mr. Laidlaw is willing to be our banker then you must play the politician!"

Casey mustered a smile. Laidlaw turned back to the mayor.

"I'm glad you raised the matter of finance. It is a delicate point. Forgive me, Mr. Casey, if I express surprise that a man of your political opinions would request the assistance of a man such as myself to help fund a campaign. I am a blood-sucking merchant, after all, and an Englishman!"

Casey flinched, and the mayor stepped in once more.

"Mr. Casey has sacrificed a great deal to achieve the public standing he has. He has not put profit before his ideals." The mayor stopped himself. "Not that I would suggest . . ."

"I have put everything into the newspaper," said Casey. "And I have put its profits into building a political base for the mayor."

He didn't mention the warehouses he owned on the docks, but then the deeds were not necessarily in his name. Neither did he mention the money he had put into his house on Park Row so that he could play the fine gentleman in his parlor. Nor the cost of having his children grow up alongside the children of New York's elite families having sworn, when Michael and Virginia were born, that they would never have cause to go to the Manhattan docks, the scene of his own famished childhood, except to sail from there to the great capitals of Europe.

"But you now intend to use the *Herald* to realize your own political ambitions," said Laidlaw. It was a blunt statement, not a question.

"It is a team effort," corrected the mayor, "My name and Mr. Casey's will appear side by side on the ticket this November. We will sink or swim together. The aqueduct will float us both home—ha ha!—But you have hit the nail on the head, Mr. Laidlaw. Mr. Casey will need lots of money if he is to beat the governor. We must buy up the newspapers we need in Brooklyn and upstate. And where none are to be bought we will have to start them ourselves. Then there are the needs of our Democrat friends in Albany. They will want generous persuading that Eamonn can win—and that he will serve in their interests."

"Oh—with money enough and the aqueduct to run on, I've no doubt Mr. Casey can win."

Eamonn Casey was very grateful to hear Mr. Laidlaw say it.

"But that said," Laidlaw continued, "if I might speak for a moment in the purely selfish terms that Mr. Casey would only expect me to use, when the glow of your victories has subsided, what reward might I expect for my efforts?"

"The satisfaction of saving the city of Manhattan for your children, and for their children," said Casey, drawing himself up.

But Laidlaw only pressed the tips of his fingers together and said nothing.

"I think Mr. Laidlaw is looking for something more constructive, Eamonn," said the mayor. "A more tangible means to serve your administration. If I might make a suggestion, he has said we will need to authorize a water company to build this aqueduct. Perhaps an appointment as director of this water company would be an appropriate honor for him. Am I right, sir? Would this position be of interest to you?"

Laidlaw turned to the mayor and smiled. Looking at them both, grinning at each other pleased as cats, Casey realized that whatever his aptitude for the strong-arm politics of the docks and the Bowery, he had much to learn about parlor-room negotiation of this kind.

He was still absorbed in this somber self-evaluation when he saw that John Laidlaw had reached over and offered his hand. He took it, almost without thinking. Only then did it strike him that the meeting had been a success. John Laidlaw, the wealthiest merchant in Manhattan and Wall Street's darling, had agreed to back him for governor! An extraordinary coup given that he had never held public office and had only just met the man. Casey smiled complacently to himself. He set great store in his own powers of persuasion and in the *Herald*'s reputation, but at the same time he decided that the special majesty of the aqueduct, as an idea, must have made the difference. What man of soul could resist it?

And then there was the mayor. Casey looked over at his old partner with newfound respect. He had thought him incompetent, a barely useful instrument to himself. But it was this fat, prosy politician who, when the critical moment came had known what to do. While he had been busy making speeches, the mayor had closed the deal. Casey made a mental note. He would not be shown up for an amateur again.

The mayor rose from his chair. "Excellent, then! Great things afoot. Great things!"

"There is one further matter," said Laidlaw.

The mayor sat down again.

"This yellow fever business. Last week in Brooklyn."

The mayor looked at Casey then back to Laidlaw. "It is over with, thank God. I had word just last night from Dr. Hosack. No new cases for a week. We have escaped very lightly."

"Nine deaths in total," said Casey, "instead of the hundreds we feared. The outbreak will be reviewed extensively in tomorrow's *Herald*."

Laidlaw turned to him. "And what is the opinion of the *Herald* on Dr. Hosack's proposal of a quarantine on shipping in the Manhattan ports?"

"Why, I believe it is a sensible precaution against a devastating outbreak here in the city. It is still July here, after all. The threat will not recede until the end of September. The doctor says that we in Manhattan are in grave and immediate danger."

"You know that Dr. Hosack has demanded a sixty-day quarantine on *all* shipping from the West Indies?"

Casey looked at Laidlaw uncertainly. It was like trying to read a book in a foreign language.

"Have you written on this issue in the *Herald* yet, Eamonn?" interrupted the mayor, anxiety in his voice.

"No, but . . ."

"You do know that the opinion of the medical community is divided on the question of the fever's origin?"

"Dr. Hosack is convinced the fever is imported by ship from the tropics, from the West Indies."

"Ah yes, Eamonn, but many would disagree with him on that point. There are eminent men of science—friends of Mr. Laidlaw—

who would argue with equal conviction that the yellow fever is produced from our local squalor, from the refuse on the docks and the open drains."

"Indeed, you are right, Mr. Mayor," said Laidlaw. "Let me put it plainly. If a quarantine is imposed on New York Harbor for the duration of this summer, my personal losses will run into the thousands. Perhaps a thousand dollars a day. I have a dozen ships in Kingston, more in Havana and Port-au-Prince. They will be idle under Dr. Hosack's quarantine, and their goods will rot unbought. I will not have money enough to pay my regular creditors, let alone support any political adventures in the fall. I'm sure you of all people, Mr. Casey, would not ask me to choose between paying my workers or funding your campaign."

Casey felt himself struggling to keep up and he only nodded his head vaguely.

"There is a Board of Health hearing on the quarantine business this Friday," Laidlaw continued. "Dr. Hosack is due to present his case then. The president of the board, Dr. Miller, is an old friend of mine and not unfriendly to Wall Street's view of things. With your permission, I will speak to him."

The mayor nodded with enthusiasm. Then he and Laidlaw turned to look at Casey. He coughed and lifted his large frame upright on the divan. There was no going back now.

"Well, I can assure you—that is—the *Herald* will be sure to point out the harmful consequences of a quarantine. After all, there isn't a working man in this city whose livelihood doesn't depend on the unimpeded traffic of sail in and out of the harbor. To put a halt to this trade would ruin some merchants and warehouse owners within weeks. Bankrupt them and their men won't be paid."

"Exactly," said the mayor. "And soon it's starving children in paper shoes on Broadway. No mayor can win reelection in November with child corpses on the streets in September. It stands to reason. Dr. Hosack must be denied."

"Better still," said Laidlaw, "the *Herald* might usefully question the motives of a man who would make such inflammatory suggestions regarding the public's safety."

"Inflammatory? You mean Hosack?" cried Casey.

"Yes, indeed. That mouthpiece of his, the *Gazette*, has been printing highly emotional pieces on the yellow fever for weeks. He exaggerates the prospects of its coming to Manhattan after all this time. The city is far cleaner than in '14. Public fears have been raised to an unhealthy extent."

"The *Gazette* has barely a thousand subscribers," said Casey, unimpressed.

"But many more readers," said Laidlaw. "As the mayor mentioned, I have eminent men of science among my acquaintance. They might provide your *Herald* with ready arguments against Dr. Hosack's myth of the fever being imported by ship."

"Excellent!" cried the mayor.

Casey nodded again. He felt he was expected to.

"But in the long run, for everyone's sake, I think it would be best to make an example of the doctor himself." Laidlaw directed another significant look at Casey. Then he rose to his feet.

"I quite agree," said the mayor, getting to his feet also. "This hero-worship of Dr. Hosack has gone on too long."

Casey could not repress a soft whistle as he sat back on the divan, while the other two men chatted over the mantelpiece. They were already planning a party to launch his campaign for governor, to be hosted by Mrs. Laidlaw herself.

Eamonn Casey experienced a tug of uneasiness in the midst of his euphoria. He had always admired Dr. Hosack. A rich man, yes, but one who had used his fortune for the public good. He had educated a generation of physicians at Columbia College to the standards of the great medical academies of Europe, built an entire Botanical Gardens with specimens brought from the four corners of the globe, and pressured the mayor and the council to build Bellevue Hospital after the terrible fever epidemic of 1814. Moreover, he had the air of legend about him, as the young attending physician that notorious dawn on the Weehawken bluff when he and his friend Alexander Hamilton, expecting to conclude a trivial dispute by firing in the air, were surprised by the murderous designs of Aaron Burr. And was the *Herald* now to turn against such a man? A man almost a saint? Glancing toward the ceiling, Casey's eyes made contact once more with the pale orbs of the martyred Hamilton and felt their unforgiving scrutiny. He looked away.

So this was politics. The politics of rich men. Casey rose heavily to his feet, plastered a smile on his face and offered his hand once more to John Laidlaw. The road to Albany passed through this man, and he promised to be a most interesting companion on the way.

CHAPTER THREE

The familiar cries of "Fire!" woke Albert from the folds of a deep sleep. From his upstairs window on Franklin Street, he looked out over the wooden rooftops of Manhattan. To the east, a half-mile away, a single plume of gray smoke spiraled into the blackness. Another warehouse most likely, on the East River docks.

Like most young city men, Albert belonged to a fire company. His was the proud Number 12 of the Bowery. He knew his comrades would already be staking a claim to the nearest water plug, beating off by force if necessary all pretenders to the honor of fighting the fire. He dressed quickly, pulling his red shirt over his head as he felt for the stairs in the milky darkness. He trod quietly in stockinged feet to avoid waking his aunt and uncle. Once outside, he pulled on his boots and ran all the way to Water Street.

He found George Bickart already there. He had put an upturned barrel over the water plug and was now sitting over it, arms folded like an Indian chief. Around him stood angry partisans of Company 6, remonstrating with him. Their engine had already arrived. They were ready to set their hose and fight the fire. This was their block by rights. He must get off!

"And which of you heroes is it will make me?" said George with a yawn and a grin.

Albert had first befriended George Bickart at Columbia, though George had left under a cloud before the honor of graduation could be bestowed on him. His father had disinherited him for his sins, and since that double downturn in his fortunes, George's interests had moved eastward across Broadway to the Bowery. No longer the Columbia gentleman, he was now the very picture of the fighting Bowery Boy: baggy pantaloons tucked in his boots, a vest and frock coat over his fireman's red shirt, a color kerchief knotted at the neck in true street-dandy style. This Bowery uniform was completed by a set of handsome racetrack whiskers and a knotty scar under his left eye, the trophy of a brawl at the Bull's Head in which he had been saved from virtual dismemberment by the whirling fists of Albert Dash.

But when Albert took his place at George's side to assist in staring down the upstart Company Sixers, they made an almost comical study in contrast. Even on his fighting toes, Albert stood a foot beneath George's bearish frame. Where George filled the fireman's uniform with impressive, even overflowing bulk, Albert was compact and sinewy. His dress, like his figure, was spare and without comment. He wore no adornments to his red shirt, plug hat and plain duck trousers. Nor did he chew tobacco as his friend did.

"Ah, here's Reade at last," said George at the sight of the familiar Number 12 engine, turning the corner from Wall Street.

With that, the Sixers accepted their fate. They packed up their hose and engine and trudged away in dejected silence, pursued by a chorus of taunts from the victorious Company 12.

Meanwhile, the fire raged unchecked. And it raged a full half-hour longer while they pumped water from the near-empty well. The men of Company 12 grunted and heaved at the wheel until finally the welcome gurgle was heard, and the hose sprouted a great flower of brackish brown water into the street. By this time, the warehouse—whose front covered more than half the block—was almost completely shrouded in acrid-smelling smoke.

"We should try the office door first," said Albert. "If we can't save the stock, we might get the owner his papers out at least."

"If I know Mr. Casey," George replied, "he has made copies of his insurance ahead of time."

"This is Mr. Casey's building?" said Albert, astonished.

"You didn't hear it from me," said George with a wicked smile.

Then they set to. When they broke down the door, fire licked out into the street sending them staggering backward. A cloud of sparks singed their hair and clothes, and they coughed and spat in the billowing smoke.

"Fetch the ladder!" cried George. "Try the upstairs window."

They mounted the window on the wall. Albert scrambled up halfway, but was soon enveloped in choking smoke. It filled his mouth and nostrils so he could scarcely breathe. Squinting upward through the haze, he saw to his dismay that the iron shutters on the windows had been fastened shut, trapping the angry flames. The shutters were red hot and had begun to crack and split. Thick curlicues of smoke in the air above him.

"Some fool has sealed these windows!" Albert shouted down.

No one responded, except for what sounded like George Bickart laughing.

Back on the street, Fire Company 12 considered its dwindling options. The fire had now taken hold of the entire second floor and was burning upward to the third, where further untold thousands of dollars of stock lay waiting to be consumed.

To the north was a small enclosed yard. George and Albert rushed the ladder to the fence and climbed over, while Reade and the others pushed the cart into position. George and Albert armed themselves with heavy iron spikes and set about breaking down the wall to expose the fire. They could not stand and deliver their blows without being scorched and blinded by the inferno above them. So they alternated with each other, running in and out with screaming battle-cries, smashing their pikes against the crumbling, fire-eaten wall.

"Look there!" cried George. They looked up and saw flames jet beautifully upward from the roof into the starry darkness. A loud combustion, and in seconds the entire roof had caught fire with the speed of a tinderbox. The sky above them was a single long bed of flame.

"Watch out!" cried Albert and several voices together. A huge gable tore free of the roof with a loud crack and came crashing down in front of them in a fireworks of ash and burning chips. A cry to Albert's left. One of the company, standing next to Reade, had been hit across the face.

"Is that Turner? Is he alright?" shouted Albert into George's ear in the confusion.

"To hell with him! That thing almost hit the engine."

Reade led the injured man back to the street, and the rest returned to the pump wheel, while Albert and George ventured as far as they dared into the burning building. They strained on the spouting hose, directing it upward as best they could toward the bright hot core of the flames. But it was not enough.

"Keep pumping, damn you!" cried George, when they felt the water pressure slacken dangerously.

"We are! We are!" came the cry through the smoke.

"Water's out," said Albert. "Well must be dry." They looked grimly at each other.

"Hey, in there! Get out! Roof's coming down!"

They threw the hose over their shoulders and began to run toward the shouting voices. Big George tripped and fell, swallowed instantly in the smoke like a breaching whale. Albert ran back to him, almost tripping himself up and so dooming them both.

"Get out! For Christ's sake!" It was Reade's voice this time, still twenty yards away.

"Get these fucking crates off me!" yelled George.

Albert kicked them away and hauled him out. Dragging George with one hand and the hose with the other, Albert ploughed back through the smoke toward the strip of open black sky. A terrible ripping sound, directly above them.

"Run, George, damn you!" he shouted.

Suddenly they were in the outside air. They ran right over Reade, and all three fell in a sprawling, cursing heap, tangled hopelessly in the hose. Just then began a never-ending crash, which drowned out all the shouting voices. The roof had fallen in.

Trapped in clouds of ash, minutes passed without breathable air. They stumbled across the yard, over the fence, and regrouped at last on the far side of Water Street. After a quick head count, Fire Company 12 turned to watch the last of the fiery destruction.

"Seemed like water made no difference. She just drank it up," said Reade.

"Biggest fire all summer, I'd say," said another excited voice. "They'll write us up for sure."

"Wait till Casey hears we ran out of water. You'll be reading about *that* in the *Herald*," said George, cleaning the soot from his whiskers.

"How's Turner?" said Albert.

"Fennell's taken him up to Bellevue."

Dawn revealed a smoking ruin. Reserves of the company, who had missed all the fun, brought food and water in a barrel. The water tasted foul, but they all drank it anyway, by the gallon. Then they sent for wine and ale. By the time the Trinity Church bells rang out, the boys had begun singing, and to the small crowd that had gathered to pay their respects to the mixed-goods warehouse on Water Street, it was obvious that Fire Company 12 were well on their way to being quite cocked.

George put an arm around Albert's shoulder.

"Me and the boys are heading up to Fraunces Tavern. Now that we're up, we figure we might as well make a day of it. Why don't you come along, this once."

Albert shook his head.

"Just one drink," said George. "The one I owe you for pulling me out of there."

"I'm late for a botany lesson."

"Miss Casey?"

"The same."

"I hope the old man pays you well."

"Not so. Miss Casey is eager to learn botany, and her schooling provided her with none. It is an act of friendship."

"Friendship! With a pretty young thing like Ginny Casey?" George laughed.

"It's not something I'd expect you to understand, George. Should I break the news to him?"

"Who? What?"

"The fire. Mr. Casey's losses."

George was silent a moment. "I wouldn't. His losses will be nothing to speak of, believe me. And besides"—he scuffed the blackened dirt with his large boot—"he pays other people to keep him informed of such things."

There was a moment's awkwardness between them. Albert felt George's bear-like arm around his shoulder. Then a single, parting slap on the back.

Albert took a last swig of water and set off back along Water Street. Before he reached the corner, he stopped and turned around.

"How did you do it, George?" he called back. "How did you get here first when you're up on the Bowery and the Sixers live right here?"

But George didn't answer. Perhaps he hadn't heard. He only laughed and waved before turning back into the circle of roaring Bowery Boys.

CHAPTER FOUR

Virginia Casey was acutely aware of being stared at. The spectacle of an unaccompanied young lady walking along Wall Street in the late morning was enough to bring a stop to conversations in front of the counting houses, and brought a group of rowdy young men (drunk already!) spilling onto the stoop in front of Fraunces Tavern.

The experience was one part disagreeable, one part frightening, one part she didn't know what. But it was a routine she was almost used to by now, and some of the banker's clerks and stockjobbers tipped their hats to her as she passed. To the male mind, a woman seen once was ripe for ogling and cat-calling. But see her twice and she was suddenly and ever after a lady. A simple system. But then, as her friend Vera said, men were such dear, simple creatures.

Virginia was not dressed as she would be for an ordinary day in the city, for shopping on Broadway or a promenade along the Battery. Such expeditions required silk and ribbons in abundance, and a low-cut bodice with flounced sleeves on especially confident days. Virginia was well known for her studiousness, but she was no prude. She was secretly proud of her light figure, which the new fashion for crimped waists showed off to a nicety. The problem with dressing up, however, was that the more successful ladies of the town read the same fashion periodicals and shopped at the same boutiques as those from respectable society. More than one careless young gentleman on Broadway had made a terrible mistake as a result and served a term as persona non grata among the friends of the insulted lady. To minimize that danger, Virginia wore a plain dark skirt with full-sleeved blouse, also dark, buttoned at the neck.

Wall Street, though bustling with business, still retained a country air about it. Upstate farmers in broad-brimmed hats guided their carts full of apples, corn and chickens to market, while pigs rooted in the vegetable mess underfoot. Virginia passed more than one man with a rifle on his shoulder and a dog at his side, intending no doubt to pass the day shooting rabbit and snipe on Lispenard Meadow only a mile to the north. Another man, resplendent in his financier's habit of dove-gray morning coat and silk cravat, carried a freshly killed turkey by his side as casually as if it had been a briefcase of bills. And Wall Street was decidedly rural in its treacherous terrain. Aside from the dangers of street garbage, the pavements were poorly kept up and impassable after rain. On either side, old wooden shanties crouched at odd angles between great marble-fronted edifices, jutting out into the street. Mr. Fenimore Cooper had called Manhattan "a hobble-dehoy metropolis," and though he afterward swore he meant it fondly, no one had quite forgiven him for stating the clear truth of the matter.

Virginia held her breath now as she passed the Tontine Coffee House, which sported a raised platform at its street entrance crowded with drinkers and a balcony on the first floor. Here the money men rested from trading shares on the Exchange floor inside. They smoked cigars and contemplated their gains and losses, as well as the merits of any young lady who might come into view. It was like walking onstage in full view of the gallery. (Vera said that the effects of coffee on young men could be worse than liquor.) A sudden wolf-whistle—but she refused to turn her head and hurried on. Then she wondered if it had been meant for her after all.

Down Fulton Street toward the market a very different order of the male sex presented itself. The men who hauled carts stacked with flour bags and barrels of molasses wore brown dungarees and shirts open at the collar in place of breeches and cravats, and cloth caps set low over the brow. Men who reeked of the sea stood behind stalls groaning with the morning's catch and wiped their hands on greasy aprons. Other vendors wandered among the stalls, sending up their cries in competition: oysters, clams, and hot corn could be had at ha'penny a basket, but also gingerbread, yeast buns and baked pears. Among the burly men in their seafaring caps, a lone black woman in a yellow bandanna advertised a tray of cakes in front of her with the shout of "Tea ruk, ruk, ruk! Tea ruk!"

English sailors on furlough, their unmistakable twin pigtails swinging on their shoulders, lounged among the stalls. They were always short of money but eager for diversion, and could be relied on to study Virginia from head to toe as she walked by. But their leering was now the least of her concerns. The chewing of tobacco being almost universal on the docks, great drops of black spit rained in the dust before and behind her as she walked. In a white dress, she would have arrived at her destination that day looking like an oil painting gone awry. But veteran that she now was, when the door at the corner of South Street was opened to her, she presented a figure of ladylike grooming and respectability, as befitted a member of the New York Society for the Prevention of Paupery.

Not that little Joshua Mosey, who opened the door with one hand while continuing to gorge himself on a ream of pork fat, cared what she looked like or who she belonged to. He took one look at her, determined that she was unlikely to offer to hunt rats with him or take him out in a boat, and ran chewing and hallooing back into the house, leaving Virginia to invite herself in.

She stepped into the smell of roast mutton and vinegar: the smells of the poor in tiny houses where the kitchen was the largest room, and there were no doors in the doorways.

Presently, the women of the house emerged, wiping their hands on their aprons. They greeted her warmly. Miss Casey was not like other young ladies from the Society, who could not see anything in a poor woman's domestic arrangements but to criticize it and made you sit through long lectures on thrift and personal cleanliness before giving up her charity basket.

Miss Casey was different. She didn't carry a basket at all, not since the first time. After greeting Mrs. Mosey, she simply reached into her pocket and pulled out a drawstring purse heavy with coins. As was the custom between them, Mrs. Mosey did not accept it, but allowed her daughter Sarah to take the purse, which she did with a brief curtsey before disappearing into the kitchen.

The floor was covered with threadbare mats, while the furniture consisted of some old-fashioned Dutch stools and a gaudy settee that Mr. Mosey had rescued from the street and fixed up on one of his better days.

"How is Mr. Mosey?" said Virginia when they were seated, while Sarah served them tea with as much decorum as if they had been in Virginia's own parlor on Park Row.

"Worse and worse, Miss Casey. There's no work for journeymen. It's all big shops now or no work at all. No man is his own master these days, as your father rightly says in his newspaper. I've tried to reconcile Mr. Mosey to the fact, but he's too stubborn and won't have it, even though it's the difference between paying rent and not. He just loafs about the docks, waiting for work to turn up, he says, but more like just sitting with his cronies, drinking his money away."

Virginia was a confirmed democrat in her thinking, as her father had taught her to be, but she couldn't help a feeling of consternation that a man like Mr. Mosey should be given the vote.

"If Mr. Mosey isn't working, what about your rent? I know it is disgracefully high. How can you possibly manage?"

Instead of replying, Mrs. Mosey made a clucking noise with her tongue and stared at the large patch of falling plaster above the pot-belly stove.

Virginia suddenly noticed that Sarah was lingering near the kitchen door, looking strangely at her. She noticed now, too, that Sarah's hair was done up in a way she hadn't seen before.

When their eyes met, Sarah bit her lip. She had meant to stand proud, be a bit saucy even, but when Miss Casey looked at her so openly and with such goodness she felt the hot tears well up. In an instant she was sitting with her on the settee, talking fast between sobs and allowing her hair to be petted and stroked.

Before she left, Virginia mentioned the rumors of yellow fever and suggested that Joshua not be allowed to run so freely around the docks in the evening hours.

"Thank you, Miss," said Mrs. Mosey. "I will certainly do what you say and keep 'im indoors." Then she added, in a confiding whisper, "You know what this yellow fever is, Miss?"

"What do you mean?"

"It's a plot to get the Irish. There's too many of us here now. The mayor thinks it for sure, and word on the docks is that if the yellow fever don't wipe us out, he's going to send us all out West to be murdered by Injuns!"

When Miss Casey had gone, the Mosey women declared her a true angel of mercy and spent the happiest day together they could remember. Sarah said she would not go out that night, and though that meant putting off the landlord another day, mother and daughter laughed and told jokes and praised Joshua for his display of dead rats, dangling like charms from a string, as loudly as if they had been ornaments in a shop window on Broadway.

Virginia had accepted their thanks and curtsies with a quiet smile. Despite every effort on her part to soften her relations with the Moseys, to represent herself as a friend and not a mistress visiting from the "great house," such as they were accustomed to in the old country, she still went away with the burden of their servile respect. Sometimes, they even managed to convince *her* that she was Lady Casey.

Mrs. Mosey was proud to claim notice from "Mr. Eamonn Casey's daughter, who visits us from Park Row," and Sarah from "the rather short but pretty young lady who was very rich, but did not give herself airs." Virginia was all these things, but she was sufficiently self-critical to recognize that she visited the Moseys more out of a deep curiosity for their lives than the impulses of her much-vaunted goodness. Because in looking at the Moseys, Virginia Casey was looking at her life as it might have been.

Her own father had grown up on these very streets. He had been one of those barefoot boys tearing by, chasing through the market stalls, harassing the clam sellers on the street corners. Perhaps he had been like little grease-lipped Josh Mosey, hunting rats along the wharf. And would have become like Mr. Mosey, a sad, defeated drunkard, had not some magical transformation occurred, a transformation she was very eager to understand.

All she knew of her father's early struggles was that at the age of nine, or perhaps eleven, he had found work as a typesetter's boy in a printing shop. It was there in a sunless room, covered in ink, working from dawn into the night, that he had learned to read: block by block, letter by letter as he placed the type onto the press, then sent it whizzing and whirring into the world as print. His hands, even now, were visibly stained by years of unwashed ink, which he carried into his unlikely future like a birthmark. Something about that printing shop and the magic of letters on the page must have unsealed the boy's ignorant mind and sent him on his way. Because now, some thirty years later, he was the most feared newspaperman in Manhattan, an uneducated Irishman who wielded the master's language like a whip.

Her father had never spoken of his childhood to her, and so had never properly explained how it was that an illiterate orphan off the boat from County Cavan, without prospects beyond a life of petty crime or further exile on the seas, learned even to conceive of a different life for himself. How it even occurred to him that he should aspire to be a gentleman, and that any daughter of his should not be sent to work as an indentured servant as soon as she was old enough to dress herself, but rather should stay at home to be waited on by her own maid, play the piano and generally be pampered like a dauphine.

Virginia longed to know the answers to these questions, but had never been able to ask her father outright. So she had resorted to investigations of her own. Her announcement last fall that the Society was sending her to a family on the docks had staggered him. It was the only time she could remember her father lost for a word. In Virginia's mind, that day had marked the beginning of the current troubled period of their relations, compounded of course by whole other circumstances in her life that contributed to a universal impression in the Casey household: that little Virginia was no longer so uncritically devoted to her father as she had once been and was now embracing something like independence. If not independence of body—she could never leave her father's home until she was married—then independence of mind. Of course, this only made her poor father love her the more, that her character should so much resemble his own.

Walking back uptown, Virginia noticed a more than usual commotion on Water Street. Turning the corner, she was confronted by a burned-out building, its foundations sticking up like blackened stumps of teeth. Smoke curled up from the ruins into the blue sky, and the air was heavy with the smell of burnt resin and coffee and ashes damped by water from the fire hoses.

It had clearly been a considerable inferno, even in a city where fires were an almost nightly occurrence, and a crowd was still lingering to relish the devastation. Two men near her were discussing the event, and she paused to listen.

"The boys did their best, but it took a half-hour to pump water from the well."

"A shame, that's what it is," said the other man, sucking on a cob pipe.

"Just when it looked like they had it beat, the flow dried up completely."

"Dry well again. A shame is what it is."

Virginia made her way through the crowd to the corner of Front Street. Passing once again by Fraunces Tavern she discovered that the firemen were well along in consoling themselves for their recent disappointment, making up for a lack of water with a surfeit of liquor and spirits. In their trademark red shirts, Fire Company 12 lounged in the doorway of the tavern, bantering loudly with a group of young, brightly dressed women across the street. Virginia recognized the loudest of the firemen and quickly wrapped her shawl about her shoulders and lowered her head. She had no wish to be recognized by George Bickart when he was in his cups.

It was safer to look at the young women strolling in front of the shop windows, who answered the firemen's taunts with bold talk of their own. Vera had told her about them: girls sometimes younger than herself who took a fee and went with men to lie with them alone. She studied them from the corner of her eye, then looked up at the shuttered windows above them. How many girls were now lying in bed behind those very shutters in the arms of young men, pleasantly tired in the noontime heat?

She thought again of Sarah Mosey, who only a year ago she had found rolling with her brother in the dirt near the hogs. Now Sarah had grown tall and full of figure and wore ribbons in her hair. She had looked out of the window at the passing crowds with a business-like air. Virginia pursed her lips. Was this the fate she herself had escaped because her father had taught himself to read by moonlight after all the other workers had gone home? Virginia quickened her pace uptown, turning her mind from this disquieting topic to the very pleasant afternoon she had in store.

For the afternoon to *be* pleasant, however, she desperately needed a bath and a change of clothes. A bath, because she felt sticky and uncomfortable from walking all the way back uptown in her dark dress, and a change of clothes because this dress was not in the least appropriate for entertaining a young gentleman in her parlor. Not that she was to "entertain" the gentleman exactly, because the appointment was for a lesson in botany, but Virginia, for reasons she kept to herself, chose to see the distinction as a very narrow, pedantic one. As she came in view of the willow trees of the park and the gleaming cupola of City Hall, she was already imagining her new white silk dress with yellow lace roses at the belt.

But in the event, Virginia had neither her bath nor her white silk dress.

"Why, there you are at last! I have been waiting half an age," cried Vera from the parlor. Virginia shot a glance at Lily Riley, who was helping her with her hat and shawl. But Lily only shrugged and gave her an exasperated look.

"Vera!" Virginia ran into the parlor and embraced her friend, whom she was sincerely glad to see despite everything.

"Ah, you're damp!" cried Vera, feeling her arms. She said it in a strangely approving way.

"Yes, I must change out of this dress."

"No, you don't. Not until you've spent at least twenty minutes talking to me." Vera threw herself on the divan and stretched out her impossibly long legs. She was much taller than Virginia. She was also very thin, but somehow this never translated into an appearance of being brittle or frail. Quite the opposite. Now, as she shook her head from side to side for no apparent reason other than to set her flame-red hair swirling in the air, she seemed more like a human firework. The young Columbia men lounged around the benches across the street for hours, waiting for a glimpse of Miss Laidlaw leaving her friend's house, or for a wave from the parlor window. They called her "The Rocket."

"This heat! It will be the death of me. You are so good to be doing the Society's work in July. I have told them I cannot volunteer again until October at least."

"I understand you," said Virginia. "It is certainly inconvenient of the poor to live in unventilated apartments, and out of season."

"You mock me, but you know I don't have your strength, Virginia. And besides, I never know what to say to them. I won't preach, you know."

"Nor do I, I assure you. Perhaps if you prepared for your visits in the way you do to play on the stage."

Vera was the most celebrated tragedienne in the history of Miss Piper's Academy, from which both young women had recently graduated. Word of her extraordinary natural pathos at school had reached Mr. Burfield of the Bowery Theater, who, after seeing her death throes as Desdemona, had enlisted her for his professional company, much to the horror of her mother. Since then, Virginia had noticed a change in her relationship with her friend. Vera seemed to pay even less attention than usual and had lost interest in the many activities they once shared, including the Society for the Prevention of Paupery. Lately, it was all theater, theater, theater.

"Besides, there is no drama in good works," Vera complained. "I wish that there were, but there isn't. And the families I visit have as little desire to see me as I do them. I think we should all just send our baskets to them by messenger and spare them the condescending ritual."

Virginia said nothing in reply because she had stopped listening. She loved Vera like a sister, but she could think of nothing at that moment but how best to get rid of her. Vera might be engaged to Albert Dash, but Virginia was his botany student, and in the strange, secret logic of her thinking on the matter, she believed firmly that Vera should think as little of disrupting her weekly lesson with Albert as she would think of breaking up their engagement.

Meanwhile, Vera talked on. "But I'm surprised you were allowed to go down to the port at all, with all this talk of yellow fever. Albert says the docks are very dangerous now. My mother is beside herself already. She is begging father to move us from Bowling Green before we all get sick and die."

Vera shared her mother's opinion of Bowling Green, which had fallen victim to the relentless push northward of the city's commerce. The red-brick colonial mansions of the Green had long been abandoned by their friends for the quieter elegance of Park Row and Lafayette Place. The parlors where Mrs. Laidlaw had once attended lunches with delicate young clergymen and visiting opera singers had been rudely appropriated by counting men with ink-stained fingers and slick-looking financiers. Great sacks of chaff and potatoes stood on the street, which was crammed with common carts, eventually making Mrs. Laidlaw's daily walk such a punishment to her that she now sometimes refused to go out at all. Unfortunately, Mr. Laidlaw did not seem to notice.

"What has Albert said to you—about the yellow fever?"

Vera rolled her eyes. "You know what a doomsayer he is."

"Yes, but it is the doomsayers who take measures against disaster that others are too careless to foresee."

"You sound just like Albert when you say that. But I worry that Dr. Hosack will put him in danger and Albert will not say no to him."

Virginia pursed her lips and said nothing. She had been in a fever of anxiety herself while Albert and the doctor had been on the Brooklyn docks.

"I have tried to tell him . . ." Vera hesitated, "to gently *suggest* to him that he drop Dr. Hosack and find some other patron."

Virginia was shocked. "But Albert would never do that! Besides, what better patron could he have? Dr. Hosack is the most important physician in the city."

"Yes, but my father says he is a man of the past, and your father thinks so too. The old order is passing away, you know. Those old families like the Hosacks—"

"And the Dashes—"

"—Yes, and the Dashes, too. The old families don't run things anymore. We all know the great things Dr. Hosack has done. But my father says he has made so many enemies over the years that he is no longer listened to and that any follower of Dr. Hosack will certainly inherit his enemies. He is not a very pleasant man, you know. Mother says so. And she says he is not quite as fastidious as he might be . . . with the ladies." She laughed as she said it.

Vera's new opinions on Albert's career upset Virginia, and her voice when she spoke showed some strain. "Have you said all this to Albert?'

Vera made a face. "He never gave me a chance. He got so angry with me for even suggesting he give up the doctor that I didn't have the courage to go on. I wanted to tell him he should forget medicine entirely and go to work with my father on Wall Street. That is where poor young men like Albert make their fortunes, not giving tinctures to old ladies and chasing about after the yellow fever. But maybe it's just as well I didn't say it."

She looked at Virginia as if wanting confirmation. Virginia nodded.

Vera sighed. "It all seems so very hard."

"Your father has not changed his mind?"

"No."

"Does he not like Albert?"

"It's not that. He says it's because there is so very little left of the Dash fortune. For us to marry, Albert must make his own money. And quickly too, if we are not to need spectacles and walking sticks on our wedding day."

Virginia made no reply, though there was so much to be said regarding love and money. She was looking out the parlor window onto Park Row. Vera watched her for a moment, then her whole face broke into a delighted smile.

"But it is Tuesday today, and you have your lesson with him! Why did you not remind me?"

"I thought—"

"I had forgotten completely. What luck! You know I have not seen Albert in two weeks, not since the business in Brooklyn began. It has been too, too long. What a surprise he will get to find me here!"

"He is coming."

As if on cue, the familiar ragged hat had emerged from the face-less rush of passersby as she watched through the window. Albert was striding along Park Row at a belting pace, which unfortunately she could not take as a compliment to her because he always tore about the city as if he were an hour late for something. The eyes of the two young women met for an instant, then broke away. They saw him leap up the stoop, three steps at a time.

"Why is he wearing a red shirt?" asked Vera. "And what has happened to his face?"

They heard three loud raps on the door, followed by Lily Riley bustling into the foyer. She subsequently appeared at the parlor door to announce the visitor. From the look on her face, her opinion of his appearance seemed to match Vera's.

"I suggested Mr. Dash go home to wash, but he wouldn't have it. You know what I think of it, Miss, appearing before young ladies—"

"Certainly, I know. You are very good, Lily," said Virginia.

"Tell him to come in. He must answer to us now," said Vera with a wicked smile.

Albert Dash walked into the parlor. He was taller than the two women, though not actually tall; slim but broad-shouldered. He looked very much like a Dash in his features, with his strong Dutch brow and squared jaw; but his pale complexion was very becomingly contradicted by his dark eyes and the rich black curls that framed his face. Across his right ear was a fresh finger-long cut roughly plastered with gauze.

If Vera had bargained on Albert's being surprised to see her, she was not disappointed. But her surprise was equal to his. She had begun by looking peeved, but at the sight of blood on his cheek, her resolution broke, and she rushed over to him. "My God, your ear! Have you been brawling, Albert?"

She reached up a hand to his face. He flinched, grabbed her hand and held it gently away.

"There was a fire on Water Street last night."

"Ooh, yes," cried Lily, who was lingering in the doorway. "I saw the smoke this morning and the sparks flying into the sky. It was better than July Fourth!"

"Lily, you may go," said Virginia.

Lily looked hurt. Virginia's maid considered it almost part of her domestic duties at Park Row to be in love with Albert Dash. But he was as oblivious to Lily's feelings as he was to her mistress's. Lily chose to leave toward the kitchen and she swung her skirt ever so slightly toward him as she passed by. True to form, Albert didn't notice. Nor did he notice the look of laughing contempt she gave the hat he belatedly handed to her.

"I have been at the fire since well before dawn," said Albert. "I apologize for my appearance. Lily was most disapproving."

Vera had an expression of amazement on her face.

"I didn't know you belonged to a fire company! No one I know fights fires! Have you been walking all over Manhattan in that red shirt?"

"I have."

Vera looked distinctly peevish now. She dropped his hand and turned toward Virginia.

"Did you know Albert belonged to a fire company?"

"Yes, I did," Virginia replied. Then, fearing she had sounded too smug, she added, "it is George Bickart's Bowery Company, I believe."

Vera rolled her eyes. "Oh, I see! You fight fires with your old Bowery rowdies. You told me you had given them up."

"Someone has to fight the fires, Vera."

"And I don't see why you should! Not when we have not seen each other for two weeks. You had the goodness to ask me to marry you this spring, and I would most certainly not have agreed to it had I known I would be competing with the likes of George Bickart for your time."

"I was intending to come to Bowling Green to visit you directly after my lesson with Virginia. I will still come, if you will see me."

"Not before a change of dress, I hope. My father will throw you out on the street."

"Yes, of course. Anything you wish."

His acquiescence melted her anger. Albert saw his chance and took her hand. He smiled at her—a long, wordless smile that seemed to signal everything he would say to her were Virginia not there and now would not have to say, because it was in smiles such as these, Virginia knew from close observation, that lovers measured their entire intimate history together in an instant. It was a freakish ability that separated them from ordinary mortals.

Vera recognized the smile and returned it—too lingeringly, in Virginia's opinion. A flicker of Albert's eyes reminded Vera of her friend's presence.

"Oh, Virginia. I am sorry to have interrupted your lesson."

She only smiled and made a weak, dismissive gesture with her hand. Albert turned to look at her properly for the first time since he had arrived. She was suddenly very conscious of her plain dress and the film of perspiration on her face. He looked on the point of saying something to her, but didn't.

Vera gave a teasing skip across the floor. "You will be gratified to know, Albert, that Virginia and I were talking of you when you arrived."

"I must know the context," said Albert with a smile, "to judge whether I should be gratified."

"We were discussing Dr. Hosack."

Virginia shot Vera a warning look, but Vera looked straight past her. "Virginia and I are both great admirers of the doctor, but we hope too that he is not leading you into harm's way. I know some would think a week spent exposing oneself to yellow fever in Brooklyn a very heroic business. But others might say that such heroics are foolish in a young man of good family, especially one with wedding plans in his near future."

Vera spoke tenderly and answered his clouded look with her most celestial smile.

Albert had to have been made of stone not to walk over and instantly take her in his arms. She leaned back confidently in his grasp, and he swung her lightly from side to side, an arch smile on his face. He spoke softly, so that Virginia had to strain to overhear. "The doctor says he has gained resistance to the fever over time. And so will I. My week there is your best possible guarantee that we will grow old together."

Vera blushed, half-struggled in his grip and looked over at Virginia as if to say, *You see how he can be when he is charming!*

"And you will be pleased to know," Albert went on, "that my

work with the doctor has not been for nothing. He has given me a position."

Vera broke from him and threw her arms in the air. "A position!"

Something about the enthusiasm of this response appeared to unnerve Albert. "I don't know if it is permanent."

"A position! Are you professor now? What are you to be paid?"

"A professor? No, not that. I suppose I am a kind of 'special assistant.' Those were the doctor's words. He didn't mention a salary."

"And you didn't ask?" cried Vera.

"No, I didn't think of it."

Vera stared at him, mouth agape. "You didn't think of it?"

After a moment's pause, she turned on her heel and moved over toward where her hat and a silk scarf lay on the piano. She said nothing as she put them on, while the others looked at her warily. Virginia saw that her friend's face was red with anger. And she must have been embarrassed, too, because she didn't say goodbye or even look at her. Her parting words were for Albert.

"What you mean is, you didn't think of *me*!" She pushed past Albert, who did not try to stop her, but looked confused and forlorn. A moment later, they heard the front door slam and Vera's quick, light steps on the stoop. Virginia went to the window, but she had already vanished into the crowd milling in the shade of the trees in the park.

She turned in time to see Albert sit himself heavily on the settee. He put his head back and closed his eyes.

"Oh, Virginia," he said softly. And it was all he said for a long moment.

Then he sat up abruptly and spoke without meeting her eyes. "Before we begin our lesson, I wish to speak to your father. Is he at home?"

Virginia was about to reply that he was not, when Eamonn Casey appeared suddenly near the back parlor door. If Virginia had thought her father capable of eavesdropping, she would have said he had just stepped out from behind the potted palm. He advanced toward them with the fixed grimace Virginia recognized as the greeting he reserved for people he did not like, but to whom he was obliged to be polite.

"You do indeed find me at home, Mr. Dash, but not for long. I must be at the *Herald* in twenty minutes. I have a special edition to produce. But I see you put me to shame. You have performed a day's work already." He spotted the gash on Albert's ear. "God's truth, you look as if you had been in a battle!"

"He has. Albert has spent the night fighting a fire," said Virginia, with a hint of pride.

Albert began to speak, but Casey interrupted him. "Ah, no doubt. Fighting the yellow fever one day, fires the next. It seems there is no end to your conspicuous heroics, Mr. Dash. Well, I can't stay chatting. I am merely a watchdog of the working people of this city, not a firefighter beloved of the ladies. And it is to my humble duties I must return. Good day, Mr. Dash."

He brushed between them and was gone from the room. They heard him call Lily for his hat and cane, and in another moment the door shut behind him. From the window, they saw him walk down the cobble street at a brisk pace, past the sedate gray columns of the Park Theater, brandishing his cane like a weapon in the direction of the *Herald* offices on Broadway.

Virginia stood in wonder at her father's unexpected appearance at home in the middle of the day. She wondered also how it was that her father managed to combine poor manners with the most fastidious politeness. Then she looked across to Albert and caught an unguarded glance from his dark eyes. In an instant, all thoughts of her father vanished from her mind.

"Please come and sit down. Over here."

The fact that Albert had come for her botany lesson rather than an ordinary social call made it permissible for Virginia to sit on the same settee with him. They must be close enough to examine the new drawing together. But something was wrong. He was running his hand across his forehead—a familiar habit.

"You look exhausted," she said.

Albert sat himself up and made a visible effort to appear alert. "I am fine. I would not want us to miss two lessons in a row. Not after the promise I made to teach you Linnaeus."

She smiled, even as she pondered the worth of a promise made only for the sake of its keeping.

"If we miss lessons, I'm sure I will forget everything."

"I doubt that, Virginia. You are too modest."

While he arranged the table in front of them, she thought again of how strange it was to hear him call her Virginia. The sound of her Christian name, by itself, in his low, serious voice. It was only because he thought her so young, still a child, that he called her Virginia instead of Miss Casey, even though she had now turned seventeen. To Virginia's infinite despair, she was short in stature: she had refused to grow. At least, not upward. Vera had sprouted tall as a willow tree, while she could still barely see over the high grass in Lispenard Meadow in summer. When Albert Dash looked at her, he saw a short person, a mere girl. And it was just as Lily Riley said: a man had to be *told* how things really were, and even then he could not be trusted to listen.

But Virginia could never tell Albert the truth of her feelings, or anyone else. She was sure it would be embarrassing news to him, not to mention a terrible betrayal of Vera to whom he was more or less engaged. She must be content, as she had had to be for almost a year now, with simply watching him in an affectedly detached manner, like the botanist he was supposedly training her to be. But her detached manner was as fake as the make-believe world she inhabited on these afternoons, a world in which she and Albert Dash were lovers, and in which a young woman like her could actually become a botanist.

His fingers moved with quick, sure care. He lifted the leaves open gently and spread the pages across the table while she, for the hundredth time, studied the still shocking difference between the paleness of his skin and his night-black hair. Black Irish blood? She cherished in private the idea of their ancestral connection, but had never dared share it with him.

"There!" He sat back.

Before her, Virginia saw the perfect image of a tall wildflower. From a single nub at its base, multiple slim stems arched upward, sprouting bold crimson blossoms. They looked like elegant fingers: the flower, a hand waving. To one side of the paper, Albert had drawn an enlarged delineation of a clover-like leaf.

"It's beautiful," she said after a long moment's admiration.

He smiled. "It is one I asked you to look up in Linnaeus."

Virginia's brow furrowed in concentration as she studied the broad swathe of the leaves and the small, nut-like buds.

"Wormwood," she announced.

"Very good."

"It is mentioned in *Hamlet*."

"In *Hamlet*, really?" He looked thoughtful and said nothing for a long moment, leaving Virginia ample time to loathe herself for mentioning it. It could only remind him of Vera.

"Linnaean name?" he said.

"*Artemisia Absinthum.*"

"Where found?"

"Europe, but here now too. New England."

"And when does it blossom?"

"Well, you have drawn one for me," she said with a sly smile, "and it is the end of July."

"Yes, but I have the advantage of Dr. Hosack's greenhouses, to cheat Nature with."

"July to October, then."

"Very good." Albert rose from the settee and strode across the room, gesticulating in his grandest Hosackian manner. "The wormwood, so called, is a particularly beneficent medicinal flower. Pliny considered its absinthe solution an efficient tonic for most stomach disorders, and it has been administered successfully in modern times in cases of gout, scurvy and certain splenetic obstructions. With the addition of vinegar, it is an excellent palliative for all manner of open wounds, bruises and common sprains. Accounts exist of its use for this purpose in the Carthaginian campaigns."

"I have heard of absinthe as a drink, taken for pleasure," she said, daring to interrupt him.

Albert frowned at her. "For pleasure? I think not. The wormwood is a bitter flower."

Yes, you have brought me a bitter flower, she thought.

Then she said, "Absinthe is an intoxicant, in fact."

Albert looked at her as if he was shocked that she should know such a word, or what it meant.

"George Bickart told me." She defied him with her steady, slate-blue eyes. "He said you have drunk absinthe together, at Columbia."

She saw Albert's mouth drop open and a cloud of anger pass briefly across his handsome face. Then all of a sudden, he collapsed on the settee and laughed. He closed his eyes and laughed until his body lay limp on the seat.

She laughed too, but mostly she watched *him* laugh, her eyes fixed on the taut gleam of his skin where his red shirt opened, the gentle meeting-place of his neck and chest. Then, in an instant, he sat himself upright and the precious declivity closed up again, vanished from sight. Now he was looking at her with his dark eyes half-serious, half-smiling.

"George never could keep a secret. You will not tell your father, I hope. I don't want to cause a scandal at Columbia. Dr. Hosack would see me hanged if he read of absinthe revels in the *Herald*."

Virginia felt too flustered to reply. He was still sitting very close to her. She shook her head and managed a weak smile.

"Why *Artemisia*?" she said at last, to change the subject.

"I beg your pardon?"

"Why did Linnaeus call the absinthe flower *Artemisia*?"

Albert looked bewildered for a moment. He shifted his feet on the floor and then cast a longing eye toward the door.

Virginia watched him, puzzled.

"I cannot tell you," he murmured.

"You cannot tell me?"

"It is not important." He took up the drawing and made as if to put it away, fussing with the folder strings.

"But how can you say so?"

"Artemis is the huntress, the Greek goddess of chastity and unmarried girls."

"I know that. But why her? Why chastity and unmarried girls?"

"Please, Virginia. It isn't proper for me to say."

Virginia felt a tug of irritation with him. "I tell you I know that you have drunk absinthe with George Bickart—and you laugh at it! What is there in the name Artemisia that could be so much worse than that?"

"I wish I had never given you this flower," he said ruefully.

"Albert!" She heard the threatening note in her own voice and relished it.

"Very well, then!" He stood up, now clearly irritated himself, and strode over to the window away from her. Then he turned reluctantly back to her and began to explain in the most detached, professorial tone he could muster.

"The *Artemisia Absinthe* is so called because Pliny"—he faltered—"because in antiquity, it was believed the flower contained properties,"—he stopped, blushed—"possessed properties advantageous to"—an agonizing pause—"to the acceleration of puberty in girls for the purpose of early marriage . . ."

When Albert had gone, Virginia fetched her Linnaeus and memorized the thirty new species he had set her for the following week. Memorization came easily to her. Too easily. She was done in half an hour. Repetition with her was unnecessary. When she had learnt something once, she knew it forever. Her father, whose memory was prodigious, called it her most valuable inheritance. *Castanea vesca*, common chestnut; *Solanum dulcamara*, the bittersweet nightshade . . . She would carry the names of these flowers with her to the grave.

Virginia closed the book with regret. That left seven days minus one half-hour. An eternity, in other words. Vera filled her days with other people, with visits and rehearsals and trips on the river. Virginia, by contrast, was fast earning a reputation among the graduates of Miss Piper's as a recluse. Jane Harvey had suggested she must be in love to be mooning about the house all day, only venturing out to go to church or do some good work or other. But everyone else, Vera included, had laughed at the idea. Virginia was too serious to be in love, they said, and besides, what young men did she ever meet? She would end up in a nunnery.

They were right. She was too serious—if being serious meant that she found the world of books more alive than the world she lived in. What was another picnic party to Weehawken compared to an afternoon in her bedroom reading Shakespeare or Dr. Johnson?

She went to the piano, determined to pass the rest of the endless morning playing to herself alone in the empty parlor. She chose the more difficult Mozart sonatas and watched her hands perform their elegant gymnastics as if detached from her, allowing her precious relief from the monotony of her own thoughts. Her father had bought the instrument for her seventeenth birthday as a kind of unspoken truce offering. Her beloved harpsichord, now obsolete, was consigned to the attic, shut up like a butterfly's wings. Playing it as a child, she had imagined herself running in the green-pink garden painted on its inside lid. When she sang, she heard her own light voice through the trees. But this new instrument was a stern, forbidding mahogany. However much she tried, she couldn't accustom herself to its masculine tones. She played a chord and the voice of a man seemed to sing out, though she pressed the keys with the barest touch. She wondered: can I learn to love this form of conversation?

She lost her place in the music, played a few ragged arpeggios, then stopped. She had no real heart for playing these days. She began to feel very wretched and continued to sit at the piano for another hour not playing a note, just sitting and gazing out the window while the pressure of the terrible heat built up in the parlor like a slow-firing kiln. She thought about the Moseys and about Vera and Albert, and her father's disliking Albert. Then she thought about herself thinking of these things, sending thoughts in pursuit of thoughts, chasing round and round until she felt she was quietly going mad.

CHAPTER FIVE

Eamonn Casey was no stranger to bawdy houses—no choirboy he—but he had never before stood in front of one in public view the very week he was to announce his desire to be governor of the state. Fate was sometimes a comedian, to be sure.

As he knocked, he saw a train of butchers' boys in their blood-ied aprons approaching through the dust of the Bowery, leading a large cow. A small but raucous band of flutes and drums pre-ceded them while a crowd of children followed behind, slapping the doomed beast and sometimes throwing stones at it until one of the butchers' boys turned around and waved his fist. The pro-cession made stops at each house they passed for the Bowery wives to come out and select their portion for that evening's meal. He watched them mark their choice of flank or loin with a circle drawn by a paint-dipped stick.

To Eamonn Casey, this butcher's parade had the air of the ancient past, a ritual of a bygone time in New York. While he waited, he began composing a five-hundred-word vignette on the theme for the next day's *Herald*. Perhaps he could make a series: "Country Scenes on the Bowery." He would amaze his younger readers in reminding his older ones of when the Bowery had been a rural road lined with stockyards and slaughterhouses. After an apostrophe to progress, he would tell how the city had advanced out to meet its farmers and stockmen, and how, while the Bowery was now a veritable Babylon of dance halls, oyster bars and gambling dens, with gigs and carts rattling up and down all day long, the ancient abattoirs still continued their bucolic labors in yards off the street, and that this olfactory residue of the old Bowery could not be escaped (the more fastidious reader should perhaps put off his visit until cooler weather). Actual evidence of butchery was left to the gaudy tavern signs of the Bowery—the Bull's Head, the Quartered Loin—while the Bowery's modern, genteel aspirations were clearly visible in the grand edifice of the new Bowery Theater with its Palladian columns and marble portico. On the subject of that theater, his readers should certainly take note of the forthcoming production of *Hamlet* there with Bowery favorite Richard Digby. The opening night promised to be the highlight of the season, for it would mark the much anticipated debut of renowned local beauty Miss Vera Laidlaw on the New York stage, as the tragic Ophelia.

Next door to the Bowery Theater stood the notorious Bull's Head Tavern. Casey looked over in time to see two young braves in matching canary yellow vests spill out onto the street, their hats spinning after them. They paused to hurl some abuse back at a brawny figure obscured in the doorway, but within a half minute, by Casey's reckoning, they had brushed themselves off and bounded across the street to accost two women only half-engaged in looking in a buttonmaker's window. Another minute, and the newly constituted foursome was laughing together and walking away arm in arm in a direction nominated by the ladies.

The *Herald* was certainly overdue for such stuff, perhaps a feature, "The Bowery Boys At Play." With the influx of the Bowery's commercial businesses had come this new generation of young bachelor residents who were now notorious in the eyes of the more genteel population of the city. It was a fact lost on most visitors that by and large the Bowery Boys were not native to Manhattan. In recent years, the struggling farmers of New England had taken to sending their younger sons south to the booming city with little advice and fewer expectations, to make their way as best they could in the countinghouses, banks and shops of trade by the docks. They invariably took cheap rooms together on or near the Bowery. From there they viewed the neighborhood and the city at large as their playground. With monthly pay as a clerk or shopboy more than they might see in a year on the farm and responsibility only for their own amusement, these young heroes of the Bowery inclined to drinking, bear-baiting and consorting with ladies no better than they should be. To distinguish himself from the Irish migrants of his age who labored on the docks and in the filth of the tanning factories, the self-respecting Bowery Boy took great care in the adornment of his person. After a recent study of the neighborhood, the *Herald* could confirm that cuff links, canes and beaver-skin stovepipe hats were now *de rigueur*. Fashion had become such the flavor on the Bowery that it was now difficult to tell the Columbia man from the miller's son from Poughkeepsie.

The activity of mental composition produced a glazed look on Eamonn Casey's face, and some passersby began to stare and point.

Those who recognized the powerfully built man with the stained hands as the editor of the *Herald*, a belligerent crusader-in-print against prostitution, chuckled knowingly to themselves to see him standing in front of the notorious Madam Camilla's.

He heard a small shutter snap open, then shut. The door opened, and he stepped gratefully into the anonymity of the hall. The door closed behind him, shutting out the brawling noise of the street. The air was cool, with the unmistakable perfumed quietness of a house inhabited exclusively by women. A smiling housemaid took his hat and invited him to follow her up the stairs. He noticed elegant prints on the walls depicting courtly dances and pastoral scenes, lovers in breeches on their knees. The rich, Brussels rug felt soft and welcoming beneath his feet. He might have been in a neighbor's house on Park Row or at the Geyers' on Lafayette Place but for the odd muffled cadence of pleasure from behind the closed doors as they passed.

Beyond the landing, second door, the maid paused. She turned the knob soundlessly, gestured with her eyes, and withdrew with a discretion worthy of a royal lady-in-waiting.

Casey walked into the room. Its two occupants turned to look at him: a pixie-faced girl naked on the bed with curiosity, her male companion with a beefy grin.

"Ah, you've arrived Mr. Casey," said the large young man, getting up from the settee and walking toward him. He held out a glass. "A very pleasant assignment this has been. Here, have some rum punch."

"Thank you, George." Casey accepted the punch gratefully, and when they had drunk off half the pitcher, he and George Bickart both turned to contemplation of the pixie-faced girl, who was improvising some light gymnastics on the bed. She smiled at Casey as if to say, *the more the merrier!*

There was a knock at the door, and the madam of the house appeared. When she caught sight of Eamonn Casey in the room—smiling at her and performing a deep, gentlemanly bow—she gave a cry of surprise. "Oh, Mr. Casey, you are here already!" Then she looked over to the bed. "I hope you are enjoying your *hors d'oeuvre*."

Madam Camilla enjoyed a reputation as keeper of the finest bordello on the Bowery, though no one had ever heard her describe it as anything other than a boarding house for ladies. She looked with contempt on the brothels of Five Points with their beds at thirty-minute rates and never a doctor in the house from one year to the next. Those were the fleshpots of Sodom, but *her* apartments, so prettily furnished, where her girls sat tastefully beneath prints of the Old Masters, played the pianoforte, and passed well-rehearsed witticisms in French (in addition to the skills for which they were principally employed), belonged to an almost respectable weave of Bowery life. She was a tall, handsome woman of a certain age and had taken to calling herself retired (she kept only one regular client, and he a gentleman of the old school). Retired, that is, until young George Bickart, one of the house's most reliable patrons when not hard up, had made her a most fascinating proposition.

Casey took her hand and brushed it with his lips. "Yes indeed, Madam, but only as a morsel sharpens the appetite for the promised feast. I will join you very soon, and we will all the pleasures prove"—he whispered these last words so close into her ear she could feel the tickle of his whiskers.

Madam Camilla had been listening to sweet nothings for a lifetime, but either because of an unfailing aptitude for her profession, or Eamonn Casey's irresistible air of wealth and influence, she blushed sincerely. "The door at the end of the hall," she whispered, then disappeared.

George was grinning at him from the couch. "You're a shining example to us all."

"And you're looking dangerously pleased with yourself, George."

"It's you should be pleased with me, more like. Weren't for me, you would never have known about Madam Camilla's gentleman friend."

Casey looked over to the bed where the pixie-faced girl was now sitting on her haunches, looking bored.

"For God's sake, keep your voice down," he hissed.

Even at Columbia, where name ranked far above intelligence, George had not been valued for his quickness. He stared dumbly for a moment, before producing a brow-lifting ah! He put his finger across his lips. "Mum's the word. Right you are." But after a moment's contrition, he whispered, "Why've you got it in for the doctor? Did he steal your girl back in the ancient times?"

"No. It's not personal."

"What then?"

"It's business."

George thought for a moment, then looked aghast. "You're not putting it in the *Herald*?"

Casey pursed his lips. George was suddenly very anxious, brow furrowed. "Albert Dash is his assistant now, you know. He is the anointed one."

"Yes, I know," said Casey.

"What happens to him?"

"If you want to help your friend, tell him to tell the doctor to back off."

"And this is why you came early today—to speak to me about Albert?"

Casey smiled and sat back. "Certainly not, George. It was to sit in contemplation of your manly beauty for these precious minutes."

For a moment, it looked as if he would say nothing more. Then he turned to George with an ambiguous, perhaps hostile expression. "But since you mention the fact, I would ask you this. Does your friend Albert's career really depend so much on the doctor?"

"Oh yes. The doctor has the power to find him a position, maybe a professorship down the road."

"He cannot aspire to these honors on his own merits?"

"He has merits enough, to be sure. But I don't need to tell you the way of the world, Mr. Casey. He needs a leg-up, like we all do." George looked directly at his patron, but Casey was gazing at the girl on the bed and rubbing his whiskers. Then he turned to him again with an intensity that took the younger man by surprise.

"Are you saying he has no independent means? A man with such a name?"

"The Dashes have long been out of favor with their bankers."

"And so he will marry a banker's man's daughter? He must think John Laidlaw a right fool."

George shook his head. "No, no, it's true love for sure. Albert wouldn't marry for money—he never thinks of it."

"A fine attitude in a son-in-law! A young man who has no money and scorns to make any will always be a burden to his wife's family."

George shifted uncomfortably on the divan, and spoke now in a tone he had never before used with his boss. "You're twisting my words, Mr. Casey. Albert Dash is the finest fellow I know. He will be a great man one day."

Casey gave George a wolfish glare. "Humph!" he said, and left the room without another word.

After Casey had left, George fell asleep on the sofa. When he awoke, it was already dark. His head was throbbing from the rum punch. Sitting there, he felt the particular misery of his condition: a young man alone and forgotten in a brothel.

He was still woozy from his nap as he bid goodbye to Madame Camilla. From the flushed expression on her face, the afternoon with Casey had gone well enough. She escorted him to the door, politely but firmly, to clear the field for the night's customers. George remembered with regret the time not long distant when he had numbered among them. That was before he lost his head at the track. Now he relied on Casey's charity for his entertainment.

The moon had risen. Another wasted day—filled with unpleasant business and already forgotten pleasures—was drawing to a merciful close. George stepped into the horse smells and twilight hurly-burly of the Bowery, only to be besieged by unhappy thoughts, an unusual predicament for him.

He passed a city watchman slumped on a stool and rapped his knuckles loudly on his trademark hat. "Hey, Joe! Old Leatherhead!" he called into his ear. "Don't let them catch you napping again. You don't want to send to old Casey for another favor. It ain't advisable."

"Right you are, George," said the old man, scratching his head and sitting up. "I'm set. Thank you, George."

George Bickart was well known on the Bowery as a carefree sporting gent of the first class, a true connoisseur of the pleasures of that neighborhood. He enjoyed riding his horse up and down the great avenue, fighting fires, screaming himself hoarse at the bear-baiting, and touring the many brothels—in no particular order.

In fact, it was his popularity among the Bowery Boys that had first brought him to Eamonn Casey's attention, as a young man who might be useful to him. George had been expelled from Columbia the previous fall—the unfortunate scheme involved the stealing of cadavers from the Nassau Street graveyard—and, when his father subsequently cut him off "until he could reestablish his character in the world," Casey grabbed his chance.

As editor of the *Herald*, Eamonn Casey had his penny-press nobs, wits and pundits to debate the affairs of the city in the light of day, but he enlisted George's aid in his second, less well-known career: the nighttime politics of ballot stuffing, barroom espionage, price fixing at the Tontine Exchange and, occasionally, arson. This work suited George for the time being. It was not in his character to speculate on why he did what he did, far less imagine where it might lead. Mr. Casey, he told himself, was simply helping him through this difficult period with his father. What he did not admit was that the longer he accepted Casey's favors, the more distant became the day that he might restore his character to Mr. Bickart's satisfaction.

Despite his misfortunes, George retained his good humor and continued to think of himself as a good, lucky sort of fellow. Certainly his friends—and he had many—had never suggested otherwise. But this bedrock of good opinion he had established for himself was now shaken. For reasons George could not fathom, Mr. Casey loathed his old friend from Columbia, Albert Dash. It seemed personal in some way. George shook his head as he walked, so that a passing whore stared at him and snickered. Nonsense, really. What could a rich man like Casey have to fear from a quiet fellow like Albert, who had little money and painted flowers all day long? It was beyond his mental powers to comprehend the business.

He was now approaching the lamp-lit flowerbeds of City Hall Park. Across the street stood his employer's house, indistinguishable in that patrician row of privilege. Behind a uniform line of green shutters and lace curtains, French governesses had bred his

Columbia classmates to their expectations. He thought of Albert once more and began to feel deeply distressed in his mind. He never dreamed that his information about the doctor's private life might finish up harming his friend, and now that it threatened to do just that, he faced a moral dilemma for which he was desperately unequipped. To be sure, he had had little choice: he relied on the boss for his income and now for protection from the city magistrates. But such excuses were no kind of balm to his conscience. The fact of his conspiring against Albert so casually, for a cause no better than his own convenience, meant that the habitual peace of mind he had never thought to prize was suddenly gone. George turned onto Broadway with a heavy tread, lost in the ruins of his former carefree self. Even now, as he turned south past the jail and St. Paul's Church, he averted his eyes from the moon's narrow gaze, while the evening mist from the river pursued him, calling itself Doubt.

CHAPTER SIX

A hundred years before Columbia College fled north into the open fields of Morningside Heights (the old maps call it Harlem), New Yorkers knew it as a handsome modern building in the English style occupying the whole length of the Church Street block. There it sat, oblivious to the city's vulgar business on nearby Broadway and City Hall, ranged like a row of seaside pleasure houses. It was fronted by a small half-moon park, ornamented with trees. In winter, it was said, the sight of the elegant sash windows through the morning mist, with the crunch of gravel underfoot as one made one's way up the winding drive, gave exactly the impression of a college at Oxford.

But now, at the height of this unusually hellish summer, Columbia's stone hearths and thick Scotch plaid rugs seemed nothing better than a cruel joke. Even the transplanted English patriots who had founded the college two or three King Georges ago and now lined the walls in portrait form seemed to concede with their bushy frowns that mistakes had been made: that the gentle-man's curriculum of Latin poems and casual buggery that made colleges of the old country such beguiling residences was some-how out of step with this New World metropolis and its dour, democratic enthusiasms. The new breed of populist newspapers constantly reminded the public that, before the War of Indepen-dence, Columbia had been King's College, and insinuated that ranting Tories still scurried through its halls like so many learned, treacherous rats. Columbia's brief alliance with the *Herald* had ended when young Michael Casey had to be withdrawn from the school after being bullied to an inch of his life. Since then, the *Herald* had become the college's most implacable enemy, calling it "an anachronism ruled over by relics."

Several former relics of King's College lined the wall of the labo-ratory of botanical medicine where, oblivious to the heat, Albert's hand swept quickly across the page stretched before him on an easel. A *Eupatorium perfoliatum*—the "boneset" flower—sat in a jar on the windowsill. It was reputed to be effective in the treat-ment of various swamp fevers, and so had made its way into the doctor's grand catalogue of botanical medicine, a quarto-sized, ever-expanding leather volume to which Albert had devoted the last two and a half years of his life.

Beside the ponds and streams of the Carolinas or in the water-logged earth of the Florida everglades, the boneset's natural cous-ins flourished to a height of four feet with as many as a dozen ribbon-like leaves on its stem. This specimen, however, owed its existence to science and had lived out its meager days in a botani-cal garden on Manhattan Island without the comfort of a marshy earth or the company of its fellows. The burdens of captivity were apparent in its stunted growth and the limp extension of its leaves.

To offset this unpromising appearance, science had borrowed the tricks of art. Albert first placed his homely subject by the window, where the generous light of the sun added luster to its colors. Then, in the same way that a portrait painter erases the march of time by imagining a dowager in her first bloom of youth, investing her with a beauty that is not her own but that of a sweet creature he once saw and whose image still haunts his imagination, so Albert now imagined his ideal flower, using the actual specimen before him as only the template of a likeness.

Two long vertical motions followed by a rapid attack of short fine strokes and a round stem appeared, with its protective carpet of tiny fronds. Then the leaves took shape, first as single prominent ribs drooping from the stem, then enlarged by a quilt of resinous dots redrawn in green watercolor. Albert paused before setting about the underside of the leaves, mesmerized for long minutes by their cottony, pubescent softness. At the crown of the image he faithfully sketched the cluster of small, sharp-tipped flowers his specimen possessed, before adding two more and redrafting them all in the wilder shades of nature it lacked. He paused again to consider. His last task was to trace enlarged illustrations of the plant's tiny fruit and flowerhead at the bottom of the page. The poor marsh flower gave up all pretensions to physical beauty under this exaggerated scrutiny of the draftsman's eye, so that when he was done, its organs of reproduction resembled a pair of angry insects with multiple eyes.

Albert was so absorbed in his work that he didn't notice the looming presence at his shoulder.

"Pretty pictures won't cure the yellow fever."

He almost dropped his brush, and turned to see the doctor eyeing his drawing. His face was red from the heat and he was tapping a rolled-up newspaper impatiently against his thigh. He seemed unhappy. Albert knew Dr. Hosack valued his talent as a botanical artist. Why else would he have employed him on the catalogue when he was still a student? But at the same time, he knew that there was something in his artistic style—his delicate attention to color, perhaps, or the texture of buds and leaves—that struck the doctor's colder, scientific eye as excessive to the purpose.

But Albert saw something else in the doctor's expression and he put down his brush.

"What news?"

"None that you're thinking. No new fever cases, here or in Brooklyn. I get reports from my men on both sides of the river every afternoon. So far nothing but a cargo of grain infested with lice and a few scurvy sailors."

"And the mayor?"

The doctor gave a snort of disgust. "He treats every report that there is no yellow fever on the docks as confirmation that there will *never* be. And he will not hear of my demand that all the captains' logs be checked. An infringement of free trade, he calls it. There is a new obduracy in our mayor. Of course, he is as impervious to reasoned argument as he ever was. But now he will not respond even to emotional appeals. I lowered myself so far as to invoke the safety of his wife and children in this fever season. Surely his paternal burden must touch him, I thought, even if his mayoral responsibilities do not. But he only grinned at me like a baboon."

The doctor walked away across the room to a desk in the corner, where he cleared the clutter of papers and specimen jars with a reckless sweep of his hand. He then sat heavily in the chair and absorbed himself in reading his newspaper. Albert studied the bent bald head. After a few minutes, the doctor cursed and slammed the paper down on the desk.

"And to cap it all, Eamonn Casey has sold his soul!"

Albert looked at him in surprise and then at the newspaper on the desk. It carried the familiar eagle crest and the motto, "To Serve the People."

"Read for yourself." The doctor pushed the paper toward him.

Albert sat down and began to read the editorial on the front page. "The Common Sense Argument Against Quarantine," was the impossible, the *unbelievable* headline. But Albert had only read two lines when the doctor reached over and pulled the paper out of his hands.

"Let me tell you what your friend Mr. Casey says. First, he repeats the nonsense about unsanitary conditions on the Brooklyn docks. It is that, he insists, caused our yellow fever outbreak. He then produces an account from Captain Quin of the *Belladonna*, who now—apparently—maintains that his ship never touched in Kingston Town or in any port this summer infected with the yellow fever."

"But that is not true," cried Albert. "I spoke to Captain Quin!"

"Which is why I need you to go back to Brooklyn today, to sort out this mess. Find out what you can about the *Belladonna* from other sources. Speak to the officers and crew, the dockhands. Any credible witness you can find. We need evidence for Friday's quarantine hearing."

Albert threw off his smock and reached for his hat.

The doctor held up his hand. "A moment before you leave. Sit down. Let me first entertain you with Mr. Casey's theories of the local causes of the yellow fever. Shall I read to you what his imaginative researches have produced?"

He gave the paper an angry snap.

"'*The sewers have been unusually pungent this summer, owing to the excessive heat.*'—Very well. What next? Ah, yes.—'*Kitchen maids in Brooklyn*'—maids, no less—'*complained of an infestation of caterpil-*

lars in May, then noted their sudden disappearance in July.'—This was at the precise time that the yellow fever appeared. Do you see the connection? But there's more.—*'No hedge warblers arrived to populate the cherry trees behind Wallabout Bay, which birds should have arrived the first of May! Nor were guinea pigs observed in their usual swampy habitats in Cobble Hill'*—Conclusive, wouldn't you say?"

Albert stood up to peer over the doctor's shoulder, as if to verify that the *Herald* article was not some elaborate satire. "But I don't understand. Mr. Casey has always supported us—supported you. His readers are the working men on the docks. It is they who will bear the brunt of the fever."

"But I have not done Mr. Casey full justice, Albert. He does not require us to rely on the evidence of kitchen maids, which the ungenerous might call nonsense. He marshals expert opinion also to put his case beyond doubt. Look here! He quotes a man named Rodgers, a resident doctor of Brooklyn, who claims an interest in chemistry.—*'Dr. Rodgers reports that soap*—bath soap, I wonder?—*when mixed with water and left to stand an hour on the third story of a house in the vicinity of the unfortunate Mrs. Little's, became unnaturally decomposed and refused to make good lather. The same Dr. Rodgers observed a flock of quails, which, on passing over Mrs. Little's chimney during the time of that house's infection from yellow fever, dropped like stones out of the sky, dead into the street.'*—Can you imagine that?"

Albert threw his hands in the air. "This is superstition from the Dark Ages!"

The doctor grabbed his arm. "One more, I beg you. It is the coup de grace—*'From his New Jersey estate, Mr. Noah Webster . . .'*"

"Dictionary Webster?"

"No less.—*'Mr. Noah Webster informs the* Herald *of his observation of a near-total eclipse of the sun on May 23rd, which was followed in July by a comet, its tail of fire distinctly visible in his telescope. Mr. Webster refers us to precedents in the historical literature, Herodotus and Pliny, etc., etc., where comets and eclipses are the proverbial harbingers of pestilence.'*—Tell me, Albert, why is it that the subject of yellow fever inspires such terror in people that they are unable to think or speak rationally on the matter, so that even intelligent men of broad education are reduced to babbling idiocy?"

Dr. Hosack's sardonic smile had vanished. He screwed up the newspaper and threw it across the room, nearly upsetting a row of camomile jars on a shelf.

"The People is an ass!" cried the doctor. It was his favorite commentary on the *Herald*, the rise of the Jackson Democrats and the new Voting Rights Act. "What can we do to turn back this tide of ignorance? What can any man do?"

"These are only the usual arguments," said Albert again, hopefully. "They have been discredited before. We will answer him in the *Gazette*."

Dr. Hosack shook his head. "We cannot match the *Herald*. It has ten times our readers. Mr. Casey has the public's ear, the confidence of the common people."

They pondered their situation for a long moment.

"But why has he done this?" said Albert.

"I was hoping you could tell me," said Dr. Hosack, raising a pointed eyebrow in his direction. It was true that Albert had become almost a regular in the Casey household. He had made friends with Eamonn Casey's son Michael at Columbia, and more recently his daughter, whom he tutored in botany. But in truth his recent encounter with the editor of the *Herald* at Park Row had been a rare event and, as usual, not a pleasant one. Casey was a bullying, unpredictable man and seemed to resent him. Albert shook his head.

"I have heard nothing. This is as shocking to me as it could possibly be."

Dr. Hosack took a deep breath. "Well, let's consider the logic of the matter. We must employ the science of human nature—as orderly, in its way, as the fructification of a flower."

He wandered about the room as if to promote the flow of thought. It was a style familiar to Albert from the lecture hall, and reminded him of his freshman year when the sight of the great Dr. Hosack first sent Possibility, like an eager god, crashing into his unguarded brain.

"For the *Herald* to have joined the Wall Street campaign against quarantine is a very serious risk for Mr. Casey. He has spent years building up that newspaper and he is now trusting his credit with its readers to a dangerous extent. For this risk to have been worth Mr. Casey's while, someone with a merchant's interest in preventing a quarantine must have made him a substantial offer, a very substantial offer indeed."

"Money? A bribe?" Albert felt the world as he knew it shift slightly on its axis.

"Such things have been known to happen, my boy," said the doctor with an indulgent pat on Albert's shoulder, "even in New York. That said, I still don't understand his motives. Casey has always been a ranting populist and a mischief-maker, but a principled one. Or so I thought. I cannot believe such a man would turn hypocrite for money alone."

"I would have said the same for Mr. Casey until last week."

"What's that?"

"There was a fire at a goods warehouse on Water Street Thursday morning. Almost the whole block burned."

"I remember hearing of it."

"I was there—and I have thought about it since. It was suspicious. The fire seemed to originate in several places at once. And all the windows were sealed and barred."

"An insurance payday? That's not unknown among our less god-fearing merchants, you know. Burning your wares is so much cheaper than shipping them across the Atlantic when there's a profit to be made from the loss. But what of it?"

"Mr. Casey owned that warehouse."

The doctor stared at him. "Are you sure?"

"My source is reliable—he works for Casey himself."

"So he *is* a hypocrite! The champion of the working man has a secret line in trade and graft! I wondered that his newspaper profits could purchase that fine house of his, with all its Italian marble. This is useful information indeed—but it doesn't explain his risky change of heart on the yellow fever." The doctor looked about the room as if to take a survey of the portrait heads ranged on the walls. Whatever wisdom they possessed, they didn't share it.

A thought struck Albert with blunt force. "Dear God."

"What is it?"

"I had forgotten. Virginia—Miss Casey—mentioned it to me one day last spring. Just in passing. It was at the time Mr. Casey withdrew Michael from Columbia. Miss Casey told me her father was especially angry about all the gossip because he was planning to run for governor."

"Governor of what?"

"New York."

"No. Incredible!"

"So I thought then. But she hasn't mentioned it since, and I forgot all about it."

The doctor bent down and picked up the newspaper from where it had scattered on the floor. He gazed at it with contempt. "So the Irish scribbler is running for office and needs the help of the money men. It's these damnable voting rights! It has Eamonn Casey flattering himself that he should be governor with no greater qualification than a love of publicity and a talent for bad, inflated rhetoric. Hamilton suffered from his kind of scandalmongery, you know, and Jefferson too. But I'll bet the founders never dreamed a puffed-up pennysheet man could ever run for governor. God's truth! If Eamonn Casey is elected governor of New York, where will it end? I tell you, Albert, he is worse than anything! The yellow fever might come every summer for the next hundred years and we will still be here, the same people, in the same city. But if Casey and his kind take over, your own grandchildren will not know you, will not understand anything that you have thought or fought for. They will think you have walked out of a storybook. This upstart Irishman must be stopped!" The doctor was as furious as Albert had ever seen him, waving his great arms in the air. But he stopped now and rubbed his beard quietly. "I fear for our quarantine, Albert. But first we must confirm Casey is actually running and find out if it is related to this dangerous nonsense he is publishing. You must get Miss Casey to confirm it."

Albert nodded. But in the event he never did ask Virginia about her father. He didn't need to because the very next day the *Herald* proclaimed Eamonn Casey's improbable candidacy for governor to the world in great bold type, with exclamations running wild.

CHAPTER SEVEN

Lieutenant Babcock, formerly of the *Belladonna*, was an angular man, full of argument. He dotted his conversation with Latin tags and quotes from Shakespeare to show his education. To demonstrate good breeding, he took snuff from a monogrammed silver box. For Albert, who sat across from him at a table at Grimm's Tavern in Brooklyn, the man's being stinking drunk took the gloss from both these virtues.

"Captain Quin once tried my snuff, you know, to show himself the gentleman. But he sneezed so hard he upturned his plate of beef soup into a midshipman's lap. He went red as a beet. Then he blamed me, of course. But I was pleased to show him for what he is: 'a filthy worsted-stocking knave, son and heir of a mongrel bitch.'—Ah, the Bard! There is no one better for capturing the essence of a bog-eater like Quin."

A young girl, dressed only in a dirty calico shift, passed by their table. Babcock grabbed her with one long arm and pulled her into his lap. The girl beat his hand away from under her skirt, even as she looked at him with no real surprise.

"How much then, for the black ram to tup this little white ewe?" The lieutenant was well tanned from his months in the Caribbean, and fully debauched.

"You know better than most, Adam," said the girl. "A quarter dollar gets you an hour, like always."

Babcock stood up, still clutching her tightly to his groin. He grinned at Albert.

"Nature calls, Dash! *Omnia vincit amor.* If you could pay my tab, I'd be much obliged to you"—he leaned forward confidentially, in a slurred whisper—"A word to the brave, Dash. Make your reconnaissance brief. Captain Quin has the manners of a highwayman."

"I will see you at City Hall on Friday, Lieutenant. For the quarantine hearing."

"You may count on it, sir. It will be my pleasure to expose the captain for a lying whoreson dog."

"Who's a whoreson?" said the girl, with a wicked pout.

"You'll see, Marcie!" he laughed. He slapped her rear so she squealed. "Oh, you'll see, Marcie my dear!"

A summer storm had emptied the Brooklyn streets and turned the dust to sticky mud. Albert waited in Grimm's Tavern until nightfall, watching the gray rain pelt down on the river. Then he walked out onto the docks, hat pulled low on his brow.

It was Sunday, and still raining heavily. But the schooners and packets and all the ships of trade rocked easily at their moorings. They were the city's reason for being, and would be tended to without regard for the rain or the Sabbath's solemnity. Shiphands struggled with pulleys, pursers counted their stores, merchants signed orders. Boys, too, in numbers like rats, scuttled through the traffic on their errands to and fro. All seemed to have forgotten there was yellow fever there only two weeks ago.

Albert surveyed the motley fleet, grim thoughts in his mind. Of all these ships that deposited their goods here, took others aboard, and sailed away again on their Atlantic circuit between England and the Caribbean, any one of them, at any time, might ship their hidden malignancy ashore until the October frosts came to choke the life from the fever. The docks, he noted, had been cleared of the usual rotting cargo, and the privy trenches leading from the shipyard were freshly dug. These were prudential measures for which the mayor had accepted the universal credit of the press. But cleanliness was nearer to the devil in this case, because it distracted the public mind from the true source of their danger. How many of these working folk, bustling across the newly cleaned docks, would pay for their peace of mind with their lives?

The rainshower had left great puddles of dark water. His boots were borrowed second hand and almost as old as himself, and his feet were soon uncomfortably damp. A couple of drunken men— Irish, from their voices—challenged him outside a tavern on Market Street. More than once, he met with offers of female company. But beyond the Navy Yard, the barroom crowds thinned to nothing. Though it was almost fully dark, with no moon, he threaded his way across the docks with a child's surety. Even now, his heart gave a boyish leap at the flash of a white sail in the gloom, the dim forest of lilting masts on the water.

Growing up, he had listened to sailors trade their stories in front of the taverns by the Navy Yard and clambered up on crates to watch the ship stores unloaded into small mountains on the wharf to be carried away by the brawny stevedores and their horses. He dreamed then of a life at sea. Not in merchant shipping, but the Navy. He heard of the glorious victories of 1812, when the raw American flotilla pummeled the pride of the British fleet, from the men who fired the guns. But it was here too that a boy in rags had found him with Aunt Mary's message that his mother and father were sick. Even now he remembered the message word for word. He fought off the memory. It was like a pain grown stale and ready to be thrown out. After that terrible summer, he had never again thought of the sea. His spirit instead turned inward. He had joined his destiny to that of his stewing, overcrammed island home.

The docks were deserted now. A rat startled him, and he became aware that his heart was beating rump-a-thump against his chest. It seemed almost audible in the nighttime silence. Crouching behind a row of barrels, he scanned the ships at anchor for the *Belladonna*. There she sat, bobbing in the crisp swell of the river. He heard a shout, then a burst of maniacal laughter at a distance. But around him it was quiet. The minutes passed. He began to think he had been made a fool of by Lieutenant Babcock when the sound of a footfall—shockingly close!—made him catch his breath. Two men, darkly clad, with leather hats and sticks at their side were no more than ten feet away, making their way among the litter of barrels, crates, and pulleys. One whistled lightly to himself as he walked. There had been no reports of trouble from the ships or on the docks. But someone had taken an interest in securing them, someone with the means and influence to employ a nighttime watch.

The watchmen were invisible to him in the profound darkness. He bent his head and listened intently until the sound of their heavy tread and that oh-so-helpful whistle passed into nothingness.

When he was sure he heard only the slap of water cradling the bows of the *Belladonna*, he stripped off his clothes and stowed them in a neat pile between two barrels. He crab-crawled to the wharf's edge and eased himself into the water. The cold surprised him, and for a moment he was paralyzed in his new element. The swell of water washed him hard against a wooden pylon girding the dock. Barnacles bit cruelly into his shoulder, but he barely felt it for the cold, and he settled into a broad underwater stroke. He worried about the flash of his white skin against the black water—something he had not thought of—and about the arrival of the next patrol, though they would not come for many minutes.

Panic, daring, what was it that made him strike out at last? He made toward the *Belladonna*, splashing hard, and by the time he reached its side he was dangerously spent. For minutes he couldn't count, precious minutes, he could only bob in the water and cling feebly to the rope at anchor. He cursed himself for his weakness and fear and set himself to climb. Once free of the debilitating grip of the water, his strength returned and he vaulted up on deck with seamanlike quickness.

Even in the soupy darkness, he could tell that the decks had been scrubbed to an inch of their life. A strong odor of soap and spirits filled the air. At the head of the ship, by the capstan, he found a mud turtle. A squat, complicated machine—the most powerful cleaning engine a ship's company could employ. No ship he had ever seen, excepting a man-of-war with a spit-and-polish captain, had ever gone to the expense of stowing one. An ordinary merchantman exercised its crew with threadbare mops. But here the turtle sat, as if resting from its unusual labors, nursing resentment. Someone must have thought sanitation on the *Belladonna* an important enough matter.

His head full of this discovery, Albert made his way down toward the hold and lifted the heavy trap. Because the *Belladonna*'s deck has been so well cleaned, it did not occur to him that the job might have been left half done. He was caught in the confused rush of the moment, preoccupied with returning to shore before the next patrol, his head abuzz, so that when he lifted the hatch door fully open on its hinge he was utterly unprepared for the noxious cloud of vapor that rose from the hold. Black forms floating in water, then the soured flesh-fruit smell engulfed him. He reeled backward, gasping. The stench dissolved the years in an instant and he was a helpless, retching child again. The door of the hold slammed with a shocking crash. He dragged himself up to the deck. For minutes longer than he could count he fought down the nausea and rising panic. Lying naked on the stern of the *Belladonna*, he broke into a cold sweat. In the vivid nightmare of that moment he felt the yellow angel's embrace. The fever had returned—she had come for him—she had taken him in her arms.

CHAPTER EIGHT

Like an odious relative on his annual visit, the summer haze had squatted down on the city and refused to move. Its sticky grasp kept the Sunday morning crowds from their usual parade along Broadway and the Battery. Only the most pious of Manhattan's citizens braved the broiling heat and made their way to church according to duty and habit. The city faithful, too, barely heard their ministers' texts and only mouthed the familiar liturgy of perdition. With Sunday-best hats ruined with sweat and petticoat cottons pasted to clammy legs, how could the mere prospect of Hell impress a congregation convinced they knew its earthly reality—Manhattan in late July?

Virginia Casey, her church-going finery in a heap on the floor, sat at her open window with petticoats drawn up and contemplated a *Syringa persica*, a Persian lilac. She put her bare legs up on the window sill, hoping for a breeze from the East River to cool her or, at least, dry the cloying skin of moisture from her body. She couldn't remember when she had last felt truly fresh and clean instead of a prisoner to this merciless heat that left her limp like an old damp rag.

But at least she had not given up the fight as her mother had. Twice already since returning from the service at St. Paul's she had summoned Lily Riley to fill her washbasin, which Lily had done with a weary smile. But now she wondered if she should have bothered, whether splashing in water drawn from Manhattan's evil-smelling wells, at five cents to the gallon, was not worse than bathing in the free balm of nature, her own perspiration. Bottle green and brackish, the water had left a disturbing sediment at the bottom of her white porcelain basin. Even now, her skin—in the places where she had washed—felt scaly and dry.

She shook her head, scolded herself for daydreaming, and returned to study of the picture resting on her lap. The long, sweet shape of the flower tugged at her mind. First, the curved stem, with leaves cupped as if to trap the rain. And at the head, a globed quartet of magenta petals bent gravely toward each other like partners in a minuet. A dozen white-tipped tendrils formed an exuberant half-circle around them, as if awaiting the outcome of their courtly dance.

She ran her eyes across the title script written in Albert's confident, almost reckless hand. She loved the enchanting language of botany almost as much as the flowers themselves. First the mysterious Latin name—elegant, murmuring, open-voweled—then, in modest parentheses beside it, the surprise of the familiar English word—*lilac, primrose, forget-me-not*. Perhaps the world was best represented in this way: everything strange translated to something brief and common, no further explanation required.

In the bottom drawer of her large Chippendale dresser, Virginia kept a neat pile of forgotten childhood dresses, pregnant with cedar to repel the moths, undisturbed for years but by her own hand. Now, she gently lifted the dimities and pinafores, stiff with disuse, and extracted the large leather folio hidden beneath them. It contained a thick sheaf of numbered sheets. On top, a magnolia greeted her eye and beneath it the *Dracocephalum*, or dragon's head, whose pulpy stamen was so effective, she had learned, in the treatment of gout. She returned the Persian lily to its place among the folio's pages and carefully closed the drawer.

This done, she stood distracted for a moment in the middle of the floor, spellbound by the heat. She caught sight of her reflection in the looking glass. It must be almost noon and here she was not dressed. With the efficiency of the unobserved, Virginia took off her petticoats, went to the closet, and lifted a simple-strapped white cotton sheath over her head. It gathered high on her waist and fell in graceful folds about her ankles. It felt roomy and cool. Turning back to the mirror, she lifted her flaxen curls to the crown of her head. After a moment's consideration, she let them fall back again over her shoulders. When it came to the point, she could not bear to straighten her fashionable Delphic ringlets for the minister's sake, or roll her hair into a bun like a spinster schoolmistress.

Virginia brushed the insistent curls from her face and considered herself once more in the glass. She stood just an inch over five feet tall in her bare feet, but she was well proportioned, with a pretty oval face and a small snub nose. It was an extraordinary nose, really. Inconspicuous enough, and yet with the power to deceive educated people into mistaking her for a household pet, a kitten to be teased with baby sounds or a ball of string. It was true this happened less of late, as she had grown out of her girlhood and assumed the wistful authority of a marriageable young woman. She had first noticed a change in the attitude of her father's friends. They did not pinch her cheeks or muss her hair as they used to not so long ago. They kept their distance, even as they watched her with their eyes. Peering into the mirror, she tried to look at herself now as they looked at her. It was true. A young woman stood there before her: newly hatched and uncertain of her charms but a woman nevertheless. The question was: what did *he* see?

When her brother Michael had first brought Albert Dash home to visit, Virginia had been too bound up in girlish intrigues to think of him. It mattered more which of her friends she could tell secrets to, and where to buy the latest bonnet from Paris. She knew him only as the young man who had fought for her brother in the quad at Columbia.

Then one day, in the back parlor, she happened to be alone in his company. Albert made himself agreeable to her, and when— simply to make conversation—she had asked about his studies, he stunned her with a passionate speech on the aesthetic and curative wonders of the acanthus flower. In his direct manner of speaking to her he crossed all boundaries of reserve and blandness of manner she had thought fixed rules in the social world. She felt in that instant as if she were being properly spoken to for the first time in her life—that her mother and father and what she had thought her closest friends had been merely gesturing to her all these years from a distance, a table's length, a mile, compared to the nearness of this dark-eyed young man. Though he never moved an inch from where he stood behind the dining chair, running his fingers firmly along its sides, he seemed to stand flush next to her, leaning into her ear, pouring his words into her brain. She had felt herself grow hot and embarrassed, but soon hated herself for it because Albert became embarrassed too, thinking he had bored or annoyed her, and before she could do anything to rectify the misimpression, Michael came back into the room. For the first time in her life she listened to her brother's stuttering without a shred of pity—she wished him dead or otherwise disposed of, anything that she might be alone with Albert. Since that day in the parlor, that first intense agitation, she had had no peace. Her life had never resumed the settled shape of her childhood but felt like something airborne and electric, susceptible to a whole new universe of shocks.

A knock on the front door broke her reverie. She heard Lily's exclamation of surprise from the kitchen at a Sunday visitor come so early. Pretending not to hear her own scurrying heart, Virginia waited a full minute, then went downstairs.

But it wasn't Albert Dash standing by the piano, gazing out the window as was his habit, only Vera and her mother, who was appraising the porcelain in a loud voice as if the Casey home were just another fancy Broadway store where she happened to know the proprietor.

"Virginia, my dear," cried Mrs. Laidlaw. "You do look glum. It is only us, I know, your unfashionable friends. But I trust you will be coming to the party I am hosting tomorrow night to help launch your father's campaign for governor. I have been wanting a party anyway this last age, but thought it not right to ask people to be abroad at night during the yellow fever scare. Now, I have the perfect occasion."

Virginia gave an inward smile. She took a genuine interest in Mrs. Laidlaw's plans—large parties with dancing were not so common as that—but knew very well that the original date had been changed for considerations other than the health of her guests. Mrs. Laidlaw and her daughter had only resumed speaking to each other in the last few days after weeks of slammed doors and tearful dinners at Bowling Green.

"I wonder Mrs. Casey doesn't host more gatherings," said Mrs. Laidlaw, running her hand along the Italian marble mantel. "For she has taken such care with this lovely parlor. It is a crime to keep it to herself, as she does. This sideboard and your pianoforte, I presume, are Mr. Casey's latest acquisitions from Paris."

"Yes," said Virginia, "they were gifts my father ordered during our visit last winter."

"You are a fortunate girl—and Mrs. Casey too—to have so generous a provider. Not that I should complain of Mr. L. in that regard. He allows me to order what I will from Merck's, never mind the expense. No, I do not complain on my own account, but for Vera's sake. Here she is, full nineteen years of age and she has not yet been to Paris, or to London."

"I don't care," said Vera, emerging from the velvet curtains where she had been fancifully draping herself. "I hate France."

"Don't let Mrs. Geyer hear such unpatriotic sentiments from you, Vera. She adores our French allies, and so must we if ever we are to be invited to Lafayette Place. It is a temple to the Emperor Napoleon's style, so I'm told. But, of course," she added, turning to Virginia, "I need not be telling *you* this, for you have seen it. You Caseys have no shortage of invitations to the Geyers."

"We have been to Lafayette Place only a few times," Virginia replied, "Father has business with Mr. Geyer, you know."

Mrs. Laidlaw clucked skeptically. "Well, if four morning visits in a month is not intimacy then I understand even less of your privileged world than I imagined."

New York's elite families had visited each other in the morning hours since the Dutch days, and these solemn rituals formed the cherished core of Eliza Laidlaw's life. All the more cherished since her bad marriage and subsequent quiet ostracism at the hands of New York society had assumed the dimensions of tragedy in her life. Though born a Ganesvoort, she had, as a girl, fallen under the spell of John Laidlaw, an obscure, ambitious English merchant with mocking blue eyes. Since then, her life had become a daily struggle to regain the social privileges of birth she had so recklessly thrown away. It was often said that Vera Laidlaw inherited her acting talent from her mother, though Eliza Laidlaw had never set foot on a stage. Fortune had limited her to the performance of her own unhappiness—but it was a role she relished and never seemed to tire of playing. In the parlors of Manhattan's newly fashionable ladies, Mrs. Laidlaw's performance of giddy despair was a familiar sight, tolerated for its value as an amusement, and because the spectacle reassured her friends that whatever their own secret miseries they had not yet been driven to publish them to the world.

"Does Mr. Laidlaw care?" complained Mrs. Laidlaw, when the conversation turned inevitably to her latest misfortune, Vera's forthcoming debut at the Bowery Theater. "No, of course not. He gives his hat and cane to the maid and locks himself in his study, and says nothing about it. But of course, I should not be surprised. Knowing what his mother and father were, it can be no shock to him that a daughter of his might go on the stage. I might have told him Vera was to be a fruit seller at the Castle Garden for all he cared. But for a Ganesvoort, my dear, for a Ganesvoort . . ." Mrs. Laidlaw gave a sigh and knowingly wagged her finger.

"Vera will be a great success, I'm sure," said Virginia. "The world admires success and is not nearly so strict about these things as it was."

"You are very kind. But you don't know the world as I know it. They will smile good morning to you on Broadway and cut you before dinner, if it suits them."

"My father has promised to do all he can to cast Vera's debut in the proper light."

"With respect, Virginia," replied Mrs. Laidlaw tartly, "what can a newspaperman do except make a bad situation worse?"

Vera's friendship with Eamonn Casey's daughter had grieved her mother, though his conspicuous wealth and splendid house on Park Row compensated somewhat for his being an Irishman of no name and a disgraceful profession. She had never forgotten the day he came to dinner at Bowling Green with ink stains on his hands. Eliza Ganesvoort would never have thought to call upon Miss Casey, as Eliza Laidlaw did, but then Eliza Laidlaw was in no position to be choosy, and "Governor Casey's daughter," should her father rise to that remarkable distinction, could not be snubbed by anyone.

"My father is very clever in persuading people to view things as he does," said Virginia.

Mrs. Laidlaw didn't reply. Instead, she turned over a blue-enameled duck from the mantelpiece as if to guess its price. An awkward silence ensued.

"And even if it is all a terrible disaster, and the world shuns us," cried Vera at last, throwing her arms around Virginia's neck, "you will never turn us away, will you, Virginia darling?"

"Please, Vera! Do not speak that way. Have pity!" cried Mrs. Laidlaw with such emotion that Virginia feared for her mother's blue duck.

Vera shrugged and drifted away. Virginia saw the look of despair on her mother's face and almost pitied her. Mrs. Laidlaw had had the good fortune to produce a captivating daughter who was welcome anywhere, but her dependence on Vera had consequences for her respectability. In Virginia's eyes, she had abdicated her maternal status for a subordinate role, something like a lady's companion, so that when Vera announced her outrageous intention to go on the stage, she had had no authority to enforce a refusal. She contemplated her wayward daughter now with deep unhappiness, then turned to Virginia with a ruffled smile that spoke the necessity of a fresh topic of conversation. She provided it herself.

"It is very exciting, is it not, that Mr. L. has decided to throw his full support behind your father in this election? Such a good thing for you girls. What do you think of being the first daughter of New York, Virginia?"

"I'm still getting used to the idea."

"It very nearly came to nothing, of course. Mr. L. was so very concerned they would quarantine the docks here on the Manhattan side. He stood to lose a fortune—a fortune! But that is all over now, thank heaven, and we cannot be kept from hosting our party any longer."

"But the Board of Health hearing isn't until Friday," said Virginia. "We won't know until then whether there is to be a quarantine."

"Oh, as for that, it has all been taken care of," said Mrs. Laidlaw with a wave of her hand. "These things are always decided ahead of time. It is too important a business to be left to chance. Dr. Miller, you know, is a great friend of Mr. L.'s. He is coming to the party, and—Vera, come away from the window! Do not encourage those boys on the street to stare at you."

While Vera answered her mother with a cold glare and a remark her mother required her to repeat, Virginia collected her thoughts on the settee. When she had first read her father's strange editorial against the quarantine in the *Herald*, she had reassured herself that such weak arguments could not possibly prevail before the Board of Health against the authority of Dr. Hosack, against scientific evidence. But now Mrs. Laidlaw was telling her that "it had all been decided ahead of time." She meant that there would be *no quarantine*. What would Albert think if he knew that?

Virginia now became aware of an inhospitable silence and she shook off her anxious thoughts. "What will you be wearing to the party, Mrs. Laidlaw? You must advise me. I have a horror of appearing improperly dressed."

"Virginia, my dear, your modest taste is a byword. *You* can be sure never to catch anyone's eye, whatever you wear."

Virginia suppressed the pang of the insult and instead thanked her for the compliment.

"I am wearing white muslin spangled with gold," called Vera from across the room, "with a china silk scarf bordered in the same way and spangled white shoes. Charlotte Harvey will just die, for all her Bath airs. I have already shown it off to Albert, and he said he was ready to propose to me all over again if I would wear it at our wedding. I had to remind him that one offer of marriage was considered quite sufficient, to which he replied he was glad a different standard applied to kissing."

"I hope you cut him off sharpish," cried Mrs. Laidlaw. "That young man is altogether too free in his opinions."

"What do you mean?" asked Virginia.

Mrs. Laidlaw looked toward her daughter, but Vera had rolled her eyes and wandered away to the family portraits hanging over the mantel, where she amused herself in mimicking their somber expressions. Mrs. Laidlaw joined Virginia on the settee.

"*Entre nous*, Virginia, Mr. L. has been so very disgusted with Dr. Hosack's crying up a quarantine on the docks that he was of a mind not to invite Albert at all to our party, simply on account of his being Dr. Hosack's student, or assistant, or whatever he is. But I begged him to reconsider for Vera's sake. Albert was much talked of during the Brooklyn affair, you know. It seems Dr. Hosack relies very much on him."

"I believe he does."

"Mr. L. blames Dr. Hosack for frightening everybody unnecessarily over this fever. After all, barely anybody died in Brooklyn."

Virginia bit her lip. "Nine people died, I believe, and two recovered. But perhaps Dr. Hosack is concerned about another outbreak of yellow fever here in Manhattan such as we had in the year '14. Many hundreds of people died that summer and the summer before it."

"You needn't remind me of that disaster, Virginia. Old cousin Ganesvoort died, if you remember. I was invited to the funeral and sat in the second row. But now it is entirely different. We have learnt our lesson. No one wants the yellow fever less than Mr. L. and the other ship-owning gentlemen. Thanks to them our Manhattan docks are clean now, unlike that Mr. Jackson's filthy yard in Brooklyn. And when your father's aqueduct is built, we will be completely safe."

Virginia had nothing to say in reply and presently Vera returned to them, dancing on her toes and whistling a tune Virginia had never heard.

"Do not whistle, Vera," said Mrs. Laidlaw.

"What are you saying about Albert now, Mother?"

"I merely suggested to Virginia that Albert has been misled into supporting this terrible quarantine. Now that I think of it, Vera, perhaps you might be useful in persuading him to think differently of the matter."

"But whatever should I say to him about *that*, when I know nothing about it?" said Vera, laughing.

"Well, my dear," her mother replied, "as he seems to be such an admirer of your person, you might begin by telling him that you rely on ships visiting our ports for the muslins and silks that so delight his eye."

"And my cotton drawers—don't forget those, Mother!"

Whatever scathing reply Mrs. Laidlaw considered, she withheld it. Instead, she left in search of Mrs. Casey, who was rarely seen outside her bedchamber before noon.

Vera threw herself on the divan and stretched her long arms. "I'm sure marriage was invented to separate women from their mothers. That is why it is such a respected and enduring institution."

Virginia had never had a cross word with her mother, so she could only nod in pretended sympathy.

"How was your lesson?" said Vera suddenly. Virginia started and tried not to look up. Her friend's habit of changing subject abruptly had never had a more unnerving effect.

"My botany lesson?"

"Do you have any other lessons, in subjects I don't know about?"

"No," she blushed, despite herself.

Vera's wicked smile told her that she saw only the opportunity for a joke and suspected nothing of her betrayal.

"Your mother doesn't seem to like Albert," said Virginia. "Or, at least, she doesn't like Dr. Hosack."

"You know, I wish I'd never heard of Dr. Hosack. I wish he didn't exist. Though as a devotee of botanical medicine you won't agree with me, I'm sure."

This was now a sensitive subject between them, one Virginia set about deliberately to avoid.

"But Mr. Burfield of the Bowery Theater is even less popular with your mother, it seems. Lily tells me he isn't even admitted at Bowling Green."

"Oh, now he is. I made a scene about it and mother gave up in the end, just as she always does. What mother doesn't understand is that by being so cruel to me about my debut, she is forcing me to marry Albert as soon as possible. Sometimes I think I cannot possibly live another day under her roof!"

"There was a time when going on the stage made a young woman unmarriageable."

"You mean the Dark Ages, when my mother was young? I know, I know! I have heard too much about it!"

"But Albert, I take it, has no objections."

Vera sighed. "How could I not love him for it? He is old-fashioned in some ways, I suppose, but when it comes to important things, he is the most liberal and forward-thinking man anyone could want. You know that it was he who first encouraged me to go on the stage when Mr. Burfield first asked me. And he told me what to say to my parents. And he has been so patient with me in learning my lines, when I know he finds the whole thing tedious."

Virginia pretended to be distracted by a band of schoolboys playing walk-the-plank on the steps outside. When she spoke at last, it was in her most unaffected tone. She had become, she realized, a virtuoso of casual deception with Vera.

"Yes, Albert is very modern in his ideas. So I can't imagine what you mean when you say he is old-fashioned."

"Oh." Vera smiled strangely, then looked away. "Well, I mean he is quite strict about . . . he is quite the proper gentleman. To tell the truth, I think I quite shocked him one time."

"What happened?"

Vera rarely ever blushed, but now she gave Virginia a look she couldn't interpret. Then she laughed. "I'll tell you when you have a lover of your own."

"I don't know when that will be."

"Well, if you would only meet some new men and learn to speak to them! You know, it is the most wonderful thing to have a lover. They say the most precious things. You can't have forgotten how Albert declared his love to *me*."

It would have been difficult for Virginia to forget a story that Vera had related to her several times a month for almost a year.

And this was not counting the many nights she herself spent lying on her pillow in the darkness, thinking of it.

It had been a warm day last fall, and Vera had taken to bed with one of her turns. Dr. Hosack being too busy (or fed up with Vera's tricks, Virginia guessed), he sent his young student in his place. The handsome Columbia graduate caught Vera's attention before she ever laid eyes on him. "Who is that pretty young man coming to the door?" her mother had asked, spying from the window. Then, at the sound of him leaping up the stairs like a stag, Vera's heart began to beat hard without her telling it to. Virginia was never sure what form Albert's examination of his patient had taken (it was too painful to think of), but within five minutes—so Vera said—Albert had been on his knees promising to devote himself to her care and happiness. Fortunately, Mrs. Laidlaw had stepped out of the room at the time.

"He said I was like a flower he had only imagined, but never seen before. It is still the most gallant thing any man has ever said to me." Vera smiled at the recollection. "So, what can money matter in the end?"

Albert had never read a sentimental novel as far as Virginia knew. Which made it all the more a wonder that, in falling in love with Vera, he should have behaved so according to type. With her it would have been different. *She* would teach him originality, if only he would let her. When she looked up from this sinful thought, Vera was looking at her with unsettling directness. She didn't meet her eyes.

"Shall we rehearse?" she said instead.

"Very well," Vera sighed. "No more scenes, though. My head aches from doing the same lines over and over. Let's practice pantomime, as Mr. Burfield said to."

Vera prepared herself in the middle of the parlor floor.

"Desire," said Virginia.

Vera's face brightened. She arched her eyebrows, opened her mouth to a half-smile, bent forward and spread her arms toward an imaginary lover.

"Love."

Vera closed her eyes, clasped her hands, and gazed mistily toward the mantelpiece.

"Jealousy."

Vera's face darkened. Her hands clawed her cheeks. She opened her mouth to speak, then stopped. "When is Ophelia jealous?" she said.

"Pretend you have the yellow fever," said Virginia quickly.

Vera laughed, then laid herself on the divan by the window. Her mouth dropped open. She put her palm to her forehead in the approved style.

Virginia shook her head. "You look poisoned."

"Juliet is poisoned, isn't she? And Lady Macbeth too?"

Virginia rolled her eyes. "No, they certainly are *not*. And you have yellow fever. First you suffer a terrible headache, then a maddening heat grips your body."

Vera thrashed her arms and groaned.

"Now you vomit."

Vera giggled. "I will never be called upon to vomit, even at the Bowery Theater."

Even so, she mimed coughing the black, bilious foam (Albert called it *melancholia*, after the Greeks). Then Vera fell off the divan with a thump.

"You are not dead," said Virginia.

"I am not?"

"No. You first walk about as if you were perfectly recovered. You remark on the weather and put on your hat to go for a walk."

Vera bounced to her feet, her long body magically renewed.

"So, I am better now?" she said, somewhat disappointed.

"No. You collapse suddenly in a swoon and are pronounced dead by a handsome young doctor. He weeps over your lifeless body and takes holy orders in despair."

Vera died with a smile at the thought.

CHAPTER NINE

"Albert says a quarantine is absolutely necessary," said Virginia to her father that night. Lily Riley, who was removing the tablecloth in preparation for the serving of desserts and fruit, looked up in surprise.

"We are all in mortal danger."

Casey puffed like a blowfish at his cigar and peered at his daughter through the haze of smoke. Virginia noted the disdain in his face and expected the worst. But he only said, "Mr. Dash is a young man of strong opinions," and stroked his whiskers.

Eamonn Casey had taken a wife for love, but when success came he soon began to despise her. His son, too, was a disappointment —an ink-spotted bookworm, a stuttering fool, a weakling. It was this son who had disgraced the Casey name by allowing himself to be bullied at Columbia. His wife and heir both frozen from his heart, Casey's feelings of blood had concentrated themselves on a single familial point. His tenderness toward Virginia was thus intense, and often interpreted by her as tyranny. Casey doubted Albert Dash's politics and prospects, and deplored his association with Holier-Than-Thou Hosack, but mostly he resented the dangerous influence the young man exerted on his daughter. From the day of Albert's first entry to his parlor, he had guessed his daughter's feelings and began plotting his response. Whether Albert reciprocated Virginia's affections, or even knew her heart—they said he was to marry Vera Laidlaw—was not the point. For Eamonn Casey, Albert's mere presence in the world represented all he stood to lose in it. As an advocate of the quarantine, Albert was merely a nuisance. But as a usurper of his daughter's love Casey wished him disgraced or dead.

"Albert's opinions are shared by Dr. Hosack," said Virginia.

"Yes, the good Dr. Hosack!"

"Whatever you have written in the *Herald*, Father, you must agree with Dr. Hosack on the main point—that all possible measures must be taken to prevent a repetition of the calamity this city suffered eight years ago, and frequently before then."

"Certainly all reasonable steps should be taken," he answered, "but this does not mean that *any* notion trumped up in the name of preventing yellow fever is worth adopting. I would be the first to support Dr. Hosack if I could be convinced, nay, even be allowed to hope that a quarantine might save the life of even one citizen of this city. But unfortunately, Ginny dear, the good doctor has offered not one particle of evidence to back up his theory of the importation of the fever. To heed his directions would thus serve the twin evils of distracting ourselves from discovery of its true cause, and ruining the shipping trade on which the prosperity of this city and the happiness of its citizens depends. We must not succumb to our fears by acceding to the irrational, my dear, to a quarantine that has no basis in science and that will not save a single citizen of Manhattan from yellow fever, but will certainly inflict grievous harm on his trade. If we are to stake our lives against our livelihoods, it must be for good reason!"

"But Dr. Hosack *has* given reasons," Virginia replied doggedly, "sound, factual reasons for believing the yellow fever was brought here by the *Belladonna*. It is just that these reasons have not been listened to."

Casey laughed. "So, we are to believe this intrepid fever stowed itself away in a ship's hold like a keg of rum, and deposited itself here at its own fancy? At the very least, this phantom disease should have been taxed on arrival!"

"Yes, we are to believe it," said Virginia, who was long since immune to his sarcasm. "The *Belladonna*'s hold was infested. Albert told me that workers on the docks knew the bilge water was foul."

Her father tapped complacently on his cigar. "I am sorry to speak so plain, my dear, but whatever illusions of the maritime life young Albert has fostered in you, the truth is that all ships smell tolerably foul after a month or more at sea. Besides, he and the doctor must confront the stubborn fact that not one soul aboard the *Belladonna* contracted the fever, much less died of it. No, indeed. All the victims were Brooklyn natives, living or working in the vicinity of John Jackson's Yard. For all Dr. Hosack's genius in medical fictions, the responsibility for their deaths is plain to the meanest intelligence. It lies nowhere but in the disgracefully unhealthy conditions of the docks. That villain Jackson had twenty men on twelve-hour shifts, without the convenience of a privy!"

Lily Riley giggled. Virginia glared at her. As a gesture of remorse, Lily instantly brought over a dish of strawberries and put the juiciest three on Virginia's plate. But Virginia did not meet her eye; she was looking at her father.

"Albert says the claims about the conditions of the docks have been exaggerated. Mr. Jackson's is one of the cleaner yards on either the Hudson or the East River."

"The Board of Health will decide that for themselves tomorrow." He butted out the cigar with a turn of his wrist.

Virginia now took a risk with an idea she had only guessed at since her conversation with Mrs. Laidlaw. "Albert thinks the board is not necessarily impartial."

"Really!" cried Casey, looking keenly at her. "That's presumptuous of him. Why ever would these men be less than impartial with their professional reputations at stake, perhaps even their own lives?"

Virginia was momentarily confused, and felt her composure slip. "I don't know why. Albert didn't say."

"Oh, he didn't? Your Mr. Dash is content then to purvey baseless slanders against his elders and betters? I envy the young man his freedom. He should be thankful that even his malignity and ignorance are liberties guaranteed by the Constitution. As the proprietor of a public newspaper, however, with fifteen thousand readers, and now as candidate for governor, I must exercise my freedoms more responsibly."

"Albert is neither malicious nor ignorant, Father," cried Virginia, crushing a strawberry under her spoon until the juice ran. "You are very wrong about him!"

"Enough about Albert Dash!" His eyes flashed at her, and he slammed his fist on the table. Michael, sitting across the table, stared at Virginia, appalled. Lily, too, looked at her with wide eyes. In that moment, Virginia realized she had gone too far.

"I will quarrel with you no more." Her father spoke in the acid monotone she recognized from when some unfortunate person he had vilified in his paper came to the house seeking explanation. The voice was implacable and frightening, and it made her hair stand on end.

"Your friend Mr. Dash is unfortunate in his choice of patron. Dr. Hosack is well known for his prejudices, and for much worse. You would be surprised to what lengths unscrupulous men will go to gain my ear and a voice for their opinions in the *Herald*."

"You say that Albert is unscrupulous?" Virginia felt anger rising in her once more.

"I did not say that. But certainly Hosack *is* unscrupulous, and a creature of his own advancement. I have heard this from his own colleagues in the medical profession. He will stop at nothing to advance his opinions. You can be sure he has found more sinister employment for his followers in his time than preying upon impressionable girls."

Virginia could listen no more. She rose from the table and stalked out of the room, leaving her brother to plead Albert's case. Michael's hopeless stammer followed her up the stairs, confusing her rage with pity. Throwing herself on her bed, she broke into tears.

As a child, Virginia had taken after her mother, and allowed herself to be absorbed by the awesome paternal presence in her home. But confidence had come with age, and because she had long ceased to find anything to admire in her mother, Virginia had begun to assert herself as mistress of the Casey household. She was now locked in a struggle with its master to be recognized as such: as an independent woman who would be mistress of her own house before long or, better perhaps, never marry at all, and teach in a school or devote herself to charity work instead. Over recent months, this contest with her father had turned to undeclared war. Lying back on her pillow, staring at the ceiling, she wondered did her father love her so fiercely because she understood him so well? Or did she understand him only because he kept her so suffocatingly near?

She knew his mind, his fears for her. But the maddening irony of it was that he had become obsessed with a relationship that did not exist. Her and Albert? How could anyone keep apart two people who were not actually together? The misery of her situation oppressed her most because she could see no end to it. Albert was as remote from her as ever, but she couldn't tell her father there was no prospect of intimate attachment between them because to say so would contradict the small hope she preserved within her that she was mistaken. The thought of her and Albert together was like a candle she trimmed in her most private soul, whose tiny flame could barely be exposed to the shifting winds of her own thoughts, let alone her father's hurricane prejudices.

Her sobs subsided, and Virginia lay back on her pillow and gazed at the ceiling. The comforting, private perfumes of her room—lavender sheets, sprigs of rose and lemon verbena in pots on the mantel, her mahogany bookcase polished by Lily that morning—cleared her head of her father's stinking cigar and slowly opened the door to her most cherished thoughts.

One extraordinary day in April, Albert had been admitted here to her bedchamber. In a springtime fit of maternal concern about the coming fever season, her mother had solicited Albert's opinion of the healthfulness of Virginia's sleeping arrangements. In the event, Mrs. Casey dearly wished she hadn't.

Albert had first insisted on the removal of the ancient moreen curtains with their heavy gimp trim. These, he said, harbored dust and vermin. He likewise dismissed her old leather clothes chest for its dust-trapping ornaments and the walnut chairs as too dark to reliably advertise their need for cleaning. While Virginia and her mother stood by in abashed silence, Albert went on to condemn her childhood washbasin for being too small, and to forcefully prescribe "a tepid showerbath at least three times a week. Tell Lily she must douse you from above and apply the scourge brush without mercy." Mrs. Casey was speechless at this instruction, while Virginia stared at the floor, the tips of her ears glowing hot red. Most pressing, Albert went on, was the necessity for an unimpeded circulation of pure air, to which the carpets as well the curtains had to be sacrificed, to be replaced with cotton drapes and plain straw mats. To deepen Virginia's agony, Albert insisted on supervising a smirking Lily Riley and two wide-eyed maids in the carrying out of his orders. Mrs. Casey, on the brink of tears, had thanked heaven her husband was not present to witness the pillaging of Virginia's childhood world: all the household stuff from before they were rich, worn with age, but as beloved of them both as the small snub nose their daughter had brought with her into the world, and the serious slate-blue eyes with which she contemplated it.

While Mrs. Casey had mourned the violation of her daughter's room by keeping to her own for three days, Virginia herself accepted the changes fatalistically. But when it came to it, she could not part with her painted bed curtains. When pulled entirely around her bed, backlit by candlelight, and not a crack between them to betray the existence of an outside world, they transformed her sleeping place into an enchanted cave of the imagination. A blue river flowed entirely around her, its banks lined with gilded minarets and pleasure palaces. On the right-hand curtain an oriental jungle flourished with bunches of oversized pink flowers. Exotic birds perched on trees no larger than themselves, and opened their beaks to seize fruits floating on the air. About them orbited strange poly-legged insects she could not name, while a turbaned man held a hammer in each of his gem-encrusted hands. He stood poised to ring a triangle of bells suspended from the branches of a pear tree. To her child's mind, it had been a perpetual wonder that the birds never devoured their fruit, and that the turbaned gentleman never sounded his bells. Some nights, when she could bear it no more, she reached out her tiny finger to remind them of their intentions, to prompt them into life and action. But always, at the last moment, she would withdraw her hand for fear of disturbing her own enchantment.

She loved most of all the scene at the foot of the bed-curtain, furthest from her, where steps led down from a sun-filled lattice house to the sparkling water's edge. Moored along the mossy bank lay a pleasure boat with a golden awning and plump purple cushions. Last summer—the summer she first knew Albert—she had been taken with a mild fever. Despite her mother's concern for the staleness of the air, Virginia insisted the curtains be drawn around her and had fallen asleep in a delirium. Waking, so she thought, in the dead of the night, she watched amazed as the door to the river house at the end of her bed slowly opened, and a Persian princess emerged in the shape of her prized childhood figurine on the mantel. The beautiful apparition looked at her and smiled before stepping lightly down to the water. In the boat Virginia had always known to be empty, a red-robed cavalier now awaited his lady. He arranged the bright-tasseled cushions, and tenderly extended his guiding hand to her. Virginia saw the look of perfect bliss in her eyes as she placed herself at his side. Then, as Virginia struggled to cry out but could not, the cavalier loosed the chain from the dock and down lay the lady with a sigh. The gentle stream bore them far away. When morning came, Virginia's fever had gone, leaving a pleasant coolness on her body.

Now she pressed her face into the pillow and cried quietly as the sky outside her window darkened to gray. Her thoughts drifted to the current crisis.

Yellow fever.

Albert was afraid it would come. He was sure it would come, despite what he said to reassure her. She thought of the fevers of summers past, and those who had died—Albert's parents and his two boy cousins, her old schoolteacher, the printer's boy at the *Herald*, hundreds of poor forgotten people in the fifth ward. She felt a strange laughing lightness in her chest at the thought of them all. How fragile life was! Her own seventeen years of life—so painstaking and real—lost in a moment, with no reason given.

And yet surely this light chill in her breath *was* a kind of fear, or at least evidence of a doubt. When the body died, did love die with it? And if it did, what could be more terrifying—in what afterlife there was—than to be among the houseless spirits of love interrupted by death? She began reciting Dante's canto in her mind—Francesca and her lover in their despondent flames, flickering alone forever.

Virginia half-opened her swollen eyes. It was dark. A noise downstairs. Lily's sing-song voice. Then silence. Falling into the folds of sleep once more, the same thought returned. If she died when the yellow fever came, Albert's life would be without the current of her love running through it, though he could not miss it, not being aware. But if *he* died, what would become of her heart and its shimmering pulse? Would it remain unanswered for eternity?

CHAPTER TEN

For twenty years, Dr. Hosack had not been able to walk down Broadway without thinking of Aaron Burr. The former vice president of the nation had diminished physically over those years, from the proud bantam gait of his pomp into a small, stooped figure with a copper-topped cane. But he was still a common sight in the city, looking askance at old acquaintances as he passed them in the street to see if they would cut him. Those who didn't could expect to be buttonholed for an hour in the open street while Burr entered on one of his nostalgic rants. Invariably, for the man whose own life had effectively stopped that misty morning in New Jersey twenty years ago, the conversation turned to "the day I shot my friend Hamilton." The periods before and after were for him, as for the doctor, like different lives lived in different worlds. To some Burr was pitiable, even noble in his suffering. But to Dr. Hosack, he was a very monster of self-pity.

There was no question of his making casual conversation with Burr. As befit the conduct of gentlemen in such circumstances, in the unfortunate event of an encounter the first to see the other would quietly cross to the other side of the street, eyes averted. On the rare occasions that Burr, largely an outcast in the city he had once dominated, attended a social gathering to which he was also invited, the doctor would simply retrieve his hat and cane and leave. The hostess could expect a sharp note from him the next morning. Very soon, the doctor's name had been added to the list of prominent New York citizens who under no circumstances should be allowed to meet with Mr. Burr. One glorious corpse under the Weehawken Bluff was enough.

So it was that Dr. Hosack strode along Broadway at his customary hurried half-trot without any serious apprehension of meeting his hero's nemesis in the flesh. But his spirit was another matter. The doctor saw him so rarely, and even then at a distance, that Hamilton's murderer had become transformed in his imagination into the diabolical intonation of his name, that single, fatal syllable: *Burr*. There he wielded more power than any wizened, bitter old man properly should. One night at the club, after a bottle of Madeira, he had told his old friend Sam Geyer the whole story: how the name "Burr" would come to him unbidden at night, without person or image attached. Just a name, a word, repeated over and over in blank dreams. Sam, who fancied himself a doctor of the mind, told him this meant that Burr was now more a symbol than a real person. That Burr recalled to him that fatal moment at Weehawken when nothing was done—a moment that the doctor could never have back, but was destined to relive over and over in different ways with himself as the city's guardian who would not fail again.

The doctor thought too much of his friend's philosophical powers to contradict him. Perhaps Sam was right, too, that whatever had driven him to the career he had made had also driven him into lifelong bachelorhood, and—because celibacy could not be expected of such a passionate man—into a series of unorthodox arrangements with women of the lower orders. The doctor had laughed at this theory, but felt better that Sam thought he understood all the darker urgings of his misanthropy and his dangerous liaisons. The doctor knew only that he could never examine either subject for very long, and never very clearly.

Walking uptown, he passed the old Nassau Street graveyard, where so many victims of the 1814 yellow fever were buried. Instinctively, he looked for signs of freshly turned earth. The graveyard had been officially closed since '14, it being too near the water table, but in recent years a clandestine traffic in corpses had reopened the yard on certain moonless nights when illegal burials and exhumations were performed for the benefit of his own students eager to advance their knowledge of human anatomy. It was an acute embarrassment to the doctor, though hardly his fault. He had been petitioning the mayor and the City Council to provide the medical school with sufficient cadavers to meet their instructional needs, but old prejudices died hard in the city. No one loved a corpse, except as an object of superstitious dread. The doctor had enjoyed more success with his arguments for the living, such as the building of the hospital. For all his influence, he had not yet been given authority to speak for the dead.

A loud sound startled him. One of his own Bellevue carts rumbled by, inches from his right foot, a lone black man at the reins, heading north toward the hospital. He saw the cart was empty—but for how long? He quickened his step, parting the crowd with his broad frame, chiding himself. The yellow fever was no phantasm of the mind. It was real, and it was coming.

He hadn't seen his assistant in two days, not since sending him to Brooklyn, and he was taking the unprecedented step of visiting Albert Dash in his home. He had reached the now unfashionable neighborhood of Franklin Street. In the midst of a row of red-brick, flat-fronted houses stood a lone Dutch cottage, a crumbling legacy of Manhattan before the Revolution. Unlike the row houses, its front yard terminated in a small picket fence set at an odd angle to the street. But the yard had not been kept up. The plots of turf near the gate displayed only a few stray upturned tubers, and an apple tree by the side of the house, a single stripe of sun across it, was picked bare of its fruit. An irony, thought the doctor, that a rising botanist should live with such a garden. He made a promise to himself: he would do more to advance Albert Dash in the world.

He knocked on the door. A shadow appeared in the window. A woman's face, suspicious. Then he heard the rumble of what could only have been Albert hurtling down the stairs on flying feet.

"Dr. Hosack!" The doctor presenting himself as a visitor to his home was so far beyond Albert's ordinary comprehension, he left him standing what seemed a full minute on the doorstep in the hot sun.

"Where have you been?" the doctor boomed at him. "I have new reports from Antigua and Port-au-Prince. Hundreds of deaths, and the entire Antiguan trade has shut down. There's anarchy in the streets and no effective quarantining. I have already been to the mayor this morning, but he says we must save it for the Board of Health hearing tomorrow. The Mayor has washed his hands of us. Must I stand here all day, Dash, or will you invite me in like a Christian?"

Even now, Albert hesitated. But at last, he stood aside and motioned the doctor to enter.

The moment he stepped inside the door and looked about him, the doctor's irritation melted away, replaced by a very different though no less powerful emotion.

Plaster hung off the walls in patches, and the floor of the main room—the most generous visitor could not have called it a parlor—was covered in dusty wood-shavings and a single cotton rug whose pattern had been worn to near invisibility. Against the far wall stood an ancient writing desk covered in drawings and scientific volumes. The rest consisted of a black potbelly stove square in the center of the floor and a collection of yellowing Windsor chairs that had been finely made some generations ago, but were now in varying states of disrepair. Albert, too, was contemplating the chairs with an expression of anxious urgency, as he wondered which of them might stand a chance of supporting the doctor's affluent bulk.

Before either of them could break the awkward silence, they heard a strange rattling sound from the kitchen. In the doorway appeared a white-haired man seated in an odd home-built contraption, a kind of chair with wheels. He did not look at Albert or the doctor, but gazed blankly ahead. Suddenly, his head lurched back and he launched into a violent coughing fit, expectorating into a handkerchief he held in front of his face. His driver, a broad woman of about fifty, reached around to wipe the saliva from his chin with a cloth of her own, before wheeling him in a rickety-rackety motion toward the front window. She put a bottle wrapped in paper on the window sill in front of him, arranged a blanket on his knees (though he must broil in the direct sun), then turned and left the room the way she had come, without uttering a word or even looking at the doctor.

"Forgive me, Albert. I had no idea you lived like this," whispered the doctor.

"He cannot hear us. But I must keep an eye on him while we work. Aunt has been worn out."

The old man in the chair let fly with another racking production into his handkerchief.

"Are you sure we will not disturb him?"

"He may seem to understand us," said Albert, "but my belief is that he doesn't hear a word, or even know that we are here. It is an act of will that has done it. There is no affliction of the body that I have ever been able to discover. Please take this chair."

"A remarkable case," said the doctor, after the suspense of his sitting down had passed. "Who is he?"

Albert looked surprised. "Why, it is my Uncle Mortimer."

The Doctor stared at the old man, then at Albert. "Mortimer Dash! Is it possible?"

"As you see."

"I'm sorry, my boy." The doctor realized his astonishment could only remind Albert of the sad truth he must face every day of his life: that his famous family was ruined. He had never imagined how complete that ruin was until this morning.

"It must come as a shock to you. You who must have seen him in his prime."

"Indeed, I did. He was at Columbia with Hamilton before the war. I saw him often at the Murray Hill house. He was . . . he cut a great figure in those days."

"Yes, but the government took all our lands even though Uncle Mortimer had supported the Revolution. It was only Mr. Hamilton who saw to it the family wasn't all hanged, and that we kept our other money, our shipping assets and such things."

"Then how did it come to this?"

"The summer of 1814."

There was a long moment of silence between them.

"Your parents," said the doctor.

"Yes. And my two cousins also died of the fever. That left my aunt and uncle here alone. So I came here to live with them. We did not live like this at the beginning. But my uncle started drinking and gambled all his money away after my cousins died. I think because he didn't want it if they wouldn't inherit it. And I'm afraid I did the same with my father's money. There wasn't much of it to begin with, but a year at Columbia and it quickly disappeared."

"Ah!" said the doctor. A certain mystery had always surrounded Albert Dash in his mind: how a rowdy, dissipated Columbia freshman of a very conventional sort had transformed himself, over the period of a single summer, into an outstanding scholar with a prodigious appetite for hard work. He saw now that it was the old answer: poverty had turned the boy's mind. The doctor smiled inwardly. The moral effects of poverty were sometimes the very opposite of what the ladies at the Society concerned with its prevention believed. It had made a scholar and patriot of Albert Dash.

Uncle Mortimer, sitting like a sentinel at his post near the window, barked another deep, liquid cough into his handkerchief, followed by an amount of sniffing. He reached for the bottle, drank a single, deep draught, then sat back with a sigh and appeared to drift into unconsciousness.

In answer to the doctor's quizzical look, Albert said, "We haven't had the heart to take the bottle away from him. It is his only comfort now."

"I certainly didn't recognize him. I remember that he had a great mane of curly dark hair, somewhat like yours. The ladies loved him, of course, though men wore it longer in those days."

"Aunt Mary says it turned white overnight at the deathbed of my cousins. Their room is still upstairs, you know. Aunt Mary has left everything it was the day they died, as if she still expects them to return. She visits their graves at the Nassau Street cemetery every day."

"Were you here? Were you exposed at the time of infection, to the same utensils and linens?"

"Perhaps," said Albert. "I actually don't remember anything about it."

For the sake of politeness, the doctor suppressed his medical curiosity in the case and simply nodded.

Albert gave an embarrassed cough. "But I may have been directly exposed more recently."

"What do you mean *exposed*? When?"

"This week."

"This week! How?"

"My day in Brooklyn. After speaking to all our witnesses, I snuck aboard the *Belladonna* after dark. I looked into the hold."

The doctor leapt to his feet, knocking the chair over backward. Albert felt his rough thumb pulling down the skin of his cheek—a big dark eye peered into his—then the joints of his hands crushed beneath the doctor's fingers. Only pride kept him from crying out in pain.

"No swelling there. Tongue!"

"Ahhh."

The doctor released him. But he did not take his angry eyes off him.

"Is that why I have not seen you? Because you thought you were infected?"

Albert looked shamefaced, and said nothing.

"You do not have the yellow fever. Though brain fever I cannot answer for. What on earth possessed you to board the *Belladonna*? You know it is a death ship!"

"We needed evidence for the hearing."

"And what evidence, short of your own corpse, could you have brought me out of such an escapade?"

"I can testify tomorrow. You may call me as a witness."

"Testify to what—criminal trespass? That you found what you were already disposed to find? You are a tainted witness. Who would believe I had not coached you?"

The doctor kicked at a pile of wood shavings on the floor.

"What did you find—in the hold?"

"It was the fever smell, for sure. I could not go in because of it. There was a dark, brackish water in the bottom of the hold, and crates and sacks I could see floating. The hold has not been cleared."

"A blatant breach of regulations. What did you do?"

"I fainted, I think. I barely know how I swam back. Also, I believe the ship is being guarded. There were regular patrols on the dock."

The doctor said, "You are a fool." But he said it more gently and with a grudging smile. "At least we know for sure in our own minds that the *Belladonna* is the guilty ship. Guarded, you say? Who can have arranged that? Perhaps it is Jackson's doing. Nevertheless, I need you alive, Albert. No more acts of bravado. In the future you will follow the letter of my orders and not exceed them. Understood?"

"Yes, sir."

Albert felt a sudden wave of exhausted relief. He had not been able to sleep for watching over his own symptoms, even though he knew he should be halfway to the grave by now had he actually caught the yellow fever. To conceal his survivor's euphoria, he invited the doctor to resume his seat.

The two men settled themselves in front of the pot-belly stove, using its grate as a table. The doctor pulled a large folder from his bag, while Albert rushed over to the writing desk in the corner to fetch his notes. Soon, all the information that could be had regarding the yellow fever outbreak in Brooklyn lay before them.

"I have never been to a hearing of the board," said Albert. "What kind of man is Dr. Miller?"

"Well, he is ancient, even by my standards. He is from an old family, though he moves in the new circles about town. When I was your age, he was looked up to by all of us—quite the best physician in New York. He had been to Europe, you know, and trained at Vienna with Gottfried. But it all went to his head. He became a slave to titles and honors and the approval of politicians—as if to compensate for having lowered himself to the profession in the first place. I find I can barely speak civil to him now. But his self-love aside, I believe he is a man of principle. He is a little doddering to be sure, but he understands his duty well enough."

"I heard he was once a strong advocate for the theory that the yellow fever has local causes. That you criticized him in print, in pretty strong terms."

The doctor gave a chuckle. "Oh, that was years ago, before we had all the proof that we have now. Besides, he's so old he probably doesn't remember we ever had a falling out." He paused for a moment, then shook his head as if to relieve himself of an unwelcome thought. "He's too much the city elder to take it personal, not with so much at stake. Now, I suggest we rehearse the depositions. Tell me, one by one, what each of our Brooklyn witnesses is prepared to testify."

Albert sheafed through his notes.

"First is John Jackson, owner of the shipyard where Duggan, Browne, and the others fell ill."

The doctor shook his head. "Jackson was very shabbily treated by the *Herald*. But he will make an excellent witness. He has a reputation and a livelihood to restore."

"He has told me he will contradict the allegations made in the *Herald* that his yard was unsanitary, and that the fever was produced by the noxious air of its environs. Jackson's yard is covered in its full extent both with fine gravel and wood chips, both drying agents. The effluvial pools described by the *Herald*, therefore, are pure fiction. Mr. Jackson likewise rejects the *Herald*'s claim that his property is unfavorable to the free circulation of air, and that its inhabitants suffered from the heat and swampy air they were compelled to breathe. Quite the contrary is true—as I myself saw when he showed me. The houses in the yard are not crowded together at all, and each enjoys an unimpeded southerly sea breeze on most days during the summer. In addition, the yard is surrounded on all sides by running salt water. There are no swampy deposits whatever. It has also been alleged that Mr. Jackson's boardinghouses were overcrowded. But he will swear that the greatest number of laborers to have shared a room is four, and all of these have remained in good health."

"Excellent," said the doctor. "First we demolish Mr. Casey's fairytales about Jackson's yard. Then onto the offensive. The *Belladonna*. Did you find Duggan's workmate? The man who survived?"

"Yes. Isaac Browne."

"I remember the man well. He recovered after five days, even after the black vomit. He is a stout fellow."

"I had a devil of a time finding him, but he is well known around the Brooklyn taverns, and I eventually came across him in the back room at Grimm's. He was regaling his mates with his heroic battle with the fever, a tale in which you, I'm afraid, played a scandalously small role."

"Well that's his right. After all, I've never cured a single man of yellow fever yet. But what story will he tell the board?"

Albert turned back to his notes. "Isaac Browne will testify that on the day Bert Duggan fell ill, they were both of them working on a ship on stilts in Jackson's yard when they noticed a terrible foul odor coming downwind from the direction of the *Belladonna*, which had just docked and was pumping her bilgewater. The bilgewater turned the sea black around the keel. This was visible from fifty yards away. The smell was so sickening that Bert said he felt ill and that he was going over to Mrs. Little's for a brandy and water. As we know, Duggan never came back. Isaac Browne meanwhile took himself over to Grimm's, where he sat in a corner drinking ale the rest of the day, feeling sick as a dog. The material point is that Isaac himself is convinced he caught the fever from the same source as Duggan—from the foul, infected air that escaped from the hold of the *Belladonna*—and he will swear to it."

"There is a point I wish to return to there. But go on for the moment. Who next?"

"Mrs. Crow."

"Ah."

Little Sarah Crow, the laundry woman's daughter, had died in terrible convulsions on her sixth day, only hours after a rally had raised tantalizing hopes of her recovery. For Albert and the doctor, it had been their darkest hour in Brooklyn, deep into the second week when they were already exhausted. The fever had almost blown the small girl's body apart and Albert had not been able to clear his head of the memory. From the strained look on the doctor's face, he hadn't succeeded either.

"Mrs. Crow will corroborate what Isaac Browne has said. The *Belladonna* docked just thirty yards from her house, and she noticed the same odor come through her windows. She saw the sea turn black, as Isaac Browne did, and noticed also that the sailors on board the *Belladonna* were refusing to unload stores from the hold. She heard shouting, and saw the captain waving his pistol."

"The infamous turncoat, Quin."

"She also saw Mrs. Little on the dock by the *Belladonna*'s berth. Her boy Jacob would often escape to that part of the dock to play among the anchor cables, and Mrs. Little would go in search of him there."

Albert paused. It was one thing to remember the hideous death-bed of yellow fever, the tortured eyes and wasted sacks of yellow skin. It was something altogether worse to think of those victims alive. A boy playing on a dock. A mother out looking for him, calling his name.

"It is useful that Mrs. Crow places them there, near the ship," said the doctor.

"Mrs. Crow will also give a detailed account of her daughter's symptoms. She says you may ask her what you will."

"That's courage. I honor her."

"In particular, she is prepared to relate little Sarah's own testimony of how she fell ill. As you know, Mrs. Crow takes in the washing of the men in Jackson's yard and the visiting sailors who dock there. That afternoon, she washed four tubs of linens out of the *Belladonna*."

"Where was the linen washed?"

"In the open air, out the back. Mrs. Crow remembers that Sarah stood with her over the tub for part of the time she was washing the linens, but that she then went away on account of the smell. Later, when she fell ill and her mother asked her how, she said, 'The tub. It was what was in the tub made me sick.'"

"This brings me to my point, Albert." The doctor sat back in his chair. "And it applies in equal measure to Browne and the

Littles. If Sarah fell sick standing over the tub, why did her mother not fall ill too? Likewise, if we are to argue that Browne and the Littles fell sick owing to their exposure to the same air that killed Duggan, how are we to explain that the Littles died later, days apart, and that Isaac Browne did not get properly sick until the second week?"

Albert smiled. "You could answer that yourself, Doctor. It is in the nature of an imported, contagious fever, as opposed to one of local miasmatic origin, to communicate itself from person to person, or from things to persons, in a systematic but not necessarily uniform manner. The impurity of the air surrounding that washing tub infected Sarah but not her mother. That we know. Why? We cannot be sure. But this in no way affects the question of origin. The source is certain: the infected linens of the *Belladonna*."

"Very good. A well-framed rebuttal. I will use those very words this afternoon. Now go on."

Albert looked down at his notes. "You will be pleased with our last witness I think, Doctor. I made inquiries in the bawdy houses along the Brooklyn docks and eventually came upon Lieutenant Babcock who is, or was, second-in-command of the *Belladonna*. As is often the case, he has nothing but contempt for his captain. There was even talk of a duel between him and Quin in Kingston Town, I believe. Called off at the last minute on account, of course, of yellow fever. Babcock swore to me that there were deaths on board the *Belladonna* en route from Kingston to New York. At least six deaths below decks from the fever."

"Really? Evidence of which you discovered yourself, and which the scoundrel Quin has since denied?"

"Yes, but Babcock will do anything to cross Quin, and will contradict his account on every point. He has left the ship and is under no pressure to keep silent."

"But a lieutenant's word against the captain's? I do not like our place on the quarterdeck."

Albert could not repress a glow of triumph. "But here's the rub, Doctor. Babcock has made a copy of the log—where the fever deaths are listed—and the captain doesn't know it!"

"God's truth, what a stroke!" cried Dr. Hosack, slapping his great paw of a hand on Albert's shoulder, and rising to his feet. "Quin is their only weapon, and you have taken it right out of their hands. We cannot lose now! We will have our quarantine!"

As the doctor and his assistant congratulated each other, they were interrupted by a violent cough from across the room and a swift, short thwack! Their sudden uproar had upset Uncle Mortimer's rhythm of expectoration. The old man's handkerchief remained inert in his lap while a small egg of phlegm, a perfect orb, sat glistening on the window pane in front of him. They all three contemplated it ruefully.

CHAPTER ELEVEN

A knock on the door.

"Regina?" Madam Camilla drew the sheet up around her.

The door opened a crack. Two dark arms appeared, holding a bottle of champagne and two glasses from the nice cabinet.

"Thank you." The door closed. Camilla opened the bottle with a deft flick, and presented the champagne with the smooth expertise of one long used to entertaining wealthy gentlemen in their leisure hours.

"Why, thank you, Cammie." Eamonn Casey lay propped up on a pillow with his vest open and his shoes off. "You are looking particularly beautiful tonight, my darling. Worthy of a toast."

For all her experience, Madam Camilla found herself charmed by the compliment. She laughed. "I want to believe you, Eamonn, but how can I when this house is filled with girls half my age, and all of them pretty?"

"But it's your bed I'm in, isn't it?"

Camilla allowed herself to be taken in his great arms. His face slid down into her bosom. She felt his rough whiskers on her skin.

"What could compare to these, Cammie? A man might idle his life away just here and be happy."

"I've plenty to spare, don't I?"

Now she freed herself from his embrace, shimmied down the bed, and turned her expert hand to the silk-sewn buttons on his breeches. Exploring inside, she was rewarded with a slight tremble. She moved further down the bed. Then she felt Casey's strong arm on her once more.

"What now, my love?" she said, looking up.

"Tell me how you do it with the doctor."

Camilla's heart fell. *Why must it always come to this?* she thought.

"You want to play doctor?"

"I want to know about the doctor. Your Doctor Hosack."

"Darling, you know I cannot tell you."

Suddenly, in an agile movement for such a big man, Casey rolled her onto her back and pinned her arms to the pillow. She looked fearfully at him for a moment, then he smiled and began gently kissing her on her eyelids and the tips of her ears.

"Oh yes, please," she sighed.

It had been many years since she had seen this kind of ardor in a man. As his strong bulk pressed on her hips, she forgot everything she had left undone that day. Regina would be waiting to go to market, the girls needed their dresses pressed and hair done, and there was money for the magistrate to arrange—but for precious minutes it was all forgotten. At the height of their raptures, Madam Camilla even forgot that Eamonn Casey was a client. His quick sighs sounded, she told herself, like a lover's desperation.

She felt his strong hands press against her neck, and then his face appeared. His eyes scanned hers, watching, she guessed, for signs of her happy convulsion. Just at that moment, when she felt she could not give more to this man, she heard him say again, directly into her ear, "Tell me about the doctor."

CHAPTER TWELVE

When the day of the quarantine hearing dawned, the Laidlaw house at Bowling Green was occupied with matters far more pressing than the contents of a ship's hold on the Brooklyn docks. It was still dark outside and Ma Dingle was already cursing and clattering in the kitchen, while the butler Shivers and the new boy Ned (fresh off the boat from Belfast) cleared the dining table. They scrubbed its ancient mahogany with beeswax until it shone. Next, they took Mrs. Laidlaw's finest damask tablecloth, folded like a bishop's robe, from the linen cabinet upstairs. After an hour's meticulous ironing, Ned went to fold the cloth over the table corners as he had been taught, but Shivers quickly slapped him, hard on the ear so it stung. The Laidlaws' head servant despised folds for a sin, and together they hung the tablecloth across a row of chairs in the back parlor until its moment should arrive.

Down in the cellar, Ned breathed the apples ripening sweetly in the darkness and the keen odor of herbs drying on the wall. On the shelves he found molasses jars from Havana, Malaga raisins with the grape's bloom still fresh on them, bags of Arabian coffee, Sumatra pepper and dusty golden cinnamon from the Spice Islands. Below these stood tins of tea with Chinamen printed on the front in smocks and long trailing hair. Next to them, tiny casks of tamarinds and guava, and ginger jars still wrapped in bamboo lattice to preserve them through their long journey from distant climes.

When he had brought armfuls of these riches to Ma Dingle, Ned returned for three cones of sugar, hung on hooks like hams from the ceiling, hard as rock and as heavy. An unknown slave's weary hand, in Kingston Town or Havana, had sealed them in purple cloth and tied a red ribbon label about the base. Ned lifted one down, cocked his ear a moment, then slowly unsheathed the sugar cone tip. He sucked the brown nib silently, drawing in his cheeks like a bellows. At the press of his moist lips and tongue, the hard grains exploded with perfect sweetness in his mouth. He smiled for the first time since leaving Ireland. He would blame this moment's pleasure on a rat.

Back in the kitchen, he found Ma Dingle bathed in a gleaming skein of sweat. A trio of saucepans frittered on the fire: one simmering, one spitting, the third singing like a bird. The charcoal smoke had turned her black, and she cursed with an energy that made Ned ashamed for her. Opposite the stove and fireplace, in an old oak dresser, stood rows of pewter plates tilted forward to save them from dust. They seemed to dance to the music of Ma Dingle's blasphemous shouts, while above them swayed a bountiful chandelier of pheasant carcasses, hares, woodcocks and gaping fish on hooks.

Ma Dingle grunted and pointed to the floor, by which Ned understood he was to scour the steel knives with brick dust to clean the rust, then sharpen them with stone. Kneeling on the floor, his eyes streamed from the smoke. From time to time, when Ma Dingle's curses turned especially fluent, he looked up to see her bent awkwardly, her arm buried deep in the brick oven. She crumpled her doughy face in pain while Shivers counted the seconds off. Forty seconds without fainting and the fruit pies and pastries could go in. Shrieking after twenty and the meats and bread lay waiting. When her arm reappeared, puffy and red, Ned thought he smelled cooked gooseflesh. He almost felt sorry for his tormentor, but when she caught him looking with his doleful eyes, she kicked him until he yelled and drove him out of the kitchen with a pair of tongs.

At three in the afternoon, in the front parlor, Ned lit the candles and the lamps with glowing tapers. Mr. Shivers opened the French doors between the two parlors to create a moderate-sized ballroom, then stood by the mantelpiece while Ned, at his say-so, tilted the looking glasses to better catch the pinpoint auras of flame. They lowered the curtains, heavy velvet burgundy over silken white. As darkness descended on the room, the candles' yellow light touched the gilt-framed portraits on the walls, and lit the brass curtain pulls. The glass-fronted rosewood cabinet, filled with silver, launched a fireworks of winks and glimmers that doubled in the mirrors and the crystal glasses on the sideboard, until the Laidlaws' wealth was multiplied beyond ordinary magnificence into an otherworldly splendor.

At five, just when they had begun to worry, flowers arrived in a great flotilla from the hothouse at Dr. Hosack's Botanical Gardens. Roses of all colors, laburnums, magnolias, iris, and the rare lady's slipper.

"He sent these," said Ned, "Mister Albert sent these for Miss Laidlaw." He gazed at the cut flowers in rows on the floor, in jealous wonder at the demonstrative powers of the well born.

While Shivers went off to dress—as the senior man, his was door duty—Ned hung clusters of laurel roses from the chandeliers, and arranged great bouquets in glass vases on the mantelpiece. Rocking on a ladder, he hung semicircle wreaths from the ceiling join and placed the largest—a masterpiece of baby's breath and pink roses—on the prominent ledge above the folding parlor doors.

He had only just come down from the ladder when the first guests arrived.

"Get out back, lad," hissed the white-gloved Shivers from behind a marble column. "If Dingle sees you she'll roast your balls."

Eliza Laidlaw believed fervently in the new informality she had heard was fashionable in London and Paris. Chairs, divans, card tables and stools, in small easy arrangements, stood in all quarters of her parlor, the better to promote circulation and lively group talk. For the convenience of her younger guests interested in more intimate dialogue, Mrs. Laidlaw ordered crimson love seats to be situated discreetly in dim corners of the back parlor.

Virginia had been sitting on one of these seats with Charlotte Harvey for a full half hour before Vera appeared, wafting downstairs into a waiting gaggle of admirers. She caught sight of Virginia and shot her a beseeching look. But as the minutes passed, Virginia saw that Vera was not making any serious effort to extricate herself and she resigned herself to the company of the elder Miss Harvey, whom she had been friends with at Miss Piper's.

Actually, Charlotte Harvey was an ideal companion. Sitting with her, Virginia did not have to be embarrassed, as she often was at parties, at the appearance of being alone, but neither was she required to make conversation. Charlotte and her sister Jane had just returned from three months' accelerated breeding in Bath. A single question about any aspect of that experience and Charlotte would happily talk away until the food arrived or the dancing began.

This left Virginia able to indulge her favorite party game: the quiet observation of her fellow human beings in their full social plumage. It was definitely a "new" Manhattan crowd. The ruffle-shirted merchants, bankers, and newspapermen, and their wives in silk-sheath dresses and feathers were all in boisterous high spirits. But the pleasure of watching them was not as great as it might otherwise have been. For one thing, their conversation lacked variety. Everyone talked only of how *delighted* they were, how overwhelmed with *relief* that there would be no quarantine of the port. This subject alone made Virginia anxious.

And then there was the spectacle of Vera herself, from which Virginia could not long be distracted. Even in such brilliant company as this, her friend was clearly the most dazzling presence in the room. With a skill Virginia could only admire, Vera managed to preserve democratic good feeling among her admirers by never outwardly singling one out for her special regard, while at the same time she preyed upon the unshakable male conviction of each in his own superior attractiveness. Crowded close around her, each young man supposed himself, on the proof of a sudden, suggestive flicker of her eye or the brush of her arm, to be the favorite.

Virginia had once been only mystified by Vera's brilliant reputation among the bachelor gentlemen of New York. What was her secret? After all, Vera could neither draw nor play the piano, and she refused to sing (except to herself, and that constantly). She knew even less of the world than she knew of books—had not been to Europe—and could not be trusted not to take off her shoes in public. Virginia, on the other hand, had labored hard to satisfy the demands of female accomplishment. French. Watercolors of

Trinity Church and the Palisades in autumn, widely admired. The pianoforte on which she accompanied herself tunefully. But somehow, it had all turned out the wrong side up. Virginia's many talents had earned her the unstinting praise of her friends and their mothers, but it was Vera, who possessed none such, who held the bachelors of the city in thrall.

Virginia watched her friend now as she laughed at one of the young men's jokes, began a teasing anecdote to another, and sent a third in quest of champagne. Was it her face that drew them like moths? But that face seemed to her unnaturally long, with strange, heavy brows and her hair a mess of curls. Her figure? But Vera said herself that she was no more than a pale thin reed—or *weed*. Was there some hidden virtue of her character? There was a time when Virginia had contemplated these questions with a scholar's detached fascination. But all that had changed the day Vera arrived in her parlor on the arm of a particular dark-eyed young man, who had run his fingertips down the sides of a dining chair when they were alone, and spoken to her of flowers.

As if summoned by her thoughts, Albert Dash now appeared, scandalously late to his prospective mother-in-law's party. At the door, Mrs. Laidlaw acknowledged him with the briefest of nods, while Mr. Laidlaw turned his head away and pretended to listen to her father.

Vera had been surreptitiously watching the door until the moment Albert appeared, at which point she fixed her attention away from it and did not turn around. Virginia saw Albert color at the sight of Vera surrounded by a posse of young men. But with a show of pride that endeared him all the more to Virginia, he did not join Vera's circle. Instead, he stood silently some feet away, within Vera's view but not meeting her eye. She left him standing in the middle of the parlor for a full two minutes by Virginia's reckoning, and for a while she thought the outcome of the struggle in serious doubt. But at last, Vera dismissed her entourage and walked over to him.

Charlotte had finally given up Bath and was asking her opinion of the young gentlemen in the room, so Virginia was not able to witness the conversation between Vera and Albert. But she did see that it was brief, and that Vera turned away from him with a toss of her head that might have been anger. Albert stood alone for some minutes before wandering toward the back parlor without making any effort to speak to anyone else.

Virginia quickly excused herself from Charlotte Harvey, promising to return very soon. She followed Albert as discreetly as she could through the French doors, spread outward like wings against the wall, and into the back parlor. It had not seemed to occur to Albert to look for her. Instead, he kept walking all the way to the most distant corner of the room where he stood with his back to the crowd. He seemed to purposely avoid looking at the fresh flowers he himself had sent, which were on display everywhere in brilliant arrangements. Instead, he was scrutinizing an artificial bouquet set inside a glass dome on a pier table. He leaned toward the encased flowers, his face almost pressed against the dome as if in secret conversation. A cloud of his moist breath formed on the glass. From where Virginia stood, the painted flowers appeared to bloom under his breath.

"I believe the stamen is missing, and the pistil quite shriveled."

"A flower in a case has no business reproducing itself," Albert replied, turning to her with a weak smile. "It is alone and believes itself unique. It has no wish for rivals."

Now he looked beyond Virginia and fixed his eyes on Vera, who stood brilliantly lit in the middle of the other room. A small flock of men had regrouped around her, glittering like peacocks.

"If you are at a loss now," said Virginia, following his gaze, "what will you be when she is a success—a famous actress?"

Albert frowned. "You speak knowingly of things you have only read in novels."

"Reading is a kind of experience."

"One learns from books, but one feels nothing. Not true feeling."

"I must lend you some of *my* books."

"I have no time for reading." In the silence that followed this abrupt statement, Virginia had a sinking feeling that their conversation was over, that he would not confide in her. She had time, now, to regret that she had so exposed her desire for that confidence by following him across the room.

"I know Vera's mother does not wish her to be an actress," he said suddenly. "Now I'm beginning to think Vera doesn't want me to be a physician."

There being no comment Virginia could safely make, she only asked him why he thought this.

"Because she made such a fuss about this party to me. That there would be a great many of her father's Wall Street friends here, and city councilmen. People I should meet. I think I see her design now. She intended me to ingratiate myself to these people, for someone to offer me a situation. You've noticed that Dr. Hosack was not invited."

"Yes."

"Now she is angry with me because I have arrived late, and that I am in no mood to do what she wants. But how could she expect me to flatter and grin at these people, especially after what happened today?"

He fell again into a brooding silence. Just then, the dancing began, as the musicians, three violins and a cello, struck up a popular bourée. The bright humming sound enlivened the room, and the chatter grew louder and more animated.

Albert was now distracted from further conversation by the provocative sight of Vera whirling about the parlor in the arms of a councilman's son, her hair spilling down her shoulders, her swan's back bent dramatically toward the floor. She had conspicuously ignored Albert's claims on her, and Virginia watched his reaction nervously out of the corner of her eye. Vera laughed as she passed them, apparently oblivious, and the whole room smiled. They were the only ones not to catch its infectious hilarity. Virginia's eyes followed her friend as she whirled past her and back again through the web of spinning couples. Then she turned back to Albert.

"I want to say how sorry I am about the Board of Health hearing," she said. "I'm sorry you did not get your quarantine."

Albert studied her, as if searching for a fault. "I almost didn't come tonight because of it. I have never seen the doctor so angry." He turned and looked grimly around the room. "It seems everyone here has heard. And they seem pleased, what's more. I am amazed—though I shouldn't be, I know. Mr. Laidlaw is a Wall Street businessman with money at stake on the docks and these are his friends."

"What went wrong?"

"Oh, everything. The hearing was a farce. None of our witnesses showed up, except poor John Jackson, and the board treated him with contempt. Dr. Miller threw out our petition in twenty minutes."

"What happened to your witnesses?" cried Virginia. "Was there some mistake?"

"Dr. Hosack says it was no mistake. Someone didn't want them to testify."

"Who?"

"I don't know."

They both scanned the room, as if the culprit were under their very noses. Virginia's eyes lit almost by accident on her father, who was deep in conversation with the mayor.

"Why would someone go to such lengths to sabotage the hearing, to suppress the truth when the city is in so much danger?"

Albert shook his head. "That is the hardest thing for me to understand. Perhaps they simply do not *care* to think of the danger, or they think more of their own profits. Either way, nothing will stop the yellow fever now—though, of course, I might be wrong," he added unconvincingly, and looked at her quickly as if he felt ashamed for alarming a young girl. He was leaning against the wall, his face illuminated by a small lamp mounted on the wall. In the pool of yellow light, he looked to her like a martyr in a religious painting. A beautiful, curly-haired martyr.

"What will Dr. Hosack do now?"

"We will keep fighting the board for a quarantine, with new petitions each week. We will find our witnesses wherever they are. We won't stop."

Albert surprised her now by abruptly taking her arm and leading her deeper into the corner away from the light. He looked directly into her eyes in a way he never had before. But this had the very opposite impact that he intended. The closeness of his face to hers made it impossible for her to comprehend anything that he actually said.

"Virginia, you must get away," he whispered. "Tomorrow, or as soon as you can. If your father scoffs at the fever, find some other excuse for leaving the city. Go with your mother and Michael up to Westchester for a few weeks, until the end of September. Say it is for your mother's nerves."

Virginia stared at him dumbly. He now took her by the shoulders.

"Do you understand? You *must* leave."

Virginia bit her lip. She could not think of what Albert was saying, only what she needed to say to him. While he still had his hands clasped on her shoulders, she said, "There is something I have to tell you about my father. And about Dr. Miller."

A loud announcement interrupted them. Mr. Shivers, dressed in a gold-buttoned naval jacket and velvet breeches, opened the doors to the back parlor, revealing the long mahogany dinner table in its full glory. A roast pig sat somnolently in the center surrounded by exotic fruits, sweet-smelling pies and pastries, cakes the size of dollhouses and two inviting brass tubs of sorbet. No sooner had Mrs. Laidlaw announced these delights than she was called to the foyer to welcome the mayor, who had arrived at the same instant.

A large, brightly dressed young man now approached them with a loud greeting, his face exhilarated from dancing. Albert released Virginia, who silently cursed George Bickart from her deepest soul. After a barely polite excuse, she slipped away to join the sea of people in the front parlor. There she found her brother, awkward and alone as usual, and set about introducing him to one of her kinder friends.

After a few minutes, Vera suddenly appeared at her shoulder.

"Will you speak to him for me? He will listen to you."

"Who?" asked Virginia, for form's sake.

"Albert—I don't have time to speak to him. The next dance is about to start and he is talking to that vulgar Bowery friend of his. Tell him how much trouble I had to have him invited at all. Father said he would not have him, and Mother was difficult too. Tonight is the perfect opportunity for him, with everybody here and in such a good mood. I know there are positions at Mr. Harvey's bank. Jane told me—"

"I don't think he will want to talk to Mr. Harvey. Not tonight."

"Why ever not?"

"Albert and the doctor lost their case for quarantine today."

Vera put a warning finger to her lips, and drew Virginia away from the crowd.

"Don't mention that name!" she hissed. "The last thing we want is for people to know that he is the doctor's assistant, or whatever he is. They will drop him instantly if they find out. The doctor's name is poison here. I just hope Albert has the good sense not to mention him."

They were interrupted by the approach of a foreign-looking gentleman in a scarlet military uniform festooned with ribbons. He wore a strange facial adornment—Charlotte had called it a "moustache" and seen them everywhere in Bath—which he smoothed voluptuously with his finger as he requested Vera's hand for the next two dances.

"Tell him not to be a dolt," said Vera over her shoulder to Virginia as she took her place in the line. "I know you want the best for him too."

Virginia felt very unsure of her mission but made her first steps toward fulfilling it by claiming one of the love seats by the French doors. From there she was screened by the parading couples and sat within earshot of Albert and George Bickart who were standing near the sideboard.

Peering at them together out of the corner of her eye, she wondered how it was they had stayed friends, having taken such different paths in their postcollegiate careers. Through his association with the famous Dr. Hosack, Albert had been invited to many an immortal evening at the doctor's Italianate villa on the Hudson

River where he listened raptly to eminent men of science, philosophy and government discourse, in multiple languages, on every possible theme relating to the improvement of mankind. The society George Bickart enjoyed in her father's study, by contrast— the racetrack gents and hard-drinking heroes of the press—cared nothing for man's progress whatever. Indeed, her father's circle prized nothing so much as lurid accounts of human degradation— bankruptcy, adultery, or the bottle—to be reveled in on Sunday nights over drinks and cards, then published forthwith on Monday in an adopted tone of moral outrage.

"I hear you've been spotted of late back in Brooklyn," she heard George say. "You are a rare bird anywhere, but in those parts almost extinct. You were talking to that ship's lieutenant at Grimm's."

"Your information is always reliable, George. Except of course at the track, as I've discovered to my own cost."

George screwed up his face and forced a laugh. It was an old joke between them, almost stale now.

"I was in Brooklyn on Hosack's orders, you know," said Albert.

"Of course, yes. This damned quarantine business." Virginia heard George give a self-conscious cough. "Which brings me to *my* business, Albert. A friendly warning to you of dangers you are facing you would do well to consider."

"What could those dangers be, compared to the yellow fever itself?" asked Albert.

"Don't scoff, please. I am, for once, in earnest." George lowered his voice so that Virginia could barely catch his words. "I will put it plainly. I know you pin your hopes on the doctor, but certain people are not impressed with his agitation over yellow fever." He looked significantly toward the assembly in the front parlor. Albert followed his gaze to where Eamonn Casey stood by the marble mantelpiece in close conference with the mayor, who was pluck-ing at the thigh of a cornish hen.

"But they have won their victory. There will be no quarantine."

"Not for now, perhaps," said George. "But as you well know, Dr. Hosack has threatened to convene the Board of Health every week, to keep at them about the quarantine. This has outraged a good many of the influential gentlemen present here this evening. Listen to them, Albert. They call him a publicity hound, a trouble-maker who depresses their trade."

"They are afraid for their fortunes?" asked Albert with a sneer. "Your Wall Street friends worry that their profits, instead of being a hundred percent, will be thirty or fifty?"

"They are not my friends. And it is more serious than that, Albert. They see the reputation of the city as a safe trading port in danger from such talk. You know I do not agree with them or take their part, but these gentlemen consider themselves at risk in this matter, and they are like badgers against a barn door when threatened."

"I assume you speak of one gentleman in particular," said Albert. "Your patron."

"Well," said George uncomfortably, "I was thinking of Mr. Casey, yes."

Virginia felt her breath catch, and she blushed.

"Did Casey send you to speak to me?" asked Albert.

She saw George now turn red, and mutter something inaudible.

"I'm sorry, George." Albert hastily held up his hands. "But you know that I am committed to Hosack's cause. Not only is he in the right, but the lives of perhaps thousands of people in this city depend on his being accepted as right. Your friends should think of this when they consider the viability of the port. A major outbreak of yellow fever in New York this summer will ruin their precious profits far worse than a quarantine. Think of it, George. Many ports in Europe have quarantines longer than sixty days. Our ships must suffer them in their waters."

"And merchants on both sides of the Atlantic suffer losses they greatly resent."

"Even at the risk of an epidemic, of absolute calamity to the city?"

"I don't wish to defend them, only to warn you," George put a hand on his arm. "You do not need to abandon the cause. But if you could just find some way of distancing yourself in the public eye from this wretched Hosack. Every report in the *Gazette* names you as his right-hand man. You are famous, Albert! You are the doctor's 'indefatigable lieutenant,' his 'Dash-ing young Columbian'!"

He laughed, but Albert remained stony-faced. "I say this seriously," George added hurriedly, "you are not safe with this sort of publicity, with your close association to the doctor. These are gentlemen with a keen sense of their injuries and ample means to avenge them."

Albert was silent for a moment. He turned toward the pier table, and looked again at the flower in its glass. Then he walked away over to the sideboard display of exotic oranges and bananas, brought from distant lands in the holds of Mr. Laidlaw's ships. George followed him. He whispered something in his ear. Virginia caught Dr. Hosack's name repeated twice, but nothing more.

A cluster of guests, drawn by the replenishment of the sorbet tubs, now wandered past Virginia into the back parlor. The sound of popping corks and increasingly raucous laughter filled the room. Virginia felt a creeping sensation in her stomach, and looked up.

Her brooding alone on a love seat was drawing critical attention. Light-footed young couples glared impatiently at her, while a passing train of slow-moving matrons tutted sympathetically. They remembered when they too were young and in want of a partner and had wished their miserable lives were over.

Virginia fought down her blushes, and stood up with an appearance of unconcern. She discreetly attached herself to the rear of a stream of guests moving in the direction of the rear parlor, where she observed that Albert was just turning away from George Bickart. She greeted his withdrawal with relief. She had long blamed him for Albert's dubious undergraduate reputation. Pranks, brawling, gambling, and worse—much worse. Now, having heard what she heard, she directed a look of more than usual hostility toward his retreating back. Then she took a deep breath and tapped Albert on the shoulder. Albert turned around, but before she could open her mouth to speak to him, the fates declared themselves against her once more. The clinking of fifty champagne glasses drowned out her words. The music had come to an abrupt halt, and her father and the mayor had taken their place on the now vacant dance floor. The mayor stepped forward to address the sparkling assembly.

"Ladies and gentlemen," he began. "First allow me to thank on your behalf the generous hosts of tonight's festivity, Mr. and Mrs. John Laidlaw. It has been an anxious day for us all, and this evening's gathering marks a celebration of that rarest of occasions: a day when sanity prevailed at City Hall!"

The mayor was known for his self-deprecating humor. Her father said the mayor reckoned it worth a thousand votes, or perhaps the twentieth part of twenty thousand votes, and had honed this skill accordingly. He was rewarded now with a general laugh and cheering.

Virginia didn't laugh, and couldn't bring herself to look at Albert. But it was almost worse to watch her father smiling and clapping next to John Laidlaw.

"But seriously, my friends." The mayor held up his hands. "Our Board of Health, under the leadership of Dr. Miller, has safe-guarded this city from disease these last eight years with a steady hand. Just as importantly, I'm sure you will agree, Dr. Miller's steadiness and wisdom has preserved us from the disruptions of unnecessary alarm, from the paralysis of fear. Today marks another chapter in the fine history of Dr. Miller's stewardship. Thanks to him and his board, we here can look to our own responsibilities: the safeguarding of our city's prosperity without check and free from fear. We owe him our thanks!"

The mayor gestured to a stooped old man with eyeglasses stand-ing by the dining table. He stood next to Mrs. Laidlaw, who tow-ered over him. In answer to new rounds of applause and cheers, Dr. Miller smiled and bobbed his head with evident pleasure. Sev-eral gentlemen went over to shake him by the hand.

"But with all due respect to Dr. Miller," continued the mayor, "I am sure he will concede that while he might be the man of the hour, he is not the man of the future."

The mayor was a past master of such jokes, which he preserved from insult by a smiling good will. Dr. Miller certainly took it in very good humor, seeming to concede his great age with an ironic waft of his hand and a deliberate, joking stagger. Mrs. Laidlaw, with her natural actress's timing, provided the perfect cue. She leaned over the old man, placed a hand under his arm with a nurse's care, then broke from the pose and threw her head back, laughing. Virginia thought it so well done it almost appeared rehearsed.

"Yes, my friends," cried the mayor over the appreciative hub-bub, "tonight marks a great occasion for the city of New York for reasons other than our deliverance from a ruinous quarantine. It is indeed a greater occasion than any of us, a week ago, could have imagined. Because it is tonight, ladies and gentlemen, that it is my honor and pleasure to introduce to you one of Manhattan's favorite sons—Mr. Eamonn Casey—as the next governor of the state of New York!"

There was a moment's stunned silence. The crowd turned, as a body, in the direction of Eamonn Casey, a man most of Mr. Laidlaw's friends knew only by reputation. Until very recently, that reputation had been uniformly bad. An air of embarrassed doubt filled the room.

The mayor had long experience of such critical moments. He now became very serious.

"I know that Mr. Casey's announcement of his candidacy has come as a surprise for most of us. And I know, as you do, that he is a Democrat. But I would ask you to put aside all you have ever thought about Eamonn Casey before tonight. Think instead of the sane, statesmanlike voice Mr. Casey has brought to the clamor over the yellow fever this past week. And then, after you have heard the visionary plan Mr. Casey has for the future of our city—its commercial future—I know you will be convinced, as I and Mr. John Laidlaw himself has been, that Mr. Casey is indeed the man of the future in this state. The man whom we must help John Laidlaw elect as governor in November. Without further ado, then, the man himself!"

There was an expectant hush as the mayor surrendered his place on the floor to the bearish, whiskered figure of Eamonn Casey. The merchants and bankers of Manhattan and their silk-ribboned wives considered him critically, as if still digesting the remarkable information: Eamonn Casey was the mayor's candidate for governor. More importantly, John Laidlaw's candidate! From the dumbfounded look on their faces, several in the assembly simply couldn't believe such a thing and were looking about for the joke.

The mayor shook her father's hand and ushered him forward. Virginia had listened to her father rehearsing his speech in his study. It was full of the engineering feats of the Roman Empire and ended with the Declaration of Independence. But now, as he stepped forward, she saw him quietly crumple up his notes and stuff them in his pocket. She felt a chill of anxiety about what he would say instead.

"Thank you, Mr. Mayor," he began in his genteel, parlor-room voice. "And thank you, ladies and gentlemen. I come to you tonight with the business opportunity of a lifetime—water."

He paused while his eyes slowly scanned the room. He had their attention, for now.

"Let me explain. We would all agree that the greatest danger to this city's prosperity lies in our lack of clean water. Without it, this great port will never reach its full potential. We cannot build northward and grow—indeed, we ourselves cannot be sure to survive here into the next generation—without new and plentiful sources of fresh water."

He looked up again. Somber faces mixed with sour. Behind him the mayor looked uneasy. Virginia saw that it would not do for him to strike too dark a note, not with everybody holding glasses of champagne in their hands. But her father had read the moment too and now raised his voice to a more rousing decibel.

"But the solution to the water crisis lies not in hand-wringing and despair; it lies in positive action! As my good friend, John Laidlaw, has many times said to me: the moment of greatest crisis is also the moment of greatest opportunity. If this is true of the business of trade, and sending ships to the four corners of the earth, it is no less true of water in New York City, my friends. What sum, do you think, would be owed to the man who could provide our thirsty city with a limitless supply of fresh water? Millions, you say? A king's ransom? Yes, there is no doubt. But the problem, of course—you will also say—is that there is no such man."

Nods. Some knitted brows. He must come to the point.

"I tell you tonight, gentlemen, that while there might be no such man, there are such *men*. And I am looking at them!"

A burst of baffled applause. He built up speed as he came to his pitch.

"As governor of this great state, my first act will be to sign into law the creation of a water company charged with building an aqueduct from the Croton River in Westchester, forty miles south along the Hudson River to a reservoir on Thirteenth Street, and from there to the streets and homes of Manhattan. When built, the Croton Aqueduct will bring millions of gallons of water a day to the city, enough to relieve all our current wants and free us from fevers and disease for a thousand years hence. But what is more, my friends, every single gallon of that water will pay a dividend to those lucky enough to hold shares in the new Manhattan Water Company I shall create. Shareholders will reap the benefits of water rates for generations to come. A supply of profit as inexhaustible as the Croton Spring itself!"

Whispering now, and excited talk. All eyes on her father.

"Now, with the image of this magnificent structure in your minds, and of the prosperity it will bring, like streams of clear gold, from the mountains of Westchester to the city, I ask you to mark this day with me as a truly historic occasion for the city of New York. Let us say that here, tonight, we convened the first general meeting of the new Manhattan Water Company with you yourselves, my friends, as visionary shareholders in the wealth of the future!"

He rode a first wave of cheers, then raised his voice in ringing tones above it.

"Fellow shareholders! It remains only for me now to introduce to you the director of our new company. A man known to the port of Manhattan as its captain, and to Wall Street as its prince—Mr. John Laidlaw!"

Casey turned to hail the host amid a chorus of cheers and stamping feet. Everyone was talking now, and did not quiet down until John Laidlaw himself made to speak. He did not step forward but remained where he was, behind and to the right of the mayor.

"As Mr. Casey has sagely remarked," he began (so quietly that everyone leaned forward, and shushed each other to hear him), "water is the future of this city." He looked around and smiled. "But water is also money. I strongly suggest to you, my friends, that you put yourselves on the right side of the flow!"

There was a burst of laughter and applause. The mayor then stepped forward and raised his glass.

"To the Manhattan Water Company!"

"The Manhattan Water Company!" cheered the crowd.

"Casey for governor!" boomed the mayor.

"Casey for governor!" came the answering cry. The mayor and Eamonn Casey were instantly submerged by the crowd. Some talked animatedly amongst themselves while others pushed forward to shake their hands, or even scribbled promissory notes on the spot on scraps of paper. The mayor was in his element. He wore a hemispheric grin of jubilation, shaking hands and slapping backs with gusto. Casey also embraced the crush, all thanks and gratitude. John Laidlaw, meanwhile, had withdrawn to a corner, to join a close huddle of older, black-suited men of Wall Street.

"Goodbye, Virginia," she heard a voice say behind her in the din. She spun around to find Albert looking fixedly at her. "Please communicate my regrets to Mrs. Laidlaw. I must go now." He began to walk away.

Virginia stopped him, grabbing his hand. He looked back at her in surprise. "I meant to tell you about my father and Mr. Laidlaw."

Albert seemed embarrassed. "It isn't your fault. Your father is an ambitious man and will put Mr. Laidlaw's money to good use, I'm sure. And he has paid Mr. Laidlaw in kind with his editorials."

"It goes beyond that."

"What do you mean?"

Virginia took a deep breath. She led him back to the corner, where they were screened by a dense arrangement of Dr. Hosack's bougainvilleas.

"Dr. Miller was on the original guest list," she whispered. "Mrs. Laidlaw did not leave it until today to invite him."

Albert did not seem struck by this information. "Perhaps Mr. Laidlaw hoped to ingratiate himself."

"No, you don't understand," said Virginia impatiently. "Tonight was planned as a victory party. My father and Mr. Laidlaw were sure in advance that Dr. Miller would rule against a quarantine."

"In advance?" Albert's eyes widened. "Your father was sure of winning in advance?"

"Yes. I'm sorry now that I didn't warn you." Virginia was almost crying as the pent-up anxiety flooded over her. "Please forgive me! I don't believe a word my father has written about the quarantine, you know."

But Albert was no longer listening. A dumb, absorbed look came over his face. He withdrew his hand from hers—she must have grasped it again, though she couldn't say when—then he turned abruptly away from her through the crowd.

Albert meant to leave by the back door, but in the hallway an angry-looking cook almost ran him down. He stumbled back into what he thought must be the library. Squinting in the sudden gloom, he found that he was not alone.

"Mr. Dash, is it?" said a portly, balding man behind a desk. A large parchment map lay in front of him, fixed at each end by an oil lamp. Albert's eyes fixed on the document with interest. "Are you come for the company secrets? Well, I am its Cerberus, and I have fangs."

"You have it wrong, sir," said Albert, coldly. "I am here by mistake. Please excuse my intrusion." He went to leave.

"Now, now, don't be put out," said the man, extending his hand, "since we both seek escape from these fierce gaieties"—he rolled his eyes toward the bubbling noise of the parlor—"let us be friends for an hour. My name is Geyer. Samuel Geyer."

"I know your name, sir. You are a friend of Mr. Casey's."

"Does that mean you will not shake my hand?"

Albert composed himself and shook hands. Sam Geyer motioned him to sit down.

"I am also an old friend of Dr. Hosack's."

Albert raised an eyebrow.

"I know I have felt the sting of his contempt in the *Gazette* of late for throwing in my lot with those who believe the yellow fever is of local origin. But I will tell you that it has not always been so between myself and Dr. Hosack. Our families go back to the old times here in New York, like your own. We have known each other these forty years. We were Columbia freshmen together. We competed for the attention of the professors and the young ladies with equal energy, no doubt much as you and your friends do now. And we drank too much. Then, after the Hamilton business, David changed, and I have barely seen him for many years. He spurns society, you know. He is the kind of man one only hears about.

But we have kept up a correspondence and talk long into the night on the rare occasion he visits the old club. But this summer, since the fever business in Brooklyn, he has been railing against all his old friends. And I'm sure he blames us for what happened today at the Board of Health. He paints us all with so broad a brush that he is no longer able to distinguish friend from foe."

"I believe the doctor would consider personal friendships of no account where the welfare of the public at large is at stake."

"Yes, you are right. But should we trust a friend of humanity who is friend to no man?"

Albert stared stolidly at him and said nothing.

"Never fear," said Geyer, holding up his hands, "I have no interest in turning you against him. In fact, it would grieve me to see it. These are only my idle philosophisms. You see, the character of the doctor has occupied my mind for many years, like a problem in hydraulics or, better, metaphysics."

"Have you solved it, sir?" In spite of everything, Albert found himself diverted by the company of this eccentric, round-faced man.

"Yes, indeed, Mr. Dash, I believe I have. May I summarize?"

Albert nodded, and Mr. Geyer began in his best lecture-hall style imitation of the doctor. Albert couldn't help smiling.

"In Dr. Hosack, we have the signal proof that your misanthrope is, at bottom, an idealist: not a hater of men, but the worshiper of Ideal Man. His foul temper, tiresome to his friends, comes from his being so consistently disappointed in the behavior of his fellow man. At the same time, however, he never allows himself to draw from the overwhelming particular evidence for their unworthiness and degradation the necessary conclusion that they *are* unworthy and degraded. So it is that Hosack the man of science is anything but with regard to the science of man. He allows his premises and conclusions to sit in contradiction like your most muddle-headed poet. But we all should be thankful for that. For where should he find that demonic energy of his except in wrestling these contradictions? How otherwise would the hospital have been built or his wonderful botanic gardens?"

Albert nodded his agreement.

"I, on the other hand," Geyer continued, with a wry grin, "I everywhere find that my low opinion of humanity is confirmed and so enjoy a perfect peace of mind. I loathe the city and spend as much time as I can in seclusion at Ambleside, my country retreat. There, with no one to contradict my opinions, I meditate on the infinitely disappointing nature of the world. I am neither troubled by it nor motivated to change it in any way. You don't see in me the irritation of an unfulfilled ideal, and ceaseless futile exertions on its behalf."

"And yet you wish to build an aqueduct, Mr. Geyer," said Albert, pointing to the map on the table. "A mammoth, some might say futile, task."

Geyer looked surprised, then laughed and wiped the perspiration from his brow. "You're a quick fellow, aren't you? I only said that I had solved the problem of the doctor. My own contradictions are another matter." He leaned his round belly against the desk. "But if I might be serious a moment,"—he lowered his voice—"Mr. Casey's aqueduct and the doctor's quarantine lie, by rights, on the same side of the question. Both promote the health and safety of the people of Manhattan. They are only brought to stand against each other by political circumstances and by the public's confusion."

"And who is responsible for that?" said Albert.

Geyer waved his hand. "I am not a political man, Mr. Dash. I'm a daydreamer—and men call me a fool for it—but I see clearly enough to the future. Perhaps the doctor is right that we need a quarantine to survive this summer. But we will need an aqueduct to survive the next and summers a century hence."

"You forget the doctor's principal argument," Albert replied. "The yellow fever does not originate here in our foul water. It is brought here by ship. Have you ever known the yellow fever to break out anywhere but at the docks?"

"No, I have not. But I might ask you, in turn, why the fever spreads more quickly in poorer areas of the city where the water is so very bad?"

"The doctor has never argued that sanitary conditions play no part, or should not be improved. It stands to reason that bad water and bad air will aid the course of the contagion. But we will not find the cure in simply improving these, sir. Nor should the public be led to believe we will."

Geyer smiled and nodded. "We may each serve the public in our own way, I believe."

He spread his palms out on the desk, and bent over the map of Manhattan Island. "If you will invent a cure for the yellow fever, Mr. Dash, I will endeavor to provide fresh water enough to keep at bay the thousand other malignancies that prey upon our beloved city."

Albert joined him behind the desk, and together they examined the plans. Mr. Geyer passed a stubby finger from north to south along Broadway, then across to the Bowery. He shook his head gravely.

"We are miserably kept here, sir. The sewers lie open, our livestock roam the streets uniting their filth with our own; our ponds and wells are almost dried. We have barely enough to drink and little to spare to fight our fires, as you know too well. I admire your botanical medicine and your quarantine, Mr. Dash, I surely do, but only the aqueduct can save us."

Albert looked at the map with intense consideration. It showed the laying of pipes along the banks of the Hudson to a central reservoir above Thirteenth Street. From there the life-giving branches spread east and west to all wards of the city rich and poor. On every lot on every street, Sam Geyer had proposed the position of a water pump with a small blue dot. One such dot stood at Greenwich Street near Canal, where Albert's mother and father had perished with baked lips and a saffron glow. Under the shifting, aqueous light of the lamp, the dots on the map seemed to him like buds of promise from which the pearly water would one day bloom and save them all, water to bathe and protect his and Vera's children. For a brief moment in John Laidlaw's study, Albert almost believed in Samuel Geyer.

"I see these plans are well advanced," he said. "This aqueduct is not the whim of a moment."

"Not at all," Geyer replied. "Mr. Casey and I have consulted almost daily for the best part of three months. He is very serious about the aqueduct, I assure you, quite impassioned. He sees the governorship as the only means by which he can bring his vision to reality, and Mr. Laidlaw as the only man who can bring him the governorship. Hence the importance of tonight. But I hate parties almost as much as I detest politics. Would you say tonight has been a success, Mr. Dash? I ask in all good faith."

"It has served Mr. Casey's purposes very well, I would say."

"Well, I am glad, though perhaps it is more like good news to me than it is to you. Nevertheless, I would ask you to assure Dr. Hosack when you next see him that Mr. Casey is genuine in efforts to bring fresh water to the city, something the doctor himself has been calling for these many years. Tell him also that I will soon be traveling with Mr. Casey through Westchester County to survey the aqueduct route. The mayor and Mr. Laidlaw will be joining us, I believe. I would invite the doctor at any time after that to come and examine our preliminary sketches and estimates. But then, he knows my door is always open to him."

They were startled by a voice.

"Let us be gone, Mr. Geyer! I will not remain in this company of these card sharps and libertines a moment longer!" A plump, finely dressed woman stood at the door. "Take me away, please. I cannot endure that woman's vulgarity a moment longer. Eliza Laidlaw has been flirting in revolting fashion with the mayor. And her daughter—Lord have mercy—she flirts with everyone!"

Mr. Geyer glanced at Albert, then coughed meaningfully in his wife's direction. "Ah, Aurelia, my dear," he began.

Albert remained impassively behind the desk, and said nothing. The thought crossed Aurelia Geyer's mind that she had been vulgar. She decided to despise Albert for it.

"Yes, of course, I suppose I should apologize to you, Mr. Dash. You are so very attached to this family. But you will thank me when I tell you that your inamorata—if I may call her that—appears to have forgotten you and has been waltzing this last twenty minutes in the arms of a foreign gentleman—a *very* attentive foreign gentleman. Well, Mr. Geyer, I will call for the barouche, if you will not. You may join me at your leisure."

She made her exit with as little prompting or grace as she had entered.

After an awkward moment, Albert mumbled a terse compliment and left the room in the direction of the parlor. He fought his way through the crowd across the room, disrupting the configuration of the quadrille, and ignoring Mrs. Laidlaw's cry of indignant surprise as he whistled by. In the entrance hall, dim and cool, he found Shivers sitting by the front door in a nest of silk hats and bonnets. He stared uselessly at Albert, who pushed past him and opened the heavy door himself. He had reached the street before the sound of his name stopped him. He turned around to see Virginia standing at the top of the steps, her small, dark figure framed by the bright lights within.

"You have not forgotten your promise for tomorrow?" she asked.

He looked at her but could not focus on her meaning.

"The rehearsal of Vera's play at the Bowery Theater. We agreed weeks ago. I shall be ready at four."

"Yes, of course. Goodnight, Virginia." He fixed his hat on his head and walked briskly away in the direction of lower Broadway before she could say anything else to draw him back.

It was a clear night, rich with stars. Despite the lateness of the hour, crowds of people still ambled about the northern rim of Battery Park, seeking respite from their stifling rooms. As he turned the corner from Bowling Green he saw the old statue of General Washington, solitary in the dark trees, looking out over the harbor where the British fleet had once sailed. The British had been filthy occupiers. Not a single street cleaned in five years. Disease ran rampant, and the population of the city fell by half. But that dogged Virginian had prevailed, of course, and been inaugurated as president of the republic he saved less than a mile away on Wall Street. As he skirted the park, Albert wondered what the old general would think of what he had just seen—of his hard-won republic handed over to newspaper hounds and johnny-come-latelies with their infinite credit and votes for sale.

At first, these thoughts running through his mind made Albert angry, and his pace quickened as he turned onto Broadway. But then something about the nighttime gloom of the now-deserted street—the sound of his solitary shoes scuffing the flagstones with no other sound but the hum of insects around his head—produced a sudden wave of despair. He wondered if the anger he felt was already mere bitterness; if Dr. Hosack was indeed a man of the past like General Washington, no more relevant to the present age than a statue on Bowling Green; and if he himself, in leaving the Laidlaws' party, was somehow renouncing the world he actually lived in for no better reason than to strike out alone, like some modern Quixote, on the lonely path of antiquated virtues, destined never to be useful to mankind, or to have his struggles remembered.

CHAPTER THIRTEEN

"They gave that scoundrel Miller a toast?"

The doctor said nothing more for a long moment. He seemed in a melancholy mood, even before Albert's shocking description of the goings-on at the Laidlaws' party.

Albert stood quietly, waiting for an explosion—potential projectiles lay within easy reach—but in the end the doctor only mumbled a curse and turned in his chair to contemplate the view over the Columbia quadrangle. Being a Saturday morning, it was empty of undergraduates, though the hot wind blew phantom figures of dust along the paths, like scholars hurrying between classes of some invisible realm.

Albert had resisted the doctor's invitation to sit, not out of formality, but because to do so would have entirely obscured the doctor from his view. His desk was piled with student work and old editions of the *Gazette*, for which his Columbia office functioned as unofficial editorial room, distribution house and archive. The doctor was notorious for wanting to run everything himself: he was not a trusting man. That fact made Albert's new relationship with him all the more unique.

"Miller's being at the Laidlaws' party galls me, Albert. It is as if they are flaunting the possibility of improper influence over the board and don't care if that is the appearance. I am surprised at the mayor. Such arrogance is not his style—though perhaps it is Mr. Casey's." The doctor raised an eyebrow in Albert's direction that seemed to say, *you would know better than I.*

But Albert only nodded. He did not want to discuss the Caseys or Laidlaws more than could be helped. His close association to those families had become the source of increasingly painful feelings.

"What can we do about their bribing Dr. Miller?"

"Nothing, if we cannot prove it. And proof will be hard to come by."

"But as long as Dr. Miller is director of the Board of Health our petition for quarantine will be denied, as it was last Friday."

"Yes," said the doctor, who then shook his head. "And yet I wonder if we are not missing the point in fixing on Dr. Miller. After all, if you were on the board, would you have granted our petition with only John Jackson's word as witness? No. Whatever Miller's predeterminations on the case, the fact of our not producing witnesses was our death knell. It made it all too easy for Miller to deny us."

"Have you heard nothing from them—from Mrs. Crow, Isaac Browne, and Lieutenant Babcock? What can have happened to them?"

The doctor turned slowly back from the window.

"I know nothing of Browne and Mrs. Crow. But Lieutenant Babcock is dead."

"Babcock dead?"

"Word came to me an hour ago. They found him in a ditch in two feet of water. Drowned, they say—dead drunk."

Albert now sat down. "When did this happen? What were his movements?"

"He had been at Grimm's Tavern Thursday night, drinking heavily. He left at closing time around two in the morning. That was the last seen of him."

"Can a man drown in two feet of water?"

"He can if he is drunk enough. But I would like to examine his lungs all the same, to see if there's water in them."

"Then we must do it. Today."

"We cannot, unfortunately. He was English and a sailor. We have no jurisdiction. Captain Quin himself requisitioned the body before noon, and his shipmates buried him at sea before the sun went down last night."

"And the copies he made of the *Belladonna*'s log?"

"With the fishes, I presume."

Albert took some seconds to digest the information. "A quick, sorry business."

"A criminal business."

"But we cannot prove it."

The doctor smiled grimly at Albert. "You learn fast. There is probably little to be gained by our investigating Lieutenant Babcock's death. But I would like to just the same. We can be sure of one thing, though. Mr. Casey and his friends are very serious about their not wanting a quarantine. We have been given our warning. We must be careful from now on, Albert. Very careful."

Albert thought immediately of what George Bickart had told him about Mr. Casey having "plans" for the doctor. But this would mean explaining who George Bickart was, and why he was still friends with a proven grave robber and disgraced Columbian. Besides, it was so vague a warning and the doctor was already on his guard. Albert let the moment pass.

The doctor continued, "Given these dangers, and your history of recklessness—I have not forgotten your antics aboard the *Belladonna*—I feel somewhat uneasy about what I am now to ask of you."

Albert stood up again.

"I want you to go back to Brooklyn. Speak to Mrs. Crow and to Isaac Browne. Find out why they did not come to the hearing Friday—whether they were paid or threatened not to appear, or both. And find out what you can about Babcock's death."

"When should I go?"

"Immediately. There's not a moment to be lost if we are to have something to bring to the board hearing next Friday, to wipe that smug look from old Miller's face."

Albert didn't answer. Instead, he began looking uneasily around the room. *An hour lost, a life lost*, he thought ruefully.

"If it is the laburnum drawings you are concerned about," said the doctor, "pray forget them. I can wait another week. A month, if necessary."

"It's not that. I'm afraid I have an appointment this afternoon."

The doctor's amazed look seemed to inquire what kind of appointment it was that could not be broken for a life-and-death matter. But Albert could hardly tell him the truth. A lifelong bachelor like the doctor could not know—or had forgotten—what true love means, especially to a young man who feels estranged from his beloved and must make it up if he is to live another day, even another hour.

Such were Albert's thoughts. "I'm sorry" was all he managed to say.

The doctor seemed vexed, and Albert died a thousand deaths in disappointing the man whose high expectations he had made a career of brilliantly exceeding. But conflict is not the same as indecision. His heart ruled the moment like a tyrant. "Tonight," he said. "I can go over to Brooklyn tonight."

"Very well then." The doctor pulled two small leather purses from a drawer and pushed them across the desk. Albert took them, felt their heft, and looked up inquiringly.

"To aid in your investigation," the doctor explained. "If there's one thing I've learned about Brooklyn over the years, it's that the truth there costs at least as much as a pack of lies."

CHAPTER FOURTEEN

Standing on her front stoop in the glaring sun, Virginia was convinced Albert had forgotten her.

But though she had been waiting for nearly an hour, she felt more nervous than impatient. She only occasionally lifted her eyes to scan the ever-shifting foam of people advancing along Park Row, the curricles of the fashionable trotting past and the bouncing horse-drawn carts laden with sacks. She had lasted precisely five minutes on the couch in the parlor designated for receiving visitors. But her stressed heart could not withstand the memories loose in that room, so she left it to pace up and down the vestibule. Barely a minute later, she ventured out to where she now stood: a study in meringue white, gold brocade on her sleeves, and a daringly cut bodice. A pink sash at her waist matched fetchingly to a broad bonnet to keep off the brutal sun. Pretty as a peony in a hothouse. Her mother would be scandalized to know she was waiting for a man in public on the steps of their home, but then Mrs. Casey was visiting friends and was not to know.

Virginia was reflecting on what she most clearly felt, despair or relief, when she saw the familiar ragged hat bobbing through the crowd. Her stomach gave a sudden circus tumble, all thoughts erased. Here he was, late as always, and in a great headlong rush.

"I'm sorry I'm late," said Albert, his head lowered from the glare.

"I don't mind if Vera does not," she said, and regretted it immediately.

"But she most certainly will."

"Then I will speak for myself. I do not mind."

Albert looked directly up at her—he shielded his eyes from the sun—and was astonished. He was like a man in a New England chapel who, expecting a simple wooden cross at the altar, finds instead a lustrous mosaic of the Madonna. Surely Virginia was too young for such a dress! Modesty aside, nothing about it promised to guard her against the grit and tar of the Bowery in July.

Virginia had considered this, but chose the dress anyway. It was worth it for the chance to feel the weight of Albert's eye upon her. She might fall in the mud now and be trampled by a pig for all she cared, because Albert, standing at the foot of the stoop, had fixed his gaze on her most intently. Uncertainty flickered in his usually steady gaze. She felt dangerously light-headed for a moment—but now he looked away, and her heart fell.

Albert showed no inclination for gallantry. He stood silent and preoccupied on the street, and Virginia was forced to make the best of descending the steps alone. Already, within these few moments, she felt everything going terribly wrong. What had possessed her to mention Vera? This was to have been her own special outing with Albert, her make-believe of their being a couple, strolling the streets for all to see—at least as far as the theater. And now he was distracted, thinking of her friend instead of her. The two young people commenced their journey north along Park Row toward the Bowery. They walked parallel, but at a distance, each in silent conference with anxious thoughts.

At the turn into the Bowery, the traffic thickened. Rough, jostling elbows, stressed horses, loud cursing. Shop windows ablaze in the sun. The heat terrible, glaring. Near them, stevedores nursed their goods in the shade, enjoying a moment's respite before resuming their desperate transit back toward the warehouses on the wharves. In the street just ahead, a young mother screamed as her little boy rolled his hoop into the path of a high-stepping horse hauling a water wagon. The barrel fell to the ground and smashed open. A small flood of precious well water spilled in the dusty street. The waterman cursed the child, who cursed back, while his mother cursed them both, providing the passing throng a moment's diversion in their frantic, joyless day.

No lightly dressed ladies here, or children in pressed tunics skipping about while their governess read a book on a bench. Instead, men everywhere. Working men in dungarees, faces strained beneath the weight of sacks, or urging horses; but also men of a different stamp, in purple vests and bristling top hats, whose eyes scanned the crowd for signs of who-knows-what. Virginia was vaguely aware of these Bowery Boys as an unrespectable class of young men, but because they played the gentleman with such spirit and nonchalance, it was often difficult to distinguish them from the real thing. She suspected that more than one of the lesser sort had been invited under her father's roof and sat across from her at table. One evening, just such a young man had made a determined amorous advance to her. Even now she wondered if she had fully understood his intentions. What she *had* understood was shocking enough. But she felt safe now walking the Bowery with Albert. She fought back self-consciousness about her dress and faced her jury of restless-eyed men, whose looks seemed to pronounce her guilty of something highly interesting. Meanwhile, Albert kept his head down as best he could. He knew too much of the Bowery that Virginia could never know, and was himself too well known there for comfort.

Up ahead, through the dust, loomed the grand columned facade of the new Bowery Theater. They battled the crowds of the adjacent Bull's Head Tavern—Albert even grasped Virginia's elbow for a few moments, quite firmly—before gratefully reaching the sanctuary and shade of the portico.

Until recently, no one Virginia knew had ever had reason to visit the Bowery Theater. Manhattan society had always been seen at the Park Theater, near her house, where Mr. Walker produced decorous accounts of Shakespeare and the females of the third tier could be relied upon to be as ladylike as those in the boxes. But on the erection of Thaddeus Burfield's grand new temple of art, with its sweeping marble staircases and spectacular sets, well-heeled patrons from the western wards had been unable to resist the novelty of an alternative to the venerable Park, Bowery or no Bowery. Nightly, they crossed the long-impermeable social borderline of Manhattan, running north to south along Broadway, to an extent not seen since the chaos of the Revolution. And Virginia was certain they would flock to see Vera Laidlaw, who was one of their own, even if only for the deliciousness of the scandal.

Stepping into the theater with Albert at her side, she was blinded for a moment as her eyes adjusted from the glare of the street.

"Well—I didn't expect this!" she said, when she began to look around.

Albert nodded. "It is very fine, isn't it? I'm sure if Mrs. Laidlaw would only come to see the theater—what Mr. Burfield has done— she would think much better of it all."

Everywhere were signs of the Bowery Theater's new aspirations: plush red seats instead of the old wooden benches, glimmering gas chandeliers hanging from the ceiling and gold-trimmed paintwork on the walls surrounding the proscenium. Each panel depicted a scene from a Shakespeare play. And at the top, where the curtain fell, Mr. Burfield had commissioned a portrait of the playwright himself that he intended to trump the famous statue in the lobby of the Park Theater. A larger-than-life Shakespeare stood between the solemn goddess of Tragedy and scantily-clad Comedy. Comedy had her arm draped around his shoulder and the Bard's eye seemed to be drifting toward her boisterous bosom. From where Virginia stood, Tragedy didn't stand a chance.

Onstage, two men with spades had begun their scene. There, while pretending to dig a grave, they discussed their profession. Virginia laughed at the familiar word play, but Albert only looked puzzled. He had been to Drury Lane once, on a tour of Europe with his uncle, but he had never seen *Hamlet*. He had made Virginia promise not to tell Vera that he had never even read the play, to which Virginia had desperately wished to reply that he shouldn't be worried: she knew for a fact that Vera had only ever read her own scenes.

When the gravediggers were done, they looked expectantly toward the wings. In vain. From the front of the pit, Mr. Burfield stood and called out a name. A boy walked out from the wings, script in hand, turned up his hands, and walked off again. The gravediggers then followed him off, muttering and scraping their spades behind them.

Before Virginia and Albert could understand what had happened to halt the rehearsal, Vera herself appeared before them in the aisle.

"Oh, Virginia! Now you see how things are. I wish I were dead!"

"But you are. You drowned already in Act Four."

"Where is Hamlet? Where is Mr. Digby?" said Albert.

"Mr. Digby is indisposed again today, and I haven't done my scenes! Mr. Burfield says that there is no use our rehearsing more as he will only lose his lines and forget his direction. You know I have played my scenes with him only twice!"

"Mr. Digby is indisposed?" said Virginia.

"Tired," said Vera.

"Drunk," said Albert under his breath.

"And what about you!" Vera turned to Albert and began jabbing his arm with her finger. "You are late! What have you to say this time?"

It required several minutes of self-recrimination from her lover before Vera would forgive him. It was a performance Virginia wished she had been spared, and she wondered why it was that betrothed couples so often seemed to swap their proper roles. Surely Vera should be on her knees begging forgiveness of him for last night! Instead, Vera dropped herself into Albert's willing arms and began to cry on his shoulder in an abandoned manner.

Virginia, a better actress herself than Vera had ever guessed, now played her part.

"But it's all coming along so well, Vera." She took a seat beside her friend and put a hand on her shoulder. "I hear many good things from Albert."

"Albert! But Albert is not impartial. And he knows nothing of the theater."

"I know enough to know you are brilliant, Vera," said Albert in a hurt tone.

"You do too." She kissed him quickly, as if rewarding a schoolboy for a correct answer.

"And what's more," said Albert, "I have been to Drury Lane and seen Edmund Leadbetter, which is more than you two have done."

"My father wouldn't let me go to the theater in London," said Virginia.

"Ah, Edmund Leadbetter," sighed Vera. "He is the greatest actor on earth. I would give anything to see him—to meet him. Tell me again, Albert, what part did you see him play?"

Albert hesitated. "King Richard."

Vera was looking at him with an arch smile. "The Second or Third?"

"I don't know. Perhaps it was *Macbeth*, after all. I don't remember now."

"Oh, you are a dunce!" She threw her head back and laughed in her merry way.

Virginia saw Albert turn bright red. She began to reach her hand out toward him but stopped herself just in time. Instead, she said, "But we have Mr. Digby, who is just as good as Edmund Leadbetter—"

"Oh please do not mention that name!" Vera cried, "Dick Digby is not fit to clean Edmund Leadbetter's shoes. He is the greatest, stupidest oaf in America!"

"He is certainly large," Virginia agreed. She remembered well the one occasion her father had taken her to see Mr. Digby perform. She had been able to make nothing of his speeches. What she *had* noticed was how his shirt became drenched with sweat before the end of the first act and clung in an extraordinary way to his torso. It had revealed a musculature beyond anything she had ever seen or imagined.

"Well, enough of this!" said Vera, suddenly brightening. "I have my friends here and that is everything. What shall we do now?"

Side-stepping the Bowery crowd, Albert hurried out into the street to hail one of the horse-drawn cabs that hurtled up and down. He waved down the most sedate of these he could see, and moved to install his two companions. The usual awkwardness over precedence when one man is in the company of two women was not evident. Albert first held open the door for Vera, who ascended to her seat with the help of his arm about her waist. With this, the business of chivalry was done. In then moving to assist Virginia, Albert's only concern appeared to be the purely mechanical problem posed by her diminutive size. For one heart-pumping moment, Virginia thought Albert was going to take her up in his hands and launch her into the cab like a hay bale. But his purpose in bending toward her was only to lower the steps of the chaise. At the last moment, as she took her seat, he briefly rested his arm under hers, brushing her wrist. Virginia experienced a warming wave of pleasure. She had long been used to satisfying herself with morsels where her friend Vera feasted: the least attention from Albert was precious to her.

Albert continued to sit in gloomy silence until Vera suggested to him that, having enlisted the aid of the cab, he might inform the driver where they would like to be conveyed.

"Yes, of course," said Albert. "It is getting late. We must take Virginia home."

He directed the driver to Park Row, and the three friends began their bumpy, dusty ride. Two of the company said nothing, while the third offered a continuous satirical commentary on the dress and physiognomy of the residents of the Bowery. Vera's opinions did not, however, prevent her from repaying the bold stares of the Bowery Boys with a bevy of gracious smiles. Virginia looked anxiously at Albert, whose jealous temper she knew, but fortunately he was not paying attention.

At their arrival at the Caseys' address on Park Row, Virginia considered how best to carry out the business of leave-taking with dignity. She began by collecting her parasol.

"Well, Albert, you are rude, I must say. Most unfeeling to poor Virginia," said Vera in a teasing tone.

"How? What do you mean?"

"I have given you countless opportunities to compliment her, and here you are playing the perfect ox, a picture of indifference. So like a man."

"Please, Vera," said Virginia.

"Compliment her?" cried Albert, not comprehending.

"Yes, silly oaf. Virginia's new dress makes her look the loveliest thing in the world, quite the grown woman, and you have said nothing, not a word of praise. It is very ungallant of you."

She gave Virginia a sympathetic pat on the arm.

It took some moments for the meaning of Vera's words to register with Albert. He then stared at Virginia up and down while she blushed crimson and cursed the vanity that made her choose the dress.

"Well, of course, I did notice the dress. She looks very fine," he said finally—then, struck by a sudden inspiration, added—"very much like a *Convolvulus*."

A look of horror crossed the women's faces. Albert hastily continued, "I mean the plant, of course. It has the same shape and color as your dress, Virginia, and a fine-looking bowl and stamen, much like your head looks with that hat on it."

The carriage rattled away, drowning the sound of Vera's happy laughter. Virginia flew upstairs to her room, and from the bottom drawer of her bureau drew out her secret folio of botanical drawings. Leafing rapidly through its pages, she came upon a rosette-shaped flower of white, pink, and gold. It was inscribed "with affection. A." But the charms of this New World specimen were lost on Virginia. Instead, she began to sob, and at the height of her frustration hurled the precious volume across the room. All she could think of was that Albert Dash had called her a particularly nauseating species of tropical weed.

CHAPTER FIFTEEN

The young lovers wandered past the tantalizing store windows of lower Broadway, which exhibited flounces and foodstuffs from all corners of the trading world. It was the part of the city that European visitors talked of as most surprising to their notions of America's republican simplicity. Not even in Paris did grocers wear calf-skin gloves in handling their wares, or decorate their windows with silk bunting. Exhausted shoppers, meanwhile, recovered their strength at one of the many French cafés, with prints of the Seine on the walls and tables drifting out onto the pavement in a satisfying imitation of the Boulevard Saint-Germain.

Vera had already made several heart-stopping orders, and Albert experienced a mild sickening feeling as they came to Merck's Emporium. Predictably, Vera flew inside.

"What do you think of this vase, Albert?"

"Very fine."

"And do you see the gorgeous picture? Can you see why I chose it for us?"

"I see a fellow chasing a girl through a garden. He seems worn out, and she is losing her clothes. It is the French idea of gardens."

"You are very bad!" cried Vera. "It is atrocious of you to think of that. We must have it for the hall. It will be the first thing you see when you arrive home. After me, of course. And I will dress just in the way of that pretty girl in the garden."

Vera's laugh rippled through the store in its infectious way. The eyes of half-a-dozen young men looked up at the sound and were held by the striking beauty of its source—a green-eyed girl with a long swan's back and a fountain of thick red hair. Even Mr. Merck's elderly, stone-faced clerks found themselves grinning in answer.

Albert joined in, smiling gamely as Vera guided him through an assortment of fine Venetian rugs, painted rush-bottom chairs, pembroke tables, muslin curtains, and mahogany divans from Mr. Phyfe's workshop. He attracted knowing attention from the staff and signs of fellow-feeling from other imperiled bachelors trailing through Merck's in the company of eager, well-dressed young women. But while they grinned resignedly, Albert's feelings were closer to sincere panic. Though his friends credited him with all the higher virtues, money did preoccupy him. Since falling in love with Vera Laidlaw, his poverty had buzzed like a mosquito at the rim of his conscious thoughts. Now his entire brain buzzed. He was making a rough computation of the costs of furnishing an average-sized parlor to Vera's taste when he tripped over a canary-yellow silk screen so delicate it almost took wing at his touch.

"You are strangely quiet, Albert," said Vera, when they had left. "I hope you are not put out."

"No, I'm not put out."

"Did I make a spectacle of myself at Merck's? Was it unseemly to covet all those lovely things when we are not yet even formally engaged? I know what Virginia would say."

"I doubt that my thoughts are the same as Virginia's."

"So you don't think it unseemly?"

"I never thought of it. It never crossed my mind."

"Thank you, darling. Thank you for understanding so completely."

From the bottom end of Broadway, they crossed Bowling Green onto the lawns of Battery Park. There they joined the dozens of young couples like them who had gathered in the congenial dusk: to taste the thrill of their partner's arm pressed close while at the same time keeping a careful, comparative watch over other couples passing by, as if estimating the partner they currently enjoyed against the image of possible future joys.

"I know what you are thinking," she whispered, touching Albert's hand.

He stopped and looked at her.

"Please don't think badly of me," Vera went on, "I have suffered so much from the thought of it. I know it was wrong—please say something now."

"I don't know what to say." He could not tell her that since deciding to repress all thoughts of his money problems, he had been preoccupied with the image of her father from last night, his head bent in a tight circle with Mr. Casey and the mayor, deep in their schemes.

Vera's face flushed. "If my sincere apology does not move you, I will withdraw it! I can tell you quite freely that I enjoyed the party very much and was flattered by all the attention."

"But Vera, what in heaven are you talking about?"

She looked suddenly confused. "Why—I mean my not dancing with you. Were you not thinking of that just now?"

"No, I was not. Should I have been?"

Vera gave a nervous laugh. "Oh, but darling, I thought—. Mother was angry with me for dancing with other people when everyone knew I had promised you first claim. And then, when I was finally released, you had gone. I thought you were angry. Now I see you were not."

"Oh, but I was, Vera."

"Then why have you said nothing about it to me?"

Albert thought for a long moment. Did he know why?

"I had forgiven you already," he said, at last. "But you are sorry that you danced with that French officer instead of me?"

"I am. I am!" cried Vera, tears welling.

Albert seized her hand and kissed it, then drew her close. Arm in arm now, they made their way along the boardwalk beside the water. They leaned over the railing and watched in companionable silence as other couples paraded up and down the narrow pier leading to Castle Garden.

Albert's father had courted his mother here for the same reasons he brought Vera. Battery Park offered the most perfect accommodation for young couples in Manhattan: the open lawns and boardwalk along the water for a public display of devotion, while behind them the web of romantic groves, with trees above and around, offered an arcadian retreat for lovers to negotiate their affections on more intimate terms.

It was here he and Vera had shared their first kiss. July Fourth, not a month ago. As the crowd whooped at the fireworks from Castle Garden, she had pulled him away behind a tree and slid herself against him. He had seen her face unbearably close, upturned and expectant. He remembered vividly the surprise of her ready lips and the thrill of his hand as it brushed the tempting swell of her breast. To this extravagant liberty (as he thought), she had only breathed her encouragement. The sudden flare of a rocket—voices nearby—and the moment was over. They ran quickly back to the boardwalk and walked home to Bowling Green in silence. They had never spoken of it since, but in Albert's waking dreams this kiss stood as an unmeasured moment of personal glory. At the same time, something haunted his memory. Was he the first to pull away from the embrace? The truth here was clouded. Sometimes, he remembered nothing after the siren sound of the flare . . .

As the water faded from green to gray in the setting sun, he was intensely aware of Vera's presence beside him, of her strange solemn brows, which a smile or laugh—to encourage her many admirers—could undo in an instant. When she turned to smile at him, it reminded him of the change of season in a dogwood tree: flesh-pink flowers where it seemed, just a moment before, only the bare tissues of winter. At the party, from across the room, he had watched the sinuous stem of her body under her dress as she moved. It was the most wonderful motion to see. Like an orchid in a fibrous sheath. A botanist's fantasy. But after the party, unable to sleep, he found to his great chagrin that he could not recall her face. If he could have committed it to paper, like a flower, he would. But Vera's beauty did not exist to be drawn. It existed only in the single form of its present vivid reality—in the dusk of the Battery, or the lamplight of her mother's parlor, dancing with another man. Many times he had seen her look plain, her face emptied by gloom or boredom, her eyes gray as ashes. He would half believe himself out of love with her until the next time, when a sudden smile opened her face and he could see inside to the wonderful living spirit.

Standing close beside her, he instinctively kept note of her breathing, the small rise and fall of her shoulders, and her long rust curls playing on the breeze. She seemed content in these attentions, but he knew she would not have been had she been able to read his thoughts. Ever since the Brooklyn fever, these promenades with Vera on the Battery had lost their charm. At the same time his heart indulged her, his clinical eye could not be kept from the ships still plowing their way on the harbor unchecked by quarantine. Any one of these could be a carrier of mortal contagion, a ship of death. Was he the only one on the Battery who comprehended the danger?

Three couples chatted and smiled as they set out together on the pier to Castle Garden. One of the young men made as if to fall in the water. His partner shrieked, then skipped and clapped her hands in thoughtless glee. Albert sighed anxiously, which Vera fortunately mistook for a lover's frustration. In the gauzy light, the stone Castle Garden ahead of him seemed to float upon its broad moat like an enchanted pleasure dome. Beyond it spread the milky dark water of the harbor. On the horizon, the twin arms of the islands curled together, never locking. Even now, a cluster of ships made its way through the strait named for the Italian who was first through the southern lane to this harbor, greater and deeper than any in the Old World. They watched together in silence as the advancing ships beat up against the wind toward the East River and Brooklyn, or tacked west toward the slips of the Hudson. For those who had first ventured here, this majestic port must have seemed not an accident of geology but a gift of Providence herself. He listened to the harbor waters sound a joyous clap against the stone sea wall of the Battery and he was suddenly convinced that their descendants belonged in this blessed spot: they were not to be evicted by some late-coming menace, by a demon fever borne in on an invisible wind.

But if the yellow fever did come . . . ? What vices, what pleasures might there be in a doomed city, with law and common order fallen away? He lay awake at night with such questions. In the Athens of Herodotus, brother turned against brother while bodies piled in the street and a war was lost. In Dante's Florence, mothers abandoned their children, and merchants left their goods to rot unsold. Respectable citizens opened their houses, broke open their wine cellars, and gave themselves over to orgy.

He watched Vera's reflection shimmering next to his in the green mirror of water, and saw gaudy visions of her in a plague city. How moral anarchy would suit her! She who was so indolent she could barely be made to rise from her bed in the morning, or hold polite conversation for more than a minute without yawning or scratching herself; she who made no distinction between her bedchamber, the stage of the Bowery Theater, or Broadway at noon, but wandered through the world just as she pleased; she who once kissed him as if she were a child sucking on a fruit. If the yellow fever came again to Manhattan, in its fullest flower, what would there be to stop the descent of this outwardly respectable yet barely civilized girl to the lifestyle of a Bacchante? In his hellish mind-painting, Vera was transformed by the glassy swell into a wild-eyed nymph. While she stood oblivious beside him, he watched her feverish reflection in the water as she welcomed the rough embrace of satyrs of the deep, and gave herself to sea beasts with the faces of his rivals . . .

He murmured something—ran his hand across his forehead. He should be in Brooklyn.

Should have been there hours ago.

An impulse to throw Vera into New York Harbor almost overwhelmed him. He raised his head and squinted into the sunset glare. The gratification of being called on to save her would be sweet indeed. He imagined her shivering and crying in his arms, her grateful head pressed against his chest. But as it was, Vera seemed barely aware of his presence. The tenderness between them of a moment ago had been forgotten. She swayed her shoulders, humming a tune he didn't recognize. Now she moved away, dance-stepping in her provocative way, claiming the crowded Battery as the private ballroom of her fancy. He raced to catch up to her, doing his best to guess the steps to the dance, but all the while cursing the humiliations of love.

CHAPTER SIXTEEN

At about the time Albert Dash finally boarded the ferry for Brooklyn, some four miles north Dr. Hosack was gulping back two full snifters of brandy in his Bellevue office. He then sat heavily in his chair and remained there, motionless, until well past the hour. When he finally began his afternoon rounds, the nurses' looks spoke their surprise. He surprised them again by his slow pace through the ward, treading deliberately between the low, white-linened cots.

It was the usual assortment: lank-haired prostitutes coughing and wiping their spittle with the backs of their hands; emaciated beggar children speechless with neglect; stone-faced farmhands with mangled limbs. The indigent and the unfortunate. A motley parade of common human suffering. On an ordinary day, they would not have cost him half-an-hour. But today, the doctor spent twenty minutes with one woman alone, bleeding her and holding cups of Peruvian bark to her bloodless lips. The starved children were too weak to bleed. So he wiped their glassy brows and reminded his nurses of their proper regimen of gruel and cheese—it was important not to overawe their pinched bellies.

The doctor felt the necessity and hopelessness of his mission with equal keenness as he looked up and down the rows of beds. That woman would die of consumption, if not now then next winter. Nor could he raise any of these children to lives worth living. The strongest of them would survive somehow back in the filthy dens and alleyways of the Five Points. The others he would see again once or perhaps twice, or read about them washed up on the banks of the Hudson. Most likely he would never hear of them at all. The doctor sighed. He could keep death at bay for them but he could not run a foundling home. Perhaps in another life, a more righteous life.

"What are you wanting me to do with him, Doctor?" He had seen Nurse Purvis almost every day for eight years, but she had never called him anything but Doctor, or he called her anything but Nurse. She was pointing at the delicate femur fracture in bed five (gangrene his initial concern) where a large, sandy-haired young man lay with his head resting peacefully on his hands. He smiled at their approach.

"Release him today, Nurse. No bill."

Nurse Purvis looked at him, then nodded.

"And all the others, too," the doctor went on with a wave of his hand, "All the breaks and contusions. Release them today. Anyone who can stand up, get them out."

They mustn't know he had been supporting the small farmers, healing their laborers without charge to the public purse. It would be "Hosack's Folly" all over again, on top of everything else.

Nurse Purvis was now standing with her hands on her broad aproned hips as if she didn't know what to say.

"And that fellow there, too," said the doctor, pointing to a black sailor by the window who had lost two fingers belaying a rope Peck Slip and been set ashore by his captain. "He goes too. Tell him to mention my name to Captain Dohse at the naval office. He will enlist him and rate him able." God knows what they would do if they found a black man in the ward under the care of white nurses.

"That one today, too?" asked Nurse Purvis.

"Yes, Nurse. Today."

He turned away to escape her searching look, and walked one last slow circuit of the main ward. He felt strangely conscious of his every step across the floor he had paced like a sentinel these eight years. The creak of the wood, the spray of sunlight on the whitewashed walls, the rough feel of the new-washed linens as he brushed them in passing. These were like extensions of himself, the household fixtures of his soul.

Back in his office, he swigged another glass of brandy before setting about his papers, piled like so many oversized anthills across every inch of his desk and the floor around it. He crammed three overflowing folders into his old leather bag and set two great piles on the sideboard for anyone to read. He took the 1814 commemoration, signed by the old mayor, down from the wall. Then, even though it was the hottest part of the day and the room was stifling, he lit a fire. He was feeding wads of paper into the flames by the handful when he became aware of a familiar white presence at the door. Nurse Purvis looked at the fire, then scanned the entire room, including entire stretches of floor she had never seen before. He saw her tongue run slowly along her lip. She craned to look past his shoulder, as if she might find an answer to the expression on his face in the contents of his desk. But it had been cleared away except for a newspaper with its broadsheet pages in disarray.

Nurse Purvis was a strict old woman with no fondness for tricks, so he met her gaze directly, as if to challenge her with the truth. Still, she didn't speak. Instead, she walked briskly to the window, opened it, and began beating at the smoke with her apron. Then she stopped and turned to him, her hand resting, not lightly, on the window sill.

"So?" she said, eyebrow raised.

From Nurse Purvis, the question carried all the weight of an Inquisition.

CHAPTER SEVENTEEN

Simba the bear had begun to limp in her hindquarters. She staggered again from the fresh assault of the circling hounds rather than lurching aggressively forward, as before, to attack the nearest dog, while warding off the others with her great paws and sudden vicious whips of her rump. She had disposed of one dog in this fashion, almost flattening it beneath her, then tossing it high in the air with a roar of defiance that encouraged her backers, who had taken her on at good odds.

But the hearts of the hopeful had long died within them. Some had already moved away from the pit to the bar, preferring to watch their wages ebb away from an amber-filled glass rather than the bleeding limbs of an overrated she-bear. But to those with no investment in the proceedings, Simba continued to offer more than passable entertainment. No one could say that this was not a game beast. Even now, in the hour of her defeat, she raised herself once more on her hind legs, shook her great black head to clear the blood and slaver from her eyes, and leered horribly at her enemies. Tethered to a stake by a rope around her neck she bellowed bravely, like an unrepentant soul in Hell tormented by a clutch of devils.

Then suddenly the dogs were on her. The leader took the bear's face, fang to fang, another hung from her ear, a third leapt on her blood-matted back. The whole tavern erupted at the humor of this final bloody reckoning. To veterans of the sport, it was gratifying indeed to see such a bear, no more than mid-size, exhaust the last of her strength in tossing and tumbling the dogs like a circus wheel across the entire breadth of the pit. It spoke of a nobility, a greatness of spirit in the bear.

But the dogs would not let go their holds and at last Simba pitched into the dust, her two weeks' celebrity at Grimm's Tavern in Brooklyn at an end. Applause rippled through the room, joined even by the more sporting of those who had money on the vanquished bear. It required some minutes for the trainer to reclaim his dogs—each one needed his jaws prized from the carcass—and only then did the boys come to untie the rope from around Simba's neck and drag her away.

The crowd around the pit now drifted to the bar, exhilarated from the battle. Drink orders flew. Pipes flickered to life. From somewhere in the raucous hubbub, a fiddle resumed.

Albert knew that another bear, the third and largest of the evening, was prowling about in the wings. So he took the opportunity now to move through the fog of tobacco and foul whale-oil smoke toward the bar. The floor of the tavern was covered in sawdust to collect the grit from the boots of the laboring men. Clouds of it flew into the air when someone was pushed or danced at a joke, and Albert's eyes were soon streaming from the irritation. He could barely see to know where he stepped. Once he almost knocked over the glass of a large, sullen-eyed sailor, who cursed and gave him the evil eye. Then he walked straight into a table. The whore sitting there alone said, "Fuck off, flat-arse," without even looking at him.

At the crowded bar, Albert took a seat next to a stocky, pock-skinned man in a cloth cap. A heap of copper coins sat on the bar in front of him alongside a glass of what the barkeep had sold to him as whisky. He was turning over the pages of a newspaper in a discontented way and mumbling under his breath. Albert recognized the paper as Eamonn Casey's *Herald*. While he watched, the man in the cloth cap downed the dregs of his glass and pushed another coin toward the barkeep with a grunt. He was rewarded with a shot of Grimm's mud-colored vintage squirted from a barrel.

"You wouldn't be sitting gawping at me for my good looks, would you?" said the man in a none-too-friendly tone, not lifting his head from the newspaper.

"Don't you remember me, Isaac Browne?"

The man turned to look at him, and grunted.

"It's you, is it? Who's got the black vomit now then?"

"Pardon me?"

"If you're here, yellow jack can't be far off."

"No new cases. Not yet."

Isaac Browne grunted again and turned back to his newspaper. He pulled an empty cob pipe from the pocket of his dockhand's dungarees and began sucking moodily on its stem. He did not seem inclined to further conversation, even with a young man who had so recently risked his own life to wipe his brow and bathe him like a baby for two nights, to save him from a horrible, fever-racked death.

"Did you lose on this bear, Isaac?"

"How'd you guess?" he replied, without looking up.

Albert looked steadily at him and decided to take a gamble of his own.

"Don't tell me you've thrown it all away on the bears."

"Threw what away?"

"That little windfall you came into for keeping your mouth shut. For not showing up last Friday at City Hall like you promised me."

Isaac Browne turned and looked at him with an arch smile.

"And how should I know what you're talking about, young fellah? Maybe I didn't feel like coming and saying my piece to some damn-fool toffs."

Albert pulled one drawstring leather purse from his jacket and pushed it across the bar. Isaac Browne eyed the purse, and reached out a tentative hand. On feeling its weight, he raised an eyebrow and chuckled softly to himself. Then he looked up at the pretty strip of a lad as if seeing him in an entirely new light.

"Catching the yellow jack sure makes a man popular."

He went to deposit the purse in his pocket, when Albert reached out and stopped his hand.

"A few questions, Isaac."

He reluctantly replaced the purse on the bar.

"Go ahead then."

"Who killed Lieutenant Babcock?"

"Who killed who?"

"Babcock of the *Belladonna*."

"Dunno. He drowned."

Albert looked at him sharply. "This purse isn't for the pleasure of conversing with you, Isaac."

"I don't know nothing about him!"

"Babcock died the night before he was due to testify at the Board of Health quarantine hearing, just as you were supposed to. Drowned in two feet of water. Don't you think that's odd?"

"I don't know. He was drunk. What do you want me to say?"

"Babcock made trouble, but you were more cooperative. You took the money and saved yourself from the same fate."

Albert found it hard to believe the idea had not crossed the man's mind before, but from the surprised look on Isaac Browne's face that seemed to be the case.

"I suppose that's right," he said more quietly, and took a gulp of whisky. "More fool he."

"Who paid you, Isaac? And when was it?"

"Last Wednesday night. Here at Grimm's. A big fellow, a Bowery Boy. He came up to me just like you did. Gave me ten dollars not to show up at City Hall on Friday. Easy money—most in life I've been paid to do nothing, I'd reckon."

A grave look came over Albert's face. "Did this Bowery Boy tell you who sent him? Did he mention other names?"

Isaac Browne's brow wrinkled for a moment. "Nope." His hand reached out for the purse, but Albert's hand was quicker.

"Just a moment. I want to give you a chance to double that." He opened his jacket and pulled out a second purse. Isaac Browne's eyes glinted at the sight.

"Go on then. Ask away."

"No more questions, for now. We need you to show up to City Hall this Friday just as you were supposed to last week. We need you to tell the Board of Health everything, including what you just told me."

Isaac Browne spat vehemently on the floor. "What do you take me for, lad? I go to City Hall and I'll end up in the ditch with Babcock, sure as eggs. Your money's no good to me dead."

"We'll protect you. A safe house with constables on watch. Guaranteed."

"Who's gonna protect me? Who's gonna guarantee all that?"

"The doctor."

"Dr. Hosack?"

"Dr. Hosack will arrange it. You can trust him."

"This his money?" he said, pointing at the purse.

"Yes."

Isaac Browne gazed at him for a long moment then, to Albert's astonishment, he began to laugh. He spat out his cob pipe and threw his head back in a roar, revealing more gum than teeth: an ugly sight.

"You can tell the Doctor"—gasps of laughter—"tell him I don't know what he pays his whores on the Bowery, but Isaac Browne don't come cheap. And I won't stroke his dick for ready money neither!" He thumped his hand on the bar and roared again until the tears ran down his cheeks.

Albert watched him in amazement. Then he grew angry.

"Damn you, Isaac, what are you talking about?"

Browne pushed the newspaper toward him, and pointed a finger at the front page.

"Your doctor's been caught with his pants down, young fellah. Eamonn Casey's got him by the balls, I reckon." He laughed some more.

The light was dim and clouded with pipe smoke, but by laying the paper flat on the bar and peering close over the print, Albert was able to read:

HOSACK MUST RESIGN!

Although we at the *Herald* are not in the business of intruding on the private lives of individual citizens, we firmly believe that to those in whom public trust has been placed—and what higher trust than the management of the Bellevue Hospital?—a higher standard must be applied. We ask, in our turn, whether the citizens of Manhattan should continue to place the bodily health of their wives and daughters, as well as themselves, in the hands of a proven whoremonger? For so it has now been proved of Dr. Hosack! It has long been a matter of popular gossip that the doctor has been from his youth a reliable patron of the many sins of iniquity that despoil this fair city, and give license to the most depraved urges of its citizens. But diligent inquiry by the *Herald* has uncovered more serious evidence of Dr. Hosack's tawdry past. Though the truth has long been suppressed, we may now reveal that Dr. Hosack was once found guilty in a court of law for breach of promise to a young lady. The unfortunate woman, we are told, afterward went mad from his betrayal, turning her hand in despair against herself. Secondly, and with apologies to the sensibilities of our female readership, we find the long bachelorhood of the good doctor has been notable for the fathering of a healthy litter of bastards, one of them a half-caste. In recent years, his companion in debauchery has been the notorious Madam Camilla . . .

Albert could read no more. The barkeep winked at him—he was in on the joke now too—and Isaac Browne grunted with satisfaction.

"Looks like the sins of the good doctor have caught up with him," said the barkeep with a grin.

"He'll be looking for work now, I reckon," said Isaac Browne. "I'm sure we can get him something here on the docks. Plenty of whores for him too, come payday." They both laughed and, in the mood of general good humor, the barkeep refilled Isaac Browne's glass without the advancement of a coin.

Albert, meanwhile, said nothing. His expression was obscured by the fog of whale-oil smoke. When at last he spoke, there was only the slightest undertone of anger in his voice.

"This Bowery Boy who came to you last week. Did he have a scar under his eye?"

Isaac Browne furrowed his brow a moment.

"Yup. Now that you say it, he did. A nasty cut, too. Seemed like a West Ward gent gone bad to me."

Albert stood up from his stool. He reached out for the purse.

Isaac Browne started up. "Hey! Wait there a minute. That's mine. Get your hands off it!" He grabbed Albert's arm. In an instant, they were toe to toe. Because the new bear had not yet arrived in the pit, a circle of onlookers quickly cleared a space for them, more than ready for some entertainment.

"Would you really hit me, Isaac? When it was I nursed you back from death's door?"

"I would if I thought you was taking what's mine!" cried Isaac Browne. He scowled at Albert. "Besides, I don't suppose you did much for me. It was Isaac Browne saved himself."

"Deck him, Isaac!" came a cry from the crowd. "Don't let that Manhattan fancy boy talk to you!"

"Do you think you've earned the doctor's money?" Albert looked directly into the man's eyes, searching for even the semblance of a soul.

"I answered your questions. The money's mine."

Without taking his eyes from him, or altering his expression, Albert punched Isaac Browne hard—a single, rapier-like blow just beneath the breast bone. He doubled over, gasping for wind. Albert leaned over him.

"Show me the man who will save another man's life then pay him to laugh at his misfortune, and you can have your purse."

Isaac Browne spluttered, half-crouching in the sawdust. "That's horseshit! I earned it." He staggered to his feet and threw out a hand to grab him, but Albert side-stepped neatly, took him under the arm and threw him back into the crowd. Soon there were three men sprawled among the barstools, spitting sawdust. Curses and dirty looks aplenty for Albert, but no one came forward. The fancy boy's punch had come from nowhere, and he looked angry as hell. Besides, no one liked Isaac Browne enough to fight for him.

"For God's sake!" cried the fallen man in protest, still gasping. But Albert had already pushed his way through the crowd and disappeared out the door.

CHAPTER EIGHTEEN

It was rare for the Geyers to be in the city during the hottest part of the summer. Aurelia would stay at Lafayette Place all year if she could—she could entertain in much more satisfying fashion there—but her husband preferred the quiet of Ambleside, their country house on the Hudson, with its contemplative views and plentiful fish and fowl for the idle sportsman. Still, Aurelia must have prevailed upon him somehow, because Eamonn Casey held in his hands a gold-embossed invitation to an "Aqueductial Affair" at Lafayette Place for that Saturday evening. It announced that the French Ambassador and author Washington Irving were to be in attendance, as well as the Democrat candidate for governor, Mr. Eamonn Casey.

His elevation to such a distinguished list did not give him the warm rush of Irish pride it would ordinarily have. He did not even read the invitation over. Instead, he sat alone in his chair in his study the entire evening, feeling no motivation to shift from it. He did not even hear the knock on the front door that came just before eleven o'clock. And he was only mildly surprised when Lily Riley came to tell him that Mr. Geyer was paying him a late-night visit.

"Thank you, Lily. Off you go."

Lily curtsied and left.

"So what has brought you down from the country, Sam, and at this late hour?" he asked, though the black look on the man's face told him the reason beyond any doubt.

"I was hoping to outrun this." Sam Geyer picked up the gold-framed invitation from where Casey had left it on the desk. He looked ready to tear it to pieces. "But the copy of yesterday's *Herald* did not reach me at Ambleside until this afternoon. When it did, I came straight here."

He reached into his jacket and pulled out the paper. Then, with a violence Casey had never suspected him capable of, Geyer slammed it down on the desk, scattering papers and quills to the floor and almost guttering the lamp.

"You should be ashamed, sir! Explain yourself!"

Casey was no stranger to irate reactions to his editorials, but this was different. It was only with a great effort of moral will that he had been able to bring the scandal against Dr. Hosack, a man he had always respected and admired. And now here was Sam Geyer, another admirable man, taking him to task for it. But he was glad Geyer had come. He must make him see the necessity of what he had done, just as he had eventually come to see it for himself.

"Will you come and sit with me, Mr. Geyer? Over here by the window?"

Geyer seemed surprised by his gentle demeanor. He had clearly expected a drag-down fight.

"A glass of porto after your journey?" Casey persisted.

"I will not drink with you, sir," Geyer replied. But he did sit down, nevertheless.

Casey joined him. Then he sat forward and looked at him earnestly.

"I know why you are here. I know what you are thinking. How? Because I have thought exactly the same things myself. You are thinking that Dr. Hosack is a great man, one of the great men in the history of this city. You are thinking too that the sins of his private life mean nothing when measured against his achievements, his many good works."

Geyer seemed startled for a moment, then looked at him suspiciously.

"Certainly. But if you think so too, then why did you publish your slander? Why have you brought him down in this disgraceful manner?"

"For one reason only, and I will explain it to you."

Eamonn Casey got up and poured himself a glass of porto. He downed it in a single gulp and savored the brief burn on his tongue. Then he turned squarely to face Sam Geyer and began to speak in well-rehearsed tones.

"Dr. Hosack is an older man now, and older men, however great they have been, can become fixed in their opinions, pursuing the same great causes they championed in their prime without seeing the urgency of confronting new challenges. It is just so with our Dr. Hosack, I'm afraid. I am speaking of his obsessive insistence on quarantining the port. He will have his quarantine, you see, even if it means scuttling all other plans for protecting the health of the city and its citizens."

"Do you mean the aqueduct? But you know your argument is absurd. Why can't we have both the quarantine and the aqueduct?"

"Political reasons."

Geyer rolled his eyes and gave a grunt of disgust. "Political reasons? Do you call it politics to ruin a man who has brought medical practice in New York to a par with the great cities of Europe? Is it politics to force a man to resign as director of the hospital he himself conceived just at the moment when the city is most vulnerable to an appalling epidemic? This is a politics of disaster, sir. Damn your filthy politics!"

Geyer ended his speech by standing up and shouting directly into Casey's face. As a younger man, Eamonn Casey would have made him pay dearly for such an insult. But he felt no animosity toward Sam Geyer. In fact, he only admired him the more. His own belated grand mission in life—the aqueduct, the governorship—had brought him a feeling of serenity under pressure that raised him above other men and enabled him to see their anger at him for what it truly was: frustration at their own limits, at the smallness of their own understanding.

"I respect your convictions. Please sit down."

Geyer sat down, still flushed with anger. "Be careful. Don't mock me."

"I am not mocking you. But listen to me. You, Sam, are like Dr. Hosack. You both stand outside the politics of this city, undertaking your good works as private men of means. This way, you are assured of your independence and a clean conscience. But I have never had this luxury."

"I see it now!" cried Sam Geyer. "The circumstances of your birth have made you bitter and you are determined to bring down those more privileged than you. It is the democratic evil sweeping this country!"

Casey shook his head. "If I were driven simply by bitterness against your class, why would I seek a partnership with you? Why would I be trying now to mend fences with you?"

Mr. Geyer looked blank and said nothing.

"You misunderstand what I am saying," Casey continued. "I only want to show you that a man of my position is always subject to being worked upon. He must take care of his own advancement, even as he keeps an eye fixed on the greater good. This is the course I have always followed with my newspaper and now in my campaign for governor. It is only by adopting this difficult strategy—filthy politics, you called it—that I am now within sight of a real opportunity to make great change, to do truly great things."

"And Dr. Hosack—you will say—is a necessary sacrifice to this ambition of yours."

"Not necessary at all. He is an accidental victim. Dr. Hosack has forced my hand in this, you see. I will spare you the politics behind it, Mr. Geyer, but the equation is quite simple: if Dr. Hosack is to have his quarantine, I cannot run for governor. And if I am not governor, there will be no aqueduct for Manhattan."

He saw Sam Geyer turn pale. His voice was faint. "If what you say is true, then I am implicated. My partnership with you has helped bring about the doctor's ruin—a man I have known for forty years. I am as guilty as anyone!"

Casey shook his head. "It is not your fault, sir. Neither is it the doctor's, except for his stubborn self-righteousness. It is simply this. You and your friend have found yourselves on opposite sides of a great historical moment. Neither side is wrong, but only one sees what is truly necessary. Console yourself with the knowledge that you are on that side, Mr. Geyer. It is time for you to embrace your destiny, as I have done. And now you must go home, for we have an early start tomorrow."

CHAPTER NINETEEN

The staff at the Deer's Head Inn at Sing Sing were accustomed to plainspoken riverboat men who removed their hats before slurping their soup, and squareset upstate farmers on their way down to market in Manhattan who were most polite when saying nothing much at all. In short, the Deer's Head Inn was a respectable overnight establishment for respectable people not at their best; it promised nourishing food for empty stomachs, clean linens for travel-weary bones, and no corrupting luxury.

So when word came that the mayor of Manhattan was leading a campaign party through Westchester north to the Croton River, and would be requiring rooms in Sing Sing, there were no reserves of splendor at the Deer's Head to draw upon. No silk settings, no silver plate to be handled by white-gloved attendants, no chandeliers to replace the smelly whale-oil lamps hung along the wall.

The innkeeper, Mr. Whitwell, was philosophical. "The mayor will find us as we are. Plain country folk, and no less respectable than his grand city friends for that."

"*More* respectable," piped his daughter Sally, who was thirteen and rode a horse as well as any of the boys in Sing Sing. "The city is full of thieves and whores. Minister says so."

"Now then, girlie," tutted her father, with an indulgent pat on her fair head.

Whether it was because she feared the imminent descent of city thieves and their whores on her inn, or because she had less confidence than her husband in its respectability, Mrs. Whitwell had fled to her hiding place in the giant elm by the river directly after lunch, leaving Sally to cook the fish stew.

The mayor's party arrived late but in buoyant spirits, and set upon the steaming dishes with gusto. Eamonn Casey's speech at the church square had been well received, and forty-three citizens of Sing Sing had signed promissory notes for shares in the Manhattan Water Company. More importantly, each had promised to find ten votes for Mr. Casey among their family and acquaintance, and to spread the gospel of the aqueduct up and down the Hudson River.

"Another grand effort, Mr. Casey. Quite majestic flights of prose, I must say," chuckled the mayor, taking a second helping of pickled cabbage.

"A second Demosthenes, truly," agreed Sam Geyer. "I'll wager it is not every day the good folk of Sing Sing hear themselves described as 'a new race of Romans set by God astride the rivers of the globe'!"

"You could be mayor of Sing Sing tomorrow were you so inclined," said the mayor.

"A toast to you, sir," said John Laidlaw.

The three men raised their glasses, while Eamonn Casey answered with a modest smile and nod of his head.

"And tomorrow, the Croton River," cried Sam Geyer, "to contemplate the prospect of our own Roman aqueduct rising from its waters!"

"Hear, hear!"

Before long, Sally was scurrying to the cellar for fresh bottles of wine, praying to the Lord to stop her ears against the gentlemen's talk of their whores, which had begun just as she served them their oyster pie.

"I knew Madam Camilla in her younger days," the mayor recalled wistfully, "and by a less exotic title. A fine, willing piece she was. Do you think one of the doctor's bastards is hers?"

"I know it for a fact, Mr. Mayor," Casey replied, with a wary look toward Sam Geyer, "but I did not publish the information out of consideration for my readers."

"Ah, I see," said the mayor.

"The *Herald* has done the public a great service," said John Laidlaw. "Mr. Casey is to be congratulated. May I inquire if Dr. Hosack has submitted his resignation from the Bellevue Hospital as yet?"

"His letter is sitting on my desk," said the mayor with satisfaction. "But it is not only the hospital—I hear that he has resigned his chair at Columbia as well. Withdrawn from the public eye completely. They say he sits alone up at his villa where he broods on his fall like Napoleon on Elba."

Laidlaw and the mayor laughed. Casey managed a weak smile, while Sam Geyer, who had been toying with the crust of his oyster pie during this conversation, lay his fork down on his plate and folded his arms. An awkward moment passed while they all looked at him.

"Mr. Geyer faults me, Mr. Mayor," Casey explained. "He believes I have erred in publishing the truth about Dr. Hosack."

"Politics is a messy business, to be sure," said the mayor. "And perhaps when all of this is forgotten—after the election—we will see Dr. Hosack's reputation restored somewhat. History might yet judge him well."

"I only hope we are judged as kindly," said Sam Geyer.

"That will depend on our commitment to the task that lies before us, gentlemen," said Laidlaw, who seemed eager to change the subject. He rose to his feet. "It is the success of the aqueduct that will secure us our place in history's pages. To that end, I have a document I wish to share with you."

Laidlaw walked over to where a large leather bag lay on a chair by the door. He pulled from it a number of scrolls bound with gold twine and distributed them around the table.

"Gentlemen, I submit for your consideration a text of the legislation required for the creation of our Manhattan Water Company. The mayor will present it to the Manhattan City Council and from there, God willing, to Mr. Casey's desk in Albany. What you have before you is only a draft, of course. I would welcome your comments and suggestions at this juncture."

They read silently. Sally Whitwell appeared at the door, but she seemed awestruck by the air of manly business in the room and ran away again.

Eamonn Casey was the first to speak.

"When is it your wish to make this public, Mr. Laidlaw? The *Herald*, I believe, might be a useful instrument for sounding public opinion of this text. It would be presented as unofficial, of course, a draft only."

"A sound idea under ordinary circumstances, Mr. Casey," replied Laidlaw carefully. "But with the election close, and your candidacy so delicately balanced, I would counsel against it. We cannot give the impression that you will conduct government through your newspaper."

"Granted, sir, but surely we cannot wait until after the election when my chances of winning ride on the promise of this legislation."

"We have three months yet."

"And so?" said Casey, with a note of unease. Laidlaw seemed strangely coy on the point. Casey's anxiety was not helped by Laidlaw's fixing him with his steeliest blue-eyed gaze.

"I would ask you to allow me to decide the precise timing both for publication of the draft and its submission to the council. Perhaps I should have made myself clearer. The draft you have before you is confidential; it must not go beyond the present company. I'm sure the mayor would agree that one cannot be too careful with such things."

"Certainly," said the mayor. "We should hold back our trump card until the decisive moment—at your say so, Mr. Laidlaw."

Eamonn Casey wondered to himself when it had been decided that matters of political strategy would be deferred to Mr. Laidlaw, the Wall Street businessman. But the mayor seemed satisfied, so he kept his misgivings to himself.

Only Sam Geyer had said nothing at all. He had not lifted his head from close consideration of the document. "I have one question," he now said, looking up at Laidlaw. "It pertains to the penultimate paragraph—'Messrs. Laidlaw and associates are hereby permitted to raise public monies for the establishment of a company, to be called the Manhattan Water Company, and to employ said monies for the purpose of providing water to the city of Manhattan, or for any other purpose.'—Pray, sir, what purposes for raising money might a water company have aside from providing water?"

John Laidlaw gave a nonchalant waft of his hand. "It is a matter of form only. I have merely followed the text of similar legislation. Mr. Mayor, the language is familiar to you?"

The mayor seemed momentarily unprepared to offer an opinion, but then said, "Oh yes, certainly. It is mere jargon," in his heartiest tones, after what was a barely discernible hesitation. "The wording is of no moment."

They were interrupted by the sight of Sally Whitwell bearing a tray of peaches and sliced apple sprinkled with brown sugar. Cinnamon had been stoutly resisted at the Deer's Head Inn as an unnecessary foreign innovation.

"Thank you, gentlemen," said Sally in answer to the coos of praise, though her look of proud unconcern seemed to say that the Deer's Head Inn saw enough mayors and governors every day of the week for her not to care a whit for their good opinion.

"Your beds are prepared, sirs. One candle for each room, if you please. Father has others if you request it, but he is never happy when someone does. Mother has put out her best peach brandy for you, too, on account of your being the mayor and his gentlemen friends. She says you may drink as much of it as you like, though not after nine o'clock when it is lights out at Deer's Head Inn!"

With that hospitable declaration of terms, Sally Whitwell departed.

Since the clock on the wall showed it already past eight-fifty, the four men first looked at each other with expressions of amusement, then at the solitary bottle of peach brandy on the sideboard, eyeing it with a lustrous regret.

CHAPTER TWENTY

It was the most pleasant part of the day when the mayor's party left the Deer's Head Inn. The rim of the sun had only just cleared the trees and dripped a clear orange light into the valley. The cruel heat it promised could be wished away for this brief hour while the night's moisture lingered in the air. The nighttime silence, too, seemed to enfold the noisy business of the day's beginning—harnessing the horses, strapping the gentlemen's trunks on the roof of the carriage, repeating directions a third and fourth time for Mr. Laidlaw's hard-of-hearing driver—in an invisible cocoon of muffled quiet.

They took the northerly road, winding along the crooked arm of the Hudson in the direction of the Croton River. Eamonn Casey and Sam Geyer rode on horseback, while the mayor kept company with John Laidlaw in his carriage. With the cautious Gibbs at the reins—who much preferred the dusty perils of city driving to this endless winding on bad, bear-infested road—they proceeded at a cautious trot. Inside, the two passengers sat with heads together, deep in conversation.

For the first few miles, Sam Geyer rode abreast of the coach, so that when they came to the crest of a hill and a view to the Hudson River opened spectacularly before them, he could give an engineer's account of its features: where the gradient rose and fell, where dynamiting would be needed, the number of laborers, the fall and flow of the aqueduct's water at feet per second.

But neither the mayor nor John Laidlaw showed much appetite for technical information or for the visual delights of the country-side. They halted their conversation out of politeness when Mr. Geyer approached and kept silent during his description, but they did not seem to look where he pointed. When he had finished, they merely nodded their agreement and returned to their heads-bent discussion—a discussion, Geyer surmised to his disappointment, that had more to do with politics than the aqueduct.

And so he left them and rode ahead. He found Eamonn Casey in a mood far more congenial to his own. It was clear Casey had not grown up with horses—he had an awkward seat—but he appeared oblivious to any discomfort. Instead, as the trees to their left opened to reveal the biblical sweep of the valley and the serene, broad river, his face wore an expression something like bliss.

"I find you are as overwhelmed as I by these stunning vistas, Mr. Casey," he said. "We must promise to help each other. If you will reassure me that the enormous engineering difficulties can be over-come, I will reassure you that our aqueduct, when it is built, will surpass anything of its kind in Europe. In years to come, foreign-ers will visit this place to admire the boldness and ingenuity of our undertaking. And we will snuff out in an instant all this fashionable melodrama of the Western expansion. Future generations will find our intrepid American genius here, in New York State!"

Casey listened carefully, head cocked. Then he broke into a wide smile.

"When I look out over this prospect, Mr. Geyer," he said in a deep, earnest voice, "I am struck with the conviction that whatever else each of us has done in his life will safely count as nothing, if only we can attach our names, in some small way, to the carrying out of this great work. Believe me, sir, I shall devote the rest of my life to it."

"And I mine," said Sam Geyer. He found himself moved by Eamonn Casey's words, which only deepened his confusion over the question of his character. Could this Irishman, who seemed at this moment to be touched with the divine spark, be the same man who had ruined Dr. Hosack with scandal and was, by many accounts he had been increasingly tempted to believe, as vile a self-seeking scoundrel as any in America?

At length they left the Hudson Valley. The road wound down into the woods, leading them from time to time within sight of some picturesque farmer's cottage with its neat terraces and flower-filled garden. Toward noon the road ascended once more, steeply this time. Horses and riders bent their heads from the exertion, and the sun disappeared at intervals behind the canopy of trees closing over their heads. Quite suddenly, they were forced to a halt. The earth ahead of them seemed to plunge into blue space. Beneath the ridge of the summit, an enormous unbroken swath of green wood, lined by steep, black outcrops of ancient rock spread into the luminous distance. They stopped in silent astonishment. Even the mayor and Mr. Laidlaw leaned out of their carriage to absorb the sight. On the bright disk of the horizon to the east, they could see a glinting vein of silver winding beneath the flank of the mountain.

"There she is!" cried Geyer, out of breath but exultant. "The Croton!"

They paused there and took their lunch. They had just remounted their horses and steadied them for the descent when they heard the sound of rapid hooves to their rear. A strapping, pink-faced girl riding bareback flew out of the trees into the clearing, hair and skirts flying. It was Sally Whitwell, who had left the official messenger from New York miles behind in her dust.

"Where is the mayor, then?" she cried, as they all stared at her.

The mayor's flabby face appeared at the window of the carriage.

"What is it, Sally? Did we leave some article behind?"

"No! I have a message. I am to tell you the news that has come from Philadelphia."

Stepping too close to the ridge, the horse shied and whinnied. Sally brought him to order with a sharp tug and a slap.

"And what is the news from Philadelphia?"

"Yellow fever, Mr. Mayor!" Sally shouted. "Yellow fever in Philadelphia! You're wanted back at City Hall this minute!"

CHAPTER TWENTY-ONE

Fate had never looked kindly on Albert Dash—he could not remember a time before there was some wreckage to survive—but nothing in his many bereavements, his intermittent poverty, and the day-to-day burden of a ruined family name had prepared him for the fall of Dr. Hosack.

He went to Columbia each day as usual, where he continued sketching and painting. He tried not to think about the fact that the Botanical Gardens catalogue, which was to have launched his career, would now never be published. Without the doctor, he no longer had a career in any proper sense. The college faculty was still recovering from the shock of the *Herald* article, but it was only a matter of time before they appointed a replacement to the post of professor of medicine, whereupon Albert's space in the laboratory would be given over to the new man's followers.

The depressing logic of the situation did not end there. Without a career at the college, Albert knew he could not marry Vera Laidlaw. That is, not this year. Not until he had found a new profession. It was when he arrived at this point in his thinking on the matter—when he contemplated the necessity of his giving up botany—that Albert's usual clarity of mind deserted him and broke completely with reality. He accepted the *theory* of giving up botany. But in practice, his mind did not offer him the slightest hint as to how he might pass his days *not* botanizing. And because the human body will not operate without instructions from the mind, or in the absence of guidance will simply revert to habit, Albert set up his easel by the window overlooking the Columbia quad every morning as usual, and continued to sketch and paint his specimens with tireless exactitude.

Then, late one afternoon, the news came from Philadelphia. In an instant, the future's hazardous glare vanished into the clear present. He had to find the doctor. All the rest could wait. He left half-mixed paints resting on the easel and ran all the way to the stables on Church Street.

He emerged now from the dark of the trees into a clearing and a view of the Palisades. The great gray cliffs loomed like gothic buttresses on the far banks of the Hudson, obscuring the last of the sun. He urged the horse on at almost reckless speed. Never had it mattered less what happened to him. Looking over the river, he imagined his life's ambitions—professor of botany at Columbia, Vera Laidlaw his wife—hung somewhere in the summer's dusk ready to vaporize in a moment, to join the legion of failed human strivings in their ghastly spirit cave. A bear cub scooting away in the brush woke him from his bitter reverie. He shook the sweat from his forehead and clung more firmly to the reins. At least for this one hour, in the act of striving itself, his ghostly sense might vanish. This galloping mare was a thing of certainty. And the dark earth beneath her flying hooves could not be called into doubt.

As the lights of the Hosack estate came into view, Albert eased back on the reins. Before him stretched the familiar abundant garden in the Mediterranean style. Ivy-clad pergolas dotted the lawn, with plaster-cast statues of Roman character. The doctor had taken his Grand Tour of Europe as an idle young man, and his interests at this phase of life (and apparently since) were reflected in statuary. No stern gods or aged Roman generals lined the main colonnade; instead, a paradise of fair flesh. Above each hedgerow stretched a downy thigh; from behind each clambering vine a marble breast heaved its distress.

He tethered the mare and approached the imposing manorial door. A woman answered his knock—the doctor's maidservant, Gertie. Her blank face offered no sign of recognition, still less welcome. "Wait here." She walked slowly back into the parlor on old discouraged legs. He did not hear her voice, but guessed she must have spoken because he then heard the gruff tones of the doctor.

"I will speak to him outside. Bring the bottle."

Gertie returned and led him through the empty parlor to the rear French doors, which stood open to the buzzing twilight.

Beyond the dim-lit porch, the lawn stretched down to the river's edge. Albert perceived a familiar shape in the gloom. The doctor, bent over in an old wicker chair, was pouring fingers of yellow liquor into two glasses. A gray cloth lay like a priestly mantle across his neck and shoulders, so that Albert could not properly see his face. He drew it now over his glistening bald head and down across his eyes, to soak up the tiny streams of sweat running across his brow. Though it was dusk, the humidity hung in the air like a moist blanket.

"Sit down."

Albert sat. Characteristically, the doctor dispensed with all preamble.

"You know, of course, that I have resigned my posts, and that the mayor has already appointed Miller to replace me at Bellevue. It is worse than I'd imagined. Miller is either senile or corrupt, and I'm beginning to doubt the mayor himself."

"Miller cannot possibly run the hospital in an epidemic," said Albert.

"He cannot, sure, but they say he will."

Without looking up, the doctor pushed the glass across the table toward him.

"You will learn to take solace in this. Today I have decided that the city deserves its fate and that we should all drink deep while we still can."

Albert held back his news, for a reason he couldn't specify. Perhaps to enjoy one last moment of stillness before the world turned upside down. The bittersweet wood of the cognac surprised his tongue, and it saved him from the awkwardness of the moment. There was so much he could not say to Dr. Hosack about what had happened, so much neither of them would want to say. It was an unease new to their relationship. Not the embarrassment of sex, but the revelation that Dr. Hosack was mortal, an ordinary, vulnerable man who could be judged like other men.

Albert took another large gulp of cognac. The golden liquid slowly ghosted into his chest and sent its goodwill northward to his harried brain. He sank an inch further into his cushion and observed the twilight on the Hudson river grow a measure more luminous. For a precious few moments the doctor's disgrace, the yellow fever, his love for Vera Laidlaw, all receded before the confident beauty of the dusk and rated his petty business as nothing.

"What news?" said the doctor at last. "I know you have not come all this way to commiserate with a disgraced old man."

The moment had come. "Yellow fever in Philadelphia. First reports came this morning."

The doctor threw off his lethargy in an instant and leapt up from his chair. "Why didn't you say, damn you? How many cases?"

"Dozens."

"Already? What has been done?"

"Well, there's good news. They have closed the port."

"That *is* excellent news! It proves that this antiquarantine insanity is confined to New York. And we may cure that yet. Have they identified the culprit?"

"A sloop from Kingston Town is under suspicion. Half her crew died on the passage. She then docked in Philadelphia without the captain declaring the sickness aboard, and now there's yellow fever all along the waterfront. The dead are lying in the doorways."

"And this unforthcoming captain?"

"In custody. He will rot in jail, they say."

"If only we could have arranged the same accommodations for Captain Quin."

"Surely Mayor Van Ness must institute a quarantine now. The fever is so close, and the Philadelphians have closed down their port. And there can be no distorting the truth as there was in Brooklyn. Everyone in Manhattan knows what is happening. There are updates from Philadelphia every hour."

The doctor rubbed his chin as he commenced his customary pacing. "You're right that the mayor will certainly feel the pressure to act on the quarantine. But we have underestimated him before. Our work is not yet done, I believe. Tell me, what did you find out in Brooklyn? Did you track down our witnesses?"

Albert grimaced. "Mrs. Crow is not to be found. Her neighbors say she came suddenly into money from a wealthy relative and, having no kin left in Brooklyn, she has gone to Connecticut or to Boston—or somewhere—and set herself up as a publican."

"Mr. Laidlaw has deep pockets."

"No," said Albert quickly, "not Laidlaw." He did not want to assume the worst of a man he still hoped to call Father. Or for the doctor to assume the worst. "I see no reason to"—he hesitated—"it's Casey. Everything points to Casey."

"Really? How so?"

"I found Isaac Browne. He admitted to taking a bribe not to appear at the quarantine hearing."

The doctor gave a grunt of disgust. "I should have expected nothing less. But how do you know it was Casey bribed Isaac Browne?"

"I recognized the description of the man Browne said paid him off. He is one of Mr. Casey's men."

"Which one? What is his name?"

Albert hesitated again—"George Bickart."

Dr. Hosack's bald brow creased in surprise.

"Your former confederate at Columbia? Bickart, your friend?"

Albert nodded, not looking up.

"And you think Casey had Babcock killed?"

"I don't know."

The doctor slapped his hand into his fist. "We must have proof. If we can prove Casey ordered Babcock's murder, we will have our quarantine. But with the fever already in Philadelphia, time is against us. The job falls to you again, I'm afraid. Hours matter now. I will find you a fresh horse so you can return to Brooklyn tonight. Find out what you can. We must have proof."

Albert's glass fell unheeded into the dark grass. The doctor intercepted him as he reached the door to the house. He stopped him with two great hands on his shoulders.

"Be careful, Albert. Do not underestimate the determination of this man Casey, as I have done. No heroics."

Albert nodded, but in the darkness the doctor could not see that he hadn't listened to a word. He was already halfway to Brooklyn in his mind.

CHAPTER TWENTY-TWO

In the wee hours at Grimm's Tavern, Albert learned where Babcock's body had been found. He slept two hours under a tarpaulin on the docks, then at first light went directly to the spot.

A barren stretch of road east on Fulton Street, between the warehouses and taverns of the docks and rows of ramshackle wood houses and falling-down fences of the little town. A no-man's-land where a small stream, meandering out from the wetlands by Wallabout Bay, came to a marshy, foul-smelling end. He found the tree that marked the place. A miserable tree, too, to have survived so many Brooklyn winters without anyone thinking it worth the labor to make firewood of.

He looked around. Just behind the tree, the banks of the stream declined steeply to the muddy pool below. A drunken man, relieving himself in the darkness by the tree, could so easily stumble and fall down this bank into the invisible water. And who's to say

Babcock wasn't so drunk that he could not gather his wits enough to clamber out again? Or that he didn't hit his unlucky head on one of the largish rocks lying about and never woke up before a stinking, soggy death claimed him?

Albert stepped carefully down the bank. Multiple footprints—no doubt the men who had found Babcock next morning and got him out. Yes, sure enough—there was the furrow in the sandy mud, the breadth of a man, where they had dragged him back up to the street.

Suddenly, Albert stopped short. He looked down at his feet and saw that he was standing in an identical furrow in the mud. It led up the bank too, in parallel fashion to the first, not five feet from it. He cursed under his breath with excitement. Either Babcock had slithered on his belly like a serpent into the water, or he had been dragged *into* as well as out of it!

Albert scrambled quickly up the bank and began searching the ground near the tree within the approximate diameter of a struggle. He had almost given up—unsure again in his mind whether he had seen proof enough—when the morning sun, edging from behind a cloud, lit the surface of a small object half-buried in the dust. He picked it up. Silver, with a clasp. A gentleman's tobacco case, perhaps. Or a snuff box? He cleaned it off with his hand. Set in fancy silverwork trim were the initials AB.

A voice behind him said, "You shouldn't touch what isn't yours, lad."

Without turning round, Albert knew there were four of them, behind him and to the left. Ahead was the ditch with its steep banks on either side, and an empty lot with no cover beyond. He leapt forward down the bank. Two pairs of arms lunged at him. Then he scrambled right, sideways up to the level ground once more, leaving one rolling into the water, a second stumbling off balance in the sand. But the other two hadn't fallen for the trick and were waiting for him. They wore plug hats. One taller, with snarling teeth, flexed a rope. The other, a shorter man with a bright pink cauliflower ear, carried a stick.

After a few seconds of ugly grappling, Albert felt the rope across his face and a painful whack on his leg. Cauliflower Ear was aiming for his knees. Albert was about to give up his ground—his instincts roared at him to roll onto his back—when the tall man slipped on the bank's edge, and a lucky back-handed punch at the same moment caught Cauliflower Ear in the throat. A split-second out of their grasp was enough for Albert to stagger forward along the bank into open space. He found his feet the very instant they lunged at him and he set out at a sprint toward the marshes of Wallabout Bay in the distance.

His pursuers regrouped and soon all four were after him. He could hear their heavy panting close behind. But his confidence surged as the breeze whipped his face. He would be very unlucky to be outrun when he had not lost a footrace in four years at Columbia. Sure enough, their grunting breaths soon grew faint, and the running steps receded.

By the time he reached the marshes' edge, they were thirty yards away. He turned and shouted abuse at them. Outraged, they picked up their lagging speed and came down toward him in a pack. When they were no more than ten yards away, Albert turned and began running across the ankle-high water with great airborne strides, clearing the reeds like a deer. He shouted back at them as he ran, exhilarated with rage and the triumph of escape, knowing full well that these Bowery Boys wouldn't follow, that whatever incentive they had been given to capture or kill him, it could not outweigh their love for their fine calfskin boots.

CHAPTER TWENTY-THREE

"Oh, Virginia, you are here!"

Shivers, who had ushered her to the doorway, now retreated. Vera was dressed in her standard convalescent's garb: a canary-yellow silk sheath. Three large goose-feather pillows supported her head. On the table beside the divan on which her suffering body was elongated, an ornate lacquer box spilled over with various baubles, gifts from her father. Suspended above, as if guarding these riches, was a parakeet in a bamboo cage.

Virginia admired the tableau, but didn't fail to remark to herself that in the equivalent spot in her own bedchamber stood a bookcase.

"How are you, Vera? How is your fever?"

"I am very ill."

Despite this bleak diagnosis, Vera got up from her sickbed and began pacing between two windows overlooking Bowling Green.

It was less crowded than usual. There were no children in the streets. Water being in such short supply, the mayor had banned the use of water carts for damping the streets, even in the wealthy wards. The dust rose like great brown storm clouds around the houses fronting the Battery, obscuring the view of the harbor. Many still believed in Dr. Hosack's theory of airborne contamination, and almost no one was willing to bet their life that he was wrong, so windows all across Manhattan had been shut up since the news from Philadelphia. Vera and Virginia certainly retained their faith in the doctor, and sweated in their own private cauldron of uncirculated heat. But it all had to be endured. Better this discomfort than the deadly heat of the fever burning inside you until the very skin blistered from your body like peel from a fruit.

"And besides, if we open the windows," Virginia observed, looking out at the great polluted clouds, "we shall certainly share the fate of the Pompeiians. Archaeologists will find us all, hundreds of years from now, preserved in a sarcophagus of dust and soot."

"Must you always be so morbid?" Vera cried. She hit impatiently at her skirts as they caught on the furniture. She stopped at the window, but as she could see nothing through it on account of the dust, her looking outward seemed expressive of some deeper desire.

"Do you know that I have not heard a single word from him in five days? We have never been apart for so long before without Albert sending me a note or a letter, to remind me that I am everything to him."

"That's too bad."

Virginia's voice was faint. She was unused to company and conversation, having spent the last week—ever since her father's sensational article about Dr. Hosack—alone in her bedchamber, solemnly renouncing the world and all her hopes in it. At first, she had thought of rededicating herself to her ancestral religion, joining a convent as the heroines often did in her novels. But even that seemed inadequate to her misery—you could only join a nunnery once.

Vera came and sat across from her. Virginia noticed a seriousness in her face she hadn't seen before and realized, with a pang of surprise, that her friend was suffering no less than she. Vera spoke quietly now, with none of her usual bravado.

"Do you know what my mother said? She said that I can never marry Albert now because Dr. Hosack is in disgrace and will not be able to get Albert that position at Columbia. And if he is not to be a professor, Albert will have no income and no standing in society. Do you think she is right?"

"Yes."

"I thought you would." Vera stood up and walked back to the window.

"Can you keep a secret?"

Virginia nodded.

"I have decided that I will marry Albert anyway. We must marry,"—she turned back to Virginia with a dramatic look that made her almost forget her own churning feelings—"Ophelia did not stop loving Hamlet though he treated her cruelly and all the world was against them. She never abandoned him!"

"No, she didn't, but it didn't end well for them all the same."

"Oh, I will not drown myself, if that's what you're worried about."

Vera's eyes lit up with a sudden idea, and she rushed back to the settee. "What do you think Albert is thinking of this very instant?"

"I don't know."

Vera took her hand and clasped it in hers. "Try to imagine! I know you have never been in love, but I tell you it is possible for two lovers to know each other's thoughts even when they're apart."

Virginia hesitated. "I believe that they wish they could."

"Oh, but they can, they can! You are too earthbound, Virginia! I would not be you for the world. I am sure in my heart, this moment, that Albert loves me as I love him and that he is thinking it just as I am. He is thinking that we will find a way to be together! I'm sure he will send me a note to tell me as soon as he can."

Vera looked at her glowingly, and Virginia realized that she had actually succeeded in convincing herself of the truth of this fancy. Finding herself to be miserable, she had wished herself to be happy. Perhaps this was an ability given only to those who were loved. The unloved meanwhile lived in a world of brute facts. This being so, Virginia could justify herself answering a little brutally.

"Still, I suppose you would prefer that he say it to you in person."

"Of course I would prefer it! And he will get the opportunity to very soon."

"You are expecting a visit?"

"Not a visit. We will see each other at Mrs. Geyer's party on Saturday. Mr. Geyer insisted on inviting him in spite of Mrs. Geyer's objections."

This information had a profound effect on Virginia, and she was speechless for a long moment. She had not reckoned on an encounter with Albert at Mrs. Geyer's party.

"Mr. Geyer," Vera went on, "thinks the world of Albert and very little of Dr. Hosack's scandal."

"Yes, I know. Mr. Geyer visited our house this week. He and Father said some very heated words."

"I've no doubt they did. Don't be angry with me, Virginia, but I wish your father had not written what he did about Dr. Hosack. You don't know how much heartache it has caused me, worrying about Albert. I'm sure it is why I am sick. I know your father was right to expose the doctor as a libertine, if that is what he is. But I wish he hadn't all the same."

Virginia gave a nod of understanding, as if the thought of regretting her father's article had just occurred to her. She watched as her friend began to stride up and down the room once more, this time more cheerfully.

"I am so impatient for Saturday to come. I will not be surprised, Virginia, if Albert actually proposes to me while he has the chance, and demands that we elope on the spot! He is just that impulsive kind of man."

They were both startled by the sudden appearance of a very different man at the open door. A moment later, Shivers appeared, out of breath and looking grieved.

"Mr. Burfield!" Vera stood to face the visitor, her hands combatively at her hips. "Is it your notion of good breeding to intrude on the bedchambers of young ladies without announcing yourself?"

"I will apologize for my presence here, Miss Laidlaw," said Mr. Burfield coolly, "if you will explain yours. Your fellow cast members await you at the Bowery Theater. We have been at rehearsal these last two hours and cannot proceed further without you."

"Can't you see I am deathly ill?"

"No, frankly, I cannot."

"Oh, but I am, I am!" Vera threw herself facedown on the divan and began to sob.

Mr. Burfield observed her blandly for a moment. "Your performance is admirable, Miss Laidlaw, but ill-timed. That is, unless you wish to make your debut here in your bedchamber rather than on the public stage."

"Virginia, tell him to go away!"

Mr. Burfield turned to Virginia, who gave him a helpless look.

"Truly, I must be unloved by Fortune, Miss Casey. On the one day that Hamlet arrives sober and in command of his lines, my Ophelia chooses to go mad two weeks ahead of schedule."

"It is true she has been ill," ventured Virginia.

Mr. Burfield sniffed disbelievingly. "Perhaps it would aid her recovery if I were to review the professional responsibilities to which she is bound by contract. You understand, Miss Laidlaw,"—he turned to address the moaning figure on the divan—"that actors who aspire to the summit of their profession must study perhaps five hundred lines every day. This will occupy even the swiftest intelligence for six hours. Added to this, your duties at the theater require four hours for rehearsal every day excepting the Sabbath. Then, of course, there are five hours given over to the evening's performance to the public when the play is running. Here are sixteen hours of labor alone, to say nothing of the time required in study of the character after the mere attainment of the words. No one, nay, not Mrs. Sarah Siddons herself, is absolved of this steadfast devotion to the Muse."

Vera ceased groaning and turned herself over. But her face was innocent of shame, and Virginia wondered if she had heard a word Mr. Burfield had said. She lay equably on the divan, her gaze directed toward the window. But did she look through it, or at her own reflection? Whichever it was, her bad mood had vanished.

"Mr. Burfield, you need not be concerned," she said, laughing. "Ophelia has few enough lines, the poor doomed thing, and I know them all. I have been practicing with Virginia here. If you allow me five minutes to repair my hair, sir, I am ready to accompany you to the theater."

"That won't be necessary. I have dismissed the company."

"Dismissed them?"

"I will be frank, Miss Laidlaw. I have not come to fetch you, but to deliver bad news."

Mr. Burfield moved a chair from against the wall and collapsed into it. The two women fixed their eyes on him apprehensively.

"When you speak of contracts, Mr. Burfield," said Vera with a note of rising anger, "you must remember to honor yours to *me*. I will not stand to be replaced. My father will not stand for it."

"Certainly, the idea of replacing you is a capital one. But my ill tidings lie in another quarter entirely."

"For God's sake, what is it?" Somehow, Vera's blasphemy sounded perfectly natural, not shocking at all.

"Has the theater burned down again?" said Virginia.

"Two words only, ladies," Mr. Burfield announced with a dramatic pause: "Edmund Leadbetter."

They stared at him.

"I, too, was speechless—but it is true. Mr. Walker, of the Park Theater of New York, has gained the services of Mr. Edmund Leadbetter for the remainder of the summer season. The newsboats brought word of his impending arrival just this afternoon. The name Leadbetter will be in every newspaper and shop window by the morning. It appears my rival Mr. Walker has grown jealous of our luring his patrons to the Bowery and wishes to put us in our place."

"Edmund Leadbetter?" cried Vera.

Virginia had seen Vera perform "astonishment" before, but this was her finest rendering.

"Yes, the same. The very darling of the English stage, London's most storied performer, coveted and caressed by all living managers. The Lion of Drury Lane. But to us, now that the Park has him, Mr. Leadbetter is a one-man invading army come to rout us. In short, we are doomed."

Vera began pacing up and down the room in agitation, while Virginia searched for something encouraging to say. Only the parakeet, sniggering to himself, interrupted the unhappy silence.

"Have you told the rest of the company?" asked Vera at last.

"No, I have not. Actors are the most excitable pessimists in creation. Besides, they will know soon enough. I make an exception for you because you are new to us."

"But you have your loyal patrons, Mr. Burfield," said Virginia. "The young men of the Bowery will come to see Mr. Digby as they always do. And when they hear of Vera, they will flock to see her too."

Mr. Burfield sighed. "Let me put it plainly to you, Miss Casey, out of consideration for the naïveté of youth. Mr. Digby is to Edmund Leadbetter as the trough at which my horse drinks is to the Atlantic Ocean." The two young women stared at him blankly. He sighed again. "In short, and with respect to Miss Laidlaw's abundant gifts, no one will think of the Bowery while Leadbetter is at the Park."

Vera gave a loud sob and fainted back onto the divan. Mrs. Laidlaw arrived, and at the sight of her apparently unconscious daughter went into some minor hysterics of her own. When Vera was removed to the bed, Mr. Burfield himself took over the divan, pleading dizziness.

At seven o'clock, the new doctor was called. He administered laudanum and ordered bed rest. Mr. Burfield returned to the theater, while Mrs. Laidlaw disappeared to her room with a vial of the doctor's laudanum, so that when darkness finally lowered the curtain on the day, Virginia found herself once more alone with Vera, keeping watch at her bedside.

A single, feeble candle on the dresser. Only the mocking chorus of the parakeet for company. Sitting silent and still in her chair, Virginia's feelings of emptiness returned. Even after all this afternoon's dramas, nothing had actually changed. Vera's saying she would marry Albert, whatever happened, only confirmed the worst of what she had already thought. She leaned forward and looked at her friend's face on the pillow, pale and serene as an angel's. But she was too exhausted with sadness, too utterly empty to feel any pangs of jealousy. Vera would recover by morning, as she always did, and return to the daylight world to love and be loved as she wished. And she, who had no one's love to command, would stumble unnoticed from the rich drama of her friend's life to the secret sad farce of her own.

CHAPTER TWENTY-FOUR

"Mr. Laidlaw," said the mayor, "you know I would do everything in my power to oblige you, but you must understand my position is as difficult as it could be."

Mayor Van Ness, arms crossed, leaned against his broad mahogany desk, which so dwarfed him that it seemed to contradict any impression of mayoral power. Directly across from him sat John Laidlaw. The Wall Street man did not take advantage of the divan to recline, but perched forward, his gaze intent on the mayor. Over by the fireplace, beneath the dead Hamilton, Eamonn Casey rested his large frame against the mantel while toying moodily with an iron in the empty grate. All three gentlemen were in evening dress, in honor of Mrs. Aurelia Geyer's reception that evening at Lafayette Place.

"By the week's end," the Mayor continued, "there will be a hundred dead in Philadelphia. All the papers, excepting Mr. Casey's

Herald, are demanding a quarantine. They say we should not be too late to do so, as the Philadelphians have been."

"Patience, Mr. Mayor," said Laidlaw.

"But we cannot stall until the election, sir, if that is your plan. If the yellow fever comes this month or next, even a small outbreak, when such obvious warnings have been given, I will be hounded from office in November. To be reelected, I must be able to point to serious measures I have taken—now—to protect the city. I'm afraid we must have a quarantine, sir."

There was a tense silence. The mayor feared the worst, but John Laidlaw only turned in the direction of the fireplace. "And you, Mr. Casey?"

Eamonn Casey replaced the iron in the grate and sat down. "I agree with the mayor. Since the news from Philadelphia, the *Herald* is fast losing credibility over its antiquarantine position. I am accused from all sides of too close a relationship to you and your Wall Street friends, of putting my own ambitions ahead of the safety of the city. I know what a quarantine signifies to you financially, but your money will be no good to me if I am a discredited candidate. The governor is getting stronger every day."

"But what of the aqueduct? I have seen your excellent coverage in the *Herald*, your publication of Mr. Geyer's sketches and estimates. The last I heard, your circulation was twenty thousand and the aqueduct was on everyone's lips."

"What you say was true until Wednesday. But the Philadelphia outbreak has changed everything. People in New York are frightened for their safety now, *this* summer, and have little attention to spare for their future well-being."

Laidlaw stood up. "Do not be discouraged, gentlemen. I believe we have a solution for our immediate concerns." He brought out a paper from inside his jacket. "Dr. Miller, in his capacity as director of the Bellevue Hospital, is ready to publish this comprehensive report that blames the Brooklyn yellow-fever outbreak on the contaminated drains at the docks. This report will contradict the necessity of a quarantine and make people think once again of the necessity for fresh water and the building of the aqueduct."

Casey glanced at the report and shook his head. "It is too late for such scientific arguments. Now that the Philadelphians have quarantined their port, it has settled the issue in people's minds."

"Granted, it might have," Laidlaw replied, "but Dr. Miller's report cannot hurt us, and it gives the mayor some plausible cover to postpone his decision on the quarantine for a few days more."

Laidlaw fixed his eyes on the mayor, who nodded reluctantly.

"A few days, yes. But no more than that—not without some turn of events in our favor."

Laidlaw pressed on. "In the meantime we must find some way of turning the people's minds back to the water shortage and the aqueduct."

"It will be difficult as long as this yellow-fever scare lasts," said the mayor, "which could be until early October, by which time the election will be beyond our reach."

Laidlaw stood up and walked a slow circuit of the mayor's fine English carpet, his head bent in thought.

"In my opinion," he said at length, "our first duty is to stop this hysteria over the yellow fever from overwhelming our chances. Do you agree?"

"Agreed," said the mayor.

"But how?" said Casey. "What could overshadow it in the public mind, with the city on the brink of panic?"

"This is where I defer to you, Mr. Casey, as a proven general of public opinion. If there is a way to distract the public, I'm sure you will find it."

Casey shrugged and threw up his hands.

"Perhaps something could be made of this Leadbetter visit," suggested the mayor. "We have never had so famous an actor of the London stage here in New York. Any ordinary summer and the papers would be filled with puffs and profiles and hullabaloo."

"An interesting idea," said Laidlaw with a small smile, "especially as you know Mr. Leadbetter's arrival has not been universally welcomed. Mr. Burfield, the manager of the Bowery Theater, is most upset. I know this from my daughter."

"And how is Miss Laidlaw taking the news?" the mayor asked. "I'm afraid Edmund Leadbetter will steal the thunder of her debut at the Bowery."

"Well, she cried for a day. But now that is forgotten, and she is all excitement to see him. She has decided they are to be twin stars of the stage, not rivals."

The mayor laughed in spite of the general mood of gloom. "What a young lady she is! But if it is true what you say about Mr. Burfield, perhaps we might beat up some controversy between the two theaters. Eamonn, what do you say to a showdown between the Bowery Boys and the Park Theater aristocrats, in which everyone must take sides and have an opinion? Could you stir up such a thing?"

"Surely, I could. But I worry that it will not catch fire with the public in the way we need. The yellow fever is life and death, you know, not theatrical byplay."

The mayor nodded. "We must find something that reminds the voters of the Eamonn Casey they know and trust. The patriot candidate and champion of the common man. Let us think on it some more." He consulted his fob watch. "But it is late. We must be off to Sam Geyer's." He picked up his hat from the desk.

"There is one more thing, gentlemen," said Laidlaw. Casey and the mayor turned back from the door. "While we may have suc-

cessfully disposed of Dr. Hosack, the same cannot be said of his
protegé, young Albert Dash. My information tells me that he is
making a great nuisance of himself in Brooklyn, spreading slan-
derous rumors about Lieutenant Babcock's death."

"What kind of rumors?" said the Mayor.

"That Mr. Casey was somehow involved."

Casey felt a sudden chill come over him. He didn't know if it
was fear or anger. One thing was certain: it was time to call in
George Bickart's debt to him with regard to Albert Dash.

"Then something must be done," he said.

"But young Dash has no credibility," cried the mayor. "Dr.
Hosack's disgrace has ruined his own career prospects. It is clearly
a desperate attempt at revenge against Mr. Casey. I think we may
safely ignore him."

The mayor saw that neither man was convinced.

"But what if he goes public in a pamphlet?" said Casey.

"Or in the *Gazette*?" said Laidlaw.

"Something must be done."

"It will not be easy to find him," said Laidlaw. "They tell me he
has gone to ground."

The mayor looked at Laidlaw in surprise. Who was *they*? And
wasn't Albert Dash betrothed to his daughter?

"Then we must find him! We must flush him out!"

Eamonn Casey said this with such an air of menace, such close-
lipped vehemence, that the mayor, who had no personal grudge to
bear against Albert Dash, hoped in his heart that Mr. Casey and
Mr. Laidlaw would not find the young man. He prayed that Albert
was at that moment on board some ship already far away, and
heading to the farthest corner of the earth.

"Well, gentlemen, let us go," he said with a sigh, "or we shall be
very late. Aurelia Geyer has a surprise in store for us, I hear."

CHAPTER TWENTY-FIVE

The exact circumstances under which Edmund Leadbetter, the famous Drury Lane tragedian, had come to New York were in dispute, but it was generally believed that he had been kidnapped by Mr. Walker of the Park Theater.

The Lion of Drury Lane had been touring the northern provinces in the summer season, while the London theaters were closed. When a severe case of the gout confined his manager to his hotel room in Liverpool, the famous actor, freed from Mr. Chidgey's strict supervision, had resorted to his usual lairs, stalking the taverns along the waterfront from before noon.

In the course of three memorable performances in his first week at the Royal Theatre, the inebriated Lion had confused the roles of King Lear, Othello, and Richard the Third into a bewildering Shakespearean farrago. On the Friday night, before a full house, the local Desdemona had refused to continue for fear of outright strangulation in Act Five. Word spread of Leadbetter's condition, and receipts dropped off disastrously in the second week. Mr. Chidgey, when not fainting from agony, did his best to placate the irate manager of the Royal from his sickbed, but could do nothing to better the situation.

It was at this moment of more than usual confusion in the career of Edmund Leadbetter that Douglas Walker perceived a golden opportunity. He too had been touring the provinces during the summer, in an effort to recruit a leading man or lady of minor fame to bring with him back to New York. It was not Walker's usual practice to go to such lengths to fill out his summer season bill, but the sudden, spectacular rise in the Bowery Theater's fortunes had him worried. Managing theaters less than a mile apart, he and his old nemesis Thaddeus Burfield were locked in a do-or-die struggle for the patronage of a suddenly promiscuous theater public. And so, he had suffered his bones to be rattled on bad roads from Newcastle to Bath, sat in dozens of drafty, crowded theaters, and witnessed a hundred debuts of young aspirants to the London stage.

Leadbetter was sharing a parting glass with his cronies from the Royal, some of whom had shared the Drury Lane stage with him in their better days, when Walker found him out. He introduced himself as an American visitor and theater-lover, and expressed a convincing surprise on meeting by chance with so famous a tragedian. A round of drinks purchased him a seat across from Leadbetter, whereupon he suggested he might accompany the actor in the coach to Warrington, from where he was to travel to London in the morning.

Upon Walker's purchase of a further round of drinks, Leadbetter grumbled his agreement. Within an hour the two men had taken their places in the Warrington coach, as ill-fated a company as ever traveled that road. They got as far as an inn called the Legs of Man when Mr. Walker began to prevail upon the Lion to take some further refreshment with him. The landlord, he said, was cousin to his wife. Mr. Holt was Leadbetter's greatest admirer in the world and he, Douglas Walker, would not be left to explain to his cousin that he had had the great man in his company and not delivered him to be toasted by one and all. In addition his wife was young and pretty, she lay a sumptuous table, and the inn carried the best stock of fortified wines in England. These last inducements made a solid impression on the Lion. After but a few minutes' more resistance, he found himself crossing the threshold of the Legs of Man with Mr. Walker's persuasive hand firmly on his shoulder.

The innkeeper, as if expecting his famous guest, greeted him with emotion. A bottle of the best Madeira was called for, and Leadbetter was soon indulging his attentive audience with highlights of his great career, from the night his Richard the Third outshone the great Kemble, to Garrick's words on his deathbed when he anointed him heir to the Drury Lane crown.

After a second bottle had been drained and a third begun, the Lion was encouraged to retell his extraordinary exploits in the war of 1776, where, though mathematically speaking still a very young child, legend placed him at General Burgoyne's side when he thrashed the upstart ingrate Yankees.

At the opening of the fourth bottle, with Mrs. Holt now on Leadbetter's lap, Mr. Walker produced a set of legal-looking papers and began to paraphrase their contents in glowing terms. As well as making Leadbetter a rich man, he explained, an American tour would secure his fame for the ages: as the first to shine the light of English genius into a land in darkness; to bring the true Shakespeare to a people ignorant of his name; to be a savior, no less, to the fragile, infant civilization of the New World. In addition, the critics would be just so many doves a-cooing, while the ladies of New York could be trusted to express their admiration in fulsome fashion.

Walker's words brought a glow to Leadbetter's forehead, and he launched into a foaming tirade against the London critics who had harassed him like dogs for years. Those whoreson scrubs!—He would boil them in their own bile! Mrs. Holt bounced up and down on his thigh, hanging on for dear life. Quickly refilling his glass, Mr. Walker attempted to persuade the Lion that his best answer to those West End dogs was to sign the papers before him, which would remove him in an instant from their fangs and restore him to his proper place as the Roscius of the age, destined to carry a beacon across the waters to the philistine hordes, etc., etc.

The instant it was done, Walker signaled to his accomplice, Mr. Holt, who called for his chaise to be brought around to the rear of the inn for the accommodation of Mr. Leadbetter. The Lion was somnolent after his recent outburst—and a pint of Madeira—and the two conspirators found him compliant. In fact, it was only the massive dead weight of his body that prevented Leadbetter's removal to the chaise and from there back to Liverpool—leaving the Warrington coachman baffled and alone by the road—from succeeding as an operation of military smoothness. In the gray light of early dawn, a snoring Edmund Leadbetter was conveyed to the docks mounted upon a stretcher and taken aboard the *Don Quixote* bound for New York.

The packet duly weighed anchor, and by the time the Lion awoke from his deeply fortified slumbers in the mid-afternoon and stumbled onto deck, she was confidently breasting the Irish coast toward the open ocean. The Lion roared his indignation at the sight of his lifelong domain receding from the ship's stern. But in vain. The smooth-talking Yankee had outwitted him, and he now found himself a king in exile upon a foreign element. The vast waters of the Atlantic—serene in the sinking light—seemed to have no opinion whatever of his leonine eminence, and answered his tantrums from the decks of the *Don Quixote* with nothing more than an occasional breeze-blown sigh.

"And where is this Digby?" Edmund Leadbetter now said to Douglas Walker, as he eyed the sherry decanter on Mrs. Geyer's marble-topped sideboard. "You said you would show me my American rival tonight. Show me this man you have set me against."

"Dick Digby is an oaf, not likely to receive an invitation to Lafayette Place," replied Mr. Walker.

Aurelia Geyer's parlor was a particularly magnificent sight that evening, redecorated for her "Aqueductial Affair." At the entrance stood a noble reproduction in plaster of the Roman aqueduct at Aix, while between the parlor and the dining room one passed beneath an enormous classical arch painted with a creditable impression of brickwork and the words "Let the Mighty Rivers Roll" inscribed across it in giant gold lettering. The taller gentlemen needed to bend their heads to get to the liquor table.

"And yet Digby has a substantial following, particularly among the young men of the Bowery," Walker went on. "They come to see him exhibit his great rippling chest and consider themselves well entertained if the man is too drunk to speak. They would rather watch him prowl and froth at the mouth than recite his part like a Christian."

"Dreadful. Pitiful," said Leadbetter, shaking his head. "If such is the extent of Mr. Digby's talents, Mr. Walker, I wonder that you have not found some local champion to mount against him. Are your own ranks so thin that you must sail abroad like some scavenging Turk slavemaster to fleece foreign nations of their treasures?"

"A fair question," Walker replied, who was not a man to take offense when business was being discussed, "and if it were only a matter of Richard Digby, I would have spared myself the trouble of recruiting you, and the cost."

"So there is another man, another American Roscius?" asked Leadbetter with a sardonic sneer. "But where is he? I see no one here but schoolboys and limp-eared old buzzards."

Mr. Walker nodded in the direction of the pianoforte. "Look to the young lady in the blue dress. Do you see her? She has been glancing over at you ever since we arrived. She is currently admiring the obscene painting of Mrs. Geyer blessing the waters, while a hopeful young swain beside her whispers in her ear. There, now she laughs at him in a most fetching manner. "

"Ah!" Leadbetter regarded Vera Laidlaw with a grin of approval. "Your Mr. Burfield has riches at his disposal, indeed. And what is this young lady's reputation—I mean on the stage?"

"She has none."

"What do you mean?"

"Vera Laidlaw has no professional reputation. Not yet. Mr. Burfield of the Bowery Theater saw her perform Desdemona while she was still at school. She makes her debut with Digby next week."

"A schoolgirl!" cried Leadbetter, turning instantly bright red, his voice rising. "Let me understand you, Mr. Walker. You have shanghaied *me*, Edmund Leadbetter, to this godforsaken hole to face a schoolgirl, a novice, an unknown!"

"She has the gift," said Walker, unmoved.

Leadbetter turned to him, eyes narrowed. "How do you know?"

"I have spies, men who understand these things. They tell me."

Leadbetter looked over at Vera again, this time scrutinizing her with a professional eye. "How good is she?"

"Divinely good. Another Sarah Siddons."

Among Aurelia's guests was a Southern acquaintance named Fairholm. When he saw that Edmund Leadbetter had slipped the close supervision of his manager and stood alone contemplating the bust of Napoleon, he seized his opportunity. Only Vera Laidlaw, by far the boldest of the young ladies present, stood nearby, and even she appeared too awed to address Mr. Leadbetter. She lingered awkwardly by the punch bowl, pretending to sip at her glass.

"Excuse me, sir, but are you by any chance related to Sir Wilfred Leadbetter, of Grimsley Hall in Dulwich?" asked Mr. Fairholm in a high voice, by way of introducing himself.

Edmund Leadbetter said nothing, but looked down at the stranger from his great height with an odd, disbelieving expression.

"Because if that were the case," Mr. Fairholm continued, "I might have some grounds to claim a blood connection with you, sir. Allow me to explain. My family, the Fairholms, have been resident in Brandywine, Maryland some eight generations. Gilbert Fairholm married one Laetitia Leadbetter, my great-great-great-grandmother, of Waverly, Virginia, who was herself derived from the noble line of Grimsley Leadbetters. Sir Wilfred, the seventh earl, is thus my third cousin twice removed. Therefore, as I say, if it were the case that you were of that clan, sir, I might be so bold as to claim some kinship with you, and to ask, in the spirit of family solicitude, when you last saw Sir Wilfred, and whether you found him in good health?"

Vera had moved as close as she dared to Edmund Leadbetter's side and saw him emit a large sigh. His nostrils flared wide to accommodate the great draft of air. He then turned to his newfound cousin with a smile.

"And you sir, Mr. Fairholm, are *you* acquainted with Sir Wilfred?"

Mr. Fairholm shook his head. "Not personally, no, sir. Sadly, there has never been the occasion for an introduction though it has been most ardently wished, for generations now, on the side of the Maryland Fairholms, as well as, if I may speak for them, by the Virginia Leadbetters. But I see, sir, that you have guessed my motive: that I cherish the expectation, in light of our fortuitous meeting, that you might suffer to be nominated an envoy of friendship between the two distinguished branches of the Leadbetter vine, currently divided by a great ocean—divided too by the late unfortunate ruptures between our nations—but happily united in our share in noble blood and the lustrous name of Leadbetter."

Vera thought at first that Edmund Leadbetter had not heard Mr. Fairholm, who now completed a deep bow to conclude his embassy. The tragedian's eyes assumed a glassy expression.

"In the course of your introduction to Sir Wilfred," Leadbetter replied at last, with eerie calm, "which I would be glad to facilitate, you will of course exchange some tokens of this noble lineage you speak of, so as to establish your connection on the firmest possible footing?"

"Why yes, of course," said Mr. Fairholm eagerly, "all will be done according to the proper form from the American side. Both the Maryland Fairholms and Virginia Leadbetters have conscientiously preserved all manner of family records dating to . . ."

"I was thinking more along the line of family jewels."

"Family jewels, sir? Might I ask for an example of what could constitute, may I say pass for, such an item?"

"Well, in your case, sir, the category may be interpreted quite liberally. You do, as I understand, *farm*, do you not?"

"Yes, sir. Cotton and tobacco. Eight hundred acres."

Leadbetter nodded with satisfaction. "As you are a landowning gentleman of the South, Mr. Fairholm, Sir Wilfred would likely make special consideration. In lieu of heirloom gems as proof of your nobility, I'm confident he would accept some assortment of the whips and chains you use to discipline your slave workers. And if you were especially eager to gratify him, you might add a black concubine for the pleasure of his sons."

Vera gasped and looked over at Mr. Fairholm. He turned pale and stared at Leadbetter, who stood smiling benignly at him. After an awful pause, he turned on his heel without a word and pushed his way to the door. The Lion chuckled for the first time since leaving London, winked over at Vera, who blushed to her roots, and moved to accost her. The danger of the moment was averted by Samuel Geyer, who just then announced dinner in the back parlor. Vera retreated in a flutter of alarm from the Lion, who growled, shook himself, and downed another glass of sherry.

Aurelia Geyer had had no reason to expect her pitiable social predicament—captive to the suicidally dull conversation of her friends over the interminable summer season (even Mr. Washington Irving could be tedious once the conversation turned, as it inevitably did with him, to New York history)—to be enlivened by the presence of a genuine celebrity. Edmund Leadbetter! It was a gift from the gods!

Mrs. Geyer's prize guest cut a magnificent figure in a blue jacket in the naval style, with a burgundy silk cravat curled at his neck and studded with a precious stone. His thick, leonine hair was stiffly brushed atop his famous tragedian's face, while a pair of brooding, poetical eyes glared at them above an impressively ridged Roman nose. His bearing as he walked about the parlor produced audible gasps of admiration, as if some famous statue of antiquity had come to life.

Leadbetter took his seat directly across from Vera and Virginia. He gave them a considering look and was struck by their almost comical contrast, like illustrations in a book depicting Temptation and Virtue. Vera wore a blue silk gown with a sequin-crusted bodice trim, illuminating her exposed bosom to a nicety. Her pretty, dour friend, meanwhile, was dressed in a dove-gray tunic drawn to the neck like a schoolmistress. He knew that women chose their friends for reasons of complement and contrast, like bracelets or a ring, and he had rarely seen a more expressive example of the phenomenon.

He smiled at the blue girl, as a form of apology. But Vera had recovered quickly from her fright. She didn't blush or avert her eyes as he expected, but smiled gaily back as if to say, *I am not fazed by you!* Then she surprised him again by laughing and turning away. His professional eye was instantly struck by the easy carelessness of the movement. Bravo, he thought, and smiled. Perhaps Mr. Walker was right to be concerned for his receipts. As a connoisseur of the fair sex, too, he was impressed. He saw no airs or awkwardness about this one, as she turned and whispered something to her little friend. None of the usual tricks of vanity or tiresome self-consciousness. Just a dazzling young woman acting her part. It refreshed him better than the sherry to see it.

Meanwhile, Aurelia Geyer was talking in a low voice to her husband at the head of the table, even as her eyes never left the adorable frown on Edmund Leadbetter's brow. "We must invite him up to Ambleside before he is snatched away from us."

Samuel Geyer appeared unconvinced. To him, this Leadbetter resembled nothing more vividly than a retired Naval officer: sozzled, embittered, and doing his best to preserve his dignity on half-pay. But he was alone in that thought. To the rest of the company, the actor's romantic appearance exceeded even those expectations set by thirty years of uninterrupted public fame.

Aurelia had been particularly concerned to introduce her famous guest to the best of New York cooking, and thus do her part in contradicting the European opinion that Americans had no notion of the finer things. She had ordered the finest wine from the cellar and given the cook her mother's old Dutch recipe for turtle soup. Not the sea-waterish consommé the newcomers to the city ate, but the true turtle, with callipash and meat balls. She watched him eagerly for signs of approbation.

For now, however, no compliments or even conversation could be elicited from the guest of honor who, after staring silently at Miss Laidlaw for a time, had confined himself to barely audible requests for water and extra salt. But as the wine made its rounds, the Lion roused himself, stiffly shook himself, and began to direct his proud gaze about the table. The Miss Harveys in particular, who sat immediately to his left, found themselves gratified by his attentions. This was well received by half of the company, but their excitement soon turned to embarrassment. Jane and Charlotte Harvey had decorated their bosoms in the Bath manner, with only the flimsiest suggestion of gauze, and it was on these that the bold eyes of the Lion were now immovably fixed. In a moment, he drained his second glass of wine with a distinct smack of his lips, directed yet another flattering remark, and while the young ladies flustered between themselves to reply, began to emit a low guttural sound that Samuel Geyer at first mistook for the empty stomach of his butler standing behind him, but soon identified as Leadbetter's accompaniment to his amorous interrogation of the Miss Harveys.

For Mr. Harvey, sitting opposite, his three months as chaperone to a pair of pretty daughters abroad had been a soul-wrenching trial. Late nights and stern lectures had been his thankless paternal lot. Once home, he had looked forward to relief from supervision of his doe-eyed charges, little guessing he would lead them directly into a lair that made Bath, with its roaming packs of fancymen and fortune-hunters, look like a home for blind pensioners. With a silent curse for his bad luck, he roused his courage to pacify the Lion.

"Your reception in New York, Mr. Leadbetter, will certainly be rapturous," he began in a nervously loud voice. "We look forward especially to your representation of Richard, for we hear you out-shine even the great Kemble in that role."

The Lion gurgled with satisfaction as he swigged his freshly filled glass, and Mr. Harvey felt emboldened to continue:

"But if you will allow me the liberty of a more general remark, as an ambassador for Shakespeare your contribution will be so much greater than the ephemeral work of any single evening's per-formance, however glorious; for by your very presence in New York you will be reuniting your American cousins with an inheritance in which we all share."

Leadbetter's brow darkened. "American cousins!" he blurted across the table. The dreadful image of Fairholm rose in his mind. "And what inheritance is it, pray, that I share with these *cousins?*"

Mr. Harvey became anxious. Somehow he had overplayed his hand, and he heard himself stutter in reply, "Well sir, begging your pardon, I meant Shakespeare. He is our common legacy. We are united in him."

"And in what else do you claim a share, sir, I wonder?" simpered the Lion, irony dripping all about his jaws, "what do you say for *your* Milton, *your* Locke, *your* Newton?"

"Oh I say nothing, sir, except that these men, like the immortal Shakespeare, transcend our merely political divisions, and"—here a rope dropped down into Mr. Harvey's disordered thoughts and he grabbed for it—"promote the mutual understanding between two peoples who are indeed one."

"But what part, may I ask," Leadbetter repeated, "has your *nation* played in the making of these men, of Shakespeare and Newton?"

"Well, sir, if I may venture a metaphor in the biblical style,"—Mr. Harvey attempted a light laugh, which failed horribly. The entire company was staring at him grim-faced—"The younger brother who leaves the paternal roof, though he does not inherit his father's estate, is heir to his fame."

The Lion's face darkened. From across the table, Douglas Walker interposed a warning look, and Leadbetter seemed to check his anger. He stroked at his mane with predatory disappointment.

"And what share do you take in Britain's fame, my friend?" he said, with chilling calm.

"Why, I suppose the year 1776 must be the historical mark of separation," replied Mr. Harvey, "I have no claim upon Britain since then, though I owe her much."

The Lion's leash broke with a snap. "And you will owe a great deal more before you are able to repay your debts!" Leadbetter roared, springing from his seat. "What will you give her, you blinking Yankee scoundrel? What offerings will you make to our Lady Britannia? Bearskins and Indian heads?!"

Here Leadbetter broke from the table in a wild imitation of a native dance, stomping and hi-ya-ing his way around the table. "Tomahawks and tom-toms! Yes, you will pay for your Shakespeare, you American lackeys! Coonskins and the scalps of savages! Lay them at our feet and we will give you the Bard!"

Aurelia Geyer and her guests watched wide-eyed as Leadbetter danced around the table, whooping loudly. He then turned with

menace toward the cowering Miss Harveys, whereupon Samuel
Geyer and Douglas Walker rose in a single motion from their seats,
restrained the rampant Lion with the assistance of a chair and led
him, still stomping and wow-wowing at the top of his lungs, out
of the room.

Never had Edmund Leadbetter left the stage to a more demor-
alized audience. In the ensuing confusion, two ladies required re-
vival with their salts, while a young Columbia man declared loudly
he would challenge Leadbetter to a duel. Only one of those present
seemed to find any humor in the moment. Virginia was watching
her father, and observed that he had a wry smile on his face as he
looked across the table at the mayor and at Mr. Laidlaw, who
seemed to smile back. Then, as Aurelia Geyer started to cry and
everyone else talked in whispers of the scandal of it all, she saw her
father set about his turtle soup with real gusto, like a man who has
just discovered the joys of fine dining.

CHAPTER TWENTY-SIX

Virginia had become accustomed that summer to opening her father's newspaper with feelings of dread. The next three days were no different. She did not want to read the *Herald* in any part of the house where her father might come upon her, so each afternoon she waited upstairs in her room for Lily to deliver it to her from the folds of her skirts.

By her open window, her legs perched up on the sill in their familiar, breeze-catching fashion, she read multiple outraged accounts of Edmund Leadbetter's disgrace at Lafayette Place. Whatever her father was up to, it was working. The Leadbetter affair was the talk of the town, Lily told her, and the yellow fever in Philadelphia entirely forgotten for the moment. The reality of Leadbetter had been horrifying enough, but her father's lurid accounts from unnamed "eyewitnesses" (merely trumped-up versions of himself, she guessed) continued to appear day after excruciating day, until the English actor's entire tour was thrown into doubt by the scandal. The *Herald* posed a question that sent chills down Virginia's neck: Would Edmund Leadbetter be allowed to perform in New York at all?

But Douglas Walker was not to have his bonanza of a lifetime taken from him so easily.

On Tuesday, after dinner, Lily brought her a copy of the *Evening Register*, her father's principal competitor and friend of the Park. From the smudged print, and the torn pages, she guessed it had already passed through dozens of hands, perhaps hundreds:

MR. LEADBETTER HUMBLY APOLOGIZES TO THE NATION

Mr. Leadbetter has been much indisposed of late, and the strain of a long season in the provinces of England has been the fateful overture, as it were, to the tragic performance witnessed at Mrs. Aurelia Geyer's, that renowned patroness of the arts and social ornament. I would ask the more sensitive spirits among you to consider the burdens of genius, and for how long Mr. Leadbetter has sacrificed his health and well-being for the laurels he so deservedly wears; how long sacrificed himself for the cause of the legacy of our brother nations. That legacy in the arts we share, as Britons and Americans, is indeed great, and yet it is sometimes for us, as merely common admirers of the Muse, to be caught ourselves amid the tempests of genius and to reckon ourselves injured by it. But I would implore the good people of New York not to judge our illustrious guest on the basis of a single incident, itself the effect of fatigue and the ill-advised consumption, on an empty stomach, of a quantity of Mr. Samuel Geyer's very excellent sherry wine. In short, Mr. Leadbetter is deeply sorry to have given offense and, in expressing his profound regret, trusts that the excited goodwill that greeted his first arrival on these shores might once again prevail.

Virginia slept soundly that night, but when Lily brought her the *Herald*'s answer the following afternoon, she read with dismay that her father disdained Mr. Leadbetter's apology. In a full page special editorial, he asked his readers if the old revolutionary spirit had died in the American people—he meant that spirit that would not hesitate to avenge the insults of an arrogant Englishman. If he were to be told it had, he resolved to withdraw at once into mourning for the great nation that was. What was more, he had not thought manly and patriotic honor so endangered that an insolent John Bull appearing in one theater could be preferred by its citizens to the sight of a true American heroine appearing in another. It could not be so, he heard his readers protest? Then why was Mr. Leadbetter's King Richard at the Park Theater sold out, while Miss Vera Laidlaw, a New York beauty of talent and renown, could be sure of barely half her house for her debut at the Bowery as Ophelia? Was not Lady Liberty herself disgraced in this? And yet the *Herald* urged its loyal readers not to be dismayed. No, indeed. They should be assured that proud American hearts would not bear it! That the sons of patriots would rise up in glory to avenge the insults of tyranny! And that the spirit of '76, which some had called dead, would revive in the democratic passions of the people, to be given their due vent that Wednesday at the Park Theater. Doors open 5 sharp.

The next morning, Lily rushed into Virginia's room, red-faced and out of breath. Virginia's first thought was that Mr. Walker had challenged her father to a duel. But Lily brought news of an entirely different crisis; her tale shook Virginia to her very core.

"I just saw him. Oh, it's terrible, Miss. He's talking murder."

"Who is talking murder?"

"Mister Albert, Miss. He is saying Mr. Casey had that man murdered."

It took some time to extract the full story from Lily of her meeting Albert at the market, where he had apparently been waiting for her.

"You said he is in disguise? What disguise?"

"He has grown a beard. And he wears a plug hat pulled down over his eyes. He looks just like a lad from the Bowery." Lily began to cry. "Oh, Miss! Mr. Casey will be ruined and he will kill Mr. Albert, and I will have to leave you and look for another place."

Virginia sat down on the bed next to Lily and began rubbing her back, what she always asked for when she was upset. She told her she would not have to look for another place.

"But did he mention me, Lily? He must have said something more."

"Yes, he did, Miss," Lily sniffed, wiping away her tears. "He said he had wanted to talk to you at Mrs. Geyer's party but didn't go because he didn't want to be in the same room with Mr. Casey. He said he meant it kindly, Miss, to spare you."

"Anything else?"

"Yes, there is. He said to give you this."

Lily reached into the hem of her sleeve, and pulled out a folded piece of paper. Virginia stared at it for a moment before seizing it. She turned the paper over in her hands. "Does Vera know about this?"

"I don't think so, Miss. Albert is not welcome at Bowling Green. Mr. Shivers himself told me he turned him away, on master's orders."

A deep breath, and Virginia opened the letter. She saw a dozen lines of the loose, artistic hand she recognized from his botanical drawings. It was the first letter she had ever received from Albert, and she needed to read it twice before its meaning began to take shape in her mind.

> Please forgive this note, which must seem like a wretched, cowardly thing to you. I wish more than anything to have had the opportunity to explain everything in person. But there is no time. You must know that my wishes play no part in the end of our friendship. I tell myself that fate is to blame. You will soon read something I have written in the newspapers. I know nothing I can say will justify or absolve me in your eyes and in the eyes of your family for what I will write. But if it can only make you hate me, I want you to be sure that in my thoughts you and I will always be friends, and that you will never cease to inspire in me a very real regard, a regard that is growing even as I think of you now, reading this note. Believe anything of me in the days ahead, but believe what I say here—I am
>
> Your friend,
Albert D.

Virginia's first thought was for her father: that someone had been telling lies about him, and very plausible lies too if Albert believed them to be true. Then she had a different, more chilling thought. What if Albert had gone mad? What if the scandal over Doctor Hosack, the ruining of his own career prospects, and what it meant for his engagement to Vera, had somehow turned his brain? What if the "murder" her father was supposed to have committed was nothing Albert had heard at all, but rather the product of a mind overstrained by disappointment? His accosting Lily at the market with his wild stories—his ludicrous disguise—this was surely strong evidence that Albert was losing his mind. Virginia felt the knot in her stomach tighten.

Whatever the truth was, she knew immediately that she must see Albert before he did what his letter promised, and stop him doing it. It took only a few moments more for her to realize where the only real chance lay for her finding Albert in time, given that he seemed to have gone into hiding. And before ten minutes had elapsed from her first reading Albert's letter, she had already surprised her father in his study with her announcement that she wished to join him and Vera at the Park Theater tomorrow after all, to see Mr. Leadbetter make his New York debut.

There was so much to consider and be anxious about what might happen next that it was only that night, as she lay sleepless in bed, that Virginia began to ponder that portion of Albert's letter where he had expressed something like his feelings for her. She repeated his words over and over in her mind. His regard for her, he said, was *growing*. And with that one word, a thousand seeds were sown in Virginia's imagination. For was it not Albert himself who had taught her that, in a propitious season, the most unlikely shoot could flourish? That the humblest flower, its roots once in place, could begin the generation of an entire garden, blooming and re-newing itself in ever-increasing splendor until the end of time?

CHAPTER TWENTY-SEVEN

The young republic did not carry half London's trade, and no expeditionary army drawn from its twenty-odd states could have confidently engaged a single well-armed duchy of Europe, but the city of New York boasted more newspapers—more pennysheets, pamphlets and bills, more broadsheets, digests and anonymous diatribes, and more literate citizens to read them—than any city in the world. And it was these vociferous organs of the public good, led by the *Herald*, that proclaimed Edmund Leadbetter an enemy of republican democracy, roused hundreds of freedom-hungry patriots from their barracks in the alleys of Five Points and oyster houses on the Bowery, and sent them marching to the unfamiliar domain of Park Row, there to pay what respect they might to the graceful columned housefronts and flourishing streetside flowerbeds of their betters.

It was true Eamonn Casey's house stood only a bowsprit's length from the Park Theater, but his heart lay with the people and their outrage. So, on the afternoon of Leadbetter's debut, he and Virginia left the house by the back way, walked three blocks to the south and west, then strode up from Broadway to be with them. When he hailed the crowd with a loud shout, his gold-topped cane upraised, and his fellow patriots roared their rebellious approval, Virginia didn't know whether to be more amazed or ashamed. But then his readers loved her father for his Irish audacity, and cared as little for the niceties of the truth as he did.

They had arrived early. It was still not five o'clock, but already all around them seethed a mass of raucous, red-faced Bowery Boys. The crowd had besieged the ticket office and now fixed its attention on opening a second door to the theater, by force if necessary. The "tramp tramp tramp" of their feet, a trademark of Bowery Boy discontent, rang along the avenue.

Vera emerged from the crowd. She was dressed in peach and carried a parasol. Twirling it and smiling, she seemed unconcerned by the extraordinary scene.

"If there is a riot here today, Mr. Casey," she shouted over the noise, "I will have you to thank for it."

"Me?" Casey replied, with a look of mock concern.

"Yes, you sir! What inspired you to publish all those terrible things that Mr. Leadbetter said, when it was only because he was tired and had been drinking?"

"It was my patriotic duty as an American."

"Do you really think there will be a riot?" shouted Virginia.

"Mr. Walker is to blame," said Vera. "He has allowed too many tickets to be sold."

"You're right, Miss Laidlaw. So you see that it is not all my fault.

The theater cannot hold half so many people as this!" Casey did not seem at all worried by this fact, however. He seemed to be enjoying himself immensely, and when someone new in the crowd recognized him, he answered their shouts with a cheery wave of his cane.

Finally, the theater doors opened and the crowd surged forward. Virginia felt herself physically jostled as she had never been in her life. There was no orderly parade of fashion into the theater as she had witnessed in her other visits to the Park Theater. It was more like a battle at close quarters on board a ship. All around them was the sweating, spitting and cursing of emotional men. The Bowery Boys had dared to invade Park Row, and the spectacle of it so shook the permanent truths Virginia had formed about the world that she hardly knew where she was.

Once inside, the three made their way as best they could to the second tier. They passed the old statue of Shakespeare at the foot of the stairs. Some rube had put a cap on his head and squeezed a cigar between the fingers resting thoughtfully on his chin. On the landing they passed some menacing-looking men in plug hats. Virginia noticed one of them, the shortest, had only a twisted pink leaf of flesh where his right ear should have been. His hat sat crookedly on top of it. The man stared openly at Vera as she passed, and Virginia consoled herself with the thought that while she might not be as beautiful as her friend, at least this protected her from the insulting attentions of ugly men. But this was cold comfort, since Albert was nowhere to be seen.

No sooner had they taken their seats and congratulated themselves on their pluck than they saw the chaos of the evening was only just beginning. A constant welling roar reverberated through the theater, accompanied by the booming tramp-tramp-tramp of the Bowery Boys' feet. Looking down into the pit, Virginia could see only a mass of heads heaving and swaying against the pressure of the crowd outside. The boys had disposed of Mr. Walker's attendants and now formed a continuous sea of humanity from the stage to the street.

Someone in the pit caught sight of them in their box.

"Hey! It's Eamonn Casey!"

"Casey for governor!" the man next to him shouted.

"And Miss Laidlaw! Hooray for our American heroine!"

As one, the entire crowd of men turned their faces up to stare at them. They waved their hats, shouting "Casey for governor!" "Hooray for America," "Down with Leadbetter and the Tory trash!" and from one quarter, "Kiss me, Miss Laidlaw!"

Whistles and foot-stamping hilarity answered. Virginia colored and hid her head behind the ledge of the box, while her father stood to receive the cheers with a broad smile. He clasped his hands together and raised them above his head. The crowd roared. Vera, meanwhile, was at first confused at the uproar on her account from hundreds of lusty-looking men she had never seen and thought of only to despise. But the American heroine recovered herself and soon perceived her duty. She smiled down on her admirers in a queenly way and waved her hand.

At ten minutes past the hour, the crowd began chanting for Leadbetter. Soon the manager himself, dressed in the character of Buckingham, appeared onstage. Hisses issued from the pit while the gentlemen in the tier boxes, hopeful yet of seeing the great Leadbetter impersonate Richard the Third, applauded loudly and cried "Hear him! Hear him!"

Mr. Walker motioned to address the audience but was shouted down. Only when he shouted at the top of his lungs did she hear him announce Mr. Leadbetter's intention to make an apology. He then signaled for the orchestra to begin playing as a desperate means, she guessed, of quieting the mob. But to no avail. The musicians performed a desperate dumb show on their violins and horns, while the Bowery Boys in the pit drowned them out with a grotesque musical mockery of their own. This amused Virginia in spite of herself. But it shocked her the more to realize that she could not hear her own laugh.

The roar reached a new pitch when Edmund Leadbetter himself finally appeared, walking slowly from the wings. He was dressed in a somber gray evening coat with a plain pin at the collar. He bowed humbly to the crowd and touched his hand to his forehead in a gesture of penitence, as if he had assumed the role of a provincial clergyman instead of King Richard.

The satisfaction of viewing the man himself, combined with his enormous size and the palpable aura about him, quieted the crowd for a moment. Before a thousand spectators at Drury Lane, Edmund Leadbetter could whisper the regrets of Richard or Othello so movingly that every member of the audience from the front row to the third tier was convinced he spoke to them alone. Even an inebriated New York mob at the height of their patriotic fury could not be expected to completely resist so awesome a machinery of pathetic persuasion as Edmund Leadbetter.

After a moment's expectant, unnatural hush, he began to speak. He did not shout as Mr. Walker had done, but addressed the crowd in a low melodious voice as if reciting a familiar lesson from the pulpit. Virginia strained to hear him.

"I come before you, my American friends," he began, "as a man in whom the spark of ambition is now extinct, a refugee in your great country, home of liberty. I come not, as might have been in former days, to walk the boards as the proud representative of Shakespeare's genius, but to seek a shelter in which to close my professional and mortal career. If, by my ill-considered words of

Saturday evening, I have given offense to my friends and handed a weapon to my enemies, I trust they will not turn it against a defenseless man. He who sits in judgment on us all will exact what debts I owe, and in no distant time from the present. In so appealing to you, the public of this great city of New York, I trust in the triumph of liberality over cruel prejudice, and compassion over the canker-sore of spite. I have done wrong, and I humbly ask your forgiveness. No man must expect more than what we offer to our God."

For a brief moment during this sublime soliloquy of regret, Virginia dared to believe that Mr. Leadbetter had won the day. But just as he opened his mouth to continue, she saw a large chunk of fruitcake catapulted from beneath her toward the stage. She watched in horror as the missile struck the penitent Lion full on the shoulder with an audible thud. Edmund Leadbetter stopped in mid-sentence and stood stunned for a moment. He stared with dismay at the stain on his jacket. She saw his face grow dark with anger as it had that terrible evening at Mrs. Geyer's.

In an instant, the Lion seemed to double in size. He roared an oath—something about Yankees—and shook his fist toward the back of the pit. In the sound of his great voice, like an amplified growl, Virginia thought she heard King Lear himself in the storm on the heath, cursing his daughters and abominating mankind.

Now that Leadbetter had proved himself a fool as well as a scoundrel, the Bowery Boys began in earnest. A battery of cakes, fruits, nuts and vegetables rained down on him and littered the stage. This fresh outburst of hostility completely astonished the Lion of Drury Lane. He stood pale and dejected, not uttering a word. Shouts of "Off! Off! Off!" assaulted his ears. From the tier boxes came isolated cries of "Silence!" and "Hear Leadbetter!" and several gentlemen took to their feet as if to make a speech. But they were roundly hooted down, and presently the Lion's champions themselves fell silent, fearing the consequences of opposition to the mob.

Mr. Walker appeared from the wings and hustled the stricken Leadbetter from the stage. He then appealed to the crowd that "the gentleman wishes to make an apology—a humble apology from the heart—but he will not do it at the risk of his life!" On the strength of this, Leadbetter made a hopeful return to the stage, but the volume of the uproar only redoubled, and under a renewed hail of vegetables he sought refuge in the green room backstage. There, it was later reported, he sat down on the floor and wept like a baby.

After a few minutes, a boy in a cloth cap appeared holding up a placard:

MR LEADBETTER DECLINES TO PERFORM.

Hoots of derisive laughter from the pit, and a fresh bombardment. Another boy inched onto the stage with a second message held before him as a shield:

SHOULD THE PLAY GO ON WITHOUT HIM?

The response to this question was more equivocal and, after another short delay, the curtain rose and the play began.

"Mr. Walker still wants his receipts," Vera shouted to Virginia.

The players soldiered on. But the provocative sight of them onstage, in costume, embarking upon the drama without consideration for them, only enraged the mob still more. Soon the actors gave over attempting to be heard, abandoned their lines, and performed the remainder of the act in an accelerated dumb show. The curtain dropped. The pit called loudly for Edmund Leadbetter. Mr. Walker then appeared on stage to announce that his leading man had left the theater.

If the beleaguered manager intended by this statement to satisfy the mob that they had achieved their object and should now disperse, he was disappointed. From her seat in the second tier, Virginia saw the good-humored rowdiness of the crowd turn abruptly savage. Just as the pull of some unseen lever behind a stage at a pivotal moment in the action of a play lowers the scene of a bloody battlefield over that of a sunlit town square, so, at the bidding of some hidden hand, anarchy overtook the Park Theater.

Scuffles instantly broke out down below them. Virginia saw one man, a supporter of Mr. Leadbetter she supposed, have his coat stripped from him and his head beaten with a brickbat. Then whole gangs of men from the pit, with bloodcurdling yells, made assaults on the stage. They were met by Mr. Walker and the Park Theater company, still in the regalia of the War of the Roses, who defended the scenery with wooden swords and the spirit of men protecting their livelihoods.

In the pit, the Bowery Boys began smashing the oil lamps and the chandeliers, intensifying the chaos by plunging the theater into a murky darkness. The smoke from the extinguished lamps filled the air, exciting the besieged occupants of the upper tiers with the fear of fire. For the gentlemen subscribers and their shocked ladies, the preservation of life itself was now their first concern. Only one occupant of the boxes appeared unfazed.

"Hooray for Mr. Walker! Go Buckingham! On Leicester! Fight like heroes!" shouted Vera, leaning out across the balcony. She shook her fists in the air and her whole being appeared lit with a mischievous glee. Casey stood grinning beside her.

A flash of flame licked the darkness. Screaming broke out and Virginia felt a dizzy wave of panic sweep over the crowd. It paralyzed her for a long moment. Then, in the deep chemistry of her veins, fear turned to vital energy. In an instant, she had grabbed her father and Vera, who were still leaning out over the ledge of the box as if mesmerized by the chaos, and propelled them back across the gallery and toward the stairs.

On stumbling down to the lobby, however, they found themselves in still worse peril. The fighting here was at its fiercest, and they were in danger of being crushed between the brawling mob in front of them and the crowd in flight to their rear. Virginia soon lost Vera, though she could hear her crying her name not far away. Then she heard her father grunt in pain behind her, and she lost the grip of his hand. She was pressed so tightly she couldn't turn her head to see what had happened, and when she tried to call out, she found she didn't have the breath. The mass of heaving bodies lifted her clean upward, swinging her like a rag doll from left to right as her feet groped for the floor.

I must keep my feet, she thought. *If I fall, I am lost.*

She strained her neck for air, but the constant pressure on her ribs from the hard, heavy bodies of the men around her squeezed the breath slowly from her lungs. Her muscles and limbs ached with exertion but could not release themselves. Time flurried and slowed. The rhythm of the brutal grip of bodies became a world in itself where she was trapped but somehow floated above. She heard voices that might not have been earthly, and briefly glimpsed the face of an old man in a beaver hat, looking at her with dread in his eyes. He gaped at her like a beached fish. She felt her strength ebbing away, a cold creep in her veins.

Then she saw Albert. In the same instant, precious, life-giving space opened suddenly in front of her as a door to the lobby broke open and twenty men fell in a heap into the street. She scrambled on her knees to the wall and took refuge behind Shakespeare, who was gazing with marble serenity over the mayhem he had authored. From there she saw Albert, in an unfamiliar beard, at the ticket office door. He was brawling fiercely, his face wild and bloodied. Nearby, the constables, who had finally arrived, were observing the chaos from the coatroom, as if waiting to make their move.

Three men struggled with Albert, who defended himself with a mad whirling of his fists. She could see that he would soon be overwhelmed and that there was no escape. The three men were driving Albert inexorably toward the cluster of constables. Then she comprehended another layer to the struggle. The men in the plug hats she had seen on the stairs were brawling around Albert and his assailants, as if trying to reach him. The short man with the twisted ear was wrestling and punching his way free from the grasp of two other Bowery Boys. Another of them whipped the air with a piece of rope, while with his free hand he groped toward Albert, grabbing at his shirt. Suddenly, a familiar bearish figure, a head taller than the rest, appeared through the chaos. He tackled the man with the rope and with a single savage blow to the jaw laid him on the ground.

At the very moment Virginia saw him, George Bickart looked up and their eyes met. The look of fury on his face broke immediately into an expression of embarrassed horror. Every dark doubt Virginia had ever nourished about George Bickart crystallized in that moment, impressing her with the vivid certainty of his being Albert's enemy. The quick-moving violence of the moment did not require reasons for this sudden conviction: the plain fact was before her and she must act on it.

With a loud shout, she raced over and threw herself between Albert and his attackers. She put her arms around his chest and grabbed his arm.

"Run, Albert! It's a trap!" she screamed into his ear.

Albert, bleeding from one eye, stared at her in wonder. "Virginia, get away!" he hissed.

He pushed her toward the open door and the safety of the street. But she had fastened herself around his neck. She felt herself swinging through the air as Albert tried to wrench her away, but she held on, pulling him with her toward the door.

"Run! Run! The police are here! It's a trap!"

At first, George Bickart's men dropped their hands in confusion at the appearance of a half-crazed girl in a torn dress screaming at the top of her lungs. But when they saw comprehension dawning in Albert's face, and the two-dollar fee for delivering their man in danger, they charged once more. Virginia felt a dozen rough hands tearing at her. Albert's arm, now tight around her waist, held her fast to him. He tried to back them both toward the open street while fending off the attackers with his free arm. But new enemies appeared to their rear, pushing them back into the lobby toward the constables. Albert's grip weakened. She heard herself and Albert cry for help in one voice. Suddenly, a blow and a great clanging sound, like a bell tolling inside her brain. She went limp and saw the floor rising rapidly to meet her. Then she no longer knew Albert was there, or who she was, and she fell into the ringing darkness.

CHAPTER TWENTY-EIGHT

When they led Eamonn Casey upstairs, arm bandaged and limp-
ing, it was already dark outside. A flickering penumbra of light
from the half-open door at the top of the landing. Strangers' voices
within, low, concerned.

They fell silent when he appeared at the door. But he did not
see the young doctor, standing in the gloom, talking to Lily. He
saw only the beloved head, motionless on the pillow. Virginia lay
perfectly still in the light of the candle. He stepped forward,
then felt his breath catch. What he had thought was shadow
playing on her face was the dark underblush of an enormous
purple bruise.

Virginia lay on her bed, still as death. Through the long hours
of that night and into the next day, while his daughter still did not
wake up, he could not be moved from her side, and did not eat or
sleep or speak. His large face looked like a slab of gray stone.

At first, Lily Riley was worried he would turn violent and harm his child with some excess of emotion. The doctor had said he could not answer for the patient's condition if she were disturbed. "But he is gentle as a lamb," she reported to the doctor the next morning.

When the doctor followed her upstairs, he saw the truth of the maid's report. Eamonn Casey was a veritable study in gentleness. The doctor saw him take his daughter's still hand from where it lay on the bedsheet, hold it like a shell he had picked up from the sand, then bend over and press his lips ever-so-lightly against her fingers. He heard him whisper nonsense words to her, endearments and pet names, and though he knew that his profession demanded a sangfroid regarding all intimate relations within a family, he nevertheless felt a strange guilt to be witnessing the scene, like he was ransacking a church.

By the next morning, Casey's arm, where it had been crushed against the wall at the theater, felt stiff as a rock, and his shoulder throbbed. After persistent cajoling, the doctor prevailed on him to accept a dose of laudanum—it had already been employed to subdue the hysterics of his wife—and once he was made pliant by the drug, Lily lifted his good arm over her own broad shoulder and brought him downstairs to his study to lie on the large divan, kept there for occasions when relations between master and mistress were more than usually unbearable.

When Lily softly pulled the door shut, thinking he was asleep at last, Eamonn Casey hauled himself upright and moved unsteadily over to his desk. He had the strange sense of doing something while at the same time watching himself do it from a distance, and wondering why. With his good arm, he opened his desk drawer and pulled out the pile of maps and plans of the Croton River aqueduct. He spread them out on the desk. As he fingered the stiff parchment pages and looked down at the swirl of lines and numbers, he decided he knew why he had thought to bring them out. Looking at Sam Geyer's work was something he was accustomed to doing every night before bed, for feelings of comfort.

He was entirely ignorant of engineering and he looked on the designs more as a symbol than a structure. The cross sections of columns and pipes, the complex notations of height, gradient, and feet per second, the geological inventories, the topographical maps—to Casey, these did not represent a set of practical problems to be overcome in the field, but rather a comprehensive vision, a single image of what the future should look like. It was a thing of beauty, like a vase in a case.

But now, looking over the plans in his nervous, drugged state, he did not experience his usual feelings. The aqueduct had lost its power to console. In fact, between the ebbing pull of the laudanum and the surges of pain in his shoulder, the Croton River scheme gradually took on a new shape in his mind: as a monument to his all-consuming vanity. He did not think of himself as a God-fearing man. He had not been raised with any idea of religion, or of anything else. But sitting at his desk now, while his daughter lay half-dead in the room above him, he was certain of a higher moral design in these events that no mere engineering marvel could obscure. Virginia was suffering in order to better teach *him* a lesson: how he had neglected to think of those he loved while he pursued the fantasies of self-love.

He gathered all the loose sheets in a pile, stuffed them back in the drawer and locked it. But the nervous fear didn't subside. He felt like a child woken in the middle of a nightmare. He reached for a cigar from the box, thinking the tobacco would settle him. But with only one functioning arm, he had no means of lighting it. To call for Lily when he was in such a state was out of the question, and so he put the cigar back in the box.

The sleepless night and the injury to his arm now caught up with him: he became deeply, massively tired. He went back to the divan, lay down and closed his eyes. But though his breath instantly fell into a kind of rhythmic wheeze, anticipating slumber, his thoughts still pursued him and would not let him rest. He could not fall asleep hating himself. A lifetime of self-belief could not be overthrown so easily. Also, the strange fear had not gone away, that half-remembered fluttering in his chest. A child's kind of fear, not a man's.

As he watched the play of light and shade on the ceiling, an image came to his mind, made gaudy and real by the laudanum. It was a bright, windy morning. He was walking down the ramp onto the strange dock, bustled on all sides by boxes and trunks and hurrying legs. He felt himself pushed to the edge of the ramp, thrust out suddenly over the gray-blue water washing against the pier. He lost his footing, was falling. His aunt yelled out and pulled him back from the brink, but the fluttering feeling had stayed in his chest that whole first day in New York, no matter how hard he squeezed her hand. The same feeling, too, at the printing shop his first day on the big machine. He saw again, with perfect clarity, the pages of black print hung to dry on the whitewashed walls and the gruff old type-man's shattered fingers pointing out the parts of the machine: where the type hammered down, where the ink fed the type, and all the hundred other incomprehensible details that he, crouching in the half dark, knew he could never possibly remember, even as he nodded his head and pretended to understand. Then the type-man had left, left him alone with the same fluttering feeling in his chest. He had known in his child's way that the big machine represented his one chance for a room and steady meals now that his aunt was dead; but he knew too that he didn't have the first idea of how to work the big machine, that he was powerless to do the very thing that it was absolutely necessary for him to do, that he was a small person in a world of big, angry people who knew how to do things but would never tell *him* how.

It was the same fluttering feeling he felt now as he had then. Anxious bird's wings beating in his chest, telling him he had no control in the world, that he would be buffeted and pushed into the water and drown, or be crushed in the big machine and his body hung up on the whitewashed wall for all to see. He thought of the riot: the unstoppable force that had dragged Virginia from his grasp into the stampede and whipped him back against the wall. He thought about his newspaper and the governor's race, and of all the power he believed was his. Until yesterday it had seemed a glorious, untroubled vision. His rising career had appeared like those scenes from the illustrated Bible he had printed over and over before he could read the words. The boy Isaac saved. Crafty Jacob wins the blessing. Glittering Jerusalem. But those bright, innocent pictures were gone. He saw now only the dangerous gray-blue deep of the water rising up as his foot slipped, and the shadow of the big machine looming over him.

Eamoun Casey had always relished his fame as editor of the *Herald*, but never until last night had he realized the full extent of his power. He had believed he could bring a great man down and, sure enough, he had brought Dr. Hosack down. But the stories he had written about Edmund Leadbetter were no more than flares, a kind of fireworks with words, distracting but harmless. At least, so he had intended. But events had proven how dangerously wrong he was. The riot at the theater had shown he could sell an idea in his newspaper, any idea, and crowds would assemble to defend it. He could talk patriotism and produce anarchy in Manhattan. If he had known he could unleash such forces, he would not have done it. But he *had* done it, and now the Park Theater stood in ruins while his daughter lay upstairs struggling for her life. What he had done appalled him. That he had been *able* to do it frightened him more deeply still. The bird's wings beat like mad against his chest as he thought of these terrible possibilities he had created for himself, and for the first time in his conscious life he looked down at his ink-darkened hands with loathing and regret.

He pulled himself painfully upright once more while his feet searched for the floor. There could be no sleeping for him today. He was sitting there on the divan, dumb with restless exhaustion and remorse, when he heard his wife give a startled cry from upstairs. He stumbled into the hall toward the stairs. He called for Lily, but she was already rushing out the door for help.

When the young doctor arrived, panting hard from running in the heat the length of Broadway, he found Eamonn Casey, who had taken laudanum enough to fell a horse, pulling aside the shutters from the window and dancing and slapping his sides. A bright stream of sunlight illuminated his patient sitting half-upright in her bed, her blond hair loose across her shoulders. When Virginia Casey looked over at him, her pupils were wide with wonder. She had a peaceful smile on her face, sitting there, as if she had never once thought of dying, and had just now woken from a fairy's sleep.

CHAPTER TWENTY-NINE

Albert heard footsteps in the hall. Two sets. Then a key in the lock and a gruff voice.

"Dash. A visitor for you."

Bridewell Jail once stood as an awesome reminder to New Yorkers of the law's ever-watchful gaze. Its two broad stories of gray stone, with high barred windows cut like eyes, had loomed over the west side of Broadway near City Hall for longer than living memory. Together with St. Paul's Church, whose graceful white spire rose just to the south, the two structures stood as a strong visual check to any Broadway pedestrian contemplating mischief; it reminded him at a glance of what judgment he might expect for his sins, both in this world and the next.

In recent years, however, Bridewell inspired less reverence for the law than mockery. The great front door was continually falling from its hinges, and the old stone walls sagged haphazardly into the mud of seventy winters. Indoors, great cakes of plaster crumbled from the walls and ceiling like an incessant rain shower, exposing a roof infested with cockroaches and vermin. Prisoners and their keepers alike knew better than to fall asleep with their mouths open.

Upstairs, in a bare holding cell where American patriots had once starved in their dozens at the hands of their British captors, Albert Dash sat despondently on a stool in the middle of the floor. He stood up on seeing the warden's bright red face through the grille, but when he saw the large figure standing behind him, he froze. Albert's right eye was folded back beneath a great blue welt of pulpy skin so that he could not see at all from it, but his left eye stretched wide with angry surprise.

"I'm sorry about that shiner," George Bickart said to him when the turnkey had gone. "Now, don't look at me like that. Just listen to me." The next George knew he was lying on his back on the hard stone floor, with a small confetti of damp plaster raining down on his face. Albert Dash stared down at him with his one belligerent eye, his fist curled at the ready.

"If you move, I'll hit you again. God help me, I will!"

"Now, now, Albert," George rasped. "I thought I told you to listen to me."

"Anything you have to say to me, you can say it from there." Albert still stood over him, his foot poised menacingly on the rim of his solar plexus.

"Just as you please, old friend. But I ask you if this is any way to treat a man to whom you are currently very much in debt."

"In debt? I have you to thank for this, that's all I know." He pointed to his swollen face, and then to the four walls of his Bridewell cell. His boot toyed with George's breast bone.

"Better in Bridey than some shallow grave off the Harlem Road."

Albert hesitated, then removed his foot. He stepped back. George made quick use of the opportunity to get up and wipe the scum off his clothes. He fingered his jaw resentfully.

"You really shouldn't hit people, Albert. You being a doctor. Whatever happened to 'First, do no harm'?"

"What do you mean—better here than in a grave off the Harlem Road?" Albert fixed him with his cyclopic glare.

There was another three-legged stool in the corner of the cell. George brought it over and set it down next to Albert's. In silent agreement to an uneasy truce, they sat down together. George was first to speak.

"You've put me to a lot of trouble for your sake, old friend."

"How's that?"

"Protecting you from yourself. I knew you were putting it about that Casey had Babcock killed, but you're wrong. You upset folks with that talk, you know."

Albert's single eye communicated suspicion, and no forgiveness. George thought it best to start over.

"On my honor, Casey's no murderer, and nor am I if that's what you're thinking. But when I heard you'd been asking questions at Grimm's, I knew the only way to convince you was if I found out who did it myself. So I went to Brooklyn. I asked around—"

"And?—"

"Quin's your man."

"Captain Quin, of the *Belladonna*?"

"Yes."

Albert grunted and stood up. He walked over to the wall.

"You see how convenient this story is. If it is only a personal vendetta between Babcock and Quin, then no one else is to blame. Including Casey."

"That was the plan. But Quin didn't kill Babcock because he loathed him, but because he was blackmailed by John Laidlaw."

"Mr. Laidlaw? Prove it!" cried Albert angrily.

"I will. Babcock was a loudmouth, as you know. You heard him at Grimm's, boasting how he would bring Quin down at the quarantine hearing. Well, Laidlaw's spies got back to him, and then he made the deal with Quin. He told him to get rid of Babcock or he would lose his ship, and end up here in Bridey. Laidlaw had already paid him a handsome sum to alter the *Belladonna*'s log to say they'd never touched at Kingston Town. He owned Quin, you see, so when he heard about what Babcock was planning to testify at City Hall for your Dr. Hosack, he put his man to use. It was the perfect solution. Make poor Babcock's death appear an accident and, if people got suspicious, they would look no further than Quin anyway. Everyone knew they hated each other."

Albert listened silently. When George finished, he began pacing up and down the cell. Six steps, then a turn at the wall. Then six steps back. At the third turn, he looked over.

"It was all Laidlaw?"

"Yes."

"And you think he had similar plans for me?"

"I know he did. Word in Brooklyn was that you were a dead man. You were lucky me and my boys got to you first."

"I don't believe it."

"Not exactly friendly in a future father-in-law, I admit. But it's the truth."

Albert rubbed his hand slowly across his forehead. "How did you know to come to the Park Theater?"

"I went because I knew Laidlaw's thugs would be there."

Albert stamped his foot. "But how did you all know *I* would be there?"

George grinned. "You're not such a mystery to people as you think. How else would you get to see your beloved Vera? And with the national honor at stake—we just knew you would be there. Laidlaw played his part well. He shut his door against you seeing Vera because he knew it would make you lose your head. I was worried you would give the game up too easily, by trying to see her or slip her a note."

"I was going to but things got out of hand too quickly. I never had a chance."

"Be thankful for that. Laidlaw's boys were waiting for you on the stairs outside her box with the lovely Miss Vera for bait. But by the time they got down to where the action was in the lobby, me and my boys were ready for them."

Albert sat down on the stool and put his head in his hands. He said nothing for a full minute. At last, he looked up with his pitiful purple eye.

"I'm grateful to you, George—though no one else will be. You only saved the biggest fool in America. The doctor warned me about Laidlaw, and I didn't listen. I wanted to believe it was all Casey. I was so sure—"

George felt bold enough to reach out a give Albert a brotherly pat on the shoulder.

"You've always put too high a store on your own cleverness, Albert. That's my opinion. Don't think too badly of yourself. You've had worse days at Newmarket."

"Bribes are one thing," said Albert. "But why would Laidlaw think it worth murdering a man? He has insurance agents and can bear the losses, and he must see that the quarantine is inevitable now that the fever has broken out in Philadelphia."

"I can't help you there."

Albert shook his head. He felt disgust with himself rise inside him like a sour taste.

"Have you seen Casey? Does he know Laidlaw's suborning murder and is looking to kill me too?"

"I don't reckon he does. I haven't had the chance to see him. Since the riot, they're letting no one in at Park Row, and Casey won't even come to the door. They've got all the shutters drawn, and doctors running in and out at all hours."

Albert, who had resumed pacing, stopped short, puzzled.

"Doctors?"

George grinned. "You don't know? That's a shame. Because I wanted to ask you how it feels to have a young lady throw herself between you and a gang of Bowery hoodlums with their blood up. Poor little Virginia got knocked on the head Wednesday night, you see, trying to help you keep yours."

Albert stared at him, disbelieving.

"My boys must have properly jiggled your brains. How much do you remember?"

"I remember seeing Virginia, but I didn't understand why she was there. I tried to throw her off. Nothing after that. Is she hurt very bad?"

"It's my fault. One of my boys tried to crown you with a brick-bat—for your own good, of course—and got her instead. She dropped like a bird hit by buckshot."

Albert groaned.

"Don't despair just yet. I've seen far worse, and she's a Casey, after all. Strong of will like her pa. She showed great pluck taking on those brutes." George paused, and gave Albert an arch look. "Though I can't help wondering why little Virginia Casey, who's a very level-headed girl if ever there was, would do such a crazy fool thing."

Albert leant his whole tired weight against the wall. He felt he could not possibly continue to stand without the support of penitentiary stone.

"I've been a fool," he said again. He shook his head, then looked over at George. "Tell me what to do, George."

George smiled. "There's a first! Well, you've got plenty of time to think up a good story for the magistrate. Make yourself comfortable here, I'd say. Streets aren't safe for you."

Albert paced up and back once more, then stopped suddenly.

"We have to get out of here," he said. "You have to get me out of here."

"Well, I could post your bail tomorrow. You can take one more night in Bridey, can't you?"

Albert grabbed his arm. "There's no time. We must get out of here, right away."

George stood up reluctantly. He knew better than to contradict Albert in this mood.

"Alright. But the magistrate won't be happy—not with either of us."

"The magistrate will have bigger fish soon enough."

George banged with his fist on the iron door. "Hey, Jack Ketch! Come get me!"

They heard a shuffling along the dark hall. A set of puffy eyes appeared through the latch, then a key turned and the door swung open. The warden's face turned a brighter pink when he saw George Bickart dangling a hefty-sized purse above the prisoner's head. He whistled.

"Now, George, what's your game? You know they'll hang me if the magistrate sends for him and he's not here."

"There's six months wages here, mate." George tossed the purse from hand to hand.

"But I need my job here, George, come wintertime." The warden was now leaning against the door, arms crossed, as if he were settling in for a long negotiation. Albert gave George an impatient jab in the ribs.

George sighed. "Don't say I didn't try." He strolled up to the warden, who eyed him with a leery grin, and punched him hard on his red nose. The man groaned and crumpled onto the floor. George leaned over him and dropped the purse onto his chest, while Albert was already out the door.

"There you are, Jack Ketch," said George kindly. "Now no one's going to believe you ever took a penny."

CHAPTER THIRTY

Eamonn Casey knew the mayor did not want to be seen with him. Not since newspapers from Boston to Charleston had got wind of the riot at the Park Theater and called it a national disgrace. As he read editorials from around the nation, he had the uncanny feeling that he had read them all before, even written them himself.

The *Philadelphia Inquirer*, even in the turmoil of that city's yellow fever epidemic, found time to ponder "how a man who would incite and applaud public riot can aspire to the highest seat in New York? What anarchy might be foisted on the citizens of that state with the full powers of the governor's office available to Mr. Casey, who can cause so much destruction from his editor's desk?"

The *Boston Globe* took the same view. Since Edmund Leadbetter had taken refuge in that city after his misadventures in Manhattan, and charmed drawing-rooms full of Bostonians with the pathetic tale of his persecution, the *Globe* editor worried for the reputation of the nation: "What will they say now at Covent Garden and Drury Lane of our much-vaunted Yankee hospitality and our Yankee taste? They will say we are ungoverned savages, with no appreciation of the courtesy due to an eminent foreign visitor or to the thespian art he glorifies, a people incapable of elevation above the violent lather of the mob!"

Eamonn Casey read these reports with a sinking heart. And they were nothing to the recriminations of the New York papers, who delighted in the *Herald*'s humiliation. After reading them, he had such a clear sense of his own notoriety that he sent a message to John Laidlaw suggesting that their hastily called meeting should not take place at City Hall or in the daylight hours, to spare the mayor any awkwardness.

It was thus around closing time at the Tontine Coffee House, on the Saturday after the riot, that he picked his way through the refuse barrels and roaming swine in the alley behind Wall Street, knocked three times, and was conducted by a houseboy with a lamp downstairs to the basement kitchen. There, on a broad wood table more used to the traffic of plucked chickens and soused trotters than urgent political meetings of the great men of the city, he joined John Laidlaw and a somber-looking mayor.

"I apologize for the circumstances of our meeting," he announced to them after a solemn exchange of greetings, "but I'm afraid our mutual association has aroused the wrong kind of talk. The mayor has his electoral future to look to, independent of mine. And I take responsibility for the unfortunate outcome at the Park Theater. If it is not too much to presume, I think the less said on that subject the better."

He did not look at John Laidlaw. It was the only way he could get through what he had to say.

"Yes, of course," said the mayor, "though before we drop the painful matter altogether, I must ask how Miss Casey is faring in her recovery?"

Casey's face tensed, but his voice remained steady.

"Better. She got out of bed this evening. She is dressed now and sitting up in the parlor, attended to by her mother."

"I'm glad to hear it."

"We're both glad," said Laidlaw. After a polite pause, he went on—"We should not deceive ourselves or each other about the difficult state of affairs confronting us. Would you agree, Mr. Mayor?"

"I would. To be frank, I call our situation desperate. This Leadbetter affair has killed our momentum. Just today I have received messages from a dozen of our upstate editors. They ask me what defense to run for Mr. Casey, or whether to ignore the riot altogether and continue to publish encomiums on the aqueduct. I will tell you honestly that I didn't know how to advise them, as both courses seem equally hopeless. And as for the city, you both know as well as I that nothing can possibly be heard above all this clamor over Leadbetter. It will take weeks to die down."

"Don't forget that we have achieved one important objective," said Laidlaw. "The quarantine issue is forgotten."

"It is a Pyrrhic victory, sir."

"Perhaps. I would agree that our situation is bad. But it is not, in my opinion, irretrievable. We have one chance left, one great opportunity—that is, if events take a particular turn."

The mayor's eyes brightened and he leaned forward in his chair.

"I'm glad to hear you say it, sir."

"What is this one chance, Mr. Laidlaw," said Casey, "this great opportunity?"

Laidlaw laid his hands flat on the table as if to steady it.

"The yellow fever."

Casey and the mayor said nothing while they waited for an explanation that didn't come.

"What do you mean?" said the mayor at last.

Laidlaw looked at them both in turn, his blue eyes glinting. "I mean the unique political opportunities afforded by a crisis, by an epidemic of this sort. It is in a public emergency that a mayor can rise above petty politics and show himself in the heroic light of the statesman: marshalling his forces, rallying morale, visiting the sick. And if you, Mr. Mayor, when the yellow fever comes, were to appoint Mr. Casey in some equally heroic capacity, to take charge of the water and food supply for instance, or the evacuation of the port, you would surely excite the gratitude of the people and be the men of the hour come November."

Casey felt the hairs curl up on the back of his neck. Looking across to the mayor, he saw that he too was stunned.

"Well, it is a macabre thought," said the mayor. "No doubt we might profit by an epidemic, somehow. But it is all hypothetical."

Casey shifted on his chair. He spoke in a dull monotone that belied the fluttering in his chest. "But you were not listening to Mr. Laidlaw. He said, 'When the fever comes.'"

"A slip of the tongue," said Laidlaw, "I meant 'if.'"

"I see," said Casey. "But still, you said, 'when the fever *comes*.'"

"I don't understand."

"Oh, but it is I who haven't understood, Mr. Laidlaw. When I hear you talk of the yellow fever *coming*, that suggests to me you believe it will come from abroad, that the source of the yellow fever is from some distant place, say, the West Indies. Might I ask whether you have recently altered your thinking on this question, or have you believed the fever is imported from the tropics all along, even while you had me attack that very idea in the *Herald* as if it were a great heresy?"

In the tense silence that followed, Casey stared at the wall, at a blank space just above John Laidlaw's head. To look at the man himself could only mean blood. At length, it became clear that his question would not be answered.

"You made a liar of me about the quarantine, Mr. Laidlaw," he said softly. "You had me conspire, too, against Dr. Hosack. Then you set me against Edmund Leadbetter, the most famous man to visit New York since Lafayette. And what have been the fruits of your advice? My honesty and integrity are challenged by every newspaper editor in the country. My campaign for governor is called a national disgrace. And now you wish me to champion the yellow fever itself as an ally against my opponents. For your sake, sir, I will pretend this meeting never happened. Our association is at an end."

He stood up, replaced his hat on his head and walked to the door. He banged on it hard, twice. There was the sound of footsteps on the stairs and the innkeeper pulling back the bolt to let him out. In an instant, he had vaulted himself up the stairs and out into the open night. It stank of chicken bones and pigs, but still he breathed deeply, as if it were the air of the freshest virgin meadow.

CHAPTER THIRTY-ONE

According to his wife, Samuel Geyer should have been in bed long ago. But he had stayed up late in his study—a room he had barely left since returning from the abortive expedition to the Croton River. Toward midnight, to the alarm of all in the household except its insomniacal head, there was a loud knock at the door.

Mr. Geyer appeared immediately in the hall, shooed the servant away who had stumbled sleepily in from the kitchen, and answered the door himself.

"Who is it, Mr. Geyer?" came the shrill cry from his wife's room upstairs. "Are we to be murdered in our beds?"

"No cause for alarm, my dear. It is only my surveyors. I told them to bring the new maps to me however late the hour. It is my fault."

There was a loud grunt of disapproval from above, then a slamming door.

"I have been expecting you, gentlemen," said Sam Geyer when he had closed the door and lit a fresh candle. He looked up in mild surprise at what the candlelight revealed. "I see now that my alarms for your safety have not been exaggerated. That eye, Mr. Dash, is an impressive sight."

He indicated seats for his two visitors by the elegant bay window.

"Pardon me, sir, but how is it that you have been expecting us?" said Albert. "I was in a cell in Bridewell Jail until an hour ago and did not think to call on you until my visit from George here."

"I don't believe I've had the pleasure," said Geyer, looking at George.

"George Bickart, sir. An old friend of Albert's. Pleased to make your acquaintance."

Geyer nodded. He was wearing a silk evening robe with an oriental pattern. Tied across his round belly, it made him look like a sorcerer in a pantomime. But the look on his face suggested nothing like comedy.

"I have been expecting you, Mr. Dash, ever since I unraveled the meaning of this."

He reached into the pocket of his robe and brought out a paper. He laid it on the small table between them. Albert instantly took it up and read it.

"'A Bill to Establish the Manhattan Water Company.' Did Mr. Laidlaw write this?"

Geyer nodded. "Read the second last paragraph, if you will. Out loud."

Albert read. "'Messrs. Laidlaw and associates are hereby permitted to raise public monies for the establishment of a company, to be called the Manhattan Water Company, and to employ said monies for the purpose of providing water to the city of Manhattan, or for any other purpose'—I don't understand."

"I think I do," said George. "'Any other purpose.' That stinks."

"Precisely," said Geyer. "Those words troubled me from the moment I read them a week ago. I knew I had seen them before. It was another context, many years ago, but the same wording exactly."

"What does it mean?" said Albert. "And why did it lead you to expect a visit from us?"

Geyer smiled. "I know you, Mr. Dash, as a very determined young man. I knew too from our conversation at Mr. Laidlaw's party that you were suspicious of Mr. Casey, and thus by association, Mr. Laidlaw too. And I knew your suspicions could only grow after the *Herald*'s attack on Dr. Hosack. In short, I knew that your inquiries would eventually lead you to my door, as a player in this aqueduct business. Though I must say that after the trouble at the Park Theater on Wednesday night and seeing your name in the papers, I wondered if you had fallen into some sort of trap."

Albert bent his head and looked ashamed. "I did, but I was fortunate enough to have George here looking out for me."

George smiled complacently.

"I'm thankful for that," said Geyer, "because I had begun to despair. I knew I could never put all the pieces together myself. It took me three days of hunting through old notes and diaries, and a trip to the archives at City Hall, but I did find my source. That phrase—*or any other purpose*—does indeed have a history in this city. It was appended to a piece of legislation introduced to the council in the year four, a petition to create a public works company for the purpose of digging wells in the vicinity of the old canal. You see, our water problems back then were almost as severe as they are now." He sighed and looked suddenly melancholy. "I'm afraid history will not look kindly on my generation. We have done nothing to avert our current disastrous water situation. It was the shame of this failure, you see, that led me to put such exaggerated hopes in Mr. Casey and Mr. Laidlaw when they approached me this summer with their plans to support my aqueduct."

Albert pitied Sam Geyer in that moment, but he had no patience for digression.

"Please, Mr. Geyer."

"Of course. Excuse me. Well, the petition for the public works company was recognized at the last minute as a fraud. In the end, it was not even formally tabled."

"Who authored the petition?"

Geyer paused. "Aaron Burr."

Albert and George looked at each other in horror. It was the name uttered to all New Yorkers in their cribs to instill in them a precocious fear of the Devil. No one spoke for several moments.

"What were Burr's plans for his well-digging company?" Albert asked finally. "What was the *other purpose?*"

"It was a typical Burr scheme. He wanted to create a finance company with himself as director. Burr never intended to dig wells at all, you see. He just wanted the power to raise capital for whatever speculative investments he chose by opening the company to private shareholder accounts. A bank, in all but name."

"And the law could not touch him?"

Geyer nodded. "As I said, the petition was never formally presented. At the last minute, one of Burr's confederates betrayed him to some members of the council. Burr was no fool. He knew when the game was up. There was gossip about it for a while—I recorded it in my diary—but it was not long after that he killed Hamilton. His foiled banking scheme, known only to a very few people, was not remembered long once he had inscribed himself in the pages of infamy with that heinous act."

"You think John Laidlaw learned of this and is trying Burr's trick for himself?"

"So it seems."

"But why should he think he will succeed where Burr failed?" said George.

Sam Geyer sat back, folded his arms across his belly and contemplated the ceiling. "I have not been able to sleep for asking myself that very question, Mr. Bickart. And I'm sorry to say I have no answer for it."

"In any event," said George, "whatever schemes he had must now be over with. His Water Company relies on Casey's election. And Casey's prospects were doomed from the moment news came of yellow fever in Philadelphia and their quarantine. Laidlaw will drop him now."

Geyer shook his head. "If that is so, then why is Mr. Laidlaw still plotting? Only this evening I received a message from him to come to a meeting at the Tontine Coffee House with Casey and the mayor. I was told to enter from the rear, unobserved. I didn't go, of course, but if the yellow fever has put an end to his hopes, as you say, what would be the use of such a clandestine meeting?"

Albert, who had wandered over to the window, now broke his silence. "If Laidlaw knows about an obscure scheme of Aaron Burr's twenty years ago, he would surely have heard the very well-known story of the Bellevue Hospital. Do you remember the circumstances of the financing of the hospital, Mr. Geyer?"

"Of course. Dr. Hosack committed a portion of his private fortune, and the balance was funded by the city."

"Yes, but it was not so easy as that. Dr. Hosack had been petitioning the council for years to help him build the hospital. But they did not vote to fund it until the year fourteen, in the summer of an election year when the city . . ."

"The yellow fever!" cried Sam Geyer, a glow of comprehension in his eyes. "1814 was the worst epidemic in a decade!"

Albert nodded. "Laidlaw has learnt from the doctor's success. A new yellow fever outbreak in Manhattan would serve him well. He could get the council to vote for whatever he put under their noses."

Geyer sat back in his chair, a palm to his forehead. "He is a second Burr, truly. That is, if what you speculate is true. But he is still taking a very great chance. The yellow fever may not come. And he can do nothing about it."

Albert turned back to the window. The blackness outside was complete, with only occasional pinpoints of lamplight visible from the wealthy wards on the west side.

"But he has done something about it, don't you see? First he has ensured there will be no quarantine. Second, he has had Dr. Hosack removed from Bellevue and installed his man Dr. Miller there in his place. Put these two things together and what do you have?"

"A greater likelihood of yellow fever in Manhattan."

"More than that," said Albert, his voice growing tense. The full realization dawned on him only as he put words to it. "With Dr. Hosack gone, Dr. Miller, and therefore John Laidlaw, has authority over all the medical services in this city. The hospital nurses, the porters. He has control, too, over all information. That information is his to withhold if he chooses."

"I don't get it," said George.

Albert looked at them. "I mean what if the yellow fever is already here—and we don't know it?"

They sat silently to absorb the idea. The candle gutted in an unseen draft of air, then flared again. Suddenly both men were on their feet. They looked at Albert.

"George, go up to Bellevue and see what you can find. Be careful—I doubt they'll welcome visitors. Mr. Geyer, you must go to

Park Row in the morning and tell Casey everything. If he is innocent, as George says, and has fallen under the spell of Mr. Laidlaw, he may yet turn against him."

"I will tell him—rely on it."

"What about you?" said George. "There's still a bounty on your head in Manhattan, you know."

Albert offered a wry smile. "They won't be looking for me where I'm going."

CHAPTER THIRTY-TWO

The ground was damp where he sat among the headstones. After half an hour of waiting, he crouched on his haunches to relieve a cramp, knees on his leather instrument bag. He watched the lamp, lit low and hidden in the grass, to make sure it didn't sputter out. In the thick darkness, he mistook a rustle of leaves for a sniffing dog, a clump of trees waving in the wind for Laidlaw's men coming. It hurt to sit here so long, too sore to move. His ribs still ached with each breath though his throat no longer burned. His eye was no better: still half-closed, weeping. He had seen it in a mirror that night at Sam Geyer's. Bruised yellow like an egg in a pan.

The porters arrived at last, four of them, the big man he knew from Bellevue at their head. Two stretchers between them. When he stood up, they dropped their loads and scattered.

"Mr. Albert, that you?" hissed a voice from behind a headstone.

"Yes," he hissed back.

"Where've you been? And how'd you get so ugly?"

"Not ugly. Old, waiting for you."

One by one, four heads popped up from behind four tombstones. They picked up the stretchers and walked over to him, to the fresh ground where he knew they would have to dig.

"What do you have for me, my friend?" he said.

The big man lifted back the sheets, damp from the rain, and he saw the bodies of a young man and a girl, looking as though they had just been dipped in batter.

"A gift to you, Mr. Albert. Fresh today."

"On behalf of Dr. Hosack, thanks." He handed him a purse.

"Thank you kindly."

"Where did you come from?"

"Hudson docks. Rector Street."

"When did they die?"

"Today. Fresh, like I said."

"Hours matter."

"This morning, early. We got Doc Miller's call at eight."

"It's midnight now. That's sixteen hours."

"So we wait till dusk. Everyone's curious in daylight hours. But Doc Miller knows no watchman's going to stop four black men carrying stretchers to the Nassau Street boneyard at midnight. Leatherhead's pay's not worth what he might find. So he sits and pretends he can't see us in the dark. Not that white people's sight improves in the daylight."

"That's right," said the others, spitting on their tools.

Before digging, they moved the bodies downwind. They worked silently except for the big man, who sang softly to himself.

After twenty minutes, the hole was neck deep and broad enough for two bodies.

"A grave big enough for a rich man," said the gravedigger, "or for a poor man and his wife. And they say money breaks up a marriage—that the poor don't make close families!"

To lay the two bodies in the grave, they had to scramble out themselves to make room. Albert gave them the oil lamp, so low it barely lit the hand that held it. He leapt into the grave, landing on one leg, twisting his ankle. But the pain freshened his mind, he told himself, sharpened him for the night's work ahead. The big man handed down his bag of instruments, then the lamp. Deep in the grave, the flame was sheltered from the wind and invisible from Nassau Street. He encouraged it more and soon, in the broader light, he could see the entire lengths of the bodies—a sinewy slim working man and his bride, little bigger than a child, still warm from the heat of the fever. The lamp tottered, almost fell into a puddle.

"I need help," he called out. "Come down and hold this lamp."

The gravedigger's head appeared above him. "I'll light your way to heaven, Mr. Albert, but not the other way. No, sir. I'll follow you to the ends of the earth but not into it!"

Then he was gone, and his men with him.

Albert took a breath and fought back the deep-running fears. *We are not an animal to relish our own dead*, he thought. *We fear our own mother, a lover, a bosom friend once we put them in the grave.*

The young man's face still bore the strain of his last terrible hours. His eyes stared up at Albert, whites upturned. Jaw locked— the rigor of horrific surprise. But his wife, the girl, might have died in her sleep a contented grandmother but for her smooth skin and light, un-used limbs. She had made her peace with the fever at the last, had turned her thoughts to the rewards of the innocent.

Albert cut—a single, decisive stroke—into the man's abdomen. He peered in with his useful eye. The fat of the body was yellow, the luster of jaundice. He felt something small, viscous, where it should not have been. The light was too poor to distinguish it. Blood vessels from the cawl? No, that was gone, burnt up, only an oily floating liquor remained. So much had been annihilated by the terrible spasms, the convulsions of the sixth and seventh days. Lower down, the liver appeared plump and healthy to the eye. But when he turned over its concave underside, he saw that it was burnt deep black like coal. Everything was corrupted by a yellow film on its outside, and inside blocked by a black, ropy coagulation. The fever seemed to have absorbed the man's organs whole. It was not bile, this black stuff. More like burnt blood evacuated from the liver.

Albert paused to wipe his weeping eye. Then he resumed. Deeper inside the stomach the tissue was all inflamed, with two dark blush-red pools against the yellow flesh. The man's final toast? A glass of wine before dying? But it could not be. The lungs surprised him too. They had not collapsed; they were inflated, in fact. A last, massive inspiration of breath, held now for eternity. All over the lung cage were black and livid spots, some as broad as the palm of his hand. He took the lamp up in one hand and began to work the bone with the other. He found blisters like a gangrene, but with a yellowish humor. He then tried to bleed the man but could not find an agreeable vessel. It was like the fever had boiled him up, burnt his veins dry of blood.

Steps above, very close. He was so caught up in the dissection, he had forgotten to fear discovery. There was no time even to extinguish the lamp, though it could not matter now. He was trapped in another man's grave, a bloody knife, nowhere to run. A white face above him in the darkness, then a scream. When he got to the surface he found Lily Riley, fallen in a puddle.

"May the Lord forgive you, Albert Dash!" she whispered as he helped her to her feet. "I will pray for that poor soul, and then I'll pray for yours, by the saints I will."

"What are you doing here, Lily?" said Albert, breathless.

"George sent me. Wanted to make sure you're still alive."

"Damn him. I told him to go straight to Bellevue. But I need your help, Lily. I need a man and a horse to take a message to Dr. Hosack. This instant."

"Alright. I'll find someone." Lily looked into the grave and then at his bloodied self, unforgivingly. "And I'll say the Devil sent me."

CHAPTER THIRTY-THREE

Early the next morning, with the sun barely midway toward its brutal zenith, two men sat across from each other in a carriage heading uptown from lower Broadway. They had been silent throughout their journey and still now, crossing Wall Street, neither seemed inclined to conversation. They might have been strangers—brought together in a cab-for-hire by the accident of shared destination—except that one of the men, a tall, broad-shouldered man, showed a very familiar interest in the comfort of the other. He was continually reaching over to secure his companion in his seat whenever the rattling motions of the cab threatened to unsettle him, and risked battering his own head against the roof.

The tall man was made less comfortable still by an indisposition. He kept a handkerchief continually pressed to his nose, as if he were suffering a nasty late-summer cold in the head. But he did not utter a word of complaint, while his partner slumped indifferently in his seat.

At the corner of Cortlandt Street, the cab suddenly stopped, causing great inconvenience to the traffic from four directions. Passersby saw a large gentleman with a streaming cold open the door in unorthodox fashion on the streetside of the cab, leap nimbly (for his age) out onto the hub rail, then vault up on the bench to sit beside his own driver who, oddly enough, also held a handkerchief to his nose while directing his nervous horses with his free hand as best he could. The gentleman's companion must be obnoxious, people thought, for him to abandon the cabin in the middle of the street and choose to complete his journey seated next to a sick cabdriver, all exposed up there to the heat and the clouds of baking dust.

The cab proceeded a further half-mile before two large granite pillars and a trellis fence overhung with willows told them they had arrived at City Hall Park. Here Nassau Street merged with Park Row and it was the turn of fashionable uptown New Yorkers in their colorful crinolines and stovepipe hats to witness the spectacle of two men (one clearly a gentleman) atop a cab, handkerchiefs fluttering like flags, yelling and shaking their fists at the traffic around them.

Even the mayor himself, seated at his desk in the east wing of City Hall, noticed something of a more-than-ordinary commotion coming from the street outside. But this was a rude, noisy city, and he thought no more than that a horse, crazed from the heat, had kicked a child senseless, or that some watermen were disputing over control of their dwindling deliveries. More to the point, he was currently engrossed in his late morning collation. Oysters, hen lobster and a glass of gleaming black porter sat on a silver tray in front of him. Commotion or no, his concentration could not safely be broken at this moment, not if he wanted to be sure of conducting the city's business at the peak of his powers until lunchtime.

"Please excuse the intrusion, Mr. Mayor," said his secretary, poking his head around the door. He did so with some trepidation because the mayor had been in a foul mood all morning.

"Next appointment isn't until noon, Mr. Fry," said the mayor, still chewing.

"No, sir. But you have an official visitor just arrived. The gentleman demands to see you, sir."

"Who *demands* to see me without an appointment?" Then a sudden, fearful look came over his face. "It isn't *him*, is it?"

"No, it isn't Mr. Laidlaw, sir. It's Dr. Hosack, sir."

The mayor looked relieved, then peevish again. "Hosack! He dares to show himself here? I'll be damned if I see him!"

"I have not made myself clear, sir," persisted Mr. Fry. "Dr. Hosack does not desire to see you himself, but for you to meet his particular friend, an ambassador from the Jamaican dominion. He has come all the way here expressly to deliver you a message."

"Message? Ambassador? I know of no ambassador from Jamaica."

"Please, sir. Dr. Hosack is most insistent. And he is drawing public attention to his business on the steps. The ambassador waits at your pleasure in his carriage."

Muttering to himself and gulping one last oyster, the mayor strode with his secretary out into the corridor.

"What is the ambassador's name?"

"Sir Mortimer Amberblood, sir."

"Never heard of him." Their shoes clacked busily across the marble-floored lobby. "Jamaica, eh? And I thought Hosack had given up his quarantine at last. No such luck."

Out on the steps, a crowd had gathered near the ambassador's carriage.

This must be an important fellow after all, thought the mayor, struggling to recall an occasion in the course of his own thirty-year public career when he had commanded rapt attention for simply sitting in a cab. He saw a boy in a cap mount the hub rail, peer insolently inside, then run away again with a loud cry. Impressed, the mayor instantly straightened his shoulders and assumed his best mayoral mien. Meanwhile, Mr. Fry cut a passage for him through the crowd where he came face to face with Dr. Hosack. The doctor was barely recognizable—his nose and eyes streaming.

"Mr. Mayor. The ambassador salutes you!" Dr. Hosack grabbed the mayor's arm and pulled him toward the carriage.

"For God's sake, Hosack!" cried the mayor with indignation. Then he recoiled violently. "What is that godawful smell?"

The mayor looked up and saw a dead man in a winding sheet pressed against the window of the cab. A single white eye stared back from a parchment-yellow face streaked with mud.

"Lord have mercy!"

He staggered away, his stomach heaving. Dr. Hosack leapt forward and opened the door of the cab. In full view of the crowd, the fevered corpse spilled out onto the steps of City Hall. A woman screamed and fainted but was left there on the steps by the fleeing, yelling crowd. In the chaos, the mayor found Fry and screamed in his ear above the din: "Bury that body immediately, then give the order to evacuate! Clear the city! Laidlaw be damned!"

CHAPTER THIRTY-FOUR

The ghost of Lord Howe landing on the Battery at the head of five thousand screaming redcoats could not have produced a more electrifying effect on the citizens of Manhattan than the mayor's proclamation of an outbreak of yellow fever. Rumor of it had spread throughout the city by ten and, by noon, every vehicle that could be found to urge the desperate exodus northward out of the city had been launched onto the streets.

The liveried carriages of the uptown moguls made the first break for open countryside. Following in their wake, a motley, sprawling caravan of heat-stressed humanity. One-horse curricles with well-dressed gentlemen at the whip joined firetrucks stacked with shouting Bowery Boys, donkey-drawn hearses and goods carts strapped to the shoulders of young men, their brawny strength purchased for the day for a month's wages. The children riding behind at first whooped delightedly among the chicken coops and upturned chairs then, as the shouting around them grew fiercer, the day got hotter and the water ran out, they began to cry bitter tears.

Behind this great jostling, lurching four-wheeled procession, the downtown poor filed along the streets on foot, carrying everything they could by way of pots and pans and clothes on their backs. Young children clung to their parents, sometimes two or three to a hand, while it fell to the eldest to carry and comfort the baby.

Some sturdy folk stood sentinel at their doors, proclaiming to passersby that they would not go and leave their worldly goods to looters. But those fleeing thought little of these speechmakers, who would just as likely turn looters themselves once their neighbors' backs were turned. Then there were others who ignored the mayor and stayed for less explicable reasons. The numberless inhabitants of the dockside shanties and cellar basements, who ate beans and stewed apple on good days and nothing on the bad, must have decided that an infected port city was as good a place as any to be miserable, and that the yellow fever was no greater enemy to their happiness than the everyday hardship of the world.

Livestock increased the confusion on the streets. Great numbers of pigs, accustomed to roaming unharassed through lower Manhattan as useful disposers of waste, found themselves cornered and squeezed into small, desperate herds. Blinded by the dust and tormented by the noise, they charged through the crowds like parties of crazed Gadarene swine. Uptown, someone with a rare flair for mayhem had unlocked the pens on Hester Street. A dozen enraged bulls now terrorized the Bowery, goring a man to death, and trampling a crowd of screaming children under their deadly hoofs.

By midafternoon, when the choking heat was at its worst, thousands had abandoned their homes for the open road, though there were not enough country inns or farmers given to charity for even a fraction of them. By nightfall every room between Greenwich Village and Cold Spring would be taken, with not even the grimy corner of a stable to be had at any price. So it was that those from the poorer wards, who had no money for accommodation anyway, traveled with easier minds than the minor burghers of upper Broadway, who flogged their horses and spent small fortunes on envoys to ride on ahead for nothing more, in the end, than a bed in a meadow under the stars beside the laboring men and their families.

For the Caseys, prospects stood better, at least at first. Within a half-hour of the mayor's evacuation order, Sam Geyer had sent messengers to the Caseys and the Laidlaws, inviting them to seek sanctuary from the fever with them at Ambleside. But Casey had waited until the last possible moment to leave the *Herald*, and he was still dictating to his copy boy as he ran home. By the time the carriage was harnessed and all were aboard, there was no room left on Broadway to exercise the advantage of their four-horse power. In fact, with the streets clogged to bursting, the horses quickly became nervous and fretful, a potentially deadly hindrance to their escape.

They sat squeezed three abreast in the carriage, red-faced and sweating, Lily and Ned inside with the family. Above them they heard the calming tones of the driver to the horses, alternating with angry shouts at those on foot and in vehicles around them to keep clear damn you and watch the hell out! Through all the shouting and confusion, death and the fear of death hung heavy in the air, mingled with the dust. Lily passed vials of camphor between them. They held soaked handkerchiefs to their faces and mostly stared down at the floor, afraid to look at the chaos out the window.

Virginia saw that her father had reinjured his arm lifting her bulky case onto the carriage roof, and was squeezing his eyes shut with the pain of every bump in the road. She glanced guiltily at

him from time to time, feeling worse that he had not blamed her
for it. It was very hard to hold onto her determination to hate him
when he sat suffering in silence simply to spare her feelings.

Her head, too, still ached painfully, and her bruised eye and cheek
felt tender. It was a long time before she felt brave enough to lift up
the shutter and look out over the great crowd streaming along Broadway. She gasped at the sight. It was like a dam had burst and sent a
mighty torrent of humanity onto the streets of New York, spilling
its way along the great avenues. At one point, Vera saw someone she
recognized—it was Mr. Burfield—trying to fight the crowd, heading south. But he was picked up and carried back the other way. She
saw his hat and cane bobbing like buoys in a storm until he passed
out of sight.

Throughout the first long, terrible crush from Bowling Green
to Prince Street, no one said a word. When the carriage was completely stalled, as it often was, Virginia felt only the agony of wanting to move, to put even a yard, a foot further between them and
the unseen menace of the yellow fever. And when the carriage did
lurch forward, forcing its way somehow through the bedlam of
traffic, the vehicles crossing crazily before and behind them filled
her with the dread of a disastrous collision. Her eyes clasped shut
in misery and fear, handkerchief close about her face, she imagined a wheel wrenched loose on some abandoned article in the
road—or one of the horses, mad with stress, choking itself in its
harness and pitching them all into the gutter.

After two terrible, interminable hours, just when her throbbing
head told her she could not take it any longer, the peril was suddenly over. The carriage began to accelerate. She heard the driver
crack his whip and encourage the horses, then felt the carriage settle
into the familiar rhythm of a country drive. When she pulled up
the shutter again, the dangerous slow-moving traffic of carts and

shouting pedestrians had gone, and she could smell the hyacinth among the waving meadow grasses. When they passed Greenwich to their left, its mayhem of little streets and hodge-podge houses, built by refugees of fever epidemics past, seemed almost peaceful. A few miles further, beyond the open fields of Dr. Hosack's Botanic Gardens stretching to the east, the road was given over to carriages like their own, with the occasional fast-flying barouche or red-faced man on horseback the only reminder, in the serenity of a summer's day in the country, of the catastrophe they had left only a few miles behind.

As evening closed in, two narrow turrets appeared above the trees, red-tiled in the old Dutch fashion. Beyond a grove of lordly chestnut trees, Ambleside itself came into view, its yellow stone walls overgrown by a green net of clambering vines.

As they turned the corner past the red-painted stables, they saw a small welcoming party waiting for them on the gravel drive in front of the house. Aurelia Geyer was pointing toward them. Beside her, her husband was distracted by the conversation of Eliza Laidlaw. Standing a little apart, the slim figure of her husband. And then Vera, waving madly.

Their host was first to greet them as they made their grateful exit from the stifling confines of the cabin. Mr. Geyer paid special attention to Virginia.

"Please take my arm, Miss Casey. What a terrible journey to have undergone so soon after your accident. Your room is ready if you wish to rest straight away."

"Thank you. I am fine," Virginia replied, though she did feel distinctly woozy. Then, when Vera embraced her with all the feelings of old, she thought she would cry.

Aurelia Geyer assisted Mrs. Casey, and they were soon joined by Mrs. Laidlaw. She and Mrs. Geyer broke into excited, overlapping chatter: how awful it all was, the terrible scenes they had witnessed, how they were all lucky to be alive . . .

Eamonn Casey was the last to step out of the carriage. John Laidlaw advanced to meet him, hand extended in welcome. After no more than a beat of hesitation, Casey took his hand and shook it firmly.

Laidlaw smiled. "I'm so pleased Mr. Geyer was inspired to invite us both to Ambleside. I'm hoping we can make a fresh start after the strains of the last week."

"I agree, Mr. Laidlaw. Yes, a fresh start."

"I have spoken to Sam. There is clearly nothing to be done today. But I will send my driver Gibbs back to the city at first light, and the three of us will meet in the study before breakfast tomorrow. My belief is that the mayor has badly overreacted and that we will be able to go back to the city tomorrow. Then we will take charge of the situation."

"Tomorrow morning it is, then," said Casey, and they walked together into the house.

Meanwhile, the women supervised Ned and Lily Riley in unloading the trunks from the carriage. Virginia's was the largest and the last. Young Ned, seeming surprised by its weight, almost toppled from the roof handing it down.

"Be careful!" cried Virginia.

They all looked at her and her unwieldy trunk with curiosity, and decided that they had underestimated the personal necessities of a shy and bookish young lady.

Virginia and Vera were to share a room upstairs. When they looked out from the window, they could see Ambleside's fruit orchards and the rows of berry vines climbing the hill to the north. Across the lawn, a stone path led down to the riverbank, framed by cypress trees. Even from this distance, they could hear the ringing falsetto of the summer insects unseen in the reeds. Beyond that, the great broad river eased effortlessly in the direction of the city and toward its greater Atlantic destination.

Virginia watched Vera unpack, leaving her own trunk unopened on her bed. They exchanged their stories of the day's dramas, stories that were much the same: hours of pure hell on bumpy roads in choking traffic, and stuck the whole time inside a crammed carriage with no chance to stop along the way. And everyone either panicking or crying or miserable.

While they talked, Virginia waited anxiously for Vera to ask for an explanation for what had happened at the Park Theater: why she had thrown herself at Albert Dash in that crazed manner and caused them both to be hurt. The tension built inside her the longer Vera said nothing about it. When Vera finally turned to her, and began silently scrutinizing her face, Virginia thought she would shrivel up inside. But Vera only remarked that her nasty bruise had faded and that with the riot and now the yellow fever, their lives were just too dramatic for words and that it was just as well that they should now have retired to the country.

Whether it was her relief in arriving at Ambleside, or some other cause, Vera looked strangely elated in the circumstances. She paused in the middle of separating her stockings into pairs and sat down on the bed opposite Virginia. She was twisting her hands together in her lap.

"There is something I must tell you, Virginia. Something has happened."

"What is it?"

Vera got up from the bed and went to her trunk. From deep under a pile of clothes, she pulled out a letter and held it toward Virginia.

Virginia was convinced it could only be a love letter from Albert, and she held up her hand. "I won't read it. Tell me what is in it— if you must."

Vera frowned. "Sometimes I don't understand you, Virginia. I'm sure *I* would want to read it. Can you guess who it's from?"

"What do you mean?"

"Oh! Well, then you are not as clever as I thought you were. But you must know. Who is it I have worried myself to death thinking about since that awful night at the Park Theater—apart from you, of course?"

"Your betrothed," said Virginia quietly, not meeting Vera's eye.

Vera appeared surprised, then embarrassed. "No, I have not seen Albert or heard from him, and he is certainly with Dr. Hosack by now."

It was Virginia's turn to look surprised. She realized in an instant that Vera must not know what had happened at the Park Theater. She must not have seen how she got hurt. And her father had lied about it to her and sworn Lily to secrecy. The idea that her father was ashamed of her pained Virginia, but her relief that he had hidden the truth from Vera was far greater. She had thought about what happened in the Park Theater lobby for hours that day in the carriage, but she still did not have an explanation for her actions, at least not one that Vera could possibly accept.

Vera was still nervously leafing through the letter, which ran to many pages. Virginia could judge from the florid handwriting that Albert was not its author.

"I only wish Albert *had* written it," lamented Vera, "for it is a very gallant letter, full of compliments to me and passionate expressions. No—it is not Albert's style at all. It is from Mr. Leadbetter."

Virginia could not comprehend for a moment what Vera had said, so she simply repeated her last words. "Mr. Leadbetter."

"Yes, but you must have guessed. He was so particular in his attentions to me at Mrs. Geyer's party. Then, at the theater, I thought him so very heroic in the face of that terrible mob—I was so worried for him. You will blame me for this, I know, but I sent a message to Mr. Walker the following day—a message for Mr. Leadbetter. Then yesterday morning Mr. Walker brought me this reply, which Mr. Leadbetter wrote from Boston."

Virginia looked at her in astonishment. "You have been in secret correspondence with Edmund Leadbetter?"

"It sounds very bad when you put it like that, when it has only been one letter each."

"Yours being the first."

Vera blushed. "I knew you would blame me and say it wasn't proper. But I felt so angry for him at the wrongs he suffered in New York. I wanted him to know that there was at least one of us who knew what was due to him, to an artist of his great standing."

"I'm sure he was grateful for your support, but I don't see . . ."

"But there is more than thanks in his letter, Virginia. This is what I have tried to tell you. He is leaving directly from Boston back to England. And he wishes me to join him!"

"Join him? As his wife?"

"No, no." Vera gave a look of horror, then could not suppress a giggle. "I hope my family will come with me. I will ask my father this evening. Oh, Virginia, how could you think I would marry him? I am to be his partner on the stage, not in life. He wishes me to join the company at Drury Lane! Can you believe it?"

Virginia took a moment to absorb the news. She shook her head.

"No, I cannot believe it. You have a contract with Mr. Burfield at the Bowery Theater. And you have not even made your debut!"

"Well, Mr. Leadbetter says I deserve better than the Bowery Theater. That I will not be appreciated here as I ought. I must return to England with him, he says, or he will throw himself into Boston Harbor in despair. But what's the matter? You must believe me!"

"I believe Mr. Leadbetter capable of writing such a letter to a young woman he barely knows. What I don't believe is that you are planning to run away with him!"

"I will not be running away with him!" Vera sounded angry, then seemed to regret it immediately. She looked pleadingly at Virginia and brought her to sit with her on the bed. "Please don't think the worst of me."

"I won't think the worst of you," said Virginia, "if you tell me how you really feel."

"About Mr. Leadbetter? I don't know what I feel. I don't know him."

"And about Albert?"

"You know that I love him."

"You love him and yet you are going to England?"

Vera took her hand and smiled. "I see what you mean. But you don't know Albert as I do. I value him more than I show sometimes, and I wouldn't give him up for anything. You think I am giddy and ignorant—don't deny it!—but I understand enough of the world and our woman's lot in it to realize that a handsome, well-born young gentleman of liberal opinions is very hard to find." She gave another little laugh and squeezed Virginia's hand. "You'll see, dearest. Albert will understand that I have to go to London. And he will wait for me to come back. Now what are you thinking?—You have such an odd expression."

Because there was nothing Virginia could say, she simply nodded. This response seemed to confuse Vera the more, but before she could inquire further Vera's mother appeared at the door, sun hat at the ready, to invite them for a walk down to the river. It was a beautiful spot, and one so rarely got invitations to Ambleside. They should definitely make the most of it.

Vera immediately got up and fetched her hat. Virginia declined to join them, pleading a headache that though it was no fabrication, was not the reason she didn't wish to go.

"Are you quite alright?" said Vera, looking at her with concern.

"Yes. I just need to rest."

When Vera had gone, Virginia went over to the window and watched mother and daughter walk across the lawn and down through the cypress trees. Vera had already taken off her hat and was skipping lightly down the lane. Watching her, Virginia marveled at her friend's amazing ebullience. Even after all the trauma of the past three days, and with an extraordinary decision on her future looming before her, Vera could still enjoy the simple pleasure of a walk to the river on a summer evening. Virginia envied her deeply. While Vera embraced the full possibilities of each moment, and the world lovingly returned that embrace, she was always holding back, thinking not of the present but the future. She had always chosen to admire it as a mark of virtuous ambition that she put so much store in her "destiny," but now she felt a hollow feeling in her stomach as she wondered if it was all an illusion: if on her last day on earth she would still be looking into her imaginary future, only to see at last the slow death she had been living all along.

Vera had often warned her against useless morbidity, and she caught herself now. She brought a chair over to the window and sat down with her legs propped on the sill, just as if she were back in her room at Park Row. She looked out at the untroubled blue sphere of sky above the trees and willed her mind-clouds away. After all, this was no time for philosophy. Whatever future she was to have was now unfolding before her eyes, with startling quickness. She had to fight from feeling overwhelmed by it all. Only a week ago, she had been living her long-running melodrama of unrequited love for Albert Dash, a drama so familiar to her it seemed to have no beginning or end, as if she had always been in love and unhappy. Now, everything was in motion. She had thrown herself at Albert at the Park Theater and almost been killed for it. Vera was setting off for England. And Albert would either wait for Vera or he would not. What had seemed the interminable course of fate now seemed contracted into the risks and feelings of a few days. Would Albert even survive this terrible fever outbreak? The hollow feeling of a few moments ago returned. There could be no comfort in thinking about Albert, of where he might be at that moment. So Virginia let her eyes drift again into the glorious indifferent blue, and imagined herself with Vera down on the riverbank, laughing and playing like two children of nature.

CHAPTER THIRTY-FIVE

Circumstances being what they were at Ambleside, no one looked for the usual forms of hospitality to be observed. Mr. Geyer told his cook to assume the guests would take dinner in their rooms, and that those venturing downstairs should be received by an informal buffet without attendants. In the event, Mr. Geyer was joined only by Mr. Laidlaw, not out of a desire for each other's conversation, but for an hour's relief from the company of their wives. After an exchange of pleasantries and a solitary failed attempt at conversation from Sam Geyer, the two men ate their meal in silence.

During the interminable evening that followed, they all felt the agony of being useless. They had found sanctuary from the yellow fever at Ambleside, but not from the idea of it. Images of disaster haunted their minds: "I'm sure Bowling Green is burned to the ground," lamented Mrs. Laidlaw, on retiring finally at eleven. And because they could do nothing to discredit them, their fears grew steadily worse: "We are all doomed!" Mrs. Laidlaw cried out, sitting bolt upright in her bed at three. With the exception of her husband, who slept peacefully beside her, Ambleside, for all its lullaby of crickets and crisp nighttime air, offered little rest for fever-jaded spirits.

John Laidlaw was the first to come downstairs in the morning. He padded quietly down the hall and into Samuel Geyer's study. It was like some mad hermit's cave. Where the walls weren't covered with maps and diagrams, bookshelves rose up to the ceiling, packed densely with leatherbound volumes and scrolled papers squeezed in at every angle.

He walked over to the desk. Amid piles of loosely stacked sheets crammed with calculations, a large parchment page was spread out flat. A work in progress. Its subject was clear even to a layman. The drawing represented Sam Geyer's answer to the perennial argument over how best to transport water from Westchester across the Harlem River to the thirsty island of Manhattan. Some had suggested that a very low, inexpensive bridge would do: traffic was scarce on that part of the river and the flood tide negligible in most years. Others had argued that the gradient necessary to maintain the aqueduct's flow required a high, sturdy structure, built of stone for the ages.

Sam Geyer clearly adhered to the second school of thought. Moreover, his design suggested that the bridge should do more than simply serve its function. His lofty, granite creation, with its graceful Roman arches and columns decorated with heroic motifs of agriculture and industry, seemed to insist that the very highest ideals of civic culture in the New World should be fulfilled by the Croton River aqueduct.

"Poor fool," muttered John Laidlaw.

The drawing was unfinished. The northern shore of Manhattan Island was not filled in, and the last section of the bridge simply projected into empty space like an unanswered question. Lifting his hand from the page, Laidlaw found a thin film of dust covering his fingers. Not only had Geyer left his vision unrealized, it was clear he had done no work on it in recent days.

Laidlaw walked over to the large bay window. It faced south, overlooking the gravel drive and the lawn dotted with drooping chestnut trees. He gazed over their lofty heights in the direction of the city, smiling to himself.

He heard a sound behind him. Casey and Geyer had arrived together. They looked solemn and unrested.

"Good morning, gentlemen. I hope you slept well." He turned back to the window. "My driver Gibbs set off before dawn. He should return with news around three o'clock. I trust both of you will be ready to accompany me at that time? We will go directly to City Hall, if there is no objection."

He smiled as he posed the question, but that smile vanished on his turning to receive their answer, which took the form of a pistol pointed at the center of his chest.

"Here is your objection," said Casey. "Please take a seat, sir. If you call out, I will take great pleasure in shooting you."

Laidlaw remained standing reluctantly for a moment. Then he sat down on a Windsor chair nearest the window.

"I hope you will excuse me if I don't raise my hands. I am rarely armed at this hour of the morning, especially when enjoying the hospitality of my friends."

"I am not your friend," said Sam Geyer.

"That's clear enough. You lured me here as a deliberate trap."

"Just so," said Casey. "Returning the favor, if you will."

"I don't know what you mean."

"Don't insult us with denials, sir," said Geyer. "We know everything. You may have made fools of us, but not Albert Dash. He saw it all. Your villainous banking scheme, the plot to cover up the yellow fever. Everything. He is a son-in-law you don't deserve."

A slight frown crept across John Laidlaw's forehead. Casey lowered the gun but did not put it away.

"If you still have your heart set on returning to the city, we can certainly oblige you there. Only there will be a slight change of destination. No more than half a block. Instead of City Hall, we'll drop you off at Bridewell Jail."

"Oh, I don't think so," said Laidlaw, pressing the tips of his fingers together. "Whatever my misdeeds may be, you both have your share in them. Who, in a court of law, would believe an independent-minded man of your stature and experience, Mr. Casey, could be practiced upon to do anything that was not of his own free will? I will bring you down with me, sir. And you too, Geyer."

A flush of anger welled up in Casey's face, but Sam Geyer stepped forward quickly and put a restraining grip on his gun hand.

"I anticipated this from him, Eamonn. What else would you expect? He is the greatest scoundrel since Burr."

Laidlaw smiled and rested his arm against the window.

"But we *will* share your cell in Bridewell," Geyer went on, "before we see you return to business in our city. You are finished in New York."

"You want me to go back to England?"

"To Hell if you'd prefer it," said Casey.

Laidlaw pursed his lips. "I will go, but only if I go freely. I want no constables at my heels and no scandal following me to London."

Geyer and Casey looked at each other, grim-faced.

"Either that," Laidlaw continued, "or we take our chances in the Manhattan courts, before judges who know me as a very generous friend."

"Very well," said Casey, "but you will leave your New York assets here."

Laidlaw raised an eyebrow. "Now I see why you are eager to stay out of the courts!"

"You've got it wrong, sir," said Geyer. "Not a penny is for either of us. Your money will go toward fulfilling your many broken promises. It will help break ground for the aqueduct. The little fraud you practiced on us will become a great reality, with your help."

Laidlaw looked at them with contempt. "You will never build it. It is a ludicrous scheme. And you two are bumbling amateurs."

"That may be. But it will be built all the same," said Geyer.

"Sam is right," said Casey. "Even if we don't live long enough to drink a single cup from it ourselves, that aqueduct will be built."

Laidlaw scoffed and muttered something. Casey put the gun back in his pocket, while Geyer walked back behind his desk and gazed at his unfinished drawing of the Harlem River bridge. Then he looked up.

"But we are left with the problem of your departure, Mr. Laidlaw. How is it to be managed?"

Laidlaw sat back, lightly tapping the ring on his finger against the window. "The truth is I already have a plausible pretext for returning to London. Vera has received an invitation to join the theater company at Drury Lane and wishes very much for us to take the next packet out of Boston. I said no to her last night, but I may yet play the indulgent father and say yes this morning."

Casey and Geyer looked at him, astonished.

"Vera at Drury Lane!"

"It is not so incredible as that," said Laidlaw. "Mr. Leadbetter might not have seen her onstage—it is true that she has never properly been onstage at all—but he has already declared her to be the next Sarah Siddons. He wishes her to play in *Romeo and Juliet* with him this season in London."

Sam Geyer could not suppress a grin. "Of all the things"—he shook his head in wonder—"I declare that girl's a marvel. You may not be missed in New York, sir, but your remarkable daughter surely will be!"

CHAPTER THIRTY-SIX

Virginia was dressing for breakfast, had just hitched her last stay into place, when she was startled by a great crashing sound and shouts coming from the front of the house.

She ran to the window in time to see Mr. Laidlaw pick himself up from a pool of shattered glass below her and set off at a run down the gravel drive in the direction of Mr. Geyer's stables. Virginia then saw her father leap through the broken study window and set off in pursuit, waving a pistol in the air. He was followed, in more cumbersome fashion, by Mr. Geyer.

Virginia didn't wait to see any more. She sped out the door and down the stairs, two at a time. She ran straight past a shrieking Aurelia Geyer at the front door and out onto the gravel path.

Her father had caught up to Mr. Laidlaw some distance from the stable gate. She saw him throw the gun away and wrap his great bears arms around Mr. Laidlaw as if trying to crush him. But the smaller man slipped from his grasp, jumped on his back and began pounding the back of his head with his fists.

Sam Geyer came lumbering up, looking for a way to intervene. "The stables, Sam," cried Casey, between blows on his ears. "Lock up the stables—I'll deal with him."

So Sam Geyer kept running past them down the hill toward an astonished stableboy who had emerged, muck bucket in hand, to watch the action. He saw his master waving his arms at him but showed no comprehension of what he could possibly mean by it.

Meanwhile, Casey had wrenched himself free. He was holding his bad shoulder and grimacing in pain but he waded in once more to launch his good fist at Laidlaw's head. Laidlaw parried it with surprising deftness and jabbed him on the very point of his shoulder. Casey cried out in pain but still reached out again, using his superior height to subdue the smaller, quicker man. They grappled awkwardly and soon tumbled brawling into the dust.

Virginia ran toward them shouting at them to stop, but they kept flailing their arms, landing blows mostly in the dirt. Laidlaw escaped once more and scrambled to his feet, but Casey tripped him up and they wrestled again, heads and arms locked in the middle of the path where they would have been run down by an oncoming carriage, hidden in a column of its own dust, had not Virginia run ahead, begun jumping up and down and screaming loud enough for the oncoming team of horses to hear her. It was clear the driver had heard nothing at all, because when the horses pulled up a yard from where Virginia stood with her eyes closed and arms raised, Gibbs looked at her as if she were an escapee from Bedlam.

"Saints preserve us, Miss," Gibbs grunted, breathing hard, "I almost runned you clean over."

Then he saw his master and Mr. Casey running toward him, covered entirely in dust. Laidlaw was bleeding from one ear, Casey from a cut above his eye. Gibbs's eyes grew wider still.

"You've all gone mad," he said under his breath.

"Gibbs, what are you doing?" shouted Laidlaw. "Why have you come back?"

"Sorry, sir. I went as far as the Canal but I reckoned my life weren't worth fishbait goin' any further than that. They've blocked the road south. A fellah told me there's hundreds dead and dying in the city. Streets filled with 'em. And you got gangs roaming about robbing the dead. I want no part of it, job or no job."

"What news from City Hall?" said Laidlaw. "What's being done?"

"No one left at the Hall, sir. Yesterday, there was word of fever on the Bowery, north of it. Since then, it's every man for himself."

"Jesus and Mary, it's happened," cried Casey. "It's an epidemic!"

"And what news from the hospital?" said Virginia.

"Bless you, Miss, that is the only good news I heard. I saw some porters on their way to Bellevue. Dr. Miller, they say, left days ago. He's gone off to Long Island, they say."

"Damn coward," said Laidlaw.

"But Dr. Hosack, you see, has taken over. He'll set things to rights. He's a good man, that doctor, for all that say he isn't."

Gibbs here gave a baleful sidelong glance at Casey, who looked very pale.

"Is Dr. Hosack all alone?" said Virginia. "Is there no one there to help him?"

"A couple of nurses stayed on, they say, and some black folks the doctor knows. They can't catch the fever, you know, the black folks."

"Anyone else?"

"I can guess who," said Laidlaw, and spat into the dust.

Casey, too, stared at the ground and turned away.

"Yes, Miss. There is Miss Laidlaw's young gentleman friend," said Gibbs. "Young Mr. Dash has been there from the start."

Sam Geyer came running up with the stableboy, who moved to restrain the fugitive. But Laidlaw cursed angrily and pushed him away, and began walking back to the house alone. Gibbs meanwhile took Virginia and her father in the carriage. She set him back on the seat and began to clean the cut above his eye with her handkerchief. He reached for her hand.

"Ginny, forgive me," he said between heavy breaths.

"Hush."

"That man—I did his bidding. The devil's business."

She squeezed his hand. "Not now. Tell me later—when it's all over."

John Laidlaw arrived first at the house and walked into the parlor. His collar and shirt had been ripped, he was shedding dust on the carpet in great clouds, and a little stream of blood flowed from his ear down his neck.

"I need spirits, Geyer, and some gauze to stop this damn bleeding," he said to his host, who had followed him inside.

"My man will tend to you, sir. You will find him in the yard."

Laidlaw disappeared into the kitchen at the precise moment Eamonn Casey wobbled in the front door, accompanied by his daughter. He held a bloody handkerchief to his forehead.

Mrs. Casey, who had heard the commotion but could get no coherent account from Aurelia Geyer, met them in the hall. She gave a small cry at the sight of her battered husband and reached out eager hands toward him. She put his great arm around her shoulder and made as if to carry him up the stairs herself. He could walk well enough, but he allowed himself to be cosseted in this way.

He gave Virginia's hand a parting squeeze, and she watched their lopsided progress up the stairs for a moment, struck by her mother's unusual animation, her lively chatter of concern. Then she went to look for Lily Riley.

Back in her room, Virginia found Vera standing at the window. She held something in her hand, concealed from Virginia's sight by the folds of her skirts.

"What has happened?"

"Your father has had an argument with my father. And Gibbs is back already. He says the situation in the city is very bad."

"It must be. I can see fires," said Vera, without turning around.

"Gibbs says they are burning the dead in great piles—and the houses of the sick where there is infection."

"So it is an epidemic, just as Dr. Hosack said it would be."

Virginia went to look at the faint smear of smoke above the tree-lined horizon. They stood in silence for a long moment. Vera bent her head. "Can there be anything more horrible than this? Virginia, what will we do?"

"You are safe here at Ambleside."

"We are prisoners here! I feel helpless."

"It is better if you stay."

"If *I* stay?" Vera turned to face her. "And what about you?"

Virginia went to the door and closed it. Then she came and sat on the bed and began to pull off her shoes and stockings.

"I must wash my clothes—be as clean as I can manage. I have time before nightfall."

"What are you talking about? Are you quite well?"

"I am leaving here tonight to go to Bellevue Hospital. Dr. Hosack needs nurses. I want to help."

"And how will you get from here to Bellevue? It is more than thirty miles. Your father will never allow it."

"I will not tell him. Lily Riley knows the stableboy here. She is going to arrange a horse for me. If I ride all night, I can be at Bellevue before noon."

Vera was silent for a moment. She walked over to the bed.

"Don't go, Virginia, I beg you. It is madness. The very air in that hospital will be a death warrant. It will be chaos."

"Dr. Hosack is in charge again at Bellevue. And he needs help."

Vera looked at her searchingly, and nodded to herself. Then, in an altered voice, she said, "I know why you are going. It is not only to help the doctor."

Virginia had stepped over to the bellpull to ring for the maid, but now she stopped. She turned and saw Vera draw her hand from behind her back and place a large sheet of drawing paper faceup on the bed directly between them. It was the picture of an orchid, with purple petals like clasped hands, the stem a long, fine, tapering arm. They both looked at the drawing.

"You love him, don't you?" There was no note of challenge in Vera's voice—it was barely a question at all.

Virginia held her breath, then exhaled. "Yes, I do."

"You have loved him for a long time?"

Virginia nodded. "You have been looking in my trunk."

"I'm sorry for that," said Vera. "But you have been acting so strangely. Last night, I began to wonder whether it might not only be your knock on the head. And this morning, as I was walking in the orchard with Michael and mother, it came to me that I would find the answer in your enormous trunk, so I came back."

She pointed to Virginia's precious leather folder sitting in full view on the dressing table. Virginia was shocked she had not noticed it. Inside could be seen the carefully folded edges of Albert's drawings. Virginia felt a sudden panic come over her, as if someone had walked in on her naked. Vera looked at her now as if she just had.

"If a girl has a single trunk to take away with her for who knows how long, she fills it with clothes, unless she has a very, very good reason to bring something else."

A long silence. A silence different from any other Virginia had known. She thought they would have to learn some whole new language in order to break it.

Then Vera said, "You cannot help it that you love him. I do not blame you for it. I should feel betrayed, but instead I feel—I feel something different. I thought I was in love with Albert—and now there is Mr. Leadbetter." She paused. "You know, I have been staring at this beautiful picture and thinking how much you must have suffered to be my friend while you were in love with him. And suffered in being his friend, too. Does he know yet that you love him?"

Virginia shook her head while a jumble of other thoughts raced through her mind. She felt amazement and gratitude and relief bubbling over her. Vera did not hate her!

"But you are so secretive and Albert is so dense!" her friend cried. "How will you ever understand each other?"

"The secrecy is all over," said Virginia firmly. "I mean to tell him as soon as I find him. Then, whatever happens, at least he will know the truth."

"When did you decide this?"

"Last night, when I realized finally that you did not actually love him. For a long time I believed you when you said you did. It was only last night I understood that you were using the word to mean something else." She went over to Vera and took her hand. "Vera, you must tell him that you don't love him, and I must tell him that I do. He needs to stop suffering for no reason and so do I. That is, if it is not too late."

Vera looked fearfully at her, then she nodded. But when Virginia turned away, Vera held her back. She put her hands on her friend's shoulders, and gazed at her earnestly.

"You may think it is hopeless, but let me be right for once and say that you are wrong. You are very pretty, you know," as she tucked an errant blond curl behind Virginia's ear. "You will not love for no reason."

Vera reached for the bellpull and tugged it hard twice.

"Now we must wash our clothes, as you say. Luckily, I thought to bring my tough cotton skirt. It rained last night and will likely rain again."

Virginia looked at her in surprise and made to speak.

"Please don't say anything at all," Vera said, stopping her mouth. "We've said all there is to say. I won't be left behind, that's all."

CHAPTER THIRTY-SEVEN

When Albert and Dr. Hosack arrived at the hospital, they discovered that Dr. Miller had already abandoned his post. They walked up the stone steps and through the great brass-knobbed doors into an eerie emptiness. The doctor turned to Albert and made a smacking gesture with his lips, a look of distaste. Albert nodded. Exploring the halls, they heard the sound of laughter from the director's office. The porters had broken into the spirits cabinet. Two of the nurses lounged on a table, one kissing a shirtless man. The doctor flew into a rage. He beat two of the men to the floor, and when one of the drunken slatterns cursed him for it, he slapped her across the face and set her down in a chair.

Mounting the stairs to the wards, they found themselves enveloped in a sickening vapor. Albert had smelt it before, at Duggan's bedside in Brooklyn, on the deck of the *Belladonna*, but never before so deep in his throat. Every breath felt like drinking a poison fluid of the air—violent pangs in his stomach—and urge to vomit—

"Come on!" cried the doctor, coming back to where he had doubled over at the turn of the stairs. "Don't think of it! And don't stop, even for a moment!"

He took him by the arm and dragged him up to the landing.

This first episode did not appall him. The fear had been in the anticipation of it. Now the fever was finally here he felt crazily invigorated. It was the pure freedom of life-in-death.

They found a line of empty coffins crowded at the door to the ward. Empty but for one whose lid had not been nailed down. A man lay in it, livid yellow, dead flesh rolled back from his bones, eyes stark open, as if at the moment of death he had seen a ghastly vision of what lay beyond.

"Leave him," said the doctor.

They stepped into the sick ward where a still worse sight presented itself. A long room crammed with cots, three feet apart. Twenty heads lifted from their pillows. "Water," whispered the nearest, motioning to his mouth. Others thrashed from side to side on their beds unaware of their presence, locked in the fever's private embrace.

"How long have they been here?" he said.

The doctor pointed to three lying motionless in stinking linen in their cots.

"At least seven days for those three and our friend outside. That scoundrel Miller has served Laidlaw well, for God knows what reward."

They walked the length of the ward, sidestepping what they could not identify on the floor.

"Call down below for those dead to be taken away. They go first. Then we change the sheets. I have sent for Gertie. She will bring her women with her to make up a washing detail. Twice a day, no exceptions, every bed—and the dead buried in their linen. God's mercy, it's stuffy. I have never breathed more putrid air."

They pulled the blankets from the windows—Miller had taken care to hide his work from the view of the street—and then opened them to a stiff hot breeze. The room flooded with light. Groans from the beds the whole length of the ward. The light distressed them more than the suffocating heat.

Now downstairs to see the porters again. The doctor announced that Albert was to superintend them while he managed the sick ward. If he heard word of a shirker or a troublemaker, he promised to personally cut them up and feed them to the fish in the East River. They were silent and subdued.

Albert walked out onto the front steps with his crew and considered the scene with a sinking heart. He had imagined this day a thousand times, lain awake at night, arranging it scene by scene in his mind. But now everything seemed unfamiliar, an impossibility. The simplest facts of the situation confounded him. He looked out over the empty lots and the meadows marked by red flags. It was a mile and a half in the sultry, dusty heat to the Bowery and the same again to the docks. He had twenty intoxicated, barely willing men to command and a shortage of stretchers and coffins, not to mention carts. How were the sick to be brought here, and in this heat? He would fail before he had even begun.

One of the men—tall, Irish—must have seen his distress and patted him on the shoulder.

"Don't concern yourself, lad. The carts'll be here soon now that the doctor's come—and we'll sober up in the meantime."

He told them to sit over in the shade to wait. He brought them water in flasks from the hospital's precious stores, which instantly reconciled them to his command. They stopped cursing him under their breath and even began to assume an air of purpose about them, like men on the eve of battle.

As the Irishman had promised, the carts began to appear. First one, then a stream of three, four. He asked the first driver if he knew where others were to be found and how many. He replied there were more than enough for the men he had, but they had stayed away since Dr. Miller's leaving, thinking they wouldn't get paid. But he could fetch them now. They would be at the river watering their horses and staying out of the bad air—but he would bring them to Bellevue within the hour or his mother weren't born a virgin.

Other carts pulled up. He recognized the crew from the grave-yard at Nassau Street.

"Well, hoot! It's Mr. Albert. We'll get paid sure enough, now. He's got that honest face and has dug graves with the black man. Stands to reason, a man who's been to the grave's end and back is good for his debts."

The other porters appeared encouraged at this report. Some even tipped their caps to him as they mounted up, four to a cart, three coffins and two stretchers.

He left the Irishman in charge of the rest with orders to go to the Bowery.

He took his seat in the cart at the head of the first party, making for the docks. He carried a pistol inside his jacket and an enormous ring of keys at his belt. The doctor would have Albert enter the houses of the sick through the front door like a Christian, not smash his way inside. They moved at a steady pace, but anxiously slow. Right onto Houston Street and its irregular spread of half-built houses and empty lots. Across the Bowery then to Broadway, heading south. At Canal Street, they crossed a makeshift picket barricade and entered the infected district. Instead of a melee of cabs and carriages and shop windows swarmed with people, they rode into an empty silence. The windows of the upper stories, just days ago filled with faces and shouts of glee or derision to the street below, were now closed up.

At Duane Street, they glimpsed a hearse cart rumbling around the corner. A boy ran alongside the cart calling out "Coffins! Coffins to fit! All sizes!" in a lusty voice, as if he were selling butcher's meat on some ordinary day in the city. When Albert heard him the memories, vivid as truth, came flooding back to his mind. A scene he had not even dreamt about in more than eight years:

He was eleven years old. A quiet afternoon in the heat of August. He sat by the parlor window at their old house on Greenwich Street. Mother was out. Only Aunt Mary was there, asleep from the heat in her chair. He was dreaming of something. He saw a man walk wearily down from the corner of Broadway. The man hesitated at the window, then lay down on the steps at the front door. He went to him. The man's face was yellow as a tanner's boots, his clothes damp with sweat. He thought to fetch his aunt, but some instinct made him secretive. He sneaked into the kitchen—past Aunt, fat and asleep in her chair—and brought a brimful jug of water to the man on the steps. He bathed his head in cool towels. By dusk, the man could no longer lift his head—he didn't know he was there. A final shocking spasm frightened him. He stood with his back fast to the wall and watched until the end. Later, listening from his upstairs room, he heard his father's footsteps on the street and his exclamation of indignant surprise. He was not expecting a body on the doorstep. Soon after, three porters arrived. They talked in rough voices. He heard hammering—a lid being nailed on a pine-board box. Then their heavy steps when they took the dead man away. The next summer, the porters returned. This time, they took away his mother and his father and his cousins.

Now the fever had come again at last, like a returning angel, hovering over the city on bright expectant wings. All along Broadway were great trenches left by the fleeing vehicles the day before. The overnight rain had transformed the street into a delta of stagnant streams marked by high soft banks of yellow mud. It made their passage slow and perilous. Below Chambers Street, they drove into a swarming, buzzing cloud. The driver slapped his neck.

"Damn mosquitoes!" he grunted.

By the time they reached City Hall Park, Albert had counted only seven people in all on the streets. Ghostly figures, wrapped in winter cloaks, cloths of vinegar held to their faces. At the approach of their morbid procession—carts filled with coffins and grim-faced thugs—these ghosts shifted course to avoid them. They watched the carts pass from beneath the shade of the shop awnings, their eyes filled with suspicion and loathing.

Albert saw no sign of the rampaging bulls he had heard rumors of. But he saw more domestic animals than he had ever seen in his life. The disappearance of much of the city's perishable food had forced the rats into the street, where a large army of cats, abandoned by their owners, had joined their feral brethren on the streets and were reclaiming their predatory birthright with a bloody vengeance. Squalling intermittently pierced the air, and rat corpses littered the road and doorways, so that a time-traveler might have been misled into thinking this was a scene from the Middle Ages, a gruesome tour of the Black Death. If a rat history were ever to be written, Albert thought, this would surely be their Waterloo.

He looked back along Broadway into the sun and gave a sudden start. In that instant of turning around he was sure he saw Death itself in an orb of light, in a crinkle of heat above the roofs. The retinal vision vanished in an instant, but it left the shape of a terrible dread on his mind. He believed, with a sudden absolute conviction, that the yellow fever had marked him out—that even now it was gliding down from the sky toward him in a flutter of soundless wings.

The party of carts gathered at the iron gates of City Hall. They had traveled with maddening slowness but even so the horses breathed hard in the heat. He sent the three other drivers further westward to the Hudson docks. They were to bury the dead in shallow graves and transport the living back to Bellevue. His cart continued alone, southward on Broadway.

"What about that there?" asked the driver.

He followed the direction of his pointing hand toward the East River, where great trees of smoke were pouring into the sky from the direction of Water Street.

"That's a three-house fire, I'd say," said the porter beside him, a nervous Irishman given to muttering under his breath and making the sign of the cross.

"It's a warehouse, for sure," said his partner, a bigger, scar-faced man. "Looters everywhere on those docks." He looked at Albert questioningly. "We could pick 'em up, no problem at all." He took out an ugly-looking club from his jacket and began slapping it in his hand.

The other porter looked alarmed. "No. Not enough time. Not enough time."

The driver turned around, and all three looked at Albert.

"Let it burn," he said.

They headed east instead to Nassau Street.

"I think we got our first customer," said the driver, pointing to a doorway near an alley. A figure stood there barely upright, crumpled against the door. Albert told the two porters to bring a stretcher. The man—young, he thought, but it was hard to tell—scarcely moved as Albert felt his hands and placed a thumb and finger on his throbbing temples. His lips were blood red, his eyes covered in a strange, rheumy film, like milk in a glass. His skin was already wrinkled, the color of candle wax. It had to be his third or fourth day.

"Take him."

They did not get much further. At the corner of Liberty Street, a man with black stains on his shirt approached to tell them that his father, wife and child were dead. Three more boxes in the cart.

On almost every block, they saw evidence of looting. Sometimes they saw the looters themselves, maneuvering furniture through doorways or throwing rugs and paintings and jewelry boxes out of the upper windows down to their confederates waiting below, who strapped the treasures onto already-laden carts. These men eyed Albert and his crew warily as they passed by, but although the big porter slapped his club into his hand with a belligerent air, and Albert would have liked nothing better than to make a bloody mess of them, he told the driver to keep steady and keep going.

Once they came across a man unconscious and bleeding in the street. He was lying in a puddle of kerosene and broken glass. He had taken a sackful of crystal lamps from a nearby house, but had not got fifty feet with his booty before the fever caught up to him and administered its quick justice.

Soon the coffins were piled head high, and they began making their way back to the churchyard. "Is that the old man from John Street knocking?" said the thin porter next to him, looking warily at the pine box under his left foot. "I swear when we lowered him in, he gave me a look that said we was early and should wait some minutes yet for him."

The other man gave the coffin a kick with his big boot. "You'll have the horse talking to us next. They was all dead."

As they pulled up and took out the spades, the nervous porter was still muttering to himself.

"Can a dead man shed a tear? God's my witness, I saw him look over at his little boy and his lips were moving too like he was praying. But you just nailed him in all the same, you godless bugger."

"I'll dig an extra pit for you if you don't stop yer mumbling," grunted the big porter, brandishing his spade.

"Dig, and be quick about it!" Albert shouted at them. "Dr. Hosack's paying you by the body not the hour!"

That silenced them both, and in half an hour they were heading back to Bellevue with two more victims groaning softly on stretchers under their feet. They had found them lying on the steps of the church.

And so it went through the long heat of the day until the light faded. There was nobody to light the street lamps, and they could not work in the dark. The rhythm of the cart beneath him blurred with the rhythm of the nails hammered into pine board and so many foreheads felt and pulses checked. By the day's end, he didn't know whether it was two trips or twenty or fifty. So many houses with the odor of death about them. They had smelled gunpowder, vinegar and the other hopeful perfumes used to ward off the fever, but acrid death overpowered them all. From house to silent house they went, not knowing if the next moment they might turn the stair to come upon the final act of some tragic play, the characters unknown, only bodies strewn in a bedroom or parlor in artistic death or near-death, as if awaiting an audience and their strange, silent acclamation.

One scene stood out: a boy, no more than ten years old, alone. He lay curled in his bed, his feet and fingers strangely cold, a terrible vapor around him. Albert felt the angel still there when they arrived, hovering invisible, a kiss's height above him. The boy's skin was not saffron-colored but yellow-green like the rind of a ripe lime. The linen beneath him, unchanged in days, was stained black. Beside him, a coffin lay ready on the floor. Who had put it there? He heard the muttering porter say *vomito prieto*—black vomit, the fever was black to the Spanish—but then thought it more likely an Irish blessing he did not understand. The other porter stood toying with hammer and nails, his gaze fixed on a place on the wall a foot above the boy, who had died before their eyes in a single, hectic convulsion.

They came downstairs to find two men rolling up the rug from the floor, while a third removed brass fittings from the wall. Albert grabbed the porter's club and laid into them with a fury, smashing the brass fittings from the looter's hands and belting him hard across the back as he turned to flee. The other two dropped the rug and leapt out the window. The big porter looked at Albert with more respect after this, though Albert knew how useless his rage had been when he later saw the same three men looting a draper's store not two blocks away. The man he had beaten simply cursed at him and went back to stacking rolls of bright blue silk.

At some point in the afternoon, on their fifth trip, or sixth, the porters stopped squabbling and the driver lost interest in everything but the condition of his horse's foreleg.

"It's these damn roads," he called from where he knelt by the road, tending to his horse. It was the third time in a hour he had stopped. "First Avenue's not fit for an old bessie like her. You can see how she's pulling up. I don't care what you're paying—it's not worth a lame horse to me."

Albert stepped down out of the cart, feeling very tired. He reached into his jacket and pulled out the pistol. He pointed it at the driver's chest.

"Get back in the cart. No more stopping."

He heard the big porter laugh grimly as the driver looked at him in angry surprise. He spat once in the dust, then got back on his seat.

After that, no one spoke at all.

Back at Bellevue, after nightfall, Albert had the strange thought that he did not know how he would climb the steps. That he would collapse half way.

A heavy hand on his shoulder in the hall. Dr. Hosack, looking impossibly fresh and strong.

"Dinner for you and your crew. Tell them they may go to Gertie in the downstairs kitchen."

"It is hot here."

"We will eat in Miller's office. It will be cooler there."

He called it Miller's office without a note of irony.

"We've had quite a day," he went on, taking off his white surgeon's coat and laying it sideways on the chair beside him. Albert sat on the opposite side of the desk, feeling intensely exhausted, a tingling buzz in his ears.

"Just a minute." The doctor returned with a lamp, freshly trimmed, which he placed on the desk between them. He must have flinched at it.

"It is too bright? I will turn it down."

The bright, starry ball grew smaller as if it were suddenly much further away, with the doctor himself across the table—talking now from the end of a long tunnel.

"A bad moment came when we thought Miller had taken all the keys, but one of Gertie's people had worked here for him and knew the hiding place. We opened the cupboard upstairs and—praises be!—it's full of fresh-washed linen, still smelling of soap. Seems Miller didn't think to bother to make use of the hospital stores himself. I cannot remember a more welcome odor than that linen, not since my mother's breath at bedtime."

The doctor's voice sounded far away, muffled by the tingling in his brain. He thought, *I haven't recovered from the beating George Bickart's boys gave me.*

In the penumbra of the lamplight under the doctor's gesturing hand, the white coat lay draped on the chair. Before Albert's astonished eyes, it suddenly shook itself, then settled again as if to make itself more comfortable there. Gertie came in with another woman. They put plates of steaming stew and potato in front of them. He couldn't eat a morsel, but felt thirsty enough to drain the Atlantic.

"I would like claret."

"Eat first," the doctor mumbled, his mouth filled with stew.

Albert's eye was drawn again to an unnatural movement at the edge of the lamplight. To his horror, he saw the white coat begin its tricks once more. The sleeve, which had hung loosely over the back of the chair, slowly lifted itself up as if a living arm gave it motion. It all happened in a blurry, dreamy haze, at the very border of the light's reach into the darkness. But he could not mistake what he had seen.

"What damn trick is this!" He leapt to his feet. "We have them listening in to our every word! Will they eat with us?"

Dr. Hosack choked on a mouthful of stew. "For God's sake, Albert, calm yourself. It is only Gertie here, and she is leaving."

Dr. Hosack was staring at him with great disapproval. He saw him nod to Gertie.

"Forgive me." He sat down again, feeling cooler for the moment. With a supreme effort, he tore his eyes away from the white coat. He blinked hard and, for the first time in his life, experienced the heavy friction heat of his eyelids passing across his eyes.

"I can explain it . . ."

"Don't worry about your report," said Dr. Hosack. "For it will be the same again tomorrow. But why are you not eating?"

"Not again, not again." He said this to defy the white coat with his nonchalance. He stared resolutely straight ahead.

"What's that?" said the doctor.

"I'd be a fool to look again!" He gritted his teeth.

"Have you been drinking? Or have you gone mad?" The doctor stood up from his chair.

The white coat heaved with malignant violence. In a moment it would rise up and smother the doctor. How could he be blind to its intentions?

"The coat! The coat!"

"What about it? What the Devil is wrong with you?"

"Under it! Kill it there!"

The doctor picked up the white coat and threw it to the floor. It lay there misshapen, motionless.

"Damn it, Albert, what of the coat?"

He tried to answer, to claim at least the credit of saving the doctor from the evil white coat. He tried to explain, but the buzzing in his brain grew angrier and drowned out his voice. He felt his skin stretch like rubber across his face and neck. An eerie faintness possessed him. It wasn't yet delirium—he knew everything that was happening, though time seemed to slow, almost stop. The doctor called out into the hall. Gertie stood over him with a jug and threw cool water over his face. The water dried in an instant. He licked his parched lips with chagrin. A chill in the bones of his fingers like a burn, a tongue of ice at his heart, and as he closed his tired swimming eyes he thought, *this is death*.

CHAPTER THIRTY-EIGHT

When at last the moon appeared, they got up and dressed without speaking. Virginia forbade Vera to bring anything but a flask of water, and they left their trunks open on the bed next to the leather folio of Albert's drawings, which they had leafed through together while waiting for darkness to fall. Nor did they say a word as they crept along the hall, down the stairs, past the maid's door, through the kitchen, lightly lifting the latch and out into the moonlit yard. From there they crept around to the front of the house, avoiding the giveaway crunch of the gravel path.

The first sound either of them uttered was in the darkness of the stable. Vera said, "Oh!" when she caught sight of Lily Riley kissing the stableboy. Virginia pinched her hard, and Vera bit her lip. Lily had pulled Mr. Geyer's boy into the shadows among the piles of hay in the corner. From where they stood, crouched by the door, they saw the flash of her white skin against the darkness and heard his grateful sighs.

The covering sound allowed Vera and Virginia to find their way to the stalls of the carriage horses, where they found two princely chestnut mares stamping quietly side by side in their straw. From the complacent look in the horses' eyes and the saddles on their backs they seemed to be expecting their visitors, as if the midnight escape of young ladies from Ambleside were a thing of routine.

It was only when she had led her unprotesting mount out into the yard and, with Vera's help, vaulted herself up, did Virginia begin to believe that her wild plan might actually succeed. Sooner than she had thought it possible they were riding away toward the cover of the trees. Up the steep bank through the orchard and Virginia suddenly realized that there was no one now to stop them, no one with power to stop them had they wanted to. It was a strange free feeling—it submerged the tense, catch-breath fear of discovery—and she rode a wave of exhilaration until they reached the Albany Road.

Vera was a better rider than Virginia and rode the stronger horse. Nor could she resist giving her mount free rein and she galloped a half-mile ahead into the buzzing darkness. Virginia, cantering cautiously behind, turned the bend to find Vera waiting impatiently for her, hidden in the shadows like a highwayman.

"Why didn't you tell me you were such a hopeless rider?" Vera complained.

"It is dark, and I do not know the horse or the road."

"But your horse knows the road."

"I'm not fearless like you."

"I have an idea."

They swapped horses. Virginia took the more confident animal while Vera persuaded the best out of the other. Now they cantered side by side at a lively pace, Virginia emboldened by the physical courage of her friend, and the horses traveling better for working in partnership as they were used to under Mr. Geyer's harness.

After some hours, they came to the haunted union of the Hudson and Harlem rivers—the Dutch called it Spitting Devil. By now, a faint shell of light marked the horizon to their left. As they clattered over King's Bridge, Virginia's childish, goblin fear of the night gave way to a glowing impression of the beauty of Manhattan Island in the early dawn. Along the river bank, at distances of a half-mile or mile, they passed country manors covered in clambering vines, surrounded by hawthorn hedges and teeming gardens. But in all their hours on the road, they never saw a soul. It was as if they were the only two people left on earth. After a brief conference under the canopy of an enormous elm, they headed eastward to join the Boston Road. This took them through winding rural lanes lined with thickets and down into little valleys where glacial masses of dark rock crowded their heads, prompting even the confident Vera to slow her pace.

There were times in the sameness of the long night's journey when Virginia thought they might simply travel forever in this way, riding without fear or care into the arms of the depthless night. But with the sunrise came the reality of what they had embarked upon. The illuminated day withdrew the excuse of fantasy, and the sun's heat bore down on their faces. Another hour passed and the cool refreshment of the night had gone completely, and with it the fragile impression of an earth renewed.

Virginia noticed her mare had slowed without her command—shivering breaths, foam streaming from the mouth. All of a sudden, she too felt her own deep exhaustion that had been masked by the excitement of their escape and the exhilaration of riding. She heard a tinkling rush of water off in the woods to their right.

"Let's stop here," she called to Vera.

They dismounted and led their horses through the tall grass toward the sound of the running water. They came to a meadow where they were met by a pair of incredulous sheep. At the first sight of the horses, they scurried away with a warning bleat to their lambs wandering heedlessly nearby.

To the left down a small grassy bank, a line of birch trees leaned over a brook glinting in the sunlight. The horses whinnied their approval and soon all four of them, woman and beast, were bending their heads into the clear running stream, feeling the relief of pure water on their faces and in their mouths.

"We should rest," said Virginia after they had washed themselves and filled their flasks. Vera looked very tired and lay down on the grass without a word.

"Just an hour." Virginia lay down beside her. "We will be of no use at the hospital if we are dead on our feet. And who knows when we will sleep when we are there. Just an hour, then."

They lay within arm's reach together in the soft grass. The sounds of the enlivening day buzzed around them as they slept. Clouds of gnats hovered above, and nearby a pair of woodcocks quarreled over something discovered in the dirt. Once, a family of deer came down to the stream to drink. They looked warily at the horses munching on the grass but strode straight past the twin figures stretched along the bank. They seemed not to consider the strangeness of coming across people there and went down to the water in quiet, orderly pairs.

The hour stretched into two, and still Vera and Virginia lay motionless in the pillowy grass. If some traveler of a romantic turn of mind had happened to pass by the spot and found them there— two pale young women side by side near a secluded stream, in the deepest of death-like slumbers—he might have been excused for thinking they were slain by some mysterious conspiracy of love, or enchanted by a treacherous sprite of the nearby woods and gently imprisoned there, waiting to be awakened by a stranger's kiss.

CHAPTER THIRTY-NINE

Dr. Hosack's father had fought the British and would sometimes try to describe for his son the strange, slow-moving terror of battle. How the enemy, whom one had imagined to be gifted with superhuman speed and deadly foresight, in fact blundered about at a less-than-average rate. How the redcoats' muskets and packs unbalanced them as they charged, bringing some to grief on the most amiable of hillocks, sending others staggering into tree trunks.

Little advantage this to the patriots, who had flailed about in their own style. Some ran into each other, while others were still messing with their powder when they should have marked their man long ago. He himself had shot off a fellow patriot's ear and stabbed another in the foot before he killed his first British soldier.

The doctor had often thought of his father's words and their lesson: Do not look for order on the battlefield, only to manage the chaos. The patriots who were forever pointing and shouting—Do this! Go there!—were invariably the first to have their heads blown off. Just watch, absorb, direct. And never stop moving, not even for a moment.

The dust of the first carts had not settled before the doctor, Nurse Purvis at his side, unlocked the door to the hidden basement where rows of freshwater kegs stood expectantly in the gloom. The two sailors he had brought with him (the doctor had great respect for the competency of sailors) understood the task before he explained it, and within an hour had assembled a pulley system even the slightest of the nurses could operate, bringing a constant flow of water to the washing tubs and privies on the first floor and to the thirsty wards above.

It was according to the same principle of constant, multiple activity that they did not *wait* for the first carts to return. They simply raised the hum of their business and absorbed the sick into their midst. Columns of stretchers mounting the stairs, fevered bodies falling, almost gracefully, into beds. Gertie and her cohort had arrived from the estate, and there were now just enough nurses for alternating shifts: fours hours at the tubs, four in the wards, a break only for personal necessities.

The doctor divided his time between the wards and the front steps where the new arrivals—groaning in their already soiled sheets—awaited him. He checked the quiet ones first and sent the motionless away to the plot of ground by the east wall. The rest he followed upstairs, directing traffic with barely a word. A nod to Nurse Purvis or Gertie to indicate the first-day cases, still vomiting, while he himself focused on those at the critical phase, those in danger, from moment to moment, of a fatal hemorrhage.

Having seen so little of the yellow fever these last eight years, the doctor was struck anew by its stark difference from the common bilious or swamp fever that he saw every summer, and with which criminal fools like Dr. Miller had chosen to confuse it. As he moved slowly but irrepressibly through the ward, he saw, in case after case, that the eyes were more muddy and inflamed than in those native afflictions, how all complained of an unusual deep pain in the sockets and a racking pain in the back and limbs. Pulses rarely exceeded one hundred, and the fevers themselves did not appear intense, but the constant rolling of the eyeballs, an intermittent hysterical restlessness, and, most distinctive of all, a despondency of mind that no kind word or admonition could assuage could not be confused with any other fever in his long experience. A man with swamp fever fought the sweats and mind-bending hallucinations with every ounce of his strength. But with the yellow jack he was just as likely to give up on the first day, to call death his friend after a single convulsion. It was as if the yellow fever were a chosen form of Doom itself, darkly beautiful, and its victims hurried to welcome it like converts trembling at the proof of angels.

Baths three times daily. Doses of calomel and jalap on the hour. The doctor to mix the more potent emetics himself. For the rest, it was only the constant changing of the patient's dress, the instant removal of all discharges, and the rotation of linens every four hours that sustained a minimum healthfulness of atmosphere in the ward itself. Through all the steady activity and the constant battle with stench and disgust, the doctor watched for signs of defeat: the telltale trickle of blood from the nose or gums meant the fever's work was done. The body must be put in one of the boxes that lined the hall outside, and the bed given up to some other poor writhing soul.

For reasons not clear—and none he could depend on—the volume of new cases slowed somewhat in the late afternoon. The porters would not work after nightfall, so he took time to greet Albert Dash and eat dinner. After that dreadful scene, when Gertie had taken the poor boy away, he did not return immediately to the ward. Instead, he poured a brimming glass of brandy (the little Miller had left), and sat in his chair staring out the window into the falling darkness. In the light that lay on the tree tops like a mantle, he could still trace the flight of the carroways and gulls. They mounted in easy order into the darkening sky before steepling downward toward the East River out of sight beyond the wood, plunging soundlessly.

He went back to the ward, where he worked through the night. At dawn he slept for an hour, sitting up in a chair by an open window. Then, when the first new convoy of the day arrived, he was back down on the steps as if the battle had just been joined. The day assumed its chaotic course, indistinguishable from the last, and Nurse Purvis was just discussing the imminent exhaustion of some of her nurses with him while trying to persuade him to take some lunch, when Gertie came to the ward with a message. Though it meant leaving a man whose skin had just turned to a deep, lustrous gold before his eyes, he went downstairs immediately. Order was unachievable. The chaos could only be managed. Keep moving.

When Dr. Hosack found the two disheveled young women waiting for him, the astonishment was palpable in his tired, gray face, and for a long moment it prevented him from speaking. Two daughters of his hatred, standing there.

"When Gertie said there were new volunteers here," he said at last, "I never dreamt she could mean you. Where have you come from?"

"Mr. Geyer's," said Vera.

"Ambleside. Near Tarrytown," said Virginia.

"That is thirty miles away! Who brought you here?" He wiped his hands on his long white apron, now stained with smears of yellow and black.

Vera and Virginia looked at each other with proud smiles.

"No one brought us," said Vera. "We came together on our own. We rode all night to get here."

"You rode?"

"People say you need help here, Doctor. We want to offer our assistance as nurses."

The doctor frowned and stared at her.

"What happened to your face, Miss Casey? Did you fall from your horse?"

"No, it's nothing." It seemed irrelevant to mention her presence at the Park Theater riot, which seemed to have happened in another age, to someone else.

"You put me in a very difficult position," said Dr. Hosack sternly. "I take it that your fathers know nothing of this."

They shook their heads.

"And if I accept your offer, how am I to explain to those gentlemen that I have been an accessory to your rebellious wishes and allowed you to be exposed to the deadly yellow fever?"

"You will have nothing to explain, sir," said Virginia. "This is all our own doing. And we cannot leave now that we have come."

"We won't get sick," said Vera. "We are in no more danger than you are yourself. And I do not see you flinching from what needs doing."

"Nor is Albert, I'm sure," said Virginia, with a discreet glance up and down the corridor.

The doctor's face turned very grave, and he looked across at Vera.

"I am a doctor, Miss Laidlaw. I built this hospital expressly for the purpose of coping with epidemic disease in the city. You see me in my element to which I have long been immune. You, however, are mere girls with no knowledge of medical practice and whose young lives should not be recklessly endangered in this way. I have others to do the work."

"I don't believe you, Doctor," said Virginia.

Dr. Hosack looked startled.

"Virginia knows about medical things," said Vera. "Albert has been teaching her. And she has nursed me many times before when I have been ill."

"Where is he?" said Virginia.

"Who?"

"Albert Dash. We were told he was here with you."

"You will see him presently," said the doctor. He looked intently at Vera, then at Virginia with a look of desperation.

"Miss Casey—I beg you for the last time to leave this place. Be assured, you have both won my eternal admiration simply by coming. For all our sakes let that be heroism enough. Take your horses and ride back to Ambleside—your families must be wretched with worry."

But both Vera and Virginia were looking at him with steady eyes, arms crossed.

"Surely, there is work for you to put us to this very minute," said Virginia.

The doctor sighed and ran a hand across his glistening bald pate. He seemed annoyed.

"Very well then. Be warned, however. Nothing I can say will prepare you for what you will see. It is on your own heads. Go with Gertie. She will provide you with an apron and nets for your hair and something to eat if you are hungry. Then I will bring you to the ward."

Gertie took them and dressed them without a word, though she looked on Vera and Virginia with more respect than she had any white persons not the doctor in her whole long life. At one moment,

Virginia was sure she was about to speak to Vera—some expression of warning or sympathy seemed poised on her lips—but in the end the old woman said nothing. Instead, she stood back and watched Vera crowd her long red curls into the cotton net in silence.

Vera and Virginia then watched Gertie crush green rue leaves into a dish and mix them into clay carafes of gin and water. She handed one each to Vera and Virginia and with a motion of her eyes commanded them to drink. Their faces soured at the bitter taste of the herb, but when the inspiriting warmth of the gin began to rise inside them, they finished off the potion gratefully.

"No yellow jack can get you now," said Gertie with a satisfied look. "You's immune."

The door opened a crack and the doctor's head appeared. He gave Virginia a look of meaning, so she followed him, leaving Vera with Gertie. Out in the corridor, the doctor took Virginia gently by the arm. He spoke in a whisper.

"I don't doubt the true charity of your motives in coming here, Miss Casey. Please don't think that I do. But I know too that we will often do the noblest things for others for the most personal of reasons."

Virginia blushed. "Please, Doctor . . ."

"You needn't explain for your friend, Miss Casey. I know why Miss Laidlaw is here. And may I express my special admiration for you, for accompanying her here on what must have been a scheme entirely of her fancy, spurred by the feelings of her heart and not your own. Your devotion to your friend does great credit to you."

Virginia could say nothing, for reasons that Dr. Hosack seemed to take for embarrassment at hearing such praise of herself. He took her hand.

"Miss Casey, it grieves me to tell you that you have further comfort to offer your friend. The most difficult imaginable . . . "

The doctor was clearly struggling to come to the point. Meanwhile, Virginia felt her heart stop and the dim world around her became perfectly still. Dr. Hosack's stern eyes looked directly into hers.

"You must perform whatever miracles of sympathy you can for Miss Laidlaw," his voice was low and sad, "because Albert is far gone. The fever is advancing rapidly on him. I don't expect him to live beyond tomorrow."

The doctor wished to spare Vera (and secretly himself) from the task of nursing Albert. So it was Virginia who followed him down the long, dim corridor to a private room near the office, while Vera went upstairs with Gertie to the main ward.

"I've forgotten something. Wait there."

The doctor disappeared back toward the office, leaving Virginia for a few empty moments by herself. He returned carrying a small bottle and a glass.

"Drink this."

She made a face at the warm, sour taste.

"Bitters," he said. "Now swallow this salt tablet."

He uncorked the bottle, upturned it in his palm and began sprinkling her with vinegar water over her clothes, her bare arms, her tangled hair.

To Dr. Hosack, this ritual was closer to witchcraft than science and he performed it in an embarrassed hurry, without speaking. But Virginia submitted to the bitter draft and the sprinkle of drops on her head as if it were a blessing.

Now that Albert is dying, I will have no other ceremony than this, she thought.

At first, she did not recognize the man in the bed. He wore a thin, unkempt beard. Clumps of curly dark hair had come loose from his scalp and were strewn across the pillow.

"He has been hallucinating since yesterday," said Dr. Hosack. "The heat of it is very cruel. He will not know you."

Albert's hand lay twitching on the sheet. Virginia reached out and took it up. It felt bloated and puffy. She put her other hand on his forehead. Hot tin. Albert groaned and seemed to say something. Little streams ran from the corner of his eyes, as if he were crying in his sleep. Then his eyes flickered open and he looked straight at Virginia.

She knew him then, and the injustice of it all came to her in a strange, selfish thought. It was not fair that she should share the intimacy of sickness with Albert when all other intimacy between them had been skipped over. How could she be asked to comfort him in death when she had not been given the chance in life?

But she fought down these angry feelings and gave Albert a strong, meaning smile. Then she took a cloth from the pocket of her apron and wiped the film of perspiration from his pasty brow.

"What can I do for him? What are my instructions?"

"There is little enough we can do," Doctor Hosack replied, "as the poor fellow himself knows. Keep the sheets close about him, no matter how hot he feels. Then every hour you must call Gertie or one of the others, and she will bathe him in cold water."

"*I* will bathe him."

"Please, Miss Casey . . ."

"Gertie is busy enough. I have come here to nurse, not to sit idly by for others to do the work."

"You must bathe him naked."

"I know that."

The doctor felt the strangeness of arguing a point of propriety with Virginia Casey, whose father cared so little for the reputation of others. He rubbed his beard and looked doubtful.

"We will say nothing of it to anyone," said Virginia. "That way, there can be no talk."

"Very well. I will leave you with him. If there is any change, send word to me."

"I will."

"One thing more," he said, when he reached the door. "You must talk to him, encourage him. He must not become despondent—or there is no hope for him."

In the corner of the nearly empty room stood a claw footbath. Next to it, a barrel of precious well water and a pail on a hook. Virginia guessed that no other patient in the hospital had been given so much and that the doctor felt deeply enough what he could not show.

Albert muttered something, and she saw a tic of blood oozing from the corner of his mouth. She wiped it gently away with the cloth.

Then she went over to the bathtub. A bath every hour meant she must conserve water as best she could. Carefully, so as not to spill a drop, she lifted five pails full and poured four one after the other into the bath. After a moment's hesitation, she poured the fifth back into the barrel.

Looking across the distance back to the bed, Virginia wondered if her bravado with the doctor had been a misjudgment. How was she to get Albert into the bath?

By focusing on the physical problem of bathing him—What weight was he? Should she drag him or lift him?—Virginia was able to forget that she was undressing Albert and handling his body. She tried to speak encouragingly to him, as the doctor had told her. But the sound of her soft, unsteady voice in the empty room frightened her. It made the necessary abstraction impossible and so she stopped.

In the end, she could do no better than drag him across the floor. He seemed awake to her intentions at first and assisted her in sitting himself upright on the bed so she could lift the nightshirt over his head. But the effort ruined his strength completely, and when Virginia put her arms under his shoulders and pulled with all her might his head lolled dangerously about from side to side almost hitting the hard floor.

Grunting and puffing like a dockhand, Virginia lifted Albert up to the side of the bath. With a huge final lift and push, she rolled him into the cool water. As he splashed down, he hit his head a sickening blow on the rim of the bath. Virginia cried aloud in alarm. For a single, stomach-churning moment, she thought that she had killed him. He lay motionless, a dead weight in the water. But then he breathed a loud sigh, and she relaxed.

As she sponged and soaked him, the fever appeared to ease. His skin took on a more natural taint, and his face lost its tight, tormented expression. But after a few minutes, these positive signs diminished. Albert began muttering again, and the perspiration bloomed across the unsubmerged parts of his body. Virginia stepped over to the barrel, lifted out a pail of water and threw it over his head.

Back on the bed, Virginia eased the light cotton shirt over his shoulders and lay him back down on the pillow. He was more awake now than before, and though he did not seem to know who she was, his rambling speech was clearer.

"Please give up—no use—I'm dying," he said, mumbling. He had his eyes tightly closed, and the seeming tears squeezed out at the corners.

"You are not dying," said Virginia, as firmly as she could manage. "You are better now than before. The doctor says you must not give up."

Albert began throwing his head from side to side on the pillow. With his teeth clenched and eyes squeezed shut, he looked like a child in a tantrum.

"No! No!" he half-shouted, half-hissed at her. "Let me die!"

Virginia was at a loss. She must fight his despondency, but quarreling with him would only distress him more. Helplessness swept over her in a wave, and she was about to cry when she remembered suddenly what she had promised Vera she would do. There could be no better time for it than now.

"Albert," she said, taking his hand in both of hers. "Albert, there is something I must tell you."

Albert's head was still thrashing on the pillow. He seemed far gone. She was losing him.

"Albert—my darling." The word emerged tentatively, barely a whisper. Having crossed that threshhold, she felt calmer, like a new person with new freedoms. Very gently, she took up his hand and put his fingers to her lips, one by one.

"It's Virginia here. Do you know me?" She stopped to wipe a smear of blood from his cheek. "I love you—that's why you must live. If not for yourself, then for me."

The words hurried out, sounding stilted to her. And he had not heard her. His whole face was burning now, rolling violently on the pillow, foaming at the nose and mouth. She took a deep breath and said it again—that she loved him, that he must live—but more slowly this time, repeating the words over and over, savoring their truth as she spoke them aloud to him for the first time. After a while, it became less awkward and strange. The sound of the words—her voice in the empty room—became like a musical phrase she could turn over and over to eternity. In the end, Virginia cast a kind of spell on herself. So she was not sure how long it was before she noticed he had fallen into a calm, still sleep. She leant over and wiped the spittle foam from his lips, quietly rejoicing that it wasn't blood.

Was he better? Could he be better?

Such thoughts brought only a dangerous kind of hope, and she suppressed them quickly. One of the first things Albert had told her about the yellow fever was that worsening signs meant death without doubt but, in the peculiar humor of the yellow fever, so did their opposite. She remembered the story Albert had told her about Mrs. Little in Brooklyn. A week after poor Duggan died, Mrs. Little had risen from her sickbed—feeling good as new, so she said. She had gone down to the kitchen to make soup for her son's dinner. There, in the middle of slicing an onion, she had fallen to the floor and died before the little boy's eyes. Albert had seen the body. He said it looked as if she had been sprinkled with gold dust by a malevolent genie. Virginia wished now that Albert had never told her about Mrs. Little, that she had not been so inquisitive, because it meant that every flicker of his eyes, every change in color or peaceful sigh, took on a terrible doubleness.

After hours in rapt study of Albert's face on the pillow, broken only by the strength-sapping ritual of the bath, then wrapping him tightly as she could in his sheets, Virginia fell ever deeper into a kind of trance. By the day's end, when she looked at him she no longer knew what she saw: whether he was better or worse, his skin more or less yellow, or even whether there had ever been another Albert who was not this sick, helpless man.

She must have fallen asleep because when she sat up again with a start it was dark outside. Albert was muttering under the sheets, his skin like a sunflower. She was about to get up to look for the doctor when the door opened and Gertie appeared with a lamp.

"Miss, there is a chair more comfortable in the doctor's office next door. Why don't you sleep there awhile and I'll look after the boy."

Virginia shook her head. She was ashamed of herself for falling asleep and when she spoke it was more harshly than she meant.

"No, Gertie. I don't need help. Leave me with him."

Gertie looked at her sadly. "I'll leave you this lamp if you promise you will trim it and take care not to fall asleep and knock it over. You won't burn us all, will you, Miss?"

"It's alright. I'm awake now."

Gertie put the lamp on a small table near the bed and turned to leave.

"Miss, you know how you keep awake?"

"How?"

"Praying. It keeps you wakeful. That's what I do."

"Thank you."

The door shut on her, and Virginia was alone with him once more. The room was perfectly silent, with only the small lick of the lamp's flame on the wall. She felt enough like a nun alone in her cell that she thought she would follow Gertie's advice. So she set to praying with the fervency of a novice. She prayed silently and aloud, sometimes to God, sometimes to Albert himself, talking away, never stopping until soon it seemed the most natural thing in the world to be chatting to herself alone in a room with a dying man about everything she could imagine in Heaven and on the wide, wide earth.

The first inky light of dawn shone in the window. She heard the sound of the door opening behind her and thought it must be Gertie come to retrieve the lamp.

But it was Dr. Hosack. She did not look up at him.

"Tell me you have not been up all night."

"I dozed some earlier."

"How has he been?" The doctor knelt next to the bed, pulled back the sheet and began examining Albert's chest and arms with rough, practiced hands.

"He has been quiet a long time," she said. "Can you tell me what that means?"

"He has cooled down somewhat."

"Does it mean he is better?"

"It means he is better for now. I will not lie to you, Miss Casey, and say it means anything more than that."

Virginia felt tears welling in her throat and closed her eyes.

"You are tired," she heard the doctor say, as if from a great distance. "I have come down to fetch you, but perhaps it is better that you should sleep."

"Fetch me?" She looked up.

"Yes. A patient in the ward is asking for you. He does not have the fever. He has a gunshot wound. Somehow he has learned that you are here and he insists on seeing you."

"I will come up," said Virginia, "if you will fetch Gertie to watch Albert."

She didn't ask for the patient's name. Doctor Hosack surmised his own reasons for this, and so compounded his earlier mistaken impression. That is, until he saw Virginia's reaction to seeing George Bickart in a sickbed. When she showed no surprise, nothing of a lover's pity, he looked at her as if to say, *you're a cold fish, alright!* Then he left her with him.

Vera came silently out of the shadows and sat beside Virginia.

"I didn't recognize him at first," she said.

Vera was smeared with stains, her head sunk down almost to her chest.

"Vera, how are you?"

"I am so tired. So tired and dirty. I have never been so tired."

Vera began to cry, not even bothering to lift her head. Buds of tears dropped one by one into her lap. Virginia put her arm around her shoulder and said what reassuring words she could think of. Then she caught Nurse Purvis's eye, who came over to them. "Take her somewhere to sleep," said Virginia. She nodded and took Vera away.

The ward was a dark and miserable place, though conditions had improved. The air was filled with the groans of the sick and dying, but the open windows and relentless washing of the linen had diminished the choking vapor in the room.

Nurse Purvis and two other nurses moved quietly from bed to bed with sponges and water, though they discreetly skirted the bed where Virginia sat bent over the broad, sunken figure of George Bickart. His shoulder and chest were swathed in cloth like a mummy. His eyes fluttered open.

"Ginny Casey," he said in a hoarse voice.

"I'm here, George."

"I remember you at the theater. You saw me." He spoke between tired, heaving breaths. "I'm sorry the boys hurt you. I tried to stop them."

"It's no time to be thinking of that."

"You've no reason to pity me. But I'm not so bad as I seem. Even your Albert has forgiven me."

Virginia looked up in surprise to find George smiling strangely at her. *Your* Albert? So he had guessed! But Virginia wasn't ready to acknowledge that he had.

"What happened to you, George?"

"It's the strangest thing, Ginny. I came up here to find out what Miller was up to. I was sneaking around the back when Cauliflower Ear steps out from behind a tree and shoots me."

"Who?"

"One of Laidlaw's men from the theater. He shot me then he fixed my wound. Then he disappeared. Funny thing was he never said a word to me. Between shooting me and fixing me up he never said a word."

George was breathing hard.

"Rest now," she said, putting a hand on his arm.

He reached over with his good arm and clasped Virginia's knee.

"Ginny, where's Albert? I've asked, but no one will tell me. I know he should be here."

Virginia's mind raced. "He's downtown. At Columbia. Dr. Hosack has put him in charge of a sick ward there."

Virginia's voice was trembling, but she must have lied well enough because George released her knee and relaxed back onto the pillow.

"You rest now, George."

Virginia could not watch George fall asleep without thinking of sleep herself.

For in that sleep of death what dreams may come.

She closed her eyes and let her head drop, wishing to feel nothing, think nothing, to drift off into a sleep so deep she would never wake from it. In the inviting well of unconsciousness, she could believe she was already dead.

"Are you awake?"

She sat up painfully to find Dr. Hosack's large, stern face peering at her.

"Yes." She rubbed her eyes.

Dr. Hosack leant over the bed and put his hand on George Bickart's brow.

"He will do nicely."

He sat back on the chair next to Virginia with a deep sigh.

"I have been downstairs to Albert. Gertie came to get me."

Virginia's mouth felt suddenly tight and dry.

"Just after you left, Albert got up from his bed and began walking around the room."

With a single heaving sob, Virginia began to cry, though she thanked God she had been spared the end.

Dr. Hosack's hand touched her shoulder.

"No tears, Miss Casey," he said, surprised. "This is no time for crying. Not a bit of it."

She looked up and saw that the doctor was smiling. It was as if twenty years had fallen from him.

"Albert has got up from his bed, Miss Casey, and he is asking for *you*."

One Month Later

CHAPTER FORTY

The doctor turned the corner from Broadway onto Franklin Street and caught sight of a trail of smoke coming from the chimney of the old Dutch cottage. He smiled. The unusually early frost had not escaped Aunt Mary's notice, and her thoughts had clearly been his own when he got out of bed that morning and felt the cold floor on his bare feet: that the invalid should be wheeled out to the front room without delay, to warm himself by the potbellied stove.

Sure enough, he found his patient situated exactly as he would have wanted. Aunt Mary herself had answered the door. She cried, "Hello, Doctor!" and smiled broadly at him until she noticed he was dressed all in black and with crepe around his hat. Without another word, she took his hat and led him into the front room, which was warm as toast and oddly empty but for the stove and the invalid in his chair-with-wheels sitting next to it, toes pointed fireward.

"Good morning, Dr. Hosack. I saw you walking up from Broadway right on time. I could set the clock by you, had we not sold it."

"Hello, Albert," said the doctor. "How are you today?"

"I feel fine. Virginia just left. I'm surprised you didn't meet her on Broadway."

"Broadway is bedlam today. I wouldn't know my own mother if she tried to sell me clams."

The doctor searched in vain for a chair, until Aunt Mary appeared with a strong Dutch straightback from the kitchen. She also brought a second blanket for Albert to put on his knees.

"Well, if you never get well again, it won't be for want of nursing."

Albert had only just recovered from the yellow fever when he was felled by the most mundane of late summer colds. It had now settled stubbornly on his chest, and the doctor felt that he was not dispatching it quite as quickly as he ought.

"We must have you better by the winter, you know."

"The winter?" cried Albert hoarsely, as if the doctor had said "the twentieth century," or some other ridiculous, far-off date. "But I am fine already!"

The doctor sighed. "It's been often observed, I know, but you are a daily reminder to me that doctors do indeed make the worst patients."

The doctor put his ear to Albert's chest and listened for a full minute to his breathing. He thought the rattling sound a little weaker and less sustained. Then he felt Albert's joints and looked at his tongue. On concluding the examination, he reached into his great leather bag and produced a small knife, a china dish, and an untidy bunch of sticks with leaves.

"These are herbs sent to me from China by a colleague. He certifies them to be most efficient in the production of phlegm. We have a packet of seeds from him also. When you are better you must sketch this curious leaf for me. But for now, I will mix you a brew from it. And then I must have some of your blood."

While the doctor searched for a plausible vein, Albert pointed to his clothes. "I hoped the season for these might be over."

"It is the last of them, God willing. In 1814, I remember attending funerals in the last week of October. We have been spared a repeat of that calamity, thank God."

"You speak as if it were the work of Providence. But I think the hospital, good nursing and a steady team of porters saved us. This was the work of men and women."

"Well, well," said the doctor.

"It is strange that I have been to only one funeral," Albert went on, "and the yellow fever was not its cause."

Uncle Mortimer's heart had finally failed him during the first week of the epidemic, while Albert was still at Bellevue. Aunt Mary had packed up the house in preparation for leaving the city to live with a family of distant Dash cousins upstate. Albert had insisted she sell his oak writing desk and all the old family china to finance a wardrobe-full of new dresses for herself and a fresh set of teeth. In the end, Albert's sole Dash inheritance was his uncle's chair, and he had secretly vowed to burn it just as soon as the doctor and Virginia would let him.

When the doctor had tapped an ounce of pendulous red drips from Albert's arm into the small china dish, he gave a satisfied grunt and expertly bound the incision. "How's that?"

Albert considered the practice of bleeding dubiously old-fashioned, but he didn't say so. Instead, he declared himself much refreshed.

"It is my opinion," said the doctor, "that your general constitution is and remains sturdy, and that you have reduced yourself to this pitiable state through the accumulation of overwork and anxiety lasting some years."

"With all respect, Doctor, I will not be convinced by that diagnosis until you sit here beside me in your very own chair-with-wheels and a blanket over your knees."

The doctor clucked his tongue. "I don't remember you ever being so contrary before you caught the yellow fever. Back then, there was never this prattling dissent."

"I will tell Virginia your diagnosis," Albert said placatingly. "She will be pleased, I'm sure."

The doctor disposed of the bloodied dish and carefully wrapped the Chinese herbs and placed them in the bag. Then, to Albert's surprise, he resumed his seat.

"I have more business here today than my usual examination. I am here to congratulate you."

"Virginia—"

"No, it's not about that. It's about you. The Columbia Board met yesterday. They asked me to extend their thanks to you for your brave work during the outbreak and to tell you that an official commendation will be presented to you in some dull ceremony or other once you are better."

"That is very kind of them."

"Yes, but you can kill a man with kindness if you don't also pay him a decent wage."

Albert looked at him inquiringly.

"I took the liberty of submitting to the board your catalogue of botanical drawings."

"But it is incomplete!"

"So it is. But our globe is a large one, and the board was willing to forgive you for not having covered it entirely. And that is not the material point. On the basis of that catalogue and your out-standing recent service, I am here to offer you the position of professor of Botanical Medicine at Columbia. The board and I were in full agreement that such a post should be created, and that you should be its first custodian."

Albert said nothing for a long moment. He tried to speak twice, but stopped. Then an enormous smile broke over his face, accom-panied by a bright red flush of pleasure. The doctor chuckled even as a sober thought crossed his mind: If this were Albert Dash's proper style of smiling, then he had never seen the young man truly happy until this moment. But then the smile died away, and Albert looked suddenly quite grave.

"What's the matter?"

"It is very kind—*more* than kind."

"So?"

"But I must decline it."

It was the doctor's turn to appear nonplussed. "Whatever for? Don't tell me you are giving up the profession! Miss Casey prom-ised me—"

"No, no. How could you think that? I am fit for nothing else."

"What then? You have worked hard for this professorship, and deserve it. The world is a fickle place, as even I, warhorse that I am, have had recent proof. Don't play Sir Lancelot with the board, Albert. You must grab your chance!"

"I intend to, Doctor. But not here. Virginia and I have decided to go out West after we are married. There are great opportunities for us there."

"Nonsense! Where will you find the resources you have here? The laboratory, the botanical garden, expert colleagues and rich endow-ments. Not to mention our many visiting Europeans."

Albert nodded. "That's all true. But we still want to go. I would like to build my own hospital, and Virginia wants to run it. She is a formidable businesswoman, you know, and easily strong enough for the frontier."

"I know it," conceded the doctor. "Miss Casey might play the demure schoolgirl, but she's actually tough as old boots. She outlasted all the nurses at Bellevue and was still fresh as a daisy at the end. Gertie speaks of her as if she were a saint."

"Yes," said Albert with a fond smile, "she has many great qualities. I was very late in seeing them, you know—almost too late."

The doctor heaved a sigh and rose to his feet. "Well, I will not oppose anything the two of you have decided upon. The stubbornness of your natures renders rational argument perfectly useless. That said, I *do* look forward to seeing the faces of the board when I tell them you've turned us down. They have been sobered by the yellow fever, but when they hear that young men are refusing Columbia professorships in favor of the prairies and the plains, they will certainly think the world has come to an end."

They talked a while longer, until the doctor had to leave for his morning lecture.

"I detest this first semester. I find the freshmen's ignorance very demoralizing. One thought inspires me, however. That perhaps there will be another Albert Dash among them!" He put on his hat.

Before leaving, he told Aunt Mary that the air had warmed sufficiently for Albert to be returned to bed, where he should sleep the rest of the day, to be woken only by a meal of beef broth mixed with Peruvian bark.

"Virginia is coming again later," said Aunt Mary doubtfully. "I think he will want to talk with her."

The doctor threw up his hands. "In that case, I will not waste my breath with instructions. Miss Casey will only listen politely then do just as she pleases."

Doctor Hosack surprised Aunt Mary with a kiss on her cheek. Then he shook Albert's hand for only the second time in their long association and, with a final, firm pat on the shoulder, he was gone.

CHAPTER FORTY-ONE

Election Day in New York was synonymous with public drunkenness. Hogsheads of rum and beer were rolled out under the banner of the different parties to every polling place in the city, to encourage its citizens' participation in the sacred rites of democracy.

Eamonn Casey would ordinarily have spent the day half-drunk as he marshalled the vote in the fourth and fifth wards, then headed to City Hall at sundown to watch the returns. There he was in easy reach of the taverns if results were good, and Tammany Hall for an angry meeting if they weren't.

This year, however, Casey spent election day in his office at the *Herald* quietly packing up his papers. It had felt strange to arrive at the printing house that morning. The shopfloor—normally a cacophony of shouted copy and whirring type—stood silent and empty. The *Herald*'s farewell edition had gone out the night before and, with a handshake and two weeks' wages, he had sent his unhappy staff on their way.

He intended to be done with his work quickly—the newspaper business was an unsentimental one and there was little he wanted to preserve—but he found himself lingering there nevertheless. His usual restless energy had abated for the time being and he felt strangely drowsy and reflective, without having taken so much as a drop.

He disposed of great broadsheet piles of back issues, then came to his most recent editions dating from the end of August. These he brought over, and though their contents were vividly familiar to him, he began leafing through the pages, rereading every word.

The *Herald* had not published on the first day of the fever outbreak when he was at Ambleside, nor during his eight days at Bellevue Hospital where he had at first gone in search of his daughter, then remained to help the doctor in the sick wards.

On his return to the city, he had devoted an entire issue to a graphic account of his Bellevue experience. Despite having barely slept since the fever first broke out, he had stayed up all night at this desk to write it, recalling the stream of groaning, yellow-skinned victims, the agonizing deaths of so many, the repelling stench of the dead and dying, the indefatigable labors of Dr. Hosack and his nurses during the period of greatest crisis when all the volunteers, his humble self included, had been ready to give in to exhaustion and despair; how the doctor's superior management of the epidemic in the absence of all other functioning civic authority (notably the mayor) had been rewarded by the noticeable decline in new cases after the fifth day, and the subsequent recovery of unprecedented numbers of the sick.

The *Herald*'s next issue, a few days later, had included the most difficult editorial he had ever had to write because it involved the publication of falsehoods for the unusual end of smearing himself. He proclaimed himself guilty of scurrilous innuendo in the case of Dr. Hosack's private life, of doing grievous damage to a great man's reputation with charges based on fancy and false witness, and that the charges of libertinism against the doctor were hereby most apologetically withdrawn as beneath the dignity of a respectable newspaper to publish or the public to read.

The consequences of the *Herald*'s retraction and Casey's public mea culpa were evident in the next issue of the *Herald*, a much jollier document, which praised the Columbia board's decision to reinstate Dr. Hosack to his position as professor of medicine, and the mayor's to put the doctor back in charge of the Bellevue Hospital. The *Herald* hoped, too, that the mayor would pursue more retributive forms of justice in the aftermath of the epidemic, particularly in the case of the scoundrel Dr. Miller, whose abandonment of his ill-deserved post at a time of the city's greatest danger was reminiscent of the worst treacheries of Arnold and Burr.

In a small paragraph at the conclusion of this issue, and without any of the usual rhetorical adornments, he had announced his withdrawal from the governor's race.

Casey sat back in his chair and reflected with a smile on how the effect of those three brief sentences had been as sudden and far-reaching as any thundering four-column tirade he had composed in thirty years in the business.

The Democratic party leaders came down from Albany by the same day's coach to request an urgent meeting with him. He greeted them affably, his wife smiling by his side, and seated them in the parlor. Lily Riley had made a great fuss with sandwiches and fresh coffee.

Once refreshed, the men had turned to affairs of state. They discussed the recent disaster in Manhattan, the great resiliency of its people, the reinstatement of Dr. Hosack, the need for new cemeteries above the water table, stricter regulation of the docks and, of course, his famous aqueduct. Casey, in turn, assured them life was getting back to normal now that all the funerals were over with and the weather had cooled. But when they asked him to reconsider his decision to withdraw from the governor's race, he only smiled and shook his head.

"But you can still win, Mr. Casey!" cried the party's president, a personal friend of Andrew Jackson himself. "In fact, I would say your chances have never been better. It's clear something must be done for New York and you have earmarked yourself as the visionary candidate, the people's man of the future."

"We have money for you to run, if that is your concern," said the treasurer.

"It's not the money."

The president persisted. "Your standing with the public is again very high, for all your troubles of the summer. Your bravery during the epidemic has atoned for any earlier missteps. And this retraction of yours was the noblest thing. A masterful stroke."

He shook his head again.

"But the people are behind you!" insisted the president.

"The People is an ass!" cried Eamonn Casey, standing up from his chair.

A week later, the governor himself had paid a visit to Park Row. Sam Geyer came down from Ambleside, and the three men spent an entire afternoon looking over maps and drawings of the Croton River Valley, doing sums.

He woke from the drift of these thoughts to see Sam Geyer himself standing at the door, his round face smiling at him.

"How is your last day on the bridge, Captain Casey?"

"Ah well, Sam, you see how it is. Even the rats have deserted me. Why aren't you out electioneering?"

"I was never much of one for that. The least scene of popular enthusiasm and I am in bed with the shakes."

"So you have come to the *Herald*. It is certainly peaceful here."

"I won't allow this brooding talk. I have come here on your last day to escort you into retirement."

"You have? In what manner?"

"In the manner of a sprightly frigate tugging a battered old man-of-war into the harbor. I'm afraid you will have to imagine the twelve-gun salute."

"The fireworks will serve well enough for that. I take it as a great kindness in you, Sam."

He put aside the papers, reached for his hat, and the new friends stepped out together into the bright noise and color of Broadway. Everyone was abroad on this unusually warm election holiday. Red, white and blue bunting hung down in their faces, stretched on windows and awnings up and down the great avenue as far as the eye could see.

They heard a loud din. Around the corner a Tammany Hall band advanced toward them playing "Yankee Doodle," their brass instruments glinting in the sun. At their head, in a horse-drawn float, four young women in diaphanous white, their long tresses unbound, carried a large banner: VOTING RIGHTS AND VICTORY! Behind them on the float stood a tall, elderly man in a white wig, wielding a hickory stick in time with the band.

"That's a poor imitation of Jackson," said Geyer.

"If I were a Seminole, I'd laugh out loud," said Casey.

They both scurried into a shop doorway to evade the multitude, mostly young, shirt-sleeved men singing lustily with the band between swigs from bottles making the rounds, or trying to engage the banner-bearing girls in shouted conversation over the music.

But the excitement of the day lifted them up despite themselves, and once the band had passed by they decided to repair to the Tontine Coffee House to soak in all the political gossip. They would see how the share trading fared as the inevitable reelection of the governor neared, and as the character of the equally inevitable new mayor was sifted and assessed according to the highly suggestible, almost childlike temperament of the Exchange, where all trade, be it in goods or reputations, was charged to the point of frenzy by the universal consumption of strong coffee.

Casey and Geyer eschewed coffee themselves, preferring instead a working man's repast of beefsteak and porter with bread. They chatted companionably about the issues of the day: housing reform in the poor wards, their new positions on the governor's Croton Water Commission, and the bright epidemic-free future for the city once the water crisis was solved. Occasionally, when the shouting of the traders around them reached a deafening pitch—an announcement that the two hundredth share had passed hands produced wolf-cries and a bone-rattling stamping of the feet—Casey and Geyer gave up talking and simply looked at each other as if to say, *What an amazing city this is!*

So caught up were they in conversation and the bubbling energies of election night, they were surprised to find on leaving the Tontine that the moon had set long ago, and that the sky above them was already emblazoned by a silent fireworks of stars. There was a light wintry chill in the air.

Sam Geyer beamed beerily at him as he waved goodbye.

"Oh, Eamonn, I forgot!" Geyer leaned his bulky frame unsteadily out of the carriage window as it drove away. He was waving his hat. "Congratulations on your news. My best wishes to Virginia!"

CHAPTER FORTY-TWO

A week after the election, Virginia was sitting in a wicker chair in Dr. Hosack's garden on the banks of the Hudson River, opening a letter she had been expecting for weeks.

After the frosts of mid-September, the fall had mellowed and now seemed ready to smile on them forever, like a fair cousin to the fiendish summer that had come before it. She and Albert had made a habit of sitting together through the long, unseasonably warm afternoons at the bottom of Dr. Hosack's sculpture garden. Behind a small privet hedge nearby, a marble Venus emerged from a bath. Her nakedness seemed a decided disadvantage in the nip of the dusk. Though the season had been so blissfully mild, every day that they came down here to their favorite spot it seemed she searched about for her robe with greater urgency. Virginia sighed. Why couldn't this day simply last forever? But then she smiled to herself and shook her head. She would never exchange all she had to look forward to for a mere sunset.

"It is addressed from the Ambassador Apartments, Oxford Street, London. Dated the first of October. Shall I read it to you?"

She looked over and saw Albert lean his head back against his cushion and close his eyes. It was no clear indication that he didn't want to hear the letter and, after a moment's consideration, she decided to read it aloud.

Dearest Virginia. When your letter arrived yesterday, I knew what it would say even before I read it. But you needn't have worried, my dear, because Edmund—Mr. Leadbetter, I should say!—has behaved like the perfect gentleman from the day we set sail from Boston. I wish everybody in New York could see how wrong they have been about him. He is humility and kindness itself. Mother says it's because Mr. Chidgey has kept him from drinking, but I am convinced it is due to his essential good nature. He is a very misunderstood man!

I must say Edmund was a little taken aback when I arrived at the dock in Boston with Mother, Father, and Shivers in tow, but how could we have known that all the time I was planning to escape to London to live, Father was thinking the same thing for all of us? It is the most extraordinary thing! The yellow fever was the last straw, Father said, and he is very happy to be "home" again.

Everywhere we go, Edmund is recognized and we are pointed out and whispered about. You would not like it at all, Ginny, but I don't mind. People are always beside themselves to know who I am, and it is very amusing to hear them try to guess. So far I have heard myself called Lady Jersey, the Countess d'Anhault, and Miss Fanny Kemble—the actress, you know. I have since met the last mentioned person, at a delightful picnic Edmund hosted in Regent's Park, which is new and very fashionable.

Edmund has been very attentive, as I said, though I have not been entirely open with you yet about exactly how attentive he has been. I won't keep you in suspense a moment longer. The truth is that Edmund has proposed marriage to me—not once, but three times already! Aren't you amazed? Or perhaps not, you being so clever. After all, he was so very taken with me that night at Mrs. Geyer's, as you saw, though some people said he liked Jane and Charlotte best. He swears now that he cannot even remember any Miss Harveys and they matter nothing to him. Isn't this gallant?

I only wish you could be here to see my first night on the London stage. There is already much talk of me in the papers. Edmund says the people here love anybody new, better if she is mysterious, and best of all if she is beautiful, too. Which I am, he insists, for all that I protest. He is full of gallant sayings like this, and I know you would say that I should do more to discourage him. After all, I have known him barely three months and we are not yet engaged.

But now the thought occurs to me that this might not be true by the time you are reading this letter! What an exciting thought that is! And now that I have thought it, I'm afraid that when Edmund arrives this morning (and I am expecting him every minute), I will not remember the advice of my dear Virginia as I ought, and will smile and flirt with him as appallingly as ever! I hope that you will forgive me, my dear, after all that we have been through together (I still have nightmares of that awful hospital!). I miss you terribly, of course, and Albert too, but the Atlantic Ocean is nothing to a bond such as ours, don't you think? I must go now before Edmund comes, but be assured, Ginny darling, that though you do not always have proof of it in her conduct, you may trust always in the fondest love of your eternal friend, Vera L.

When she had finished reading the letter, Virginia laid it open on the small table, wondering if Albert would want to read it over. She looked over to him sitting in his chair, the familiar blanket over his knees. But he did not turn to look at Vera's letter, or show any interest in reviewing it for himself, so Virginia took it up again and put it in the pocket of her skirt. She followed the direction of his gaze out over the gently shifting waters of the Hudson and across to the sheer cliffs of the Palisades in the distance, aflame in the last of their autumnal reds and golds. So engaged did he seem in contemplation of the view that for a moment Virginia thought he had not listened to Vera's letter at all. But then he said,

"There are no colors like these in Regent's Park, I think."

"No, there aren't." She smiled.

They heard a crunch of gravel, and Lily appeared from behind Venus's bare torso.

"The doctor has just arrived home from Columbia, Miss, and wishes to convey his concern—not for the first time either, to be sure—that you two should be sitting out so late because he is expecting a frost. Might I add, Miss, that now I am out of doors myself, I myself feel a certain dampness in the air and am in full agreement with the doctor's opinion of the case, bless him."

During their stay at Dr. Hosack's villa, Lily was very often observed to be in agreement with the opinions of the host. Lily had ridden down with Mr. Casey in the carriage the day after her mistress's nighttime flight from Ambleside. They both stayed to help in the fever ward, and Lily had been deeply affected by her experience there. One consequence was she now looked upon Dr. Hosack with the veneration she had once reserved for Wolfe Tone.

"Everyone's a doctor around here," said Albert grumpily, hunching under his blanket.

"Excuse me, Mr. Dash, but Dr. Hosack says I have a natural attitude . . ."

"Aptitude."

". . . aptitude for diagnosis, and that the hospital never ran so well as when I was there, and that he will find me a place there whenever I should think to leave Mr. Casey's service. And I'm grateful for the doctor's good opinion, that I am."

"You deserve it too, Lily," said Virginia. "But we would be sorry to lose you. You have become quite indispensable."

Lily smiled with knowing pride.

"Shall I tell the doctor you will come in very soon?"

"Yes, Lily. Thank you. Oh, wait. Is my father back from his paddling yet?

"Yes, Miss. He and Master Michael arrived back some little time ago. The two of them have just sat down with the doctor in the parlor and opened a bottle of porto. If you will pardon my saying so, Miss, if you don't come up soon to put a stop to their stories and theories on things, Mrs. Casey says they will drink the whole bottle dry just like they did two nights ago when Mr. Bickart was here. It's a bad example for Master Michael, she says, who was sick all of yesterday."

"Did Mr. Casey find his canvas-back duck?" asked Albert.

"Yes, that he did. He has brought home a fine-looking duck. Gertie says it would look just as well plucked and braised on the table for dinner, but Mr. Casey insists he wants it for a specimen."

Because the preliminary work of surveying for the aqueduct lay entirely in the hands of Sam Geyer's team of engineers, Eamonn Casey had found himself with little to do in the past month except pursue his new passion for ornithology. He was unusually inventive in his reasons to visit his daughter at the doctor's villa, where he spent his days on the river in search of water fowl in the company of his son (who was back studying natural philosophy at Columbia), and the long nights drinking and disputing with the doctor. Mrs. Casey loved the villa but hated the roads and the travel. She was now encouraging her husband in his plan of buying property on the river, on the single condition that they never move again for the rest of their lives.

"Tell my father Mr. Geyer called with his latest survey maps, and that they are sitting on the piano."

"Yes, Miss."

"How is Mrs. Geyer?" asked Albert, when Lily had returned to the house.

"Still in mourning, I hear."

Aurelia Geyer attended her share of funerals in the aftermath of the epidemic, as they all had. But when news came shortly after of Lord Byron's death in Greece, she had resumed her stylish widow's weeds in the name of art and poetry.

"Mr. Geyer is so often away at the Croton river with his engineers, I do not believe her own husband has even noticed that she is always wearing black!"

Albert was silent for a moment. Then, in a clumsy way that both surprised and pleased her, he said, "On the subject of husbands, Ginny, what will you tell Vera in your next letter?"

"What do you want me to tell her?"

He thought for a moment. "That we shall expect a very expensive gift from Oxford Street if she is not to be here as your bridesmaid."

Virginia laughed. "Can you never be serious? I will *not* say that. I will tell her we will all miss her very much, and that our wedding day will not be the same without her."

"Oh, but it will be the same, Ginny," he said with a smile. "In all the important particulars."

Virginia gave a pout of pretended disapproval.

"Come here," he whispered in the familiar gentle-but-insistent tone.

She went to him. And while she made as if to settle the blanket more comfortably on his knees, she felt his half-expected hand around her waist, pulling her onto his lap. She turned her face to his, and their lips met in the lingering way she had grown very quickly to depend on for who she was, for feeling her place in the world.

"How long will you keep up this pretense, this sham?" She broke from his embrace and held up the blanket as if it were an exhibit in a courtroom.

"What pretense?"

"You don't seem very ill to me, that's all. If Lily were here, I'm sure she would say that you are in a very dangerous state of good health."

He drew her back to him and kissed her harder this time, just to prove her right.

"You kiss by the book, Professor Dash."

He looked hurt, and she laughed at him.

"We should go in." She stood up as if she really meant it.

"Just a few more minutes," said Albert.

So she went and brought her chair next to his, and together they looked out toward the declining light on the river. They tilted their heads upward to the darkening sky where they saw the first faint impression of stars.

Sitting with Virginia in this way, Albert felt a wave of contentment come over him. It was like a drug, this new feeling, stronger than any flower's balm. During the endless afternoons of this long, blissful month together, he had come to love Virginia's presence as much as he had ever loved Vera's being beyond his reach. Listening to her letter just now had been like listening to a foreign language he once had studied but barely remembered anymore. His love for Vera Laidlaw had been real, but it had made him a stranger to himself.

He looked over at Virginia now and felt again the glow of a new happiness, the stronger for all the death and misery they had seen together. As he listened to the birds in the reeds strike up their twilight song, he told himself that he would need far longer than a single lifetime to express his love for his soon-to-be wife, to repay her for seeing the truth when he himself had not understood it. It was because of her that the stars no longer defined him.

As if reading his thoughts, Virginia reached out for his hand. He took it, and she smiled at him. It was awkward holding hands through the arm of the chair, and the dusk air had grown quite chill, but they held on until the sun went down over the river—held on fast.

AFTERWORD

A dozen novels could be written from the life of David Hosack, a man even the quiz kids and history jocks have forgotten. His achievements were, fittingly, Hamiltonian in proportion: Bellevue Hospital, the Columbia College of Physicians and the first Botanical Garden in New York (located where Rockefeller Center now stretches skyward in deco glory) were all founded by Dr. Hosack.

But alas for the good Doctor—he lived too soon for the age of statues! While every Civil War general, incompetent or inebriated, has his marble remembrance, barely a plaque records Dr. Hosack's deeds in the modern city he helped create. His ghost will blanch at the liberties I have taken with his private life, but his extraordinary public career is here memorialized in its larger-than-life truth.

I have been faithful, too, in my account of Dr. Hosack's students (represented in the character of Albert Dash), who worked at his side during the devastating yellow fever epidemics, fearlessly entering the infected areas of the city to treat the sick and dying, whose ranks they very frequently joined. To bring to life these long-forgotten acts of civic heroism in New York, and to re-imagine one terrible summer in the 1820s when the city could so easily have succumbed to disease and disease-friendly corruption (never to enjoy its glittering future as capital of the Western world, our modern Rome . . .) was my inspiration for this book.

Largely through the efforts of Dr. Hosack, the threat of yellow fever to New York gradually receded through the 1820s. But neither he nor any of his students lived to see the mystery of the fever solved. It was not until 1881 that a Havana doctor named Carlos Finlay identified the origin of the yellow fever in a tropical mosquito, the *Aedes aegypti*. Bred in the swamps of the Caribbean and migrating north along the Eastern seaboard in the holds of trading vessels, it routinely devastated the Atlantic ports for three hundred years, before modern science and sanitation brought its reign of fear and the controversy over its origins to an end. There has not been a major outbreak of yellow fever in the Americas for over a century.

The Croton River Aqueduct was completed in 1842. It saved New York from drought and further epidemics on the scale of yellow fever and cholera, and played a major role in the city's astonishing growth in the second half of the nineteenth century. Nevertheless, the aqueduct did not last the thousand years its creators imagined. The booming modern metropolis outgrew their visionary contribution in barely three generations. Today, only the aqueduct's northernmost section is still in operation, delivering Croton water to Ossining (formerly Sing Sing): further proof, if it were needed, that New York has always been greater than the sum of its dreams.

ACKNOWLEDGMENTS

This historical novel has itself a long history, much of it too painstaking to record. But my sincere thanks are due to many for its
happy ending here in print. First, the late Catherine Voorsanger,
of the Metropolitan Museum of Art, met me on the day I first
conceived the novel. It was a bright omen. She gave me encouragement and some invaluable research leads, and my only regret is
that she is not here to enjoy the fruits of that chance New York
encounter all those years ago.

On the matter of research, I am very grateful to the staff at the
Columbia University archives where I spent one long, absorbing
summer getting acquainted with the redoutable Dr. Hosack. I am
grateful likewise to other scholars I have never met: to Professors
Burrows and Wallace for their remarkable *Gotham*, a book with a
thousand novels in its pages, and to Gerard Koeppel for *Water for*

Gotham, the book I relied on most in reconstructing the politics of water in early nineteenth-century New York.

To those who read drafts of the book—Anna Brickhouse, Audrey Petty, Rick Powers, Miranda Sherwin, and David Wright—I will forever be in your debt for the generosity of your advice and your indulgence when the manuscript was struggling through its "awkward age."

Once in the publishing realm, it was Victoria Sanders who first saw the promise of the book and Rosemary Ahern who, with tremendous expertise and always sensitive insights, collaborated with me in its vital last year, bringing that early promise to its maturity. This book would not exist without Victoria and Rosemary.

Nor would this book, and much else besides, exist without the care and support of my family. If there is a second dedication for *Hosack's Folly*, it must go to my family in Australia, who missed much of the firsthand drama, and to my wife Nancy, who missed none of it, and who thus deserves my last and best thanks for suffering the trials of novel-writing with me. The rewards for those trials are now here, and I look forward to our reading this book together with our son, whose birth came sometime after chapter fifteen and is the source of all the joy to be found in its pages.